A Fire
Within

A Fire Within

Kathleen Morgan

These Highland Hills
Book 3

Revell
Grand Rapids, Michigan

© 2007 by Kathleen Morgan

Published by Revell
a division of Baker Publishing Group
P.O. Box 6287, Grand Rapids, MI 49516-6287
www.revellbooks.com

Printed in the United States of America

Library of Congress Cataloging-in-Publication Data
Morgan, Kathleen, 1950–
     A fire within / Kathleen Morgan.
          p.   cm. — (These highland hills ; bk. 3)
     ISBN 10: 0-8007-5965-6 (pbk.)
     ISBN 978-0-8007-5965-0 (pbk.)
     1. Scotland—History—16th century—Fiction. 2. Highlands (Scotland)—
Fiction. I. Title.
PS3563.O8647F54 2007
813'.54—dc22   2007018776

13   14   15   16   17   18   19   9   8   7   6   5   4   3

Your heart was proud . . . you corrupted your wisdom . . . you profaned your sanctuaries. So I brought out fire from within you; it consumed you, and I turned you to ashes on the earth in the sight of all who saw you.

Ezekiel 28:17–18 NRSV

I

Perthshire, Scottish Highlands, May, 1568

Since she had grown from girlhood into a woman, many men had looked at Caitlin Campbell. None, though, had ever looked at her quite the way this man did. Yet, unlike the rest, his gaze wasn't filled with lust. His look went far deeper than that. Far deeper. As deep as her soul.

"He's a bold one, and no mistake," her cousin Janet Campbell muttered beside her as they walked that afternoon among the stalls of colorful wares and tantalizing foodstuffs on display at Dalmally's thrice weekly market. "Ye should find Jamie and set him on that cur. Jamie would soon have him on his knees, begging yer pardon."

For a fleeting instant, Caitlin considered then discarded that suggestion. From the looks of the dark-haired stranger, Jamie might well have his hands full attempting to bring that one to his knees.

He looked to be in his late twenties and was tall, broad of chest and shoulders. The bulk of his nondescript belted plaid did little to hide the fact he was powerfully built. His glittering blue eyes, as his gaze yet again boldly met hers, were alight with a dispassionate intelligence. An intelligence that was both chilling and, conversely, compelling.

Aye, Caitlin thought with a most unnerving thrill, Jamie would indeed have his hands full with that one. Besides, there was nothing served in starting a fight with a man solely because he chose to stare overlong at her. It wasn't the first time, after all, nor would it likely be the last.

With a final, derisive look in the tall Highlander's direction, she turned back to her cousin. "It matters not. He's hardly worth our concern. Why, he's likely just some broken man, if his threadbare plaid's any indication. And any man without a clan to call his own has problems enough."

"Aye, problems enough," Janet said, "that mayhap he shouldn't seek more by casting disrespectful glances at the local lasses. And, in the bargain, especially not at the clan chief's sister."

Caitlin laughed. "Well, he might not know that, might he?"

She drew up before a long table filled with fine woolen shawls, embroidered handkerchiefs, and sashes. "Now, let's get back to the task at hand, shall we? I've a birthing day gift to buy. And we promised Jamie we'd not be at this all afternoon, like we were last time we came to market."

Janet nodded. "Aye, I suppose ye're right. Still, for all his dark, braw looks, I think that boorish stranger oversteps himself . . ."

Almost of its own volition, Caitlin's gaze strayed in the direction the man had been. He was no longer staring at her but had turned his attention to another man who now stood beside him. Though tall himself, his compatriot was still half a head shorter. Red-blond of hair, he was slighter of build, with narrow shoulders and long, almost delicate fingers, and looked to be several years younger than his dark companion. Slung over one shoulder was a large, leather bag that appeared to contain some triangle-shaped object.

Just then, the dark Highlander glanced her way. A piercing,

steel blue gaze locked with hers. Somehow, she had once again attracted the increasingly insufferable man's notice.

She nearly looked away but knew it would be cowardly. It would also lead the chestnut-haired Highlander to imagine she had been intrigued by his earlier appraisal.

Instead, as if in warning, she scowled fiercely. He grinned in return.

Hot blood filled her cheeks. Why, the arrogant boor! How dare he! He was so far beneath her as to be a mere spider scuttling across the ground.

With a haughty flounce of her long, black hair, Caitlin wheeled around, grabbed the first colorful shawl that caught her eye, and pressed sufficient coin into the startled shopkeeper's hand. "Wrap this if ye will," she said. "It's past time we were on our way."

Five minutes later, the package tucked beneath her arm, Caitlin, with a bemused Janet scrambling behind her, made her way through the bustling throng of shoppers. They soon found Jamie snoring softly in the back of the small pony cart, one end of his dark blue, yellow, and green plaid slung over his face to shade his eyes. Janet shot Caitlin a mischievous glance, then grabbed the young man's foot and gave it a tug.

"Wake up, ye lazy lad," she cried. "M'lady Caitlin wishes to depart."

With a snort, the robustly built Scotsman sat up and began trying to untangle his considerable bulk from the plaid that had somehow become twisted about him. Janet laughed, and even Caitlin couldn't help a giggle. Finally, nearly as red in the face as the auburn locks that tumbled to his shoulders, the young Highlander managed to extricate himself, tuck the remaining plaid left over from his kilt across his shoulder, and pin it in place.

"Ye could've given me some warning of yer return," he groused. "I'd imagined ye'd be another hour or two, after all."

"Och, dinna fash yerself," Caitlin said by way of reassurance as she tossed her parcel beneath the pony cart's seat. "We just finished early for a change. And, because of it, ye're soon to be a free man, just as soon as we get . . ."

From around the village kirk, where Jamie had parked the cart, two tall men strode out, headed in their direction. Caitlin went still. It was the dark-haired man and his blond companion. What could they possibly want?

She looked to Janet, met her gaze. Her cousin opened her mouth to speak, but Caitlin gave her head a quick, warning shake. Janet's mouth snapped shut.

Jamie returned from untying the pony from the tree where he had tethered it. When he finally caught sight of the two men bearing down on them, his kind, open expression didn't change.

"Good day to ye," the dark stranger said as he and his companion at last drew up before them. "I was told ye're from Kilchurn. Are ye mayhap heading back that way?"

"Aye, that we are." Jamie paused, too polite to prod with further questions.

"My friend and I wish to gain an audience with the Campbell. Might we accompany ye on the way?" Briefly, his gaze swept once again over Caitlin. "It's a good hour's journey, from what I've heard, and two more men along would offer additional protection from any outlaws or robbers."

"As if any would dare attack the Campbell's—"

A quick hand on the arm immediately silenced Janet.

Caitlin managed a smile as she then surreptitiously let her hand fall back to her side. "And what would be yer business with the Campbell? If ye don't mind me asking, that is."

Glittering eyes the color of blue silver captured hers. "Nay, I don't mind ye asking. My friend here is a traveling bard. He thought yer chief might enjoy some song and story this night. Unless he already has a bard of his own."

"Alas, he no longer does. Arthur Mackenzies died barely a year ago, and the Campbell has yet to find a suitable replacement. He'd likely be verra pleased to offer yer friend the hospitality of his home." Caitlin paused and cocked her head. "But what of ye? Yer friend's worth is apparent. What do *ye* have to offer the Campbell?"

Something hard and cold flashed in the tall Highlander's eyes, then just as quickly disappeared. He chuckled and gestured to the claymore, a sword as long as a man was tall, that he wore fastened to his back.

"Naught, save that I go where my friend does, providing companionship as well as protection. Bards aren't generally given to swordplay, whereas I am. Besides, the harp he carries is verra finely wrought and, hence, verra valuable."

Caitlin eyed the claymore. In times such as these, his claim to serving as an armed escort rang true. Still, there was something about him that didn't set well with her. Indeed, there was something about the dark-haired man that both attracted *and* repelled her.

Gazing up into his mesmerizing eyes, Caitlin felt like a moth drawn to a flame. A flame that possessed a promise of sanctuary and warmth, yet at the same time threatened danger.

And well it should, she fiercely reminded herself. She had known such men before—men undeniably attractive in a dark, rugged, roguish sort of way. Men who, unfortunately for any lass who fell prey to their masculine charms, knew well how to use that power over a woman. There was little honor to be found, however, in such men. If Caitlin had learned anything in the past year, she had learned that well—*painfully* well.

"Ye look able enough indeed to provide protection," she said at last, belatedly coming to the realization that everyone was waiting for her to reply. "And I suppose there's naught wrong with permitting ye and yer friend to accompany us. It'd be the hospitable thing to do, ye being strangers to Campbell lands."

The dark man exchanged a glance with his friend then, turning back to Caitlin, nodded. "Aye, that we are. Strangers to Campbell lands."

He extended his hand. "My friend's name is Kenneth Buchanan, and mine's Darach MacFarlane. Friends call me Dar. And the rest either grant me a wide berth or don't live long enough to call me aught."

Of a sudden, he grinned, and the change was devastating. It was as if the sun, which heretofore had been muted, had burst into brilliant radiance. Caitlin's pulse gave a great lurch, then quickened. It took all the willpower she possessed to grasp his hand for a quick shake.

"Well, Darach MacFarlane, my name's Caitlin Campbell, and Janet and Jamie Campbell are my friends," she forced herself to say before releasing his hand.

Turning, she made her way to the front seat of the pony cart. "Still, since I've just barely met ye, I can hardly call us friends. I'm hoping, though," she said as she settled herself on the seat, then shot a quick glance over her shoulder, "one way or another, we'll never be enemies."

"That'd be my desire as well, lass." His firm, well-molded lips quirked up at one corner. "Indeed, my most *fervent* desire."

✝

She was a bonny lass, and no mistake, Darach thought as they walked along on one side of the pony cart. A lass who would drive most men to distraction, sending their thoughts careening off in wild, illogically hopeful directions. Directions that, ultimately, were doomed to humbling rejection and disappointment. Most men . . . but not him.

Indeed, a passionate tumble with the ebony-haired beauty with the blue-green eyes was the furthest thing from Darach's mind. He wasn't on his way to Kilchurn to seduce the local lasses or provide Niall Campbell and his ilk a pleasant interlude of story and song, even though, of necessity, such was the guise under which he must travel in order to infiltrate the stony fortress's defenses. Infiltrate and rescue his older brother from the depths of the Campbell's dungeons.

It didn't matter if Athe was innocent or guilty of the charges brought against him. It never had. Even now, Dar, who at the time hadn't been anywhere in the vicinity of the incident that had been the MacNaghtens' final undoing, wasn't certain who had truly instigated the brutal slaughter. All he knew was his father, brother, and other clansmen had managed to kill a much larger force of MacNabs in their own Hall during a feast. Killed them and now, almost a year and a half later, were still paying a horrible price.

Thanks to the act of proscription placed on them because of that fateful night, all MacNaghtens, be they man, woman, or child, were now hunted criminals. On pain of death, Mac-Naghtens were forbidden to wear their distinctive clan tartan or use their clan name, and must assume the name of another clan. Their lands had been seized, their weapons confiscated, and no other clan could take them in or associate with them.

Blessedly, there *were* a few clans still willing to offer them food and shelter, and to permit them to use their own clan name. The Buchanans and MacFarlanes were two of them.

Nonetheless, it stuck in Dar's craw every time he was forced to claim to be what he wasn't. Stuck in his craw to shame himself and the MacNaghtens by cowardly hiding behind the guise of another clan and its name. Stuck in his craw and burrowed deep in his soul, fueling a bitter rage against any and every man remotely responsible for the persecution that, in due course, was intended to wipe Clan MacNaghten from the face of the earth.

Niall Campbell was part and parcel of the travesty. It had been his men, after all, who had hunted down Athe in Hell's Glen, a rocky, narrow stretch of valley deep in Campbell lands between the towering peaks of Stob an Eas and Cruach nam Mult. It had been Campbell men who had brought him back to molder in Kilchurn's dungeon while awaiting sentencing and execution.

It mattered not that Niall Campbell was of the Breadalbane Campbells, a separate house of Clan Campbell, and that it had been the Argyll Campbells who had actively sought the act of proscription from the Scottish Crown. He had willingly enough joined forces when the proscription had been signed. He had willingly enough turned his back on Clan MacNaghten.

Still, Athe's rescue would be very difficult. Niall Campbell was no fool. Athe was most certainly heavily guarded, and Kilchurn was a well-fortified castle.

A frontal and far more honorable attack was impossible. Clan MacNaghten, like most of the neighboring clans, was no match for the might of even the Breadalbane Campbells. And any who dared attack Breadalbane would soon have Argyll to deal with as well.

Subterfuge and deceit were the only true weapons Dar possessed. But then, it was all any of his clan had left. There was no honor left them—the proscription had stripped that away just as surely as it had robbed them of their name, lands, and even their lives. There were no rules anymore save to win at all costs.

It was a dirty, despicable mess, to say the least, but whenever had condemned men had any options? And if innocents must suffer in the doing, Dar thought, his gaze turning to ice as the white stone towers of Kilchurn Castle finally came into view, it was no better or worse than what Clan MacNaghten had already and would continue to suffer.

✠

It wasn't long into their trek home when Caitlin noticed the bard beginning to limp slightly. By the time they topped the final hill separating them from the first view of Kilchurn, the man's steps were heavy, and he had moved close to the cart to grip its edge for support. She finally turned to Jamie, who sat between her and Janet.

"Pull up on the pony. Stop the cart."

Jamie did so immediately. "Aye? And what are ye needing?"

Caitlin glanced back at Kenneth. "Climb in. Whatever's wrong with ye, I cannot bear to watch yer pain a moment longer."

The bard shook his head. "It's naught, lass. I but stepped on a thorn last eve, and it festers a bit."

"Then more the reason to spare yer foot and not aggravate it further." She indicated the bed of the cart. "When we reach Kilchurn, I'll see to yer wound. I'm a healer, ye know."

"Nay, I didn't know that." Kenneth managed a wan smile, then looked to his companion.

The dark Highlander hesitated, then nodded. "Best ye do as she asks, lad. We'll need ye fit and hearty before we must next resume our journey."

He's the leader of the two, Caitlin thought as she watched Kenneth climb gingerly into the cart and settle himself. Not that the realization was especially surprising. Beneath Darach MacFarlane's affable if taciturn demeanor, there ran a vein of cold, hard resolve. She only wondered what he was so grimly resolute about.

Some instinct warned her that MacFarlane was a man on a mission. Problem was, the fulfillment of that mission might have unpleasant consequences for any who dared stand in his way. Yet he seemed to bear them no enmity. She supposed she should be grateful for that.

Several farm carts loaded with firewood clogged the road leading to Kilchurn's gate. The oxen pulling the wagons were notoriously slow as they traversed the slender spit of land now connecting the shore to the former island whereon the castle stood. At long last, though, they entered the outer courtyard and drew up in the south corner near the kitchen. Even as Jamie drove the pony cart into the yard, several clansmen had arrived to help unload and stack the wood near the kitchen door.

"Pull up as close to the main entrance of the keep as ye can," Caitlin instructed Jamie. "There are several empty rooms available below stairs in the servants' quarters. Janet and I can put the pony and cart away while ye and Darach carry Kenneth to one of them. I'll find ye there, just as soon as we finish and I fetch my bag of herbs and salves."

"That won't be necessary, lass," Dar was quick to say. "We needn't be imposing on ye and yer time. I can see to Kenneth's foot well enough, I'd wager."

"It's no imposition, just simple hospitality," Caitlin replied as Jamie halted the cart before the main entrance and she climbed out. "Besides, the Campbell might well be interested in having Kenneth do some harping this verra eve. The sooner we've a bard whose foot is beginning to heal, the better."

"As ye wish, lass," the big Highlander said with a shrug of his broad shoulders. "I yield to yer far better plan."

Jamie choked back a laugh. "Ye're a fast learner, laddie. She'll have her way sooner or later, at any rate."

Dar smirked. "A masterful woman, is she?"

"And why not?" Janet chose that moment to interject. "She is, after all, the Campbell's—"

"Enough, Janet." Some instinct warned Caitlin not to reveal just yet who she really was. Perhaps she was being overly wary, but something about the two strangers urged her to caution.

She took her cousin by the arm and began tugging her along. "We've chores aplenty to see to, and no time to waste on further yammering. We'll leave that, instead, to these men."

"He's verra full of himself," Janet muttered once they were out of earshot and headed into the keep. "I can't say as I care much for him."

16

"Aye, and ye've made that most apparent from the first moment ye saw him."

"And ye *do* care for him?" Her eyes wide with disbelief, Caitlin's compatriot halted and turned to face her. "After what David Graham did to ye, I'd have thought yer tastes had taken a turn for the better. But if ye now find that vagabond appealing—"

"He's verra braw." With an exasperated roll of her eyes, Caitlin cut her cousin off. "But just because I can admire a fine piece of man flesh doesn't mean it goes any further. I'm well aware that pretty faces and forms oft hide empty heads and hard, scheming hearts.

"Besides," she added as she took Janet's hand and again tugged her forward, "whatever does it matter what either of us thinks, one way or another? I'd wager Darach MacFarlane and his friend will be gone within the week."

"Then ye'd better see to young Kenneth's foot posthaste," Janet said, beginning to climb the stairs leading to the second floor bedchambers. "The sooner he's healed, the sooner we're well rid of them."

Aye, that we are, Caitlin thought as her cousin entered her own bedchamber and she continued down the long stone corridor. *Well rid of them, indeed.*

For already, in spite of common sense and painful experience, every time she looked at Darach MacFarlane, Caitlin's thoughts turned to what it would be like to melt into the powerful circle of his arms and kiss those full, firm, and most sensual of lips. Thoughts she had resolved never, ever to contemplate—much less allow to become reality—again.

✛

"Have a care with that one, Dar, or yer propensity for a comely lass will again get ye into serious trouble," Kenneth pleaded once Jamie had taken them to a spare chamber in the dark labyrinth below ground and departed. "The task before us is difficult enough without ye complicating it by coupling with one of the Campbell's servants."

As he closed the thick oak door and latched it shut, Dar gave a disparaging snort. "And do ye think me so lust-driven that I'd let a bonny lass—and truth be told, that blue-eyed beauty *is* one of the bonniest I've ever laid eyes on—endanger our mission to free Athe? Hardly." He turned and strode over to the simple, straw-stuffed mattress he and Jamie had deposited Kenneth upon. "If the opportunity arises for a quick tryst in some private corner or leaf-shaded bower, then I'll be the first to seize it. But aside from such a fortuitous occurrence, her only value is to provide us with whatever information might help us gain access to the dungeon and the keys to Athe's cell."

Kenneth settled back on his bed and sighed. "I'd hoped ye'd see it that way. Ye've always been a generally sensible sort, but the way ye were looking at her . . . well, I haven't seen ye look at a lass like that in a verra long time."

"I can admire an especially comely female, can't I?" Dar grinned. "Tell me true. Can ye claim ye didn't find Caitlin the bonniest lass ye've ever seen?"

"She's verra bonny. I just don't see how it's the time or place to be paying *any* lass much attention, that's all."

Kenneth leaned down and pulled his clarsach from its leather bag. With a gentle, loving touch, he stroked the tautly strung wire strings.

"Now, this harp . . . I confess I can hardly keep my hands or eyes off it for verra long. But then, it'll never betray me, or toss me aside for another, or break my heart."

"Fine. Fine," Dar muttered in disgust. "Ye're right. It's past time we drop the matter entirely. Once ye begin spouting honeyed words about yer harp, trying to discuss women with ye is already a lost cause."

As clear, ringing notes began to rise from the bronze strings, Dar strode over to his own bed, dropped his traveling bag beside it, and lay down. Beneath the woolen blanket, the mattress gave a little atop its rope supports, but the wooden frame was sturdy and easily supported his weight. Pillowing his arms behind his head, the big Highlander settled back and closed his eyes.

There wouldn't be much time for rest, he wagered, before Caitlin arrived to treat Kenneth's foot. Still, after a journey that had begun before dawn, with a day that was now fast fading to sunset, even a brief respite was welcome. He needed time to sort through the myriad options that now presented themselves, ensconced as they finally were in Kilchurn Castle.

In the end, all the decisions that mattered were up to him. Kenneth was as brave and loyal as they came, but he lacked the head for complex strategies. His value in this adventure was to serve as a plausible reason to get into Kilchurn, and then as a distraction while Dar freed Athe from his prison cell. Each man, however, was vital to this plan, and Dar gave his cousin his due.

He wondered if Caitlin might be of any use in this undertaking. She claimed to be a healer. As such, she surely moved about the castle freely and had the trust of all. He'd have to tread carefully with her, though, in attempting to extract information and access to places he would never easily be able to visit himself. She was clever and quick. He had ascertained that pretty much from the start.

There was just something in those striking, turquoise blue eyes that bespoke a keen intelligence overlaid with a natural wariness. Caitlin wasn't a woman easily misled, and it was already apparent she didn't suffer fools easily. It was also quite evident she didn't trust him.

Not that her suspicion disturbed Dar in the least. He had charmed women far more worldly and jaded. And Caitlin Campbell, for all her bold words and apparent confidence, was still a maiden in every sense of the word. No man of any experience could've missed the truth in her eyes whenever their gazes met.

Still, on further consideration, her lack of experience could well play to his advantage. Dar also knew when a woman was attracted to him, and Caitlin didn't hide that attraction as successfully as she might have imagined. All he had to do was woo her a bit, and she would be his. With Kenneth sure to be laid up with his infected foot for at least several days, Dar now had sufficient excuse and opportunity to remain at Kilchurn.

Sufficient excuse and opportunity, as well, to lay siege to a black-haired beauty's heart. Once he had scaled that wall, he would use her to gain access to the information he needed to free his brother. It might not be honest or honorable, but such fine aspirations had died with the act of proscription against the MacNaghtens.

Dar's mouth quirked in black humor. If the truth were told, for him at least, such fine aspirations had died long before the act of proscription. Died when his father had refused to believe his claims of innocence and banished him from the clan, cast him out to roam the Highlands as a broken man.

It was the greatest of all ironies. An outlaw, a broken man, was now the last hope of Clan MacNaghten. Indeed, if his father had lived, he most likely would've refused Dar's aid. But his obstinate, unyielding sire hadn't survived the brutal night that had brought their clan at last to its inevitable downfall. And, like it or not, there wasn't anyone left who possessed even the remotest chance of saving his father's favorite son.

No one, save the other son. The one who had been a never-ending source of disappointment and despair.

No one, save Dar.

2

Her head buried in the depths of a wooden barrel as she scraped out the last handfuls of dried marigold flowers, Caitlin at first didn't hear Anne's greeting. After a quick tap on her shoulder finally alerted her to another's presence, she levered herself up out of the barrel. Her fists full of the pungent petals, she wheeled about. Niall's russet-haired wife stood there, with Brendan, her chubby, fifteen-month-old son, perched on her hip.

"Janet said I might find ye here." Anne's glance strayed to Caitlin's hands. "Are we already out of marigold ointment? If I'd known, I would've made up a fresh batch."

Caitlin could feel the heat steal into her cheeks. "The fault's mine. I used the last of it on Maudie's hand after she burnt it grabbing that poker someone had left overlong in the fire. I meant to make more ointment, but I forgot."

The chief's wife smiled. "Well, no harm done, I suppose. But a good healer is also a prepared healer."

"Aye, so she is. That's one lesson I still need some work on, I'm afraid." Caitlin held out her fisted hands. "Not that there's much left to work with. Fortunately, springtide is well upon us, and the flowers are finally beginning to bloom."

"We *have* gone through a lot of marigold ointment this year, haven't we? Mayhap we should see about growing a larger bed to harvest this summer."

"Either that, or encourage the castle folk to take greater care not to injure themselves quite so often." Caitlin grinned. "As if that would ever happen."

"That's verra unlikely, ye can be sure. Especially with our men. A more clumsy, careless bunch of lads never existed. Still, if we run out of marigold ointment, we've always other herbal remedies at hand."

Caitlin nodded, her gaze lifting to the rafters of the modest-sized, stone chamber a few feet down the hall from the kitchen. The room had once served as an additional kitchen storage closet. Soon after Anne and Niall were wed, though, Anne had appropriated it for a healer's storeroom.

Myriad bundles of dried plants hung from the wooden beams. Two tall, sturdy cabinets, on the far wall on either side of a slit of a window, were filled with bowls, several small cast-iron pots, and all sizes of stoppered jars, each carefully labeled. On the narrow wooden table sitting in the middle of the room, a stone mortar and pestle took center stage. Several sharp little knives in a jar, a stack of thin, smooth boards, and ten glass decanters stood neatly lined up alongside the mortar and pestle.

"Fortunately," she continued, meeting Anne's glance, "we've got a good supply left of nettles to make nettle tea for burns, and St. John's Wort for festering wounds. Still, I am partial to marigold ointment."

"As am I." Anne paused to heft her black-haired son a bit higher on her hip. "Janet also mentioned we've two new visitors—some bard and his personal guard. And that this bard has an injured foot."

"His name's Kenneth, and I think his foot may be infected from a thorn he stepped on. Mayhap, though, he left a bit of the thorn tip in when he tried to pull it out, and that's what's paining him. I won't know until I examine his foot. Once, that is," Caitlin added as she walked to the table and dumped the marigold petals into the mortar's rounded stone bowl, "I get some fresh ointment made."

"Well, then, I won't detain ye." The other woman turned to go, then paused. "The bard's companion . . . What did Janet say his name was? Darach, I believe?"

"Aye, that's his name."

"What do ye make of him?"

Caitlin tensed. Just as she feared when first Anne had made mention of Janet, her cousin had gone and blabbered her concern about the dark Highlander. And likely, as well, made mention of what she viewed as Caitlin's improper interest in the man.

Needing a moment to gather her wits about her, Caitlin dusted off the petals still clinging to her hands over the mortar. Moving to the nearest cabinet, she took down two jars, one containing beeswax and the other imported olive oil. She next found a small cast-iron pot, added a cupful of beeswax and a spoonful of olive oil to the pot, and stirred the two together. Then, because she knew she couldn't delay the inevitable discussion without stirring her sister-in-law's suspicions all the more, Caitlin looked up.

"He's big, braw, and holds most things closely to himself. Yet, for all his threadbare clothes, he carries a finely made claymore. And his speech isn't that of a common peasant."

"So, ye think he bears watching, do ye?"

"Aye. Kenneth is likely what he claims to be—a traveling bard—and Darach could just as likely be his guard, but no harm's done keeping a close eye on them. Time will tell the truth of their claims."

"Janet made mention of this Darach's interest in ye." Anne cocked her head. "And, more to the point, of yer apparent interest in him."

So, here it comes.

Caitlin expelled a long, exasperated breath. "I already said he was braw. Indeed, I'd wager he'd catch even yer eye, if ye weren't so besotted with my brother. But the act of admiring a man's looks is hardly the same thing as swearing undying love and devotion to him."

"I just don't want to see ye hurt again, like yer were over Lord Graham. And neither does Niall."

"So, Janet's gone to Niall as well, has she?" Anger swelled in Caitlin. This time, her well-meaning but loose-tongued cousin had gone too far. She would soon hear a few choice words on that topic, and no mistake.

"Nay, as a matter of fact, Janet hasn't," Anne replied calmly. "It was difficult enough for her even to come to me. As for Niall, he isn't even here. Shortly after ye all left for Dalmally, he was called away to Inveraray for some pressing business. I expect he'll be gone at least two or three days."

Inveraray Castle—the seat of the Argyll Campbells. Caitlin could only wonder what plot the wily old earl was concocting this time. Another attempt at a land grab from some smaller, unsuspecting clan, no doubt. But since Niall had so far managed to avoid involving his branch of the clan in such underhanded dealings, Caitlin had to surmise this trip involved some other issue altogether.

"Well, it's for the best then," she said as she took up the mortar and pestle and proceeded to grind the dried marigold petals into a fine powder. "The main reason I invited Kenneth and Darach to stay here was so we—and especially Niall—could enjoy some harping and song. But now I'll have a chance to see to the bard's foot and get it on its way to healing before Niall's return."

"Aye, Niall does like his music. And ever since little Brendan came along"—Anne cast her son a loving glance—"I've had little time even to take down my clarsach, much less play it. Not that," she added with a laugh, "I was ever as proficient as dear old Arthur. Why, the sounds he could coax from his harp surely gave the angels pause."

"I suppose we can't expect such expertise from Kenneth, considering his age and all, but hopefully he can at least earn his keep. Darach claims the bard owns a very finely wrought clarsach. That would lead one to believe the man himself is worthy of it."

"One would think so." Anne transferred Brendan up into her arms. "I'd love to see the harp and meet both men, but just now I have a soggy bairn to attend to."

"Well, depending on the condition of Kenneth's foot, mayhap they can join us for the supper meal. Two hours' time should be more than enough to see to his foot. Once I get this ointment cooked over the kitchen fire and cooled, that is."

"Then I'll be going and not keep ye from yer task."

Caitlin sniffed the air delicately and grinned. "Nor will I keep ye from yers, for I'd lay odds that wee Brendan has more than a wet diaper to change."

✠

"Luck is with ye," Caitlin said as she finished wrapping the bandage about Kenneth's foot and tied it off. "Though there was a wee tip of thorn left in yer sole, which was beginning to inflame, there's yet no sign of festering. What with removing the thorn, cleansing it well, and the marigold ointment, we may soon have ye on the mend.

"Meanwhile," she added as she gently laid his injured foot atop two pillows, "I'd like ye to stay off that foot as much as possible. Ye must also elevate it to ease the swelling and improve the flow of blood."

Kenneth sighed but nodded his acquiescence. "I'm not a man given to inactivity, but I'll do as ye ask, lass. And at least I can practice my clarsach while abed." He grinned. "I've several new tunes I'm working on, so it'll be time well spent."

"Aye, it will. And we'll expect to enjoy the fruit of those labors in a few days." Caitlin began replacing her supplies in the large, leather bag she carried for her healing visits. "Which will work out perfectly, as Niall isn't even in Kilchurn at present and won't return for the next few days."

"Niall Campbell? Yer clan chief?" Darach asked abruptly from his bed, where he had been watching Caitlin care for his friend.

She nodded, more than a bit curious over his sudden interest after such a long span of silence. "Aye, one and the same."

"Och, what a disappointment! I'd hoped for the chance to meet him." He rose and walked over to stand beside them.

"Well, ye can at least make his wife, Anne's, acquaintance, if ye wish to sup with us this eve. She expressed a desire to greet the both of ye." Caitlin glanced back at Kenneth. "Unfortunately for ye, however, the walk would be too much for yer foot. My suggestion is to have someone bring ye a tray of food, and ye remain here for all yer meals. At least for another day or two anyway."

"As ye wish." The younger man looked to his friend. "There's no reason ye need hole up here, though. Go to the supper meal, have a look around, and meet the Lady Anne."

"Mayhap on the morrow." Dar smiled down at Kenneth. "But not this eve. I'll go up with the lass and have her show me about"—he glanced at Caitlin—"if ye think ye can spare me a bit of yer time, and then bring down a tray of food for the both of us."

"Supper should be served in a half hour or so," Caitlin replied, not so sure she cared to spend more time than was absolutely necessary in the disturbing Highlander's presence. "Once I put away my bag, I can only manage a wee tour of Kilchurn before we must gather for the meal."

"That should suffice for today." Dar reached for her bag and slung it over his shoulder. "It'll take me awhile to learn my way about a castle this large. Just being able to navigate the labyrinth of corridors down here, back up to the first level, and then mayhap my way to the kitchen, will likely be all I can handle on this first try."

Though Caitlin seriously doubted Darach MacFarlane would have any difficulty learning his way through a maze at first try, she decided it wiser to keep her opinions to herself. Better to play along for the time being. The truth of his abilities would become evident soon enough.

Since Niall wasn't even in Kilchurn and Anne was preoccupied with their son and the day-to-day running of such a large dwelling, the task of watching these two men must of necessity fall to Caitlin. Or, leastwise, until her suspicions proved correct and the help of others was indicated. After all, the responsibility was first and foremost hers just *because* she had been the one to invite them into the sanctuary of their home.

Unfortunately, that also required Caitlin to spend far more time than she cared to, keeping close watch over them. Or, to be more precise, over Darach MacFarlane.

"Well, then if that plan suits yer needs," Caitlin said, climbing to her feet, "let us be off." She smiled down at Kenneth. "It can get a wee bit chilly down here. Besides yer supper, I'll see that ye both get some extra blankets."

"Ye're kind to think of our comfort," the bard replied. "I thank ye for that, lass."

"Aye, that we both do," Darach added as he walked to the door and opened it. "All that's ever been said of Campbell hospitality has certainly proven true."

"It's no more than what any Highlander would grant to a stranger." She brushed past him, then waited until he had closed the door. "And no less than what I'd expect of ye and yer clan, if ever I was to pay ye a visit."

Something flickered in the depths of the man's silver blue eyes, then was gone. "Aye, no less," he muttered. "It's the Highland way, after all."

He almost seemed bitter, Caitlin thought as they made their way down the torch-lit corridor. As if he resented having to adhere to the ancient Highland code requiring anyone—even an enemy—who requested the shelter and hospitality of another's home be granted it with all good grace.

She could only wonder at what circumstances had turned him against the custom. It was as inbred in a Highlander as the love of clan, the stirring of the blood whenever the bagpipes played, or the unfettered joy of traversing the wild, untamed mountains and glens. Somehow, in some way, she sensed he had been deeply hurt, or even betrayed, by the code.

"If ye count the torches," Caitlin said, deciding to file that little observation in the back of her mind for future reference and move onto the task at hand, "ye'll discover the easiest way to discern which corridor to turn at to make yer way back upstairs. And, as ye can see"—she indicated each widely spaced, pitifully flickering torch hanging from a rusted iron bracket on the wall—"ye turn at the third torch."

They halted where the corridor intersected with yet another corridor. A dank, musty scent wafted by on a chill current of air.

"That seems simple enough." Darach turned to gaze down the hallway that continued along the way they had already come. "And where does the rest of that corridor lead? It seems to go on forever."

"To more servant's quarters, additional storerooms for foodstuffs, and, finally, to more steps leading down to the dungeon. None of which ye'll need to be visiting, I'm certain, in yer short stay here."

He glanced back at her and smiled. "Nay, I suppose not." He gestured ahead of them. "Shall we continue on then? I'm eager to see the rest of Kilchurn."

"Aye." Caitlin stepped out once more. "Let's be on our way."

Wordlessly, she led him down the connecting corridor until they reached the staircase leading to the main floor. After the dimness and stone-muffled silence of the underground level, for a moment Caitlin was overwhelmed with the brightness and hustle bustle. Servants hurried to and fro, some with trays of victuals meant for the Great Hall, where they usually ate the supper meal, and others with armloads of fresh, folded laundry or sheaves of dried rushes to scatter on newly cleaned floors.

Caitlin smiled. Anne had quickly grown into the efficient, meticulous chatelaine that Kilchurn had lacked since the death of Caitlin and Niall's mother now eight years past. But, even more importantly, Anne had brought such joy not only to Niall but to Kilchurn and its inhabitants as well.

"That most pleasing smile on yer face . . ." Darach chose that moment to interject, dragging Caitlin from her contented thoughts. "Dare I presume my company played a part in yer happiness?"

She shot him a bemused glance as they walked the short distance from the stairs to the healer's storeroom. "Hardly. My thoughts weren't even concerned with ye." Then, realizing how unkind her words may have sounded, she grinned a bit sheepishly. "No offense meant, of course."

"No offense taken. I suppose I am, after all, hardly the sort to interest a lass like ye."

At that less than subtle attempt to garner a compliment, Caitlin couldn't help but laugh. "If ye hope to interest any lass, much less a lass like me, ye really must put some additional effort into yer conversational stratagems. All but asking for flattery is hardly the way to intrigue a woman."

Darach arched a dark brow. "And do ye truly imagine that was my plan? I'd have taken ye for a far more astute lass than that."

His question gave her pause. If he hadn't been seeking a favorable reaction from her, what, indeed, *was* he about?

"Well, playing games with me also falls far short of the mark." Caitlin drew up at the storeroom door. "I've neither the time nor the patience, so why don't ye just tell me what yer plan actually was?"

"To make conversation, of course. To get ye to talk with me. How else is a man to learn more about a woman he finds verra attractive on so many levels?"

For once, Caitlin found herself short on words. Well, momentarily, at least.

"Ye're quite the gallant, aren't ye?" she finally asked. "And I'll wager, as well, that ye're used to having all the lasses swooning at the verra sight of ye."

He laughed, and the deep, rich sound sent a most involuntary ripple of pleasure through her. "Not *all* of them, it seems."

"Losing yer touch then, are ye?"

"Evidently."

She gave a derisive snort, turned, unlocked the storeroom door, and walked in. That was her first mistake. Darach followed her, closed the door behind him, and slid the interior bolt into place.

Caitlin set her bag on the table and began removing its contents. "And what do ye have in mind, to lock us both in like that?" she asked, masking her rising apprehension with a false calm. "Because I don't take ye for a fool, and the stone walls aren't so thick that my cries for help wouldn't soon bring me aid."

"Not to mention any unseemly conduct on my part would besmirch the Highland code of hospitality," he added with a wry twist of his lips.

"Actually, I believe the expectation of hospitality falls primarily on the host, not the guest."

She began to replace the jar of marigold ointment, roll of extra bandages, a bowl that held a small sponge, and her box of surgical instruments, which—besides the needles and thread used to suture wounds, a cautery iron, a pair of shears, several sizes of probes used to dig out arrows, pistol balls, and various and sundry other objects that might penetrate the flesh—also held several razor-sharp small knives. That box she put on a lower shelf within easy reach, then turned to face him.

"So, ye feel then, do ye, that the tragedy nearly a year and a half past when the MacNaghtens turned on the MacNabs in their own home *didn't* step outside the bounds of hospitality?"

"Hardly. What the MacNaghtens did was reprehensible. Besides all the other despicable things they'd already committed, it well and finally justified their proscription." Caitlin smirked and shook her head. "So, if ye're of a mind to choose *that* incident as validation for whatever dark and dirty acts ye seek to do while at Kilchurn, yer intent is sadly muddled."

"Ye'd hear no argument on that from me," he said as he moved toward her, "if my intent truly was dark and dirty. But surely a wee kiss from a bonny lassie wouldn't be such a dastardly thing."

Darach drew up before her. Instinctively, Caitlin backed away until she was pressed against the cabinet. She couldn't help it—no woman could.

From even across the expanse of a room, the big Highlander exuded a powerful, intimidating presence. But up this close . . . Suffice it to say, the vast disparity in their size and relative strength froze the blood in her veins and choked the breath from her body. Surprisingly, though, at the same time Caitlin felt her heartbeat quicken with anticipation.

The realization angered her. He was the most handsome and exciting man she had ever met, yet he nonetheless presumed far, far too much. In the past, she—not the man—had always determined the pace of a dalliance, *if* there even was to be one. Indeed, even that disastrous business with David Graham had initially been of her doing.

She slid her hand behind her back and gingerly placed it in the box of instruments. Immediately, her fingers grazed one of the knives. With the greatest care, she moved her hand down until she felt a smooth metal handle and gripped it.

"Nay, a wee kiss wouldn't be such a dastardly thing," she replied, forcing the response past a throat gone tight and dry, "*if* the lass were of a mind to accept it. But this lass hasn't the least interest in being kissed, and especially not by the likes of ye."

The smile on Darach's fine, firm lips didn't waver, but a wolfish gleam flared in his eyes. She had tossed down the gauntlet, challenged him. Caitlin belatedly admitted that was her second mistake. The big Highlander was quite obviously a predator—and his favorite prey appeared to be women.

"On the contrary," he said, his voice dropping to a husky whisper. He leaned close, propping both hands against the wall on either side of the cabinet, enclosing her in the prison of his arms. "I think ye *are* interested, and especially by the likes of me."

Darach's head lowered toward her. No amount of reasoning or protest would stop him now, Caitlin realized. Nothing, save one thing. She pulled her hand free from behind her and pressed the knife to the side of his throat.

"Think again, ye arrogant knave," she growled. "Think again, or suffer the consequences."

He paused a hairsbreadth from her lips. "And would ye truly slit my throat over a wee kiss?" He smiled. "I think not."

With that, Darach MacFarlane took her mouth, covering it in a gentle, achingly tender, and most practiced way. It was as if a bolt of lightning shot through Caitlin, from her lips to the tips of her toes. She went rigid, couldn't breathe. Yet, at the same time, she wanted nothing more than to arch up to meet him, to deepen the kiss, to press into the length of him and never let go.

She whimpered, and the blade lowered to her side, then fell to the floor. First one arm, then the other, snaked about Darach's neck. She couldn't help it. And it was, after all, but one wee kiss.

His mouth opened hungrily over hers, his lips slanting in ardent, demanding possession, his arms moving to encircle her and pull her yet closer. Caitlin met his onslaught with a fiery one of her own. It was foolish, mad even, but for a glorious instant more she couldn't help herself. Then reason, traitorous and most unwelcome, crept back in.

He was no better, indeed, likely worse, than David had been. David, leastwise, had treated her with a circumspect restraint for months, courting her with the most gentlemanly overtures. He, at least, had paid her respect, even if it, in the end, had been mainly due to her Campbell name. But this man—this Darach MacFarlane—barely knew her.

There was nothing he wanted but a brief, sordid tryst behind a locked door. A wee kiss indeed! He wanted that and so very much more.

With an angry, frustrated sound, Caitlin wrenched first her mouth and then her body free of his possessive, controlling clasp. She brought her hands up, placed them on the hard-muscled expanse of his chest, and pushed.

It was like trying to move some huge boulder. Darach released her but didn't budge.

"Had enough for now, have ye?" he asked, his voice rough and raw.

"Enough for a lifetime, were we to live a hundred years and more!" Caitlin glared up at him. "Ye got yer wee kiss. Now go before I change my mind and use my knife on ye anyway."

Darach laughed but began backing away. "Dinna fash yerself, lass. I'm a patient man and verra satisfied for the present. There'll be other times, and no need to make idle threats with that wee knife of yers."

"Wee knife? Other times?"

This man was insufferable! Caitlin stooped, picked up the knife, then straightened and advanced on him.

"Are ye daft? Make no mistake. There'll be no other times. Not now and not ever!"

"Have it yer way then," he said as he reached the door, slid back the bolt, and swung the portal wide. "But we all know how oft a lass is wont to change her mind, don't we? And especially one who kisses a man like ye just did me."

With an outraged cry and knife held high, Caitlin flung herself across the room. Darach was far too swift for her, though.

By the time she reached the door and hurried into the corridor, the fluttering edge of his kilt disappearing around a corner was all that remained of the dark Highlander. To her chagrin, however, their exchange apparently hadn't been totally private. Anne and her cousin Janet stood transfixed just outside the kitchen door, their eyes wide and mouths agape.

3

"I take it that was one of our guests?" Anne inquired once she had sent Janet on her way, escorted Caitlin back into the storeroom, and closed the door. "Considering his quite admirable agility and speed, I can only also assume he was Darach MacFarlane and not the bard."

If she had walked into the Great Hall dressed only in her nightrail, Caitlin couldn't have been more humiliated. Curse that vile, contemptible, loathsome man! At every turn, he managed to shame her in some manner or another. Shame *and* trick her, if the truth were told.

But nothing was served making excuses to Anne. Her sister-in-law was too quick of mind for such futile ploys.

"Aye, that was him," she muttered, not quite able to meet the other woman's gaze. "Would ye like for me to go after him and fetch him back so ye can finally make his acquaintance? Then ye could take over his friend's care, and I could be well and finally rid of him."

"From what I overheard—thanks to yer wide open door—it didn't seem to me that ye or he were all that disposed never to see each other again. Leastwise, not for long."

Hot blood flooded Caitlin's cheeks yet again. "It was but a wee misunderstanding, and naught to trouble yerself about."

An auburn brow arched, and Anne eyed the knife still clenched in Caitlin's fist. "And which misunderstanding might that be? The threat to his life and limb or the kiss? And do one or both necessitate a talk with yer brother upon his return?"

"Neither, Anne. Neither, I beg ye!"

Caitlin laid the knife on the table and rushed back over to her sister-in-law. She grasped both her hands.

"Please, Anne. Don't tell Niall. Och, don't tell him!"

"He's not some ogre, lass." Anne's silver eyes warmed with concern. "He just cares for ye and doesn't wish to see ye hurt again."

Caitlin gave an unsteady laugh, released the other woman's hands, and took a step back. "Then more's the reason not to unduly upset him. Darach MacFarlane means naught to me. I despise the man. Indeed, I rue my shortsighted folly even in inviting him to Kilchurn."

Anne graced her with a disbelieving look. "I think, instead, the folly began but a short time ago, when ye invited a stranger into this room and closed the door behind ye." She sighed and shook her head. "Truly, Caitlin, it's past time ye learned to be more cautious with men."

Listening to Anne's well meant and quite accurate words, Caitlin could feel her eyes begin to burn and knew the tears would soon follow. She was so frustrated, so ashamed, she could hardly think straight.

Darach MacFarlane had instigated this whole sorry mess. He, not she, had closed and locked the door, then demanded a kiss. Yet it was *her* motives that would be suspect, *her* honor that would suffer because of it.

Why, oh why, did the man always seem to increase his stature in the aftermath of such incidents, while the woman always paid the price? It wasn't fair, and she was mightily sick of it!

"It was only a one-time kiss, Anne," she finally replied, knowing full well she was as culpable as Darach in that kiss. It wasn't, after all, as if he'd had to force her to do anything. "And it's not as if I'm betrothed, much less wed, to anyone."

"Aye, well I know that. I just worry about ye, Caitlin. Ye seem so at a loss, so restless and searching, especially since Lord Graham withdrew his offer of marriage . . ."

"And pleased I am that he did," Caitlin cried even as tears stung her eyes. "David was never worthy of me!"

"He indeed was never worthy of ye. And neither was young Rory nor some of the others who came after him, even before ye met David Graham." A faraway look clouded Anne's eyes, and she smiled. "I'll never forget the look on yer face when Niall caught ye kissing Rory that day in the rose bower. I'm still not certain which emotion was stronger in ye—the shock or the high indignation at being caught."

"Though I hadn't the wisdom to see it then, Rory was never the man for me either."

"Aye, wisdom." Anne took her hand and gave it a squeeze. "Please accept this in the spirit it's intended, for I love ye dearly, lass. But that's exactly what concerns me. Yer continued lack of wisdom when it comes to men and to other things entirely."

Caitlin dragged in a deep, steadying breath. She knew she was proud and impatient and prone to think more of herself than of others. She also possessed a restless spirit. A part of her was always searching for something better, something more exciting and fulfilling—whatever that *something* might be.

She knew those were her deepest flaws. She didn't need Anne, her brother, or even the local preacher repeatedly reminding her of them. Besides, recognition of a flaw didn't seem to make it any easier to eradicate. Nor did it make it any easier to accept as a failing requiring one humbly to beg forgiveness.

"I need a good, strong man to rein me in," she said, wiping away the tears. "I've known it for a while now, but good, strong men seem in short supply of late."

"A good, strong man is a blessing indeed," the auburn-haired woman replied. "But the motivation to change—*and* the change—must ultimately come from within ourselves. Ye must be yer own woman, Caitlin, and do the changing because *ye* feel the need, not because another wishes ye to do so. Ye must die to yerself because the Lord asks it of ye, because it's the right thing to do. No matter how hard the task seems—and och, at times it's hard, painfully hard, indeed—ye must always strive for what's right and good."

"There's no sin in a simple kiss."

"Nay, there isn't. But we must guard our emotions and our fleshly desires, lest they lead us into an occasion of sin." Anne cocked her head. "From the looks of that braw young MacFarlane and the alacrity with which ye apparently responded to him, I think it wise to step back. Step back and reconsider where this might be headed."

"That's not as easy as it may seem."

As much as she hated to admit it, Caitlin couldn't help but speak what she knew in her heart to be true. Even now, as furious as she was with him, try as hard as she could, she couldn't quell the thrill of anticipation she felt at the consideration of next seeing Darach.

"I, of all people, know it's not easy. If only ye knew all the times before we wed that I was sorely tempted just being in Niall's presence." Anne sighed. "I burned for him, Caitlin. Och, *how* I burned."

"Leastwise Niall was an honorable man. But Darach . . ." She threw up her hands. "Och, why am I even bothering with this? He's leaving soon, likely never to return and even less likely ever to want to. I mean naught to him but some passing dalliance."

"More the reason to guard yer heart, lass. In truth, ye know naught about him. And, if I recall correctly, ye earlier made mention that ye weren't even sure of his real reasons for being here."

Caitlin frowned. "Aye. True enough. I *am* being played for the fool, aren't I?"

Anne smiled. "I hope he isn't quite that coldhearted and conniving. But mayhap it's wise to take a bit more care."

"Best I not associate with him again, leastwise not by myself, until he departs Kilchurn." She nodded with resolve. "Aye, it's for the best not knowingly to place oneself in temptation's path. Will ye see to Kenneth's foot from here on until it's healed? Then they can both be on their way."

"Gladly. When will it next need care?"

"On the morrow. If all goes well, it should heal quickly." Caitlin paused as a thought struck her. "They'll still need their supper taken down to them this eve. I was in the process of giving that *man* a tour of Kilchurn before sending him to the kitchen to fetch their supper, when we got waylaid in here. In fact, I don't know where Darach has even gone to."

"Dinna fash yerself. I'll send someone down with their meal. If he hasn't returned to their chamber by then, Jamie can find him, wherever he has gone to."

A heavy weight seemed suddenly to have lifted from Caitlin's shoulders. Aye, she thought, it was best simply to avoid any further interaction with Darach MacFarlane until he finally walked out of her life forever. For reasons she couldn't quite comprehend, he attracted her like no man ever had. Not even David had disturbed or drawn her like he did.

That wasn't, however, she realized with a tiny shiver, necessarily a good thing. Not a good thing at all.

✠

The further Dar got from the outraged little spitfire, the more his pleasure at besting her dissipated. But not, he was swift to assure himself, because he had been at all affected by their brief if surprisingly passionate kiss. Or, leastwise, no more so than he had ever been by any other bonny lass he had kissed.

It was only his self-disgust at playing such a cad that rankled him. He wasn't above taking what was freely offered; yet, despite Caitlin's barely disguised attraction to him, he *had* pushed harder than he was wont. Though he had little enough honor left him these days, he did prefer to imagine himself more honorable with the lasses than he had been with that black-haired beauty.

He could blame her, he supposed. The looks she sent him . . . those brilliant, flashing eyes . . . and her lips!

By mountain and sea, but she had the most red, ripe, and succulent of lips! It would take a saint to deny those lips, especially when they were lifted so willingly to a man.

The lass stirred his blood, and no mistake. But it wasn't just her slender, womanly form or eager response. Beneath her carefully guarded demeanor there lay sharp intelligence, a clever wit, and a good and caring heart. There was also, Dar added with an amused quirk of his mouth, a headstrong willfulness and deep-seated pride. All things considered, she was the most exceptional and exciting woman he had ever met.

The realization was of meager comfort as he made his way back down the stairs leading to their underground quarters. The likelihood was very strong now that they would have no supper, and it wasn't as if Dar could explain that his impulsive assault on Caitlin in the storeroom was the reason. Kenneth had already warned him to have a care with the lass. To now explain what he had done would hardly go over well with his friend.

In retrospect, it went over no better with him. He had been a dunderheaded fool. If he didn't have a care, he might even jeopardize the success of their plan to free Athe. And all because of a spur-of-the-moment impulse to kiss that fiery-tempered little wench!

Well, Kenneth didn't need to know any of this, Dar decided

as he reached the bottom of the stairs and took a seat on the lowest step. He would simply wait here a bit until supper was served in the Great Hall. Then he would pay a visit to the kitchen and put together a meal of sorts from the leavings. His friend would be none the wiser when he walked in with a tray full of food.

A chill breeze wafted up from the corridor intersecting the one he now sat in. Caitlin had mentioned providing them with extra blankets this eve. After what he had done, Dar had an inkling she would as soon let them freeze to death down here as starve. It might be a more difficult undertaking, though, to filch blankets than it would be food.

Not that it mattered much to Dar. He had endured far more frigid temperatures with only the protection of his plaid. But Kenneth, being a bard, wasn't quite the outdoorsman that he was.

In the bargain, there was his foot to consider. It was vital Kenneth recuperate posthaste. For that to happen, though, Dar had to ensure everything necessary was provided.

With a sigh of resignation, he stood, turned, and headed back up the stairs. There was nothing to be done for it but find Caitlin and beg her pardon. But not because he truly regretted kissing her. In his heart of hearts, Dar would never regret that.

Sometimes, however, one must humble oneself for the sake of others. And it was, after all, only fair recompense for being such a dunderheaded fool.

✝

"Might I help ye find what ye're seeking?"

Dar jerked to a halt. He had just exited the kitchen and was about to enter the Great Hall when a woman's voice behind him caught him up short. He turned.

A pretty, russet-haired woman with silver eyes who looked but a few years older than Caitlin stood there. In her arms was a chubby little boy. From her bearing and simple but elegant green dress, Dar knew this must be Anne Campbell.

He managed an awkward half bow, acutely aware of how long it had been since he had been party to such courtly manners. "Aye, lady," he said as he straightened, feeling like some bumbling oaf who had wandered where he wasn't welcome. "I'm looking for the healer, Caitlin. Would ye know where I might find her?"

"She has gone to prepare herself for supper. Might I be of some assistance in the meantime?"

Dar shook his head. "Nay, I'm afraid not. For one, I owe her an apology and, for another, I need to procure something to eat for my friend and myself. Also, at least a blanket or two extra for him for the night."

She smiled, and he was struck with the compassionate understanding that flared in her eyes. There were at least a few Campbells in Kilchurn, it seemed, who were kind, decent folk.

"Well, I can't say as how I can help ye with yer apology," Anne said wryly, "but I certainly can see to some victuals and blankets for ye and yer friend. Come"—she indicated he should follow her back to the kitchen—"first we'll address the matter of yer meal."

Even if Dar had wished otherwise, there wasn't anything he could do but accompany her. She was, after all, Kilchurn's lady. He didn't dare risk, leastwise not yet, crossing Niall Campbell.

"We've yet to be introduced, Lady," he said as they headed back into the kitchen. "My name is Darach—"

"I know who ye are," Anne Campbell gently interrupted him. "The news of ye and yer friend's arrival is all over Kilchurn. And I suppose ye know by now who I am, as well, don't ye?"

He grinned. "It wasn't hard to surmise, Lady."

"I'll take that as a compliment."

"It was most certainly meant as such."

The kitchen was empty, save for a serving girl hurriedly dishing up what looked to be a mess of boiled potatoes into a large pottery bowl. When she saw Anne, she curtsied, then returned to her task.

"I'll have these out to table in but another few minutes, m'lady," the girl said. "Cook had us bring out so many bowls tonight, I confess I couldn't keep up."

"Dinna fash yerself, Sally." Anne gave a dismissing wave of her hand. "No one has yet to starve at Kilchurn because a bowl of potatoes was last to be served." She turned to Dar. "Now, let's see to yer meal, shall we?"

"Tell me what I can do to help, Lady."

He glanced around the enormous kitchen. At one end stood a large stone hearth that took up most of that wall. Two *swees*, or right-angled iron bars attached to an upright bar set in the base of the hearth, stood swung out with empty iron pots hanging from them. At the other end of the room, another hearth bore the remains of a pig that had roasted on a spit.

Numerous shelves covered whatever free wall space there was in the room. They were filled with pewter plates, mugs, bowls, pots, a wide assortment of cooking utensils, as well as pottery jars of all sizes. Several staved barrels were tucked beneath the large work table. Dar guessed them to be filled with salt, flour, and other essential and frequently used staples.

It was the kitchen of a prosperous castle, overflowing with abundance of every kind. Harking back to Dundarave's pitiful kitchen when last he saw it, Dar couldn't help a small stab of bitterness. Thanks to Scotland's regent, James Stewart, the First Earl of Moray, and several of the more influential Highland clans—the Campbells being prime among them—MacNaghtens were on the brink of starvation, if the active efforts to hunt them down and slaughter them like animals didn't extirpate them first.

But now wasn't the time to remember such things, he reminded himself fiercely. Now was the time to win his way into the confidence of Niall Campbell and Kilchurn's folk. Now was the time to rescue his brother. But later . . . later there would be retribution, and it would be as swift and brutal as what had been meted out to his clan.

"Why don't ye take some of those potatoes before Sally delivers them to the others?" Anne suggested as she took a large wooden tray off the bottom of one shelf, placed it on the table, then added two pewter plates. "In the meanwhile, I'll carve ye and Kenneth a portion of the remaining pork on the spit. And there's some greens and carrots over there in that bowl"—she gestured with the knife she had picked up—"that ye can also dish onto yer plates."

In the next ten minutes, Anne had put together an enormous spread of food, including bread, two foaming mugs of ale, and thick slices of custard tart. Finally, she handed him the now overloaded tray.

"Why don't ye take this down to yer friend? I'll join ye shortly, just as soon as I fetch some extra blankets from upstairs. I'd like to officially welcome Kenneth to Kilchurn as well."

Dar accepted the tray and nodded. "As ye wish, Lady. I'm certain he'll appreciate the visit, as well as everything else ye and Caitlin have already done in taking us in."

"It's the verra least we could do for any stranger asking our hospitality."

As he turned to go, Dar couldn't help but wonder if there hadn't been an underlying emphasis in the woman's voice on the issue of hospitality. Perhaps it was but his oft-ignored sense of guilt—whenever he was forced to use or deceive—giving him a passing twinge of conscience.

Unfortunately, guilt and a conscience were treacherous burdens these days, a luxury for those who falsely imagined themselves aggrieved as they continued to live in safe, warm, well-appointed castles surrounded by powerful friends, and not, instead, constantly in fear for their lives. For those who didn't continually wonder if the next man they met might discover their shameful secret, their open warrant of instant death anytime, anywhere, and all within the legal bounds of the law.

But such thoughts were pointless and only clouded the mind to the task at hand, Dar reminded himself as he headed down the corridor leading to the stairs. He must remain clear-headed and single-minded. Athe depended on him, and Clan MacNaghten depended on Athe to lead them. It didn't matter what Dar's feelings were about the disgraceful events that had led to his clan's proscription. It didn't matter that the truly guilty were either already dead or imprisoned.

All that mattered was that he do everything in his power to see the innocent survive. And, for any hope of that happening, Clan MacNaghten needed their chief. A chief who was totally unworthy of them and their trust, but a chief who they had nonetheless confirmed upon the death of their old one. Athe, whether Dar thought it wise or not, was now the rightful heir and chief of Clan MacNaghten.

╬

Dar didn't realize how ravenous he was until he finished serving Kenneth and finally sat down and began his own meal. Indeed, both men had all but finished their supper by the time Anne Campbell appeared with an armful of blankets. Immediately, Dar laid aside his plate and mug and hurried over to her.

"Thank ye for these," he said as he reached for the blankets. "Between our overfull bellies and these warm coverings, we'll sleep like the dead this night."

"It's the verra least we can do for ye." Anne smiled, her gaze moving to where Kenneth lay. "This must be yer friend then."

"Och, aye." Dar laughed. "Pray, forgive my poor manners." He turned to glance at his friend. "Lady, this is Kenneth Buchanan, my friend and a verra accomplished bard and harper. Kenneth, this is the Lady Anne Campbell, wife of the Campbell clan chief."

The younger man set his tray of food on the hard-packed dirt floor and made a move to swing his propped-up foot off the pillows. With an upraised hand, Anne halted him and hurried to his side.

"Nay, don't trouble yerself over me," she said as she bent and offered him her hand. "I see Caitlin has wisely instructed ye to keep yer foot elevated, and that's indeed for the best."

Kenneth grinned. "That she has, Lady, and did a most excellent job treating my foot as well. Thanks to her, I'm certain I'm on the mend."

"Then I hope ye won't be too disappointed to be seeing me from now on for the care of yer foot?"

Dar laid the blankets on his bed, then moved to stand beside her. "It's an honor, and no mistake, to have the lady of the castle waiting on us. Isn't it, Kenneth?"

A puzzled expression on his face, the bard slowly nodded as his glance moved first to Dar and then back to Anne. "Aye, it is indeed. Not that I wouldn't gladly accept Caitlin's aid if ye're ever too busy to assist me."

"I'm never too busy to assist a guest." She looked to Dar. "If there's naught else ye'll be needing, it's time I join the others for supper."

Preoccupied with his troubled thoughts, Dar didn't immediately realize she was talking to him. "Ah . . . nay, there's naught we're now lacking, Lady," he finally said, before striding to the door and opening it for her. "Pray, allow me to escort ye back."

"It isn't necessary. I well know my way about Kilchurn."

"Then, if ye will, permit me to walk with ye a bit. I've something I'd like to discuss with ye."

She shrugged. "As ye wish."

They set out and, almost as soon as they were beyond earshot of Kenneth, Dar halted. "Is it my fault that Caitlin can't return to care for Kenneth's foot?"

"Aye, to some extent." Kilchurn's lady steadily met his gaze. "Caitlin's young and not always the best judge of men. And Campbell hospitality only extends so far, especially when it concerns the welfare of my sister-in-law."

Momentarily, Dar was struck speechless. "Y-yer sister-in-law?" he managed at last to stammer out. "But that would make Caitlin—"

"Niall's sister, of course." She quirked an auburn brow. "Didn't ye know who she was?"

"Nay." Dread rose like some turbid mist to curl around his heart. "She introduced herself as Caitlin Campbell, of course, but Janet and that lad Jamie were also Campbells. I thought they were all members of yer clan, but likely servants. And then when she said she was a healer . . . well, that all but confirmed she was a common lass of some sort."

"I'm a healer as well, and have been long before I ever met Niall Campbell or came to Kilchurn." She smiled. "Caitlin's my apprentice."

Dar felt his face go red with shame. "Truly, Lady, I didn't know. It was foolish of me to presume aught, but I did. I beg pardon—for my stupidity and for my audacity in kissing the Campbell's sister."

"No harm was done, I suppose. Still, I hope ye can understand now why I feel it prudent that Caitlin and ye not be left alone anymore." Anne paused to wet her lips. "I care for my sister-in-law deeply. Even more importantly, her brother is verra protective of her. Indeed, *fiercely* protective, to say the least."

4

Dar laid awake deep into the night, awaiting the time when Kilchurn's inhabitants would all be abed. In the meanwhile, his mind was amply supplied with chaotic thoughts to keep him wide awake, if ever he had feared dozing off. To his chagrin, however, they all involved a certain bonny if exceedingly exasperating young woman.

Caitlin was Niall Campbell's sister. Of all the sorry, misplaced fortune to pursue the sister of the man Clan MacNaghten considered one of their worst enemies. Even if Niall Campbell—save for Athe's capture and imprisonment—hadn't played an active role in the persecution of Dar's clan, he was still a Campbell and part and parcel of those who had led the successful push to have Clan MacNaghten proscribed.

Caitlin had also admitted to a low opinion of the MacNaghtens. In the doing, she was as much a participant in this despicable travesty as the rest of her kin.

He knew it was daft to feel a sense of betrayal, even pain, at that admission. By mountain and sea, he had kissed the lass but once! And it had meant nothing—neither to him *or* her. Yet, despite repeated attempts to put Caitlin out of his mind, especially the surprising intensity of their kiss and the unnerving shock the kiss had stirred of something akin to recognition, of some uncanny connection even, Dar's thoughts kept returning to her over and over and over again.

Had she bewitched him then? It didn't seem possible. She had given him no potion to drink. He hadn't seen her make any strange signs or mutter any unintelligible words that might hint at spell casting. But healers were known—leastwise some of them—to dabble in the black arts.

Indeed, hadn't Anne Campbell, born a MacGregor, once been called the "Witch of Glenstrae"? And she had admitted to being a healer well before she ever wed Niall Campbell. Were both women, then, but a witch and her apprentice?

With a disgusted grunt, Dar rolled over, pulled the blankets back up to snug high against his shoulders, and clenched shut his eyes. Had it come to this now? That he was so overcome by the strain of the past two and a half years of living like some wild, hunted animal, he now imagined his enemies were worse than cruel and heartless? That they were actually satanic beings? Without mercy and forgiveness in the world, there certainly was no God. But did such an absence still permit the presence of Satan?

Somehow, Dar doubted that. Nevertheless, witchcraft seemed the only plausible explanation for how swiftly Caitlin Campbell had gotten under his skin. She was but a wee wisp of a lass, beautiful, it was true, but there were many beautiful women in the world.

Yet, somehow, she was different. Within that small frame burned a fiery, indomitable spirit, a courage equal to that of any man. There was a passion there as well and a hunger to give herself, heart and soul, to an all-consuming, unconditional love.

He knew that with a deep certainty. He knew that because he recognized a kindred soul. He knew that, because in the deepest depths of his heart, it was the same way with him.

Dar opened his eyes to pitch blackness and sighed. When

would he ever face the reality of his life, and what he would and wouldn't have no matter how he wished it otherwise? Most times now, he managed to keep those niggling, ridiculously futile desires firmly at bay, walled off in a secret, impregnable place in his mind.

Indeed, he hadn't had to face them for months now. The daunting tasks of staying alive and finding the next meal, shelter from the driving rain, or a safe spot to sleep for the night had been quite effective at banishing less primal needs. An outlaw in constant fear for his life had little spare time left for futile hopes and dreams.

But coming to Kilchurn, enemy territory though it was, had apparently provided the respite sufficient to lure him back where he chose never to go again. That, and the ardent desires meeting Caitlin Campbell had stirred in him.

There was but one remedy, Dar decided, tossing aside his blankets and moving to sit on the side of his bed, and that remedy was action. He felt around for his cuarans and pulled on the soft, knee-high leather boots, lacing them snugly. They were beginning to wear thin again, especially the soles, and would soon need patching. Dar didn't know how many more times he could sew on another sole to the ever thinning leather sides, before even they would give way. It would be barefoot after that, he supposed, which was no worse a fate than that already suffered by most of his remaining clan.

Once, as the second son of the clan chief, he had never lacked for any necessity. Though Clan MacNaghten had never been a prosperous clan, they had managed well enough. But Dundarave Castle was now an empty shell.

Once the proscription had been imposed and it had been necessary to desert the castle and take to hiding in the hills, its former possessions were soon plundered by marauding, neighboring clans. Indeed, the Argyll Campbells with their headquarters at Inveraray, located just four miles southeast, had lost little time in initiating the rapine.

Dar rose, adjusted the belted plaid he had chosen to sleep in this night, and quietly headed for the door. Once out in the corridor, the faint light of pitch-soaked torches illuminated the long expanse leading to the dungeon. All was silent, just as he expected it would be at this late hour. Nonetheless, Dar kept his hearing acutely attuned for any untoward noise.

Several times, he caught the scratching of tiny feet, startled squeaks, and skittering sounds as he surprised rats along the way. Denizens of dark, undisturbed places, they were common enough. The last time he had dared visit Dundarave one cloudy winter's day just three month's past, the place had seemed infested with the vermin. But then the entire castle, a four-storied, L-shaped tower house enclosed by a high wall, had already fallen into disrepair.

Wooden shutters hung from broken, rusted hinges, if they still hung at all. Snow had piled in various nooks and crannies in rooms left unprotected by shutters, and the wind whistled unimpeded through the chambers and down deserted hallways. What tapestries hadn't been carried off hung in tatters on the walls. And not only rats had added to the carnage. Birds had built nests in the ceilings and covered the floor with their droppings.

It was the damage done to the entrance at the foot of the stair tower, however, that had most sorely torn at Dar's heart. Not only had the finely carved front door been all but hacked to shreds, but over the portal, the dog-toothed molded ornamentation and family motto, "I hope in God," had been so defaced that one could now hardly read it.

The callous and calculated desecration had not only added further insult to an already broken people, but also struck at the very heart of the last comfort and strength they could call upon—the Lord God Himself. For without hope in God, no men, including the MacNaghtens, had anything left to keep them going, keep them fighting on when all seemed lost.

Not that he mourned that loss for himself, Dar thought as he neared the barred, iron-grated door that separated what looked to be the dungeon's guardroom from the main corridor. He had given up on a just, merciful, and loving God years ago.

Nonetheless, he mourned that loss of hope for his people. Many of them, even to this day, clung to their religious faith like those drowning might cling to a passing bit of flotsam. And, as flawed and ineffectual as he himself might view those beliefs, Dar didn't have the heart to take that away.

The rise and fall of voices coming from beyond the iron door drew him up short. Dar slipped into the shadows beyond the last torch and listened. There were two men in the guardroom, wide awake and, by the sounds, playing a game of dice.

He edged closer until he reached the wall at the end of the corridor and moved until he was to the very frame of the iron door. On close inspection, Dar noted a thick iron padlock hanging from a stout hasp and staple, locked from the inside. Not only was the dungeon well guarded, but it was also very well secured.

Examining the door, Dar found the hinges were fastened by huge bolts driven into solid rock. A quick glance around the frame into the guardroom revealed, besides several doors that likely led into small prison chambers, a pit cell carved deep into the earth and equally protected with a padlocked iron grate. This was most certainly where Athe was being held.

Dar choked back a savage curse. His only hope of freeing Athe had been to threaten the guards with his dagg, but the short, heavy, wheel-lock pistol held only one shot. Even if he could take down one guard if he refused immediately to surrender the keys, the second guard could ring the bell Dar had seen hanging in the corner, calling for help long before Dar could reload again. And with the alarm sounded, it would be impossible to pry loose the door from its hinges before help came. *If* it were even possible at all.

Few castle dungeons were as impregnable as Kilchurn's apparently was. He had counted on a much simpler task than this one presented. Short of using gunpowder to blast down the guardroom door, Dar couldn't think of any quick way to get in and free his brother.

Smuggling in the necessary amount of gunpowder to do the job through Kilchurn's keep undetected, however, would be next to impossible. Indeed, it *would* be impossible.

With heavy heart, Dar crept back the way he had come. When he reached the stairs leading to the upper level, he took a seat on one of the lower steps. His mind raced, trying to make sense of all he had observed, picking through every detail to find a flaw that might yet yield a viable plan for rescuing Athe.

If his brother had been imprisoned in some above-ground cell, even perhaps in a freestanding guardhouse, there might have been a chance. Perhaps then there might have been a way to smuggle enough gunpowder in to blow down the cell door or even the outside wall. But it was impossible, leastwise in the short period of time in which they could continue to make their excuses to remain in Kilchurn under Campbell hospitality.

Drugging the guards' food would only leave them unconscious inside the guardroom and of absolutely no use. Getting his hands on the keys long enough to make a copy also seemed futile. To do so, he would have to learn the guards' routines. And that necessitated asking too many questions that might easily arouse suspicions.

His plan to woo Caitlin, then ply her for information, had flown out the window the moment he learned her true identity. Indeed, if the truth were told, Dar had already begun to suspect he would never be able to tease much useful out of her at any rate.

No, it was indeed impossible. With a frustrated groan, Dar leaned down and rested his head in his hands. There had to be some other way, but what? What?

His old mentor, Feandan MacNaghten, captain of Dundarave's guards and his uncle, had once told him when one problem seemed to present insurmountable difficulties, step back and look around for a clever, fresher approach. And if Dar had ever needed to do that, he needed to do so now. But what other clever, fresher approach was there to this problem?

He inhaled slowly, deeply, willing himself to calm the tortured thoughts roiling in his head. A direct assault in battle against Campbell might had always been unfeasible. Taking Kilchurn by stealth and deception had seemed the only alternative. Now that, too, had come to a quick and ignominious end. Dar needed another plan, one that would strike at the heart of all Niall Campbell held dear.

The memory of Anne Campbell embracing her son—Niall Campbell's son—flashed through his mind. Did the Campbell chief hold his family as close as Dar had once tried to hold his own? If so, the woman and bairn might well be invaluable in a trade for Athe.

He certainly couldn't just kidnap the child alone. The bairn still needed his mother. Dar couldn't fathom how he would care for a squalling babe as he made his way through the hills and glens to put a safe, negotiable distance between an enraged father and himself.

Yet taking Anne Campbell alone would leave the child motherless. Even for the sake of his clan, Dar realized he lacked the stomach to stoop to that particular form of cruelty. And he most definitely didn't care to deal with mother *and* child!

But what if, he thought, his head jerking up with a surge of excitement, he instead abducted Caitlin, holding her as hostage in exchange for Athe? According to his wife, Niall Campbell was feradiously protective of his sister. Surely she meant more to him than some point of honor that might compel him to hold a man prisoner until he could be brought to trial. And Caitlin seemed of a strong enough bent to withstand the rigors of several days' hard ride, not to mention the minor indignities of spending a time in his company without the services of a lady's maid or the comforts of a soft bed and finely cooked meal.

It went without saying he would treat her with all respect and consideration and return her as pure as he had taken her. Even if his earlier intentions toward Caitlin hadn't been all that honorable, once he took her hostage, the situation—and the rules—would change. Sister though she was to one of Clan MacNaghten's direst enemies, Dar had no intent purposely to make her suffer.

Though he imagined, he thought with a sardonic smile, his loathsome presence would be indignity and suffering enough. She wouldn't take kindly to being abducted, of that he was certain. Caitlin Campbell was, after all, a headstrong, fiery-tempered vixen.

On second thought, perhaps the custody of a squalling bairn might indeed be a far more agreeable undertaking.

✟

"Are ye daft, man? Has reason finally and completely fled yer brain?" Kenneth raged at Dar the next morning. "It wasn't enough to learn yestereve that Caitlin is the Campbell's sister, and *now* ye propose to abduct the lass and hold her hostage for Athe?"

Dar shrugged. "Is it any worse than our original plan to steal my brother right out from beneath Campbell's nose?"

"Aye, it is indeed. Breaking Athe out is a lot like reiving cattle. No one likes it, but no one's overly surprised by it. Besides, it's the Highland way. Taking a man's sister, however, touches on family and clan honor. And ye know how prickly a subject that can be."

Kenneth rose from his bed and gingerly placed his weight on his sore foot.

Dar frowned. "Ye're not supposed to be walking on that, ye know."

"Have I any choice? It seems we'll soon be on the run again, *if* ye truly aim to carry out yer lack-witted plan."

"It's the only option left us." Dar sighed and shook his head. "Ye know that as well as I."

"Aye, that I do." The bard took several careful steps, then looked up and grinned. "Besides, my foot feels surprisingly good. That thorn tip must have been what was causing most of the pain."

"I wasn't planning on making ye walk all the way back to Glenshira, ye know."

"Och, and wouldn't that be a sight, with me on yer back, and you dragging a squalling lass behind ye!"

Dar rolled his eyes. "I was thinking more like filching a couple of Campbell horses. We'll need to put as much time between us and Niall Campbell as we can, as fast as we can. Once he discovers what we've done, ye can be sure he'll come after us on horseback, with a pack of bloodthirsty clansmen at his side."

Kenneth gave a disparaging snort. "And horse thieving sounds about as easy as getting that little wench out of here undetected. But, as ye said. What choice have we? Tell me what ye need of me, and I'll do it."

"Well, that's still the part I haven't quite worked out yet. I'll need today to nose around a bit and see what comes my way."

"See to it then." His friend walked back to his bed and lay down, propping his foot on the pillows. "First, though, something to break our fast would be most appreciated."

"Right. I'll get to it." Dar strode to the door. "Might as well also begin the nosing around."

"Aye," Kenneth muttered dryly as Dar opened the door and walked out. "Ye do that, lad. Ye just do that."

He was no more happy than Kenneth, Dar thought as he headed down the corridor, to have to change plans and stoop now to an abduction. Freeing his brother from prison seemed a far more honorable undertaking, but that idea had died a final and ignominious death last night.

At least, though, that particular plan had been fairly straightforward and simple. Now all he had to do was find some way to steal horses without getting caught, spirit Caitlin from Kilchurn undetected, and then outrun her enraged brother with a woman who would fight him every step of the way in tow.

Not long thereafter, however, what some might call the work of a merciful God, but Dar chose rather to consider fate, presented the perfect solution to at least part of his dilemma. Just as he was about to exit the stairs and turn toward the kitchen, Caitlin's voice, coming from the nearby storeroom, caught him up short. Immediately, he halted and drew back into the shelter of the staircase. She stood in the doorway, apparently talking to Anne.

"It's such a lovely morn," she was saying. "I think I'll go for a ride around Loch Awe to where that burn empties into the loch beneath those big oaks. I'll get Maudie to pack us a picnic, and bring along Janet and Jamie."

"I suppose that'll be all right," Dar heard Anne reply from inside the room. "Ye'll still be in sight of Kilchurn, though barely so, and Jamie's a most intimidating presence for any who might think to cause mischief. Still, I always feel best when Niall's at home, though from the message I just received this morn, it seems it'll be another day or so before he returns."

"We'll be fine, Anne." Caitlin laughed. "And I'll see what I can find of any flowers or herbs we might need for our healing."

"Aye, be vigilant especially for the love-idleness flowers. They're likely blooming by now. I could use them to boil up a batch for those with fever. And also the leaves of the hart's tongue fern. Ye know how well it helps old Edith with that constant cough of hers. Och aye, and if ye happen on some cuckoo's shoe flowers anywhere . . ."

"I can see this is rapidly turning into a plant-gathering expedition," Caitlin said with a chuckle. "We might be gone most of the day then. Not that I'm complaining, mind ye. Already, it promises to be a beautiful day."

"Aye, that it does. When do ye plan to depart?"

"In a few hours. I need to first find Janet and Jamie, get Maudie to pack our midday meal, and then have the horses readied. We'll be back before supper, though."

"Remember to pick up an extra basket for all the plants and flowers. And a good, sharp cutting knife."

"I will." Caitlin paused. "Is there aught more, or may I see to my tasks?"

"Go. It sounds as if ye've got plenty to busy yerself with."

Dar decided it was past time to turn and disappear down the stairs back into the darkness. He had the information he needed to set his part of the plan into motion. And he didn't want anyone to see him and suspect him or his motives.

Leastwise not, he thought with a satisfied smile, until it was too late.

☦

Three hours later as she galloped her horse down the road leading from Kilchurn, Caitlin almost laughed out loud. It was a glorious day, the sky deep blue and streaked with high, windswept clouds, the sun warm, the grass green and lush. She felt so alive, so attuned to nature, and God, and every living thing. Something momentous was about to happen in her life, and she was ready, no, eager, to embrace it.

Nudging her mare in its side, she signaled the already fleet animal to widen the growing distance between her and her compatriots. Not that it was difficult. Janet wasn't overly comfortable on a horse, and Jamie, though his big gelding was a strong beast and nearly the equal of hers, was too polite to leave Janet behind.

Caitlin wasn't about to ride like some old woman plodding along, though. Not today and likely not ever. And it wasn't as if she would keep such a fast pace overlong. Soon enough, out of the same need for politeness, she would turn her horse around and rejoin the others. But not just yet.

The day was fresh and new. Her blood ran hot with the exhilaration that springtide always stirred, and she was free. Free of castle life strictures. Free of the tall, closed-in walls. And free, most of all, of that maddeningly arrogant Darach MacFarlane.

Already, Caitlin felt lighter of heart and mind. Dar was exciting, of that there was no doubt. But the feelings he stirred in her were so dark and unsettling, so unlike any she had felt for any other man. And the truth was that he frightened her. Frightened her with his intensity, his veneer of self-assurance when even she could see that a deep pool of pain shimmered just below the surface.

She was well and tired of pain. In the past eight years, she had lost her mother, then her father, not to mention Niall's first wife—who had also been named Anne—in childbirth. Lost the best friend she had ever had and her little nephew, Niall's first child, a stillborn son.

And then there had been that debacle with David. Even now, Caitlin shuddered at the humiliation he had caused her, when—in his exact words—he "had suddenly lost interest in taking her as wife." The truth of the matter had surfaced much later, when they had learned he had been offered a prestigious position at Court. A position that necessitated he wed another woman.

Niall and Anne had been surprisingly accepting of the broken betrothal, both finally confessing they'd had their doubts about

David all along. Still, it had been the end of the world for Caitlin. Or, she thought with a mocking grin, the end of the world leastwise at the time.

But that disaster was over and well behind her now. She was glad to be free of him. She was glad just to be free. And free she intended to remain for a long while to come.

Glancing over her shoulder, Caitlin noted she had left Jamie and Janet far behind. With a resigned sigh, she reined in her horse, turned it around, and cantered back to them.

"So, finally decided to rejoin us, have ye?" Jamie asked, a slight smile on his lips.

"Likely only because *ye* carry the basket of food," Janet muttered through tight, white lips as she clung to the saddle and her horse's mane with a death grip. "Otherwise, if she had been the one in possession of the basket, we'd have caught up with her an hour later to find the food all eaten and her sound asleep beside the loch."

Caitlin laughed. "Och, Janet, ye're such an old prune at times. Can't ye, just once, relax and enjoy an outing?"

Her cousin scowled. "Of course I can and do! I just don't enjoy doing it from horseback."

"Suit yerself."

Caitlin turned back to the road ahead. The first glimpse of the big oaks, shading either side of the little burn that emptied into Loch Awe at this particular spot near Kilchurn, came into view. For a fleeting instant, she imagined she saw something move in the shadows beneath the trees, then thought better of it. Few frequented the area, so it was likely a bird or squirrel, if even that.

Constrained now to the pace Janet had set, another fifteen minutes passed before they finally reached their picnic spot. Immediately, Caitlin jumped down from her horse and tied it close to an especially succulent patch of grass where it could graze. By then, Jamie had also dismounted, untied the basket of victuals for their midday meal, and set it atop a nearby boulder. He then turned to help Janet with the major undertaking of climbing down from her mount.

Knowing that little ritual would involve the good-hearted man for another few minutes, Caitlin walked over, picked up the basket, and headed for a flat, shady location where the burn emptied into the loch. However, as she passed a particularly ancient and very large oak, a hand snaked out from behind the massive trunk and settled over her hand that clutched the basket. With a gasp, Caitlin lurched to a halt.

"My thanks for bringing food for the journey," a deep, masculine voice said. "We'll be needing it, ye can be sure."

She wheeled about. There, standing beside the tree, was Darach MacFarlane. Behind him stood a wide-eyed and very nervous Kenneth. Caitlin released her hold on the basket and leaped back.

"Wh-whatever are ye d-doing here?"

The corners of Darach's mouth lifted, but the smile never quite reached his eyes. "Why else, sweet lass? I've come to take ye away with us."

As he spoke, the hand that still hung at his side moved, lifting to reveal a rusty old dagg that he pointed directly at her. "Ye will be a good lass now, won't ye? Because I'd so verra much hate to have to use this. And, like it or not, ye *are* going with us this day."

5

Caitlin's eyes widened in disbelief. Then, just before anger narrowed them to glittering slits, Dar saw a fleeting glint of pain.

The pain surprised him, stirring an answering swell of anguished guilt, before he hardened himself once more to the task at hand. Indeed, he was grateful when the anger came.

"Whatever do ye mean, to spurn the hospitality that's been so freely given ye and yer friend," she demanded in a low, enraged voice, "to think now to take me away with ye? And for what reason? What have I—or any of us—done to ye to deserve such vile, ill-conceived treatment? For ill-conceived it indeed will be, once my brother learns of it."

"I'm well aware of the consequences," Dar replied as he stooped to place the basket on the ground. "As to why the need for me to take ye, it was never my first choice. Unfortunately, Kilchurn's dungeon is far too difficult for just Kenneth and me to break into, and I need to free my brother. So, my bonny lass, ye're the next easiest solution to my dilemma."

"Yer brother?" Caitlin's brow furrowed in puzzlement. "But we hold no man named MacFarlane prisoner. The only man in the dungeon is Athe Mac—"

Her mouth dropped, then clamped shut. She glared up at him.

"Ye lied about yer true name, didn't ye? Ye're no MacFarlane, are ye? Ye're a . . . a *MacNaghten*!"

A smirk on his lips, Dar stared down at her. "Och, but the lilting way ye speak my name warms the verra cockles of my heart. But have a care, lass. It's death for anyone to mention such a foul, ill-fated clan or its name."

"Death to ye and yer kind, but not to me!" Caitlin looked to where Jamie was finally finishing the task of guiding a squirming, arms-and-legs-flailing Janet safely to the ground. "Well, MacNaghten or no, I don't believe ye'd actually shoot me," she said, turning back to eye his dagg with disdain. "Ye're too much a coward for that. Best ye slink back the way ye came, before Jamie's forced to thrash ye for yer insolence."

This had gone on far enough, Dar decided. He was beginning to get irritated. He grabbed her arm as she set out toward her two friends, and jerked her back.

"We'll just see how cowardly I am," he growled, pulling her close and pressing the pistol to her temple as the big, red-haired man finally seemed to realize there were a few more people here than he had first imagined and, a scowl on his face, headed in their direction.

"Ye'll be verra sorry ye did this," Caitlin hissed back as Jamie advanced on them. "Verra sorry indeed."

"I already am," Dar replied. "And likely to get more sorry as time goes on."

"What are ye about, MacFarlane?" Jamie demanded as he finally halted before them. "That dagg isn't loaded, is it?"

Dar cocked his head. "And do I look like a fool, to press an unloaded pistol to someone's head? Aye, Campbell. The dagg's loaded. Unless ye turn around, get down on yer knees, and allow Kenneth to tie yer hands and feet, I'll use it on the lass."

"He's not a MacFarlane, Jamie," Caitlin cried. "He's a villainous MacNaghten, he is! And don't believe him. He won't shoot me. He knows ye'd kill him if he did."

Jamie eyed Caitlin, then the pistol, and finally Dar. "A MacNaghten, is he? Well, that changes everything, doesn't it? He'd kill ye, and no mistake. The man's got naught to lose."

"At last, someone with a shred of sense," Dar muttered. "Now, do as I say."

He jerked his head toward Jamie. "Get over here now, Kenneth, and tie him up. I haven't the time or patience for any more blathering."

Janet ran up just as Jamie turned, knelt, and offered his hands behind his back. "What are ye doing, MacFarlane? If this is some daft game ye're playing, it's gone too far! Ye do know by now who Caitlin is, don't ye? Niall Campbell will have yer head, he will!"

"Wheesht, woman!" Dar snapped, silencing her. "Of course I know who she is. Why else would I be taking her as hostage?"

"Hostage?" Her face purpling, Caitlin's cousin fairly shrieked out the word. "How dare ye? *How dare ye?*"

At Janet's histrionics, Caitlin sighed in apparent exasperation. "Och, he dares, and no mistake. He's a MacNaghten, after all."

Dar had never seen someone turn white so fast.

"A-a MacNaghten?" Janet whispered. "Och, what are we going to do, Caitlin?"

By now, Kenneth had Jamie on the ground, trussed like some pig ready to roast on a spit. It was now Janet's turn, Dar decided.

"Take care of the woman," he said to his friend. "Only, once ye've got her good and tied, put a gag in her mouth as well. I'd wager, once we leave, her screeching will be heard all the way to Kilchurn."

"N-nay!" Janet wheeled about and set off at a run.

Kenneth looked to Dar. "Er, my foot might not be able to handle a race to catch that wee lass."

"Here." Dar shoved Caitlin to him. "Can ye at least hold on to her?"

He chuckled. "Aye, and enjoy every moment of it as well."

"Enjoy all ye want, but keep yer hands to yerself." Dar shoved the dagg into his belt and set off after Janet.

It didn't take long to catch the fleeing woman. Janet was really not that fast a runner and was soon winded. She screamed, though, when Dar grabbed her about the waist and lifted her into the air to sling over his shoulder.

"Put me down, ye rogue!" She kicked wildly and pounded on his back. "I knew all along ye were a smarmy cur, I did!"

"Well, ye'll soon be free of me," Dar ground out as he strode along. "That should be of some comfort, if naught else."

Janet soon tired of her tirade and flailing. Dar wasn't to enjoy the respite for long, though. Kenneth had his hands more than full with Caitlin, who seemingly had taken advantage of Dar's departure to engage in a wrestling match with his friend. Indeed, Dar's arrival was most fortuitous.

At that very moment, Caitlin managed to trip Kenneth and escape his tenuous hold on her. She sped off in the direction of the horses.

Dar spared but a moment to deposit Janet before his friend. "Tie her up, if ye can, then join me at the horses," he said, shooting the bard a long-suffering look. "And don't forget the basket of food, will ye?"

Lingering just long enough to make certain Kenneth now had a good hold on Janet, Dar turned and raced after Caitlin. This was swiftly becoming a farce of an abduction, he thought in disgust. In the bargain, they were losing valuable time in which to make their escape.

But not for long. He'd had all he could stomach of wild Campbell women for one day. Like it or not, Caitlin would now bear the brunt of his ire.

She was surprisingly fleet of foot, however, and he barely reached her in time. As it was, she had untied her mare and mounted when he managed to grab the horse's reins with one hand while, with the other, taking hold of a fistful of the cloak she wore and tugging hard. With a cry of dismay, Caitlin fought to break free by wheeling the horse around, but Dar nimbly stayed with her.

As they circled in tandem, bit by bit he jerked on her cloak until she began to lose her balance. She kicked out at him and missed. She kicked again, and that was her undoing. At that same instant, Dar wrenched hard on her cloak.

Caitlin tumbled from her mount, her trajectory sending her sailing to land right on top of him. Dar took the brunt of the fall, rolling away to avoid the horse's hooves, and came to a halt atop Caitlin. Her blue eyes blazing, she glared up at him.

"Get off me, ye lecherous knave!" she cried. "Get off me!"

"Gladly," he snarled in turn. Rising, he took a firm grip on her arm and pulled her to her feet. "Ye won't get away from me quite so easily, though."

He pulled two lengths of rope from where he had tucked them inside his shoulder plaid and clenched them in his teeth. Dar swung her around and grabbed both of her hands. Though she squirmed and fought to break free, he managed finally to secure one rope around her wrists. Next, after forcing her back to the ground, he bound her ankles.

Though she fought him with all her strength, it was evident she was already winded by her battle on her horse. "Ye w-won't get away w-with this," Caitlin gulped between panting breaths even as he finished and pulled her to her feet. "And when my br-brother comes for ye and skewers y-ye on his sword, I'll laugh, I will. I swear it!"

"Aye, I imagine ye will." He stooped slightly and bent her forward to toss her over his shoulder. "Even for a lass, ye do seem the bloodthirsty sort."

Kenneth, apparently at last successful at binding Janet, ran up at that moment. He carried the basket of food and the leather bag containing his harp.

Dar indicated Caitlin's mare. "Tie up yer harp and the basket to that horse. That one's yers from here on out."

He then headed to where Jamie's big gelding was still tethered, placidly grazing. Without any pause or explanation, he slung Caitlin face down over the horse's withers, untied the reins, and led the animal back to where Kenneth stood.

"I doubt she'll be able to escape now," he said, handing the reins to his friend, "but just in case, hold her horse for me. I need a moment more to speak with Jamie."

The bard nodded and took the reins. Dar spun on his heel and walked back to where Jamie and Janet now lay beneath the trees. The girl shot him a murderous look but, thanks to the gag Kenneth had provided, she couldn't put to voice what she was most evidently thinking. Dar turned away from her and knelt beside Jamie.

"Don't harm her, I beg ye," the big man pleaded, looking Dar straight in the eye. "For all her headstrong ways, she's a good lass. And it isn't her fault what happened to yer kin, or yer brother. That's the work of men, not women."

"Aye, well I know that," Dar replied, steadily meeting his gaze. "And I give ye my word I'll treat her gently. Or, leastwise," he added with a quirk of his lips, "as gently as she allows me. She's going to be a handful, and well I know that too."

He extracted a small packet from a pouch on his belt and tucked it in Jamie's shoulder plaid. "Give that to yer chief. It'll explain what must happen if he wants his sister back. We'll await him at Dundarave. And no tricks or treachery. Just have him bring my brother—alive and well—and do so posthaste. I've no stomach for this sort of thing, and wish it over and done with." Dar pushed to his feet. "I'm sorry to leave ye two like this, but I need to buy time before it's discovered what I've done. It can't be helped."

Jamie sighed. "Nay, I suppose it can't. Nonetheless, this'll go verra poorly for ye. Niall isn't the sort to take such an affront lightly."

"And what does it matter?" Dar shrugged. "Any way ye look at it, we MacNaghtens are all dead men. As ye've already said, I've naught to lose."

He turned then and strode away. When he reached the horses, Kenneth tossed him his mount's reins. Wordlessly, Dar threw them over the animal's back. A second or two more and he had leaped into the saddle.

Reining the horse around, Dar pointed in a northeasterly direction. "Let's be off then. We've miles of hard riding before dark, and the further we are from Kilchurn by then, the better for us."

Caitlin chose that moment to try and fling herself backward off the horse. Maintaining his seat with the pressure of his legs, Dar all but lifted her in the air and, slipping an arm beneath, flipped her over to sit beside him. Then, pulling her close, he signaled the gelding forward. The big horse leaped out into a canter that soon quickened to an all-out run.

"Ye were right, ye know," he said, releasing his tight grip on her a bit.

"Wh-what?" came her muffled reply as she shoved back a bit from his chest to glower up at him. "Whatever are ye talking about?"

"When ye said I was too cowardly to shoot ye. Ye were right. I don't shoot women. Even lasses," he said, a wolfish grin spreading across his face, "in desperate need of more sense not to insult a man with a pistol pressed to their heads."

They rode hard that day, stopping only twice to refresh themselves and water the horses. As the rolling hills gave way to narrow glens, dense patches of forests of rowan, oak, and birch, then open meadows, Caitlin watched with sinking heart as they moved farther and farther from home. They forded countless rushing burns that Darach frequently had them remain in for a mile or two before breaking back onto dry land.

She knew why he did so. It would make their pursuers' task in tracking them all that more difficult. He was used to being followed, which, upon further consideration, Caitlin knew shouldn't surprise her. Everyone in these parts had heard the tale of how Darach MacNaghten had been banished from his own clan, even before his people had been proscribed.

Rumor had it he had lain with his older brother's betrothed and gotten her with child. The hapless lass had been the only living get of Clan Colquhoun's chief. Her marriage to Athe MacNaghten would've greatly enriched MacNaghten fortunes.

But once Athe had learned of her illicit liaison with his younger brother, he had refused to wed the lass. The MacNaghten chief was so enraged that he turned on Darach, banishing him. That, unfortunately, so the story went, wasn't the end of it. A month later, the Colquhoun heiress was found dead at the bottom of a cliff near Dundarave Castle, her neck broken.

Rumor also had it that Darach MacNaghten, promising to make the now unmarriageable girl his wife, had lured her from her home one cold, late autumn day. The lass's serving maid had even produced a note to that effect, signed by Darach, so there was no doubt in anyone's mind that the ill-fated girl had gone out to meet him. His intent, however, had evidently not been that of a lover's. He had instead supposedly killed her, some said for being the unwitting cause of his exile.

In the end, in addition to his new status as a clanless, broken man, Darach MacNaghten had also accumulated the title of murderer and outlaw. An outlaw with a price on his head. An outlaw who now had once more stepped outside the bounds of decent, God-fearing folk and added abduction to his charges.

A shiver rippled through Caitlin. He had said that he didn't shoot women. But then a man as powerfully built as he didn't need any weapons other than his hands. Hands that had already broken the neck of one innocent lass.

From his earlier conduct with her, she could see that he had no morals, that he would seize what he wanted when he wanted it, and not suffer a moment's compunction in the doing. And, to add insult to injury, he had taken full advantage of the Highland's hallowed code of hospitality, using it for his own nefarious ends. He was a thief, liar, and heartless fiend. Somehow, some way, she must find a way to escape him . . . before it was too late.

Caitlin glanced down at her bound hands and feet. As long as she remained in this condition, escape was impossible. At the very least, she would need her feet untied. She must find some way to convince her captor to do that and, once done, not feel the need to bind them again.

A plan began to form in her mind. Darach MacNaghten was a man, after all, and a particularly arrogant one at that. All she had to do was allow him to imagine she was cowed and of no threat to his greater intelligence and cunning. A task, Caitlin thought with a tiny smile, that should be simple enough for a woman of her cleverness and mettle.

They made camp at twilight beneath a rocky overhang deep enough to provide shelter from the light rain that soon began to fall. With the cover of the rain, it was safe to build a small fire with wood Kenneth managed to gather before it became too wet. After tethering the horses and bringing in the saddles and other gear, Darach set about rifling through the contents of the food basket.

"Quite a feast for such a wee outing," he said as he unwrapped cloth parcels of a strong, white cheese, a loaf of fresh baked bread, a generous slab of sliced roast pork from last eve's meal, and a dried apple tart, before extracting a large leather flask of cider.

"Not that I'm complaining, mind ye." He glanced up at Caitlin with a grin. "With all the switchbacks to throw off our pursuers, it may be awhile before we reach a village where we can buy provisions. In the meantime, this fine meal will provide us with at least supper and tomorrow's breakfast."

"I'm pleased we could be of service," she muttered, glaring at him.

Darach produced a knife and hacked off a piece of bread and cheese. To that, he added a slice of pork. "Here," he said, offering it to her.

Caitlin wrinkled her nose and shook her head. "I've lost my appetite. Something about the company, I'm sure."

"Suit yerself." With a chuckle, Darach instead handed the food to Kenneth. "Of course, growing weak from hunger won't sit well with yer plans to escape, ye know." At the angry look Caitlin sent him, he smiled and shrugged. "I'm no fool, and well ye should understand that first and foremost. I've taken yer measure a long ways back. But it suits me fine to have ye weak and helpless. Makes this sorry affair all that more easy on me, it does."

"Give me that!" Caitlin leaned toward Kenneth and, with bound hands outstretched, demanded the food Darach had just given him. "Far be it for me to make aught about this any easier for either of ye!"

"Och, now ye've gone and done it, Dar," the younger man said as he handed the meal back to her. "Ye just can't help but always make things worse, can ye?"

"Dinna fash yerself," the dark Highlander curtly replied, slicing off another hunk of cheese to add it and a piece of pork to a fresh slab of bread, before handing that to Kenneth. "She's just angry I've so quickly seen through her little ploy to make good her escape."

With arched brow, he glanced up at Caitlin. "Aren't ye, lass?"

He was insufferable, he was. But she would sooner die than admit anything to him, especially that he was right.

"And why would I be telling aught I was thinking to the likes of ye?" She smiled sweetly at him, then broke off a corner of her cheese, popped it into her mouth, and chewed it slowly and thoroughly. "Och, but this is so tasty. I believe my appetite's returned. I might even have a second helping when I'm done with this. To keep up my strength and all, ye know?"

Kenneth exhaled a long, frustrated breath. "Ye're both a pair, and no mistake. In the bargain, I'm thinking ye both deserve each other." He gave a vehement nod. "Aye, that I do!"

Caitlin scowled but decided it best not to say anything more. Darach quietly returned to his own meal, which he had been preparing even as they talked. The thoughtful look in his eyes, however, made her uneasy.

He was planning something. Whatever it was, she doubted it bode well for her. But then, since the first moment she had laid eyes on him yesterday in Dalmally's market, had anything gone well for her?

Still, she had never let anything—or anyone—keep her down for long. And she certainly wasn't going to permit a crude lout like Darach MacNaghten to be the first. He wasn't as clever as he imagined. He would soon discover he had met his match in her.

"Care for more?" Darach asked just as soon as Caitlin swallowed the last of her bread and began brushing the crumbs from the skirt of her blue wool dress.

Her head snapped up and her gaze narrowed. "Aye, that I would. A bit more cheese would be nice."

A smile hovering on his firm, well-molded lips, Darach cut

her a far too generous chunk of cheese. Leaning across the fire, he placed it in her open hands. Caitlin was strongly tempted to grab him and pull him into the fire but managed to squelch that most uncharitable of impulses. Instead, she murmured a thank-you and accepted the cheese.

Finally, when all seemed sated, Darach rewrapped the food and placed it back in the basket. "Looks from what's left we'll have enough to break our fast on the morrow, and mayhap some even for a midday meal," he then said. "Hopefully, by afternoon, we'll find a village from which to purchase additional provisions."

"What do ye think, Dar?" Kenneth asked as he pulled over his harp bag and began untying the leather fastenings. "Another two days' travel, what with all this going around in circles to cover our trail?"

"Aye, if the weather doesn't get any worse and we don't run into any opposition, we should be at Dundarave by then." The big Highlander put away the basket, then looked to his friend. "By we, however, I mean Caitlin and myself. I want ye to make a beeline for home on the morrow. Uncle Feandan and the others need to know what's happened and the change in plans. Since Niall Campbell and his men will be hot on our trail by then, ye'll need time to prepare the castle."

Caitlin gave a derisive snort. "As if that meager tower house and walls will hold long against my brother! Indeed, is much of it still standing these days?"

Fury flared in Darach MacNaghten's eyes. "Enough to give ye and yers a wee pause, to be sure. And that, sweet and gentle lass, is all the time we'll need."

She had struck a nerve, Caitlin realized. Best to back off before she set him into a full-blown frenzy and he killed her right here and now.

"Er, mayhap I misspoke myself," she said. "I didn't mean to ridicule yer home."

"Aye, ye did, and did just that!"

Picking up a long twig, he poked angrily at the fire. Sparks rose in the air and the flames leaped high.

Finally, apparently having mastered himself, Darach looked to Kenneth. "Have ye a few tunes to ease the tensions of the day? I feel a need for some music, and Caitlin has yet to hear how fine ye play."

The bard smiled and pulled his clarsach from its bag. Caitlin's breath caught in her throat. A lap harp of the finest workmanship, the soundbox decorated with four small holes inscribed with intricate knotwork within ever-widening circles, was made of wood that appeared to be some sort of willow. The pillar and neck looked to be of dark walnut. A variety of mythical beasts were carved thereon.

"It's beautiful!" she breathed. "What do they signify? The beasts, I mean?"

"The animals are all religious symbols." Kenneth pointed to the top of the right side of the pillar. "This is a lion and is associated with the Resurrection. Tales have it that young lions are born dead, only coming to life three days after they're born, after being breathed on by their sire."

Next, he indicated the lower right side. "And this is the unicorn, one of the most common and potent symbols of Christ. Its strength and white color represent purity, and the belief that though it was extremely wild and fierce, it could be captured by a virgin of spotless character. Like our Holy Mither Mary in the Incarnation of Christ in her body."

The bard next turned the harp to reveal the left side of the pillar. "This is a griffin," he said, pointing to the top. "It has both the body and fierce nature of the lion and eagle, and represents Christ the Conqueror. And the dragon"—he indicated the final creature at the pillar's bottom—"though usually thought of as representing the Devil, in this case is placed here to signify the foot of the cross where Evil has been overcome. The plant work twisting up both sides of the pillar, with its stems sprouting tiny crosses, is meant to represent Christ, the 'true vine.'"

Jewels of various kinds—emeralds, rubies, and sapphires—glinted in the eyes of the fantastical creatures, as well as being embedded in the knotwork surrounding the soundbox holes. Caitlin understood now why Darach had claimed that not only the bard but also his harp needed a protector. It was indeed a costly, even priceless, instrument.

"Yer clarsach looks verra old," she said. "Was it passed down, then, from yer father?"

Kenneth nodded. "Aye, from my grandfather through my father, who never became a bard, from my great-grandfather, and his father, all the way back for at least two hundred years. Or, leastwise, that's how the tale goes. It was a gift from some ancient king, in repayment for loyal service."

He settled the instrument in his lap, nestled it against his left shoulder, and lightly stroked the strings. A bell-like ripple of sound rose in the air. Then, he looked to Caitlin.

"Would ye like to hear a few songs?"

Despite the gravity of her situation, despite the fact she was the prisoner of at least one if not two dangerous men and sat here this night far from home and family, Caitlin couldn't help but get caught up in the eager anticipation of hearing some music and song. It was time better spent, after all, than constantly dwelling on her misfortune.

"Aye, that would be verra nice," she replied.

He plucked a few chords, and the rich tones carried a haunting sustain that floated out into the night. "Mayhap a lively jig or two then?"

She nodded. "Aye."

For the next half hour or so, Kenneth played one tune after another, each one seeming better than the last. Caitlin found herself tapping her foot in time to one particularly spirited song, then leaning forward for a softer, more lyrical one. From the corner of her eye, she caught Darach watching her, but she didn't care. Indeed, as best she could, she tried to block him from her sight and thought.

Finally, though, as the latest melody died away, the dark Highlander loudly cleared his throat. Two heads turned to him.

"It's past time we retired for the night," he said. "We've a long ride ahead of us on the morrow."

"Och, just one more, I pray." Pointedly ignoring Darach, Caitlin glanced imploringly at Kenneth. "Please?"

The bard looked to his friend.

"Fine. But only one more," Darach muttered from behind her. "Play away. It's evident ye've beguiled the lass, as ye manage to do with them all, once they've had a taste of ye and yer harp."

Kenneth grinned. "And can I help it the lasses far prefer a man of gentle sensibilities over a brutish lout like ye?"

Darach mumbled something that Caitlin thought might well be a foul word or two.

"Well, be that as it may," the bard said with a chuckle, "this last tune is an English one that I recently learned. Indeed, this is the first time I've ever performed it. The song's a particularly touching one and speaks to life's vicissitudes. It's called 'Fortune, My Foe.'"

He strummed a few, soft chords and then began to sing.

Fortune, my foe, why dost thou frown on me?
And will thy favors never greater be?
Wilt thou, I say, forever breed me pain?
And wilt thou ne'er restore my joys again?

Fortune hath wrought me grief and great annoy,
Fortune hath falsely stol'n my love away,
My love, and joy, whose sight did make me glad;
Such great misfortunes never young man had.

In vain I sigh, in vain I wail and weep;
In vain mine eyes refrain from quiet sleep;
In vain I shed my tears both night and day,
In vain my love my sorrows do bewray.

No man alive can Fortune's spight withstand,
With wisdom, skill, or mighty strength of hand;
In midst of mirth she bringeth bitter moan,
And woe to me that hath her hatred known.

If wisdom's eyes blind Fortune had but seen,
Then had my love, my love for ever been;
Then, love farewell, though Fortune favour thee,
No Fortune frail shall ever conquer me.

As the bard strummed the last few chords of the ending, Caitlin thought she had never heard a more tenderly heartrending song. She sighed and smiled at Kenneth.

"Why did ye play that?" Darach demanded harshly just then, his angry voice slashing through the poignant mood the song had stirred. "What did ye imagine ye'd accomplish?"

For once, his friend didn't back down. "Ye need to face yer loss and put it away once and for all. And I thought, mayhap, to help ye along a bit." His glance moved to Caitlin. "The lass needs to begin to understand as well."

Darach gave a ragged laugh. "Och, aye, and why would that be? What does aught of what has happened to any of us matter to her? When all is said and done, she's a Campbell. Remember that, my friend, if ye remember naught else!"

He climbed to his feet.

"And where are ye off to?" Kenneth set aside his clarsach and looked up at him.

"I'm going for a walk. I need some breathing room, and I see I'll not find any here!" With that, the big Highlander wheeled about and stalked out into the darkness.

Caitlin watched him go, then turned to her companion. "What was all that about?"

"Ye heard the song and surely know the tales about Dar and his lost love." Kenneth shrugged. "Figure it out yerself."

She stared at him for a long while as he carefully placed his harp back into its bag, tied off the leather strings, and laid it aside. There was something between these two men that went a lot deeper than friendship. Something, she wagered, that had to do with the murdered Colquhoun lass . . . and even more.

"Men kill even in the name of love," Caitlin finally said. "A misguided love, more for oneself than for the object of one's affection, to be sure, and then blame it on the dead or even misfortune. No matter the reasoning, it doesn't justify the act or absolve the killer."

"True enough." He lifted his gaze to hers. "Such isn't the case with Dar, though. He's no murderer, though some of his own kin would've gladly had him so."

"And why would that be?"

Kenneth looked down and sighed. "Why else? To divert the blame from them, of course."

6

"This, I'm sure, will come as a big imposition on yer grand plans for the day," Caitlin announced to Dar the next day, "but lasses need a bit more time to prepare themselves each morn than do the lads. And a bit more privacy in the doing, as well."

The dark-haired Highlander glanced up from the breakfast he and Kenneth were preparing. "Indeed? And did ye imagine that, as a hostage, ye'd have any privacy afforded to ye? To make yer escape, I mean?"

High color flooded Caitlin's face. At the sight of her this morn, tousled of hair and still heavy-lidded from what was likely a restless night spent on the hard ground, Dar thought her the most beautiful and seductive creature he had ever seen. And also the most dangerous.

Still, the consideration of what it would be like to awaken each day beside her for the rest of his life filled his mind before he savagely banished the traitorous thoughts. He must have a care. The wench was likely well aware of the effect she had on him and, at every turn, would use it to her advantage.

"Ye'd watch me perform my morning ablutions, would ye?" Fury filled her voice and suffused her features. "Then ye're no gentleman, and I spit on yer highly vaunted claims of honor!"

"Er, Dar," Kenneth offered uneasily as he glanced from one

angry person to the other. "Surely there's some way we could offer her a bit of privacy and still keep her safely contained. Even a hostage deserves time alone for, er, private matters."

Dar smiled grimly. "There are indeed ways. But the lass has yet to ask nicely. And the sooner she learns that haughty demands and insulting accusations won't win her aught but more trouble, the sooner she may get what she wants."

The bard sent Caitlin an imploring look. "See, lass? Ye must just ask nicely, that's all. Is that such a hard thing to do?"

Her icy gaze riveted on Dar, who unwaveringly stared back. "To ask *ye* aught is easy enough, Kenneth. But not him. Never him!"

Dar laughed. He couldn't help it. He had never encountered such a proud, stubborn lass as Caitlin Campbell.

"But Kenneth isn't the master of ye, sweet lass, and I am. Haven't ye realized that yet?" Dar sighed and shook his head. "And here I was giving ye far greater credit than ye seemingly deserve."

"Ye're not my master, and never will be!" Caitlin cried. She held out her bound wrists. "Untie me, if ye dare, and discover the truth of it!"

"Och, is there to be no end to yer squabbling?" Kenneth threw his hands in the air. "And it's glad I'll be to set out on my own just as soon as I can. Though I'm beginning to doubt either of ye will survive the journey to Dundarave without me."

Dar opened his mouth to reply, then thought better of it. Instead, he withdrew his knife and strode over to Caitlin.

She eyed him warily. "What are ye about now?"

"If ye promise not to kick me in the face," he said, "I'll cut yer feet free. Then, since I see there's no hope of ye ever being mannerly about aught, I'll escort ye to the burn where ye can wash up and do whatever else ye've a need to do."

"Fair enough. I promise not to kick ye. Or, leastwise," she added with a saucy grin, "not *this* time."

She lifted her skirt enough to reveal her ankles. Dar squatted and swiftly sawed through the ropes.

"It'd help"—as she rose, Caitlin extended her hands to him—"if ye'd remove these as well."

Dar chuckled. "Aye, I imagine it would, but I think I've compromised as much as I care to. Now, it's yer turn."

Anger flashed in her eyes, then she appeared to master it. "Fine," she muttered. "I suppose I can manage." She arched a slender brow. "And ye can stay near, just as long as ye give me some privacy. I can't outrun ye at any rate."

"Nay, ye can't. And I suppose a bush or two between us should work well enough."

Caitlin expelled a deep breath. "If that's the best ye have to offer, I'll take it."

"Aye, it is."

Dar turned to his friend. "Slice us some bread and cheese to go with that herb tea ye're making. We'll be back shortly."

He turned and took Caitlin by the arm. "Come along, lass. The day draws on, and we must soon be on our way. I'll give ye ten minutes, and no more, to do what ye must."

"That'll suit me nicely," she said as they began to walk from camp. "It's not as if I need to squander much time on my appearance to please the likes of ye. As far as ye're concerned, I'm little more than a slab of meat to be traded. My brother, of course, will see it differently."

"To my great remorse, I'm sure."

"Most certainly."

He was getting tired of being threatened with what Niall Campbell would do to him. Still, it seemed to entertain his sister in the saying, and she did have little else to occupy her. He supposed he could cede her that wee pleasure without further losing his patience.

They soon reached the burn, which was little more than a

swiftly coursing rivulet of water. Dar pointed to two densely leafed bushes a few yards upstream.

"See to yer 'private' needs. Keep talking to me the entire time, though, or I'll be quick to join ye in those bushes." He smiled thinly. "Whether ye want me there or not."

Caitlin rolled her eyes. "I think I understand what ye meant, without ye having to add that last threat."

She turned and headed toward the bushes. "Why must men be so thick of skull all the time?" she whispered under her breath as she walked away.

"What's that, lass?" Dar asked with a grin, even though he had heard her clearly. "Ye must speak up a little louder, and do so until ye're once more at my side. My thick male skull doesn't pick up sound quite as well as yer far thinner one does, ye know."

"It appears to me," Caitlin muttered as she disappeared behind the bushes, "that ye hear well enough."

They kept up a spirited banter until Caitlin finally exited the bushes and rejoined him. In the interim, he had quickly scrubbed his face and washed his hands, then run wet fingers through his short, unruly locks. She eyed him disdainfully, then moved past him to kneel beside the burn.

He watched her splash icy water on her face then, with bound hands, awkwardly finger comb her long, black mane. Next, pulling the mass of hair to one shoulder, she wove it into a rough braid. After breaking off a piece of tough, long grass that grew beside the burn, she rose and walked back to him.

"Would ye tie off the end of my braid for me?" Caitlin handed Dar the strand of grass. "It's not the best braiding in the world, but it'll at least keep the hair out of my eyes today."

He moved close, took up the braid that had already begun to unravel, and deftly rewove it. As he tied off the end, a faint breeze stirred. On its passing, Dar caught her scent.

She smelled of sweet grass and lavender. His nostrils flared, and he sucked in the scent of her. It was his undoing.

Just being in her presence never failed to stir him. But standing so close to her was beyond stirring. It was intoxicating.

Her hair felt like raw silk. Her skin was milky white, her cheeks washed with rose. And her lips, so full and lush and red, were like a ripe cherry or big, succulent raspberry. Lush, ripe, succulent, and begging to be touched, tasted . . . taken.

"If ye think, after what ye've done, after what I know about ye and who ye truly are," Caitlin's frigid voice slashed through the warm haze that had engulfed him, "I'll ever again want to kiss ye, ye're a bigger fool than ye already make yerself out to be."

He jerked back his head, a head that he belatedly realized had already begun to lower toward her. His face grew warm. Aye, he indeed was a fool and, once again, she had lured him into making an even bigger fool of himself.

"Fool I may be," Dar said through gritted teeth, "but ye risk being an even greater fool by continuing to ply yer feminine wiles. Especially," he added with a hard twist of his lips as he took her arm, "knowing what ye claim ye now know about me."

His barb must have finally struck home. Caitlin paled and her mouth clamped shut. Dar didn't waste further time. He wheeled her around and, half dragging her, escorted her back to camp.

Kenneth took one look at them and sighed. "A pleasant outing was had by all, wasn't it?"

"Hardly." Dar led Caitlin to where his friend had laid out her breakfast. "Sit and eat. We leave in fifteen minutes, whether her ladyship is done with her morning repast or not."

"Her ladyship, is it now?" The bard shook his head, then sat and took up his slice of bread and cheese. "The tea's ready. Shall I pour her a cup or will ye?"

"I'll take care of it." Dar walked to the fire, grabbed the small pot with the edge of his plaid, and headed back to where Caitlin now sat. "Before I pour ye the cup of tea, though, I need yer word ye'll not immediately toss it back into my face."

She picked up the cup in front of her and held it out to him. "Fear not, my braw warrior. I wouldn't waste a good cup of tea on the likes of ye."

He made a disgusted sound and filled her cup, then poured out his own. Turning next to his own meal, Dar ate in silence, glaring at her all the while.

For the most part, Caitlin kept her gaze focused on her food. From time to time, however, she glanced up and glowered back at him. To add to his chagrin, from the corner of his eye, Dar saw Kenneth fight the smile that kept creeping onto his face.

They were soon on the road. Compliments of last night's rain, the mists were heavy that morn and the air thick with dampness. It didn't take long before their clothing was coated with a light dew. As the sun rose higher and higher into the sky, however, the mists began slowly to dissipate.

Up ahead, Dar noted thin trails of smoke rising past the trees. Relief filled him. They had finally come upon a village.

He turned in his saddle to look at Kenneth. "Since it would appear far too suspicious to ride into the village with a bound and verra disgruntled woman, not to mention she'd shriek to the high heavens that we've abducted her, it's best ye go in alone and obtain the provisions."

His friend laughed. "Aye, I can imagine it now if we brought the lass along. What would ye like me to purchase?"

"Ideally, several days' worth of oat or barley bannocks already baked, but, if not, the flour, lard, and other ingredients to make them. Also, some smoked salmon or salted herring, two good-sized rounds of cheese, and a bit of butter. We've enough tea left to make five or six more pots, and we *are* on the road, so the meals must of necessity remain simple affairs."

Kenneth nodded. "I shouldn't be more than an hour."

"We'll await ye here under the shade of the trees. Just do what ye must and be quick about it. The sooner we're gone from here, the better."

"So, ye think I'm a shrieker, do ye?" Caitlin inquired as they watched the bard ride away.

Dar glanced down at her. "I think ye're capable of whatever it'd take to make yer escape. Though I'll admit I've yet to hear ye shriek."

"The only shrieking I'll be doing is from joy when my brother catches up with ye."

"And that keeps me awake at night, it does, sleepless with worry."

"He's a braw warrior, my Niall is."

"And ye imagine I'm not?"

She tilted her head back to look at him. "Och, ye're braw enough, I suppose. Leastwise from the looks of ye. But since I've yet to see ye in any fight, man to man, that is, I really cannot say what kind of a fighter ye are."

"If all goes as I hope," Dar said, chuckling, "ye'll likely be spared such a grisly sight."

Caitlin turned back to stare at the road ahead. "Ye mean the grisly sight of ye being hacked to pieces, I assume?"

He laughed. "Och, lass, but ye never fail to amuse me. That is, when ye're not driving me to the brink of aggravation."

"Well," she replied with a sniff, "I can't say as how ye do aught for me *but* aggravate. But then, who'd find any pleasure in being ripped from their home and family, and being subjected to all ye've subjected me to so far?"

Immediately, Dar sobered. "Truly, lass, I wouldn't have done it like I did, if I'd had any other choice."

"And why is yer brother so important in all this? Rumor has it ye two haven't been the closest of friends since . . . since even before his betrothed died. I'd wager ye're the last person he'd expect to come to his rescue."

"Aye, that may well be." Dar hesitated. He really didn't care to go into some long explanation about his clan's welfare. What would Caitlin care, one way or another? "He's now clan chief, of a clan proscribed and doomed to extinction to be sure, but chief nonetheless," he said at last. "And, despite what the rest of ye may hope *and* in spite of ye, we MacNaghtens are determined to survive."

Caitlin turned to glance back at him. "Do ye imagine I wish ye and yer clan dead?"

"Why not? Isn't there already a plan afoot to seize our lands and make them part of Clan Campbell's?"

"Mayhap by the Earl of Argyll, but not by Niall and our family. My brother isn't the sort to covet the ancestral lands of another clan. He believes in the commandment not to steal or covet one's neighbor's goods."

"A good Christian, is he?"

"Aye, that he is," she snapped, an edge of defensiveness in her voice. "Still, even a good Christian is permitted to bring evildoers to justice."

"Evildoers such as my brother?"

"Aye, and ye as well, now that ye've gone and taken me away!" She flounced back around to gaze down the road. "Though I imagine he might go a bit kinder with ye, as long as ye return me unharmed, than he will with yer brother. Athe MacNaghten, after all, was as actively involved in the MacNabs' slaughter as was yer father. Indeed, rumor has it that it was yer brother who instigated that horrific plan and all over some perceived affront by a MacNab."

Caitlin shook her head in revulsion. "Attacking and murdering over a third of a clan who has offered ye the hospitality of their home. And at a feast, no less. For shame!"

Aye, there was indeed shame—deep and abiding shame—in such a dastardly deed. Outlaw though he had already been a year and a half ago, and far away when the act had been perpetrated, Dar still burned with humiliation every time someone made mention of the massacre.

It had been hard enough to hear of it the first time from Kenneth. Kenneth, as the clan bard, had been an unwitting participant. Unarmed and not well versed in battle techniques at any rate, his cousin had barely escaped with his life.

"Aye, shameful it was," Dar replied, glancing down. "That's one crime, however, ye can't lay at my feet. A broken man doesn't get much opportunity to visit his family, much less join them for meals with other clans."

"I know that." She sighed. "So why risk yer life for someone who doesn't care a whit for ye or what happens to ye anymore? As if banishment from a proscribed clan wasn't bad enough, now ye've gone and directed even more attention on yerself, as well as the ire of the entire Clan Campbell. Darach MacFarlane might have been able to live out his life in some peace and safety. But not Darach MacNaghten. Now"—she shook her head—"now the pursuit and intent to capture and kill ye will never let up."

"Wouldn't ye do everything ye could to try and save yer clan? Even at the verra risk of yer life?"

Caitlin sighed again. "Aye, I would. But leastwise my clan would love me for it. I'm not so certain ye've aught to gain in what ye're attempting to do."

How swiftly she cut to the heart of the matter, Dar thought. And if only she knew how many times he had questioned his sanity in attempting to carry out such a plan.

Dar released a long, slow breath. "It doesn't matter. As hard as it may be for ye to believe, the MacNaghtens are still my family, and I love them. Love them and will do aught it takes to save them."

"Against a royal decree to the contrary? Against insurmountable odds?"

A deep, heavy sadness welled up and engulfed him. How could he make Caitlin understand? The task ahead did indeed seem impossible, but what choice was left one, when one loved like he did? No choice whatsoever.

"Aye," Dar replied, his voice husky with emotion. "Against a royal decree to the contrary *and* insurmountable odds. Until the fire of retribution burns itself out or it finally consumes me."

✠

With a sinking heart, two hours later Caitlin watched Kenneth head directly south while they headed out on a more circuitous southeasterly fashion. What she had dreaded most of all since they had begun this journey had finally come about. She was alone, once again, with Darach MacNaghten.

No matter how hard she tried, no matter her intentions to the contrary, it seemed fate conspired against her. She wasn't meant, it seemed, to flee her unsettled feelings for the big Highlander. Whether she wished it or not, she was going to have to face—and resolve—them all by herself.

Anne had encouraged her, that eve she had discovered Caitlin and Darach in the storeroom, to change her ways because *she* felt the need and not because someone else wished her to do so. But change wasn't an easy thing for Caitlin, especially when it came to the matter of her high emotions.

She had always wanted things her way. Though time and maturity had tempered those selfish desires into a more socially acceptable manner, most times Caitlin still managed to get everything she really wanted. Most times, she still felt as if she controlled her own fate.

She wasn't so certain, however, she really wanted to continue on the path she had apparently been set on yesterday, when Darach had taken it into his head to abduct her. Caitlin feared what lay ahead, and feared it greatly. Feared the battle that might well evolve between familial loyalty and love, and the ever strengthening call of her heart.

How could a woman hate a man one instant, then in the next feel so drawn to him? He was toying with her. He must be and he, with his greater age and experience, knew how to manipulate her like a puppet. Perhaps that was what frightened Caitlin most of all. That Darach was in control and she wasn't.

But she was fooling herself, she realized with a sudden burst of insight, if she imagined she had ever truly been in control of anything. She had never been able to control life's tragedies, much less stop them. She had never truly been the one driving her disastrous romance with David Graham. And she most certainly wasn't leading the events of her life since Darach MacNaghten had entered it.

But if she had no real control over what happened, leastwise not events that truly mattered such as what transpired with family, friends, and the search for a true love, what *did* she have control over? Anne had encouraged her to surrender her life—and will—to the Lord. To die to self so that she might be reborn to the only existence that really counted—a life of faith and dedication to God and one's fellow man. The only existence, in the end, that she really *did* have some control over. Yet, try as she might, Caitlin remained uncertain how to accomplish that.

And Darach MacNaghten surely didn't seem the sort who would be willing or able to teach her.

With a sigh, Caitlin settled back against his strong, solid form and closed her eyes. It was indeed a surety that this man wouldn't teach her of God. She doubted he even believed in a Creator, much less a Savior. But he was quite capable, her woman's intuition warned her, and equally willing, to teach her of more fleshly pursuits.

If the truth were told, such considerations excited her. She burned for the dark, dangerous Highlander as much as she imagined Anne had burned for Niall. But at least Anne had chosen wisely. Caitlin knew her desire for Darach wasn't wise, or even right and good.

Then there was always the additional issue of where her true loyalties should lie. Before, as an outlaw of some unfortunate clan with a death warrant on its head, Darach had been of little personal concern to Niall. Now, in taking his sister from Kilchurn to hold as hostage, Darach had become Niall's enemy. And enemies, when they finally clashed, inevitably forced others to take sides.

There seemed no way she could halt the inevitable, headlong collision of these two men. It was yet another instance of her inability to change the events of her life. Problem was, whoever came out the victor, Caitlin feared the death of the other would surely break her heart.

✟

Neither spoke to the other for much of the day. It was almost as if Kenneth's presence had provided the safety net their two battling temperaments had needed. In his absence, both feared that anything they began they might not be able to end.

The midday meal was a brief, short-on-words affair. Then Darach silently lifted Caitlin back up on the big gelding, and they set off again.

By evening, Caitlin was so weary of the silence and the rigors of the long journey, all she wanted to do was find a soft spot upon which to lie and fall asleep. Dar must have sensed her exhaustion. He gathered wood for the fire, lit it, filled the little cast-iron pot with water from the nearby burn, and asked nothing of her.

Supper was more herb tea, bread, a slice of smoked salmon, and a wedge of tangy, soft, goat's milk cheese. Caitlin barely had the energy to eat but forced herself to do so, knowing she would need all her strength for the next day's ride. No sooner than she finished, however, she curled up in her cloak on the bed of pine boughs Dar had made for her, and promptly went to sleep.

Sometime much later, for it was dark and the fire had died to glowing embers, Dar shook her awake. Caitlin jerked to instant alertness and froze at the sight of him looming over her. Before she could ask what he wanted—fearing what the answer might be—he put a finger to her lips.

"Wheesht, lass," Dar whispered. "We're not alone. Three, mayhap even four, men are out there just beyond that stand of trees. And they've been watching us for the past hour or so."

Caitlin tried to sit up. His other hand, still on her shoulder, kept her firmly down.

"Do ye know who they might be?" she whispered back when he finally moved his finger away. "And why have they been waiting all this time? That makes no sense."

"They're no friends of either ye or me, ye can be sure. And, on the contrary, it does make sense to wait, when they can bide their time and better take us by surprise in our sleep."

"Then what do ye want of me? I can't do aught with my hands tied."

Surreptitiously, Dar slid the hand on her shoulder down to the knot that bound the rope. "I'll free ye on one condition. Ye must give me yer word that ye'll not run. Ye'll not find yer way to safety out in the dark, leastwise not before they overtake ye. Besides, ye'll only spoil my plan to sneak up on them."

"Ye-ye're going to try and take on three or more men?"

His mouth quirked sardonically. "Have ye any better ideas?"

"And ye'll leave me here alone and defenseless?"

"Give me yer word, and I'll leave ye untied, and with the extra knife I keep in my cuarans. In the meanwhile, best ye pretend ye're sleeping until that ruse doesn't serve ye anymore. That way, if any get by me, ye'll at least have the element of surprise."

Caitlin swallowed past her suddenly dry, tight throat. *If any get by me . . .*

Somehow, she knew that wouldn't happen unless Dar died in the doing. And she didn't want him to die. She wanted to be free of him, but she didn't want him dead.

"Ye've my word I won't run. Leastwise, not until it appears I'm left to my own devices."

He smiled grimly. "Fair enough." With deft fingers, Dar untied the knot but left the bonds loosely around her hands. "Leave them this way so they'll suspect naught. And pretend to slowly go back to sleep. I'll sit by ye for a time, then get up and amble off."

She dragged in an unsteady breath. "As ye wish."

His hand moved to his boot, then a knife was slipped beneath her hip. "Use this well, if ye must."

Caitlin's mouth lifted at one corner. "Fear not. I know how, and I will."

He stroked her cheek and then, almost before the act could even register with Caitlin, Dar pulled back and stood. She watched him move a few feet away and sink to the ground. Legs crossed, he stared into the dying fire.

The sensation of his fingers on her face didn't fade, however. With but the merest of touches, it was as if he had branded her as his own. Her flesh tingled, burned, sending a fire searing clear through to her heart. Never before had she felt anything like it. Never felt anything like it . . . and didn't want it ever to end.

Tears flooded her eyes. Caitlin clenched them shut. She wouldn't cry, indeed almost never did so. But this man, this hard-hearted, calculating, desperate man had stirred such confusingly intense emotions in her. And that in spite of what he had done and how short a time she had known him.

Och, but she hated him, she did! He had put her in the most untenable of positions.

When the time came to choose between him and her brother, though it might break her heart in the doing, she would have to choose her brother. She would have to. The ties of clan and family ran that deep.

But that time would come later. First, they must face the present task before them, and it was great enough. First, they must survive this night.

After a time, as Caitlin pretended to fall back to sleep, she heard Dar rise and walk away. As the sound of his footsteps faded, she lifted a prayer. A prayer not for her safety, but for his.

Yet as she prayed, for the first time in her life Caitlin accepted that the outcome wasn't hers to command. Not for her or for Dar. The outcome was in the Lord's hands, as it should be.

And in that realization, that submission, she discovered the most surprising peace she had ever felt in her life.

7

It seemed an eternity before the pistol shot rang out in the darkness, followed by an anguished cry. Caitlin startled and pushed herself to a sitting position. Anxiously, she scanned the area in the direction of the trees where Dar had claimed the intruders to be.

There came scuffling sounds. Fists thudded on unprotected flesh, then the sharp rasp of steel on steel. Another cry. Then the sound of someone crashing to the ground.

Two, she mentally counted. If her prayers were being answered, Dar had finished off two of the men. But how many more must he yet fight? Another one or two assailants?

A sudden thought struck her. What if these men weren't brigands but had come to rescue her? She had only Dar's word that they meant them harm. What if they, instead, had hoped to minimize injury to her by trying to take Dar unaware while they slept?

Muttering in disgust at her gullibility, Caitlin shook free of her bonds and dug beneath her skirt to grasp the knife. There was no further reason to pretend she was a helpless captive. Indeed, it was best to ready herself for what was likely an imminent rescue. She stood, took up several sticks of firewood, and tossed them on the coals. Within seconds, the wood caught fire. Flames leaped into the air, and light bathed the little campsite.

A man broke into the clearing, an ill-kempt brute with wild hair and even wilder eyes. He skidded to a stop and looked around. As his gaze settled on her, an expression of feral delight lifted his lips.

Her stomach gave a sickening lurch. These weren't Campbells or any friends thereof. She clenched the knife, still hidden in the folds of her skirt, and feigned a terrified mien. As the man advanced on her, she backed away, luring him ever closer to the fire.

There was no time to dwell on what had happened to Dar, or if this man who faced her was the last one standing or not. She would have one and only one chance to surprise him and win the advantage. She must concentrate on when that exact moment might arise, and strike fast and hard.

"And aren't ye a bonny one?" the man growled, only feet now from the fire. "Ye'll be worth all the effort and—"

He slid to a halt. An expression of surprise, pain, and finally horror passed over his coarse features. Then, like some huge tree toppled in the forest, he fell forward into the fire. Wood cracked; ash flew, and sparks exploded in the air. From his back, the handle of a knife was all that could be seen.

"Dar?" Her voice hoarse, Caitlin strained to see who moved in the shadowed trees. "Is that ye? Och, say something!"

"A-aye, it's me, l-lass."

Bruised and bleeding, he staggered into the clearing. What looked to be a blade cut wound its way down from his left temple onto his cheekbone. His lower lip was split. A rapidly purpling bump marked his jaw. But it was the hand clenched to his right side that gave Caitlin the greatest concern.

Blood drenched his shirt and seeped through his fingers to dribble by big, agonizingly slow drops onto the ground. She ran to him.

"Are there anymore left?"

"Nay, the last one ran off when I finished with his companion. He was but a lad, at any rate." Dar glanced down at the knife Caitlin clenched in her fist. "Ye could manage him, I'd wager, if he was fool enough to return."

Before she could even guess his intentions, he reached out and grabbed her wrist, twisting it until she was finally forced to drop the knife. Then, after wiping his bloody palm on his plaid, he grabbed her by the shoulder and spun her around.

"What are ye about?" Caitlin gasped out the question.

"The danger's over, and ye're once again my prisoner." As he replied, Dar held her two hands in one of his while he leaned down and picked up the rope Caitlin had dropped earlier.

"And do ye know what a despicable, slime-ridden varlet ye are?" she cried as she fought to break free. "And to think I was passing afraid they'd killed ye!"

"Were ye, lass?" He deftly looped the rope around her wrists and pulled it tight, then tied it off. "It does my heart good to hear of such tender concern. The next thing I know, ye'll be begging me for a wee kiss or two, ye will."

Her hurt fueling her rage, Caitlin broke free and, hands bound behind her, faced him. "I'd rather die than kiss the likes of ye! And I hope ye bleed to death from yer wound, I do! Because ye will, unless ye let me care for it!"

"It's but a wee scratch, but thank ye for yer concern." He shook his head. "Twice in one night. I'm beside myself with gratitude."

Frustrated tears sprang to her eyes. Was she speaking to the same man who, just after he had untied her and left her with his knife, had tenderly stroked her cheek? It didn't seem possible.

"Why are ye acting like this? I don't deserve this sarcasm or mockery."

"Nay, I suppose ye don't," Dar said, clutching his side once more. "But there's no help for it. We're still on opposite sides, and I'm no fool to imagine yer loyalty will ever be with me. So best we not delude ourselves that it can go any differently than it must. Aye, neither ye *nor* I."

Dar turned then, walked to where the bag of his belongings lay beside his blanket, stooped, and proceeded to dig through the contents until he pulled out a clean linen shirt. Unfastening the brooch that fastened the excess of his plaid on his left shoulder, he knelt, tugged his torn and bloody shirt free, then pulled it over his head.

From her nearby vantage, Caitlin watched him rip his old shirt into a continuous strip of fabric, sufficient, she knew, to wrap around his middle and bind the remaining fabric in place as a pressure bandage. Studying his bare chest, she saw that the knife wound ran for about six inches, from high on his right ribcage to the middle of his upper torso. It was likely a half inch deep at its worst, slicing through tautly muscled, smooth-skinned flesh.

She had known he was a well-built man, but with his upper torso exposed, Caitlin saw Dar was in superb physical condition. His chest was broad and solid, his abdominal muscles cleanly defined, his arms bulging with sinewy power. Firelight danced over his satiny skin, caressing it in illumination then shadow. Caressing it as hungrily as her gaze caressed him.

Then, with a furious shake of her head, Caitlin turned away. He was nothing to her. He had made that clear over and over. She must accept that reality once and for all. She hated him. She had to, or he would surely break her heart.

After a time, Dar rose, bandaged and fully dressed once more. He stuffed his blanket into his bag, grabbed up the other bag that held their foodstuffs, and dropped them beside the saddle. Then, walking far more slowly than usual, he untied the gelding, led it back to where the saddle and bags lay, and began preparing the horse.

Caitlin saw him grimace as he lifted the saddle onto the horse's back, then stiffly bend to fasten the girth. His movements were equally slow and stiff as he tied the bags to the back of the saddle. She knew he was in pain, and wondered how he thought he could mount the horse, much less get her atop the animal.

After how he had just treated her, she had no intention of helping him in any way. As he had said, it could go no differently than it ever had, for two with such divided loyalties.

Dar led the gelding to a boulder about two feet high, then glanced back at her. "Ye've got a choice," he said, his voice thick with pain. "Either come here and mount the horse on yer own, or I'll toss ye over its withers and ye'll ride that way from here on out."

"And what if I refuse both options?"

The gaze he riveted on her was weary but resolute. "Then ye'll walk all the way to Dundarave, with me herding ye on horseback like some recalcitrant piece of livestock. And don't doubt that I can do it. Ye're not nearly as fast as a horse, nor do ye possess the stamina to play an evasion and dodging game for long."

Fresh blood was already beginning to stain through his make-shift bandage onto his shirt. Unless the bleeding stopped soon, Dar would eventually weaken enough that he wouldn't be able to remain on his horse. Even someone who wasn't a healer could see it was but a matter of time. And even if blood loss didn't finally bring him down, the very real likelihood of infection surely would.

"Ye're a fool to set out right now," Caitlin said at last. "Better ye rest, leastwise until dawn, and give yerself time for yer wound to clot over a bit. But if ye're of a mind to head out now, I'll be happy to ride along. After all, once ye finally tumble from the horse, I'll need it to get me back home."

He made an impatient motion for her to mount. "Then get on the blasted animal, will ye? We'll make Dundarave this verra day, I tell ye, or we'll never make it at all."

✠

Dar hadn't wanted to treat Caitlin so callously, or tie her hands again, but he'd had no choice. He was weakening rapidly. With her healer's knowledge, she would've discerned that soon enough and known the time had come to seize the advantage and escape him.

He was likely a fool to imagine he could hold on long enough to reach Dundarave. Indeed, the chances were high he would meet up with Niall Campbell and his men who, by now, were probably heading in the shortest direction for the MacNaghtens' ancestral home. It was a risk he had to take, though.

No matter what became of him, either way Caitlin would be safe. Safe with his uncle at Dundarave, or safe back in the care of her brother. Far safer than if she managed to escape him and set off on her own.

It might not be much, or not nearly the success he had originally envisioned when he had first abducted her, but it seemed his options were fast evaporating. Draining away as inexorably as the blood seeping from his body.

After a time, Dar found he couldn't quite keep himself upright anymore, and began to lean a bit against Caitlin for support. She didn't comment or complain. Instead, as if to shore him up, she even leaned back against him. And, after a time more, he began to rest his head on her shoulder.

Just before dawn, Dar reined in the horse. "Forgive me," he whispered. "I don't wish to seem forward, but I need to hold ye tightly with one arm to brace myself while I untie yer hands."

"Do what ye must. It's past time ye did so. If I'm to support yer weight much longer, I need my hands to help me."

"Och, I lean on ye a wee bit, and already ye're complaining," he weakly said by way of a jest as his one arm gripped her about her waist. "And here I thought I was but keeping ye warm."

"More like I'm keeping *ye* warm, MacNaghten," Caitlin snapped back. "Ye're still losing a lot of blood, aren't ye?"

"A bit. Dinna fash yerself, lass." He began to fumble with the knot of her rope. "Indeed, I can't fathom why ye're so angry over me slowly bleeding to death. I'd think, on the contrary, it would make ye verra happy."

"Aye, ye would think that, wouldn't ye?"

As soon as the ropes around her hands loosened, Caitlin tugged herself free. Bringing her stiffened arms around to the front, she took the reins from Dar's hand.

"It fits equally well with yer dunderheaded refusal to let me see to yer wound. I could've cauterized it, ye know, with a burning stick from the fire."

"And isn't that a pleasant scene to consider?"

"Pleasant or not, it's the only thing that'll save ye."

He glanced to the eastern hills, where the first faint rays of light were easing the darkness of the night toward dawn. "We've only another two or three hours' ride, and we'll make Dundarave. Time enough to speak of such things then."

"I'll lay odds ye won't last that long."

"Well, then the victory will be yers, won't it?"

She didn't reply and, after a time, Dar realized she was weeping. Softly, to be sure, but even in his increasingly befuddled state of mind, pressed as closely as he was to her, he couldn't miss the periodic tremors that shook her or the failed attempts to hide the sniffles.

Her tears bemused him. Some instinct told him Caitlin wasn't one who cried easily. Had the rigors of the journey, coupled with last night's attack, finally broken down her resolutely proud façade? That had to be the answer. Any other consideration would be more than he could acknowledge, much less accept.

Even the slightest intimation that Caitlin might be weeping for him sent Dar into a panic. It was hard enough to admit he had placed her in grave danger, especially now that he would be of no protection if anyone else who wished them ill came upon them. And if he should fall unconscious, or even die, before he got her safely to Dundarave . . .

He had already failed—and failed dismally—one woman whom he had cared for. He didn't want to fail yet another.

That nagging little truth had followed him ever since he had abducted Caitlin. That he might, for all his intentions to the contrary, endanger yet another woman. And that, as the hours and days passed, he was becoming more and more taken with Caitlin Campbell.

Dar knew it wasn't love. It couldn't be. They had shared but three days together. Three days of such intense emotions, ranging the gamut of outright antagonism to such ardent attraction that it seemed more like three years. Any way he looked at it, what he felt for her was powerful. So powerful it terrified him to contemplate it at all.

He felt certain she considered him far beneath her. Why wouldn't she? He was outlawed from his clan, suspected of murder, and that without even taking account of the desperate circumstances of the people whose name he still bore.

"Wheesht, lass," he finally murmured, a wave of utter exhaustion swamping him. "It won't be long now, and ye'll be safe back with yer own. Hold on but a while longer, and it'll be over. I promise."

"Och," she said, strong sobs overtaking her now, "but ye're such a fool, ye are, Darach MacNaghten! Such a blind, stupid fool!"

"Aye, a fool I am. But I never—"

Up ahead to the left, cradled in the convergence of two rocky hills and behind the cover of several tall pines, Dar caught a faint glow. He squinted, trying to make out the source of the light. At that instant, a fleeting scent of wood smoke wafted by.

"Over there," he croaked, lifting an arm that felt as if it weighed a hundred pounds. "I think . . . I think I see a cottage."

Caitlin reined in the horse and looked in the direction he was pointing. "I don't see aught . . . wait, that could be a light from a window."

She turned the gelding to the left, leaving the road to head toward the source of the light. Dar opened his mouth to order her back onto the road that led to Dundarave, then realized he hadn't the strength to force her to do anything. He had been a fool even to point the little dwelling out to her.

He only hoped whoever lived there would treat her kindly and help her make it safely home again. It was the least he owed her, and even that aid was rapidly dissipating with each passing second.

For Caitlin's sake, Dar even raised a despairing prayer heavenward. It wasn't much, especially coming from the likes of him, but it was all he had left to offer her. And, if there were indeed a God, perhaps even the prayer of a godless man might be heard.

Especially if the prayer was for someone else's welfare.

☩

Heart hammering in her chest, Caitlin reined in before the little stone cottage. *Please, dear Lord,* she prayed, *let whoever lives here be kind enough to help us. If we have to ride on, Dar will surely die.*

She knew that with the surety of having attended countless deathbeds. Not only had his blood long ago soaked through the back of her cloak and into the cloth of her gown, but she had felt him grow steadily weaker. His breathing was shallow. The skin of his hands clasped around her middle was pale and, even with her support, he could now barely manage to keep himself astride the horse.

They were fortunate Dar hadn't fallen from the gelding on the uphill trek to the cottage. A less well-conditioned man would've succumbed hours ago. And perhaps, she thought with a wistful little smile, a less stubborn one as well.

The door suddenly opened. Bright light spilled from inside, outlining the form of a tall, bald-headed man with a scraggly mustache and beard. He wore simple trousers, a long-sleeved, hooded tunic, and soft, ankle-high shoes.

"I was expecting ye," he said as he stepped out and walked toward her, "ever since I saw ye down on the road. All is in readiness."

The man paused at Caitlin's side and smiled. In the light of the early morning sun, she saw a gap between his two top middle teeth. His beard and mustache were dark brown and heavily threaded with gray, his blue eyes crinkled up at the corners, and he had a kind look to him. She guessed he was past four score and ten years old.

"Y-ye were expecting us?" she stammered out, taken aback by the man's friendly manner. "And what's in readiness?"

"Why, the preparations to treat yer friend's wounds, of course." He lifted his hands to take Dar down from the horse. "Ye'll be needing the cautery iron, and healing salve, and water and bandages, ye will, if ye're to have any hope of saving him."

How this man knew so much about them, Caitlin couldn't fathom. But none of that mattered just now. What mattered was getting Dar cared for as quickly as possible.

"Have a care with him," she said as she pried Dar's tight clasp from her waist. "He's verra weak and might not be able to keep his footing once ye get him down."

"Fear not, lass," the man said with a chuckle. "I'm stronger than I look from all the chopping of firewood and working the garden that I do. One way or another, I can hold him until ye can dismount and help me get him into my wee house."

"Then have at it."

Caitlin turned slightly in the saddle to assist in helping Dar off the gelding. And, as she feared, as soon as the big Highlander's feet touched ground, he sagged in the man's arms. She swung her leg over the horse's withers and jumped down.

Even together, it was an arduous task getting Dar into the cottage and over to the simple wooden bed in the single-roomed dwelling. He seemed to be on the verge of unconsciousness, and his entire right side was saturated with blood all the way down his kilt to his leg. Caitlin helped lay him on the bed, then glanced around.

"The cautery's in the fire, already heating," the man said. "And here's the bowl of water and bandages, plus the salve." He indicated the small, rough-hewn chair drawn up at the head of the bed, whereupon laid the supplies he had mentioned.

She nodded. "I'll fetch the cautery. In the meanwhile, could ye pull up his shirt and wipe away as much blood as ye can, so I can better view the wound?"

He nodded. "I'll see to it."

Turning on her heel, she strode to the hearth at the far end of the cottage, picked up the thick pad lying there, and used it to pull the red-hot iron from the fire. Her host was just then beginning to wipe away the blood from Dar's wound. Fresh blood welled up, though, as fast as he could dab it away.

"Step aside, if ye please," Caitlin briskly ordered him. "Only fire will quench that bleeding."

The man moved back.

"Dar," she said as she stepped close. "If ye can hear me, I want ye to know I'm going to burn ye now. It must be done, though, or ye'll surely die."

His eyes fluttered open. "Do what y-ye must," he whispered.

She inhaled a deep, steadying breath. "Hold tight then. Hold tight."

In the next instant, Caitlin laid the cautery to the length of his wound. Dar went rigid and hissed in pain but didn't pull away.

Heated iron against raw flesh sizzled and popped, and the scent of burning meat filled the air. And still Caitlin held the cautery to him, turning it about to make certain all the bleeding was stopped.

Finally, Dar went limp, blacking out. She was glad for that. There would only be more pain as she next cleansed and dressed the wound. At long last, she pulled the iron away, carried it back to the hearth, and shoved it into the flames. Until she had a chance to examine his wound, she couldn't be certain she might not need the cautery another time or two.

Thankfully, though, Caitlin found no freshened sites of bleeding when she began to cleanse his wound. Dar remained unconscious, so with their host's help she removed his shirt, belt, and kilt, and covered him with a threadbare blanket.

"Do ye have any more blankets?" she asked, looking up at her new assistant. "He'll need to be kept verra warm."

"Aye, that I do." The man hurried to a rough-hewn kist, lifted the lid of the chest, and pulled out two more, equally threadbare, blankets.

Caitlin wondered how the man managed to keep warm in winter, if those were all he had. Still, they were gratefully accepted and quickly used to cover Dar. She then turned back to cleaning him as best she could before applying an ointment she noted was made from marigolds. Finally, she pressed a thick wad of clean cloths over Dar's wound.

With the older man's assistance, they were able to wrap several long strips of cloth around Dar's torso to anchor the bandage securely. Caitlin finished bathing him, then covered him with the extra blankets and treated the cut on his face and his split lip. Finally, she leaned back on her haunches, where she had knelt the entire time, and sighed.

"I've done all I can. The rest is in the Lord's hands."

"Aye, so it is," the man said. "As it has always been. *Vocatus atque non vocatus Deus aderit.*"

Caitlin looked up at him. "And what does that mean?"

"Bidden or not bidden, God is present."

"That's Latin, isn't it?"

He nodded.

"I haven't heard that spoken for many years now. Not since Clan Campbell drove out the papist priests and accepted the Reform preachers."

"Yet it's still spoken in many areas of the Highlands, by clans who refuse to turn from the old religion."

She was tempted to ask him if he followed the old religion but knew it didn't matter. He had offered them the hospitality of his home and may well have saved Dar's life in the doing.

"My name's Caitlin Campbell, and this is Darach," she said, extending her hand to him.

"I know of the lad and his true clan, so ye needn't worry about using his full name with me." He smiled and took her hand for a brief shake before releasing it. "I'm called Goraidh. And I'm also of Clan MacNaghten."

Goraidh. It meant "God's peace" in the old language. God's peace . . . something she—and likely Dar as well—desperately needed. Caitlin prayed that it would be so, leastwise for the time they must spend here.

That he was a MacNaghten shouldn't surprise her either. They were probably in MacNaghten lands by now. And, on closer consideration, Goraidh did have a familiar look about him. He reminded her of both Kenneth and Dar. At the very least, she guessed him to be some distant relation.

"Thank ye for taking us in," she said. "Dar may yet die from his wound and blood loss, but at least now he has a chance. A chance ye gave him."

"I but follow the call of the Lord." Goraidh grinned, and the act lit his weathered face with an almost luminous beauty. "He sent ye and the lad here, and that's enough for me."

"As it will be for me," Caitlin murmured, not quite certain what to think of the man's pronouncement.

She suddenly recalled the horse she had left when she had helped bring in Dar. She climbed to her feet.

"If ye'd be so kind as to stay near him, I must see to my horse's needs. Is there some spot I could tether him, where he might find a bit of grass and mayhap some water to drink?"

Goraidh lifted a hand. "Dinna fash yerself, lass. Stay with the lad. I'll see to yer mount's needs, unsaddle him, and bring in all yer belongings. But first, let me make ye a cup of herb tea sweetened with clover honey. It'll warm ye and give ye a bit of strength. From the looks of ye, ye're on the verge of exhaustion yerself."

He pulled the now empty chair close to Dar. "Sit, while I get yer tea."

Gratefully, Caitlin sank onto the chair and watched as her host prepared her mug with tea leaves, then added hot water. After allowing the leaves to steep for a time, he laid a tarnished old tea strainer over another mug and poured the pale golden fluid through it. A generous dollop of honey was next stirred into the mug before he carried the steaming brew over to her.

"Thank ye ever so much." Caitlin smiled up at him. "For everything."

"Dinna fash yerself. To love the invisible God, we must first love our visible neighbor." His glance strayed to Dar, and his expression softened. "Some, though, from the start, are just easier to love than others."

He turned then and walked from his cottage, leaving Caitlin, mouth agape, to watch him depart. She had learned her lessons well at her mother's feet, and knew of Christ's admonition to love one's neighbors if one wished to truly follow Him. And she tried to be kind and considerate of others. Well, most times, anyways, she thought as she glanced at the unconscious man lying in the bed. But, if the truth were told, so many times she failed to do so with Christ in mind.

She cupped her hands around the warm, thick pottery mug and took a tentative sip of the steaming brew. It tasted so good. It reminded her of home and comfort and love.

Her eyes filled with tears. Och, how she missed her home! Missed Niall, Anne, and little Brendan. And missed the life she had once taken for granted. A life, Caitlin realized as her gaze strayed once again to the dark Highlander lying there, as weak and pale as death, that would now never be the same.

To love the invisible God, we must first love our visible neighbor . . .

As much as she was loathe to admit it, Darach MacNaghten was as much her neighbor as were any of her family. Leastwise, in God's eyes. Yet Dar, of necessity, because of what he had done to her and the insult he had heaped on Clan Campbell's honor in the doing, was also her enemy.

It seemed an impossible task to reconcile one with the other.

8

To add insult to injury, Dar developed a fever by early afternoon. From time to time, he had brief moments of lucidity just long enough for Caitlin to get a few swallows of water down him, before drifting off into a rambling delirium. Atop the severe weakness the loss of blood had caused, she greatly feared the additional drain of the fever might well be enough to kill him.

"N-Nara, Nara . . ." Dar mumbled the name over and over. "I'm sorry . . . so verra, verra sorry . . ."

"It's the name of his lost love, ye know," Goraidh said as he ambled over the first time Dar mentioned her. "Nara Colquhoun."

Caitlin glanced up at him. "I didn't know her full name, only that she was a Colquhoun lass." She looked back to Dar. "I wonder why he's saying he's sorry."

The gray-bearded man shrugged. "Likely because he failed her."

"Do ye think he caused her death?"

"It doesn't really matter what I think, does it? What matters is what ye think."

Irritation, exacerbated no doubt by weariness, surged through her. "Ye're just like his friend Kenneth! He also told me to figure it out myself. And he claimed Dar was no murderer, though some of his kin would have him thought as such to divert the blame from them."

"Kenneth isn't just Darach's friend, ye know. He's also his cousin." Goraidh sighed. "But, be that as it may, there has been much unhappiness and unrest in Clan MacNaghten for a long while now. Long, long before Dar fell in love with his brother's betrothed."

She looked back up at him. "But naught ye'd care to share with me."

"Nay, naught, leastwise, I'd care to share just now." Her host smiled regretfully. "Best ye get the truth of most of it straight from the lad here." He gestured toward Dar. "Ask him when he finally comes around and is feeling better."

"If he ever does come around."

Caitlin reached over and took Dar's hand in hers. His hand was so big, his fingers long and strong. As strong as he had once been in mind and body.

"I'm so afraid for him, Goraidh," she said at last, her voice as tear-clogged as her eyes. "Not only that he won't survive this injury, but for what may happen to him if he does. If my brother doesn't kill him, someone else with a grudge against his clan surely will. Or even one of his own clan."

"Like mayhap his own brother?"

Tears coursed down her cheeks. "Aye, like his own brother. Not that Dar's people seem to care what he's risking in trying to get Athe back, either. For all practical purposes, Dar embarked on this grand scheme of his alone. Kenneth, as loyal and good-intentioned as he may be, served naught of any real benefit save as a decoy to get them into Kilchurn."

"There are some, though, I've heard told, who'd rally behind Darach if he asked. But the same ones who tell me that, also tell me he won't."

"Won't?" Caitlin swiped her tears away. "But whyever not?"

"Because he refuses to recognize, much less accept, his true destiny. A destiny that is naught more than the will of God."

"And what destiny might that be?"

Goraidh's gaze was sad but knowing. "What else? To lead Clan MacNaghten, of course."

She nodded warily. Though she wasn't so certain God's will really was involved, there was one thing they most definitely agreed upon.

"Aye, his father did indeed choose poorly, in naming Athe his tanist," Caitlin said. "Eldest or not, he never deserved to be the chosen successor."

☩

Even as exhaustion began to take its toll on her, Caitlin stubbornly sat by Dar's bedside, repeatedly dampening cloths with cool water to place across his hot brow and wipe down his chest and arms. Thankfully, his thrashings weren't severe enough to cause his wound to break open, and his bandages remained free of blood. As midday passed, Caitlin remained so firmly fixed on Dar that only Goraidh's persistence finally induced her to eat some bread and cheese and drink a mug of cider.

Caitlin managed to stay awake until just past sunset. When she began dozing off in her chair, wet cloth in hand, Goraidh at last laid a gentle hand on her shoulder.

"Enough of this, lass," he said, a firmness in his voice she had never heard before from the kindly man. "I've made a pallet over there in that corner near the hearth. Go, take yer rest, before I've two rather than just one patient to care for."

She opened her mouth to protest that she could hold on for several more hours. However, when she initially couldn't even get the words to come, Caitlin was forced to admit he was right.

"Promise ye'll wake me if he takes a turn for the worse, or if ye need my help for aught," she said as she rose and made her way to the pallet.

"Ye know I will. Now, sleep, lass. Rest and fortify yerself for the morrow."

Barely had her head hit the pillow than Caitlin was sound asleep. Sometime much later, she awoke to blackness outside the window and a soft murmuring coming from the direction of Dar's bed. It took all her strength to push aside the heavy lure of slumber and open her eyes.

Head bowed, hands clasped before him, Goraidh knelt beside Dar in the dim firelight. Though Caitlin couldn't quite make out the words, she knew the older man was praying intently. Storming heaven, she realized as she levered to one elbow and fixed her gaze on Dar's face.

He was breathing rapidly, his countenance slack, his skin deathly pale. He was dying.

Caitlin rolled from the pallet, climbed to her feet, and hurried to Goraidh's side. She sank to her knees to his right, closest to Dar's head.

"Wh-what happened?" she croaked out, her heart pounding in her chest.

"He took a turn for the worse. Only God can save him now."

With that, Goraidh returned to his prayers. Caitlin watched him for a few seconds, then looked back to Dar. What she had dreaded had finally come to pass. She was going to lose him.

Anger welled in her. It wasn't right. It wasn't fair. He deserved better than this!

She picked up Dar's hand, a hand that had gone cool, the fingertips blue. Clasping it to her, Caitlin vigorously rubbed his hand between hers, trying to warm it.

"Ye're not going to die, Darach MacNaghten," she cried. "Do ye hear me? Don't give up. Don't ye dare die! Ye've still got too much left undone, and too many folk need ye." Her voice wobbled. "I need ye!"

His hand felt a bit warmer now. Caitlin used one hand to rub up and down his arm.

"What of all yer fine plans?" she demanded. "Are ye such a coward that ye'd turn from a fight, no matter how hard it might seem? For shame! And after all yer fine words, yer boasting and cocksure attitude. But I suppose they were only meant to impress me and never held a shred of truth in them!"

Dar's breathing rate increased, and he moved slightly. Caitlin began to use both hands to rub his arms and chest, all the while continuing to alternately berate and cajole him. After a time, Goraidh paused in his praying to nudge her.

"Keep up what ye're doing, lass. Between the two of us, it just might be working."

As if in confirmation, a low groan rose from Dar's lips.

A fierce satisfaction filled her. "Och, so now ye try and argue with me, do ye, after giving me such a fright? But that's always been yer way, it has. And I say again what I said that night we were attacked. Ye're a despicable, slime-ridden varlet!"

Dar's lids fluttered open. He blinked, trying to focus.

"A-a varlet . . . am I?" he rasped thickly, finally appearing to see her there. "Wh-what are ye . . . a-about? N-need a wee kiss . . . or two . . . do ye?"

Joy flooded Caitlin. "Aye, that I do." She released his arm and stroked his cheek tenderly. "That I do."

Leaning down, she gently touched her lips to his. "And it's past time I take what ye've all along been wanting to give," she whispered when she drew back at last.

He licked his dry, cracked lips. "Th-that tasted . . . sweet, it did. Might I have . . . another?"

Caitlin laughed, then with all the passion she had felt but kept so tightly contained for the past days, she kissed him yet again.

As she did, Dar's hand, so cold and lifeless but a few moments ago, lifted to cradle the back of her head.

✠

By the next morn, it was evident Dar had taken a turn for the better. His fever had broken; the color had returned to his face and body, and his breathing had slowed to its normal pace. Caitlin returned to her pallet for several more hours of sleep, waking just after midday. For a time, she lay there thinking, mulling over what should be her next course of action.

Dar would recover. She felt certain of that now. If the time had ever come for her to make her escape, before he became strong enough again to stop her, it was now.

Part of her was decidedly reluctant to leave him. To do so would be like tearing a piece of her heart from her body. Yet a larger and far wiser part told her she must.

If she could reach Niall in time, Athe MacNaghten would never make it back to his clan or ever be chief. And, if Goraidh was right and Dar's true destiny was to lead his clan, Dar might then be forced to face and accept that destiny. A destiny that, as Goraidh had also claimed, was nothing more than the will of God.

It seemed the only thing to do. Besides, Caitlin thought, in the doing she could prevent the inevitable clash between Dar and her brother. Perhaps her influence with Niall could also be brought to bear in discovering some way for them to aid Dar and save his clan. Once Niall learned the truth about Dar, and that he really *was* a brave, honorable man . . .

With a pensive but resolute sigh, Caitlin finally rose, performed her ablutions, then crept over to check on Dar. He slept deeply, but now it was a healing sleep. She squatted beside him and stared at him for a long, yearning moment.

"Farewell," Caitlin then silently mouthed the words. "God be with ye in all yer endeavors."

Rising, she walked over to one of their travel bags. She took it up, gathered a two-day supply of food, and shoved it into the bag. Dar's knives lay on the nearby table along with his claymore, dagg, powder horn, key or "spanner" to wind the spring of the wheel-lock pistol, and bag of shot. After a moment's hesitation, Caitlin took one knife and the empty pistol and shoved them both into the bag.

It was pointless to take the powder, shot, or spanner. She had never learned how to load, much less use, a dagg. Though, Caitlin thought with a grim smile, no one had to know that if the need came to point the pistol at anyone in self-defense. Next, she grabbed her cloak from where it hung on a peg by the door and donned it. With one final, agonized glance back at Dar, Caitlin turned and left the cottage.

Goraidh was working in the garden not far from the little dwelling, planting seeds in the neatly hoed rows of rich, dark earth. One by one he would take a seed from a bag slung across his chest and place it in a hole he had formed with a small, smooth stick. Then, ever so carefully and lovingly, he would cover the seed with dirt. After he had planted as many seeds in holes as he could reach from one position kneeling between the rows, he would stand, walk a few feet, then kneel again.

A passing impulse to go to him and bid him farewell washed over her. The sense that he would urge her not to leave, however, kept her from doing so. Best to make a clean break with both men.

She headed to the small shed on the far side of the cottage, where Goraidh had informed her he had put up their horse. There, stabled along with the gelding, Caitlin also found a rather sway-backed, black and tan mule.

After bridling and saddling the big horse, she tied on the bag of provisions and led him from the shelter. Once more, she checked the girth for tightness, found it a bit loose, and cinched it one notch further.

"Going for a wee ride, are ye?"

At the unexpected sound of Goraidh's voice, Caitlin gasped and wheeled around. "Aye, I am. Now that Dar will recover, it's past time I return to Kilchurn as quickly as possible. I need to stop Niall from delivering Athe to Dundarave."

Hoe in hand, he angled his head and gave her a quizzical look. "Are ye certain ye're not, instead, running away?"

Her eyes widened, and irritation rippled through her. "Running away? Instead, I'd call it trying to prevent further bloodshed and ruin to Clan MacNaghten. In the bargain, I'm also attempting to save Dar's life yet a second time. I'd hardly call that running away!"

"It is if it's not what the Lord wishes of ye," the gray-haired man replied calmly. "And He wishes ye to stay the course, the same course He has set Darach upon. He wishes ye to work this out together."

"And, pray, how do ye know with such certainty what the Lord wishes of me, or of Dar, for that matter?"

Goraidh shrugged. "How else? I've prayed for the answers and they were given me. And I don't make light of this, when I tell ye the Lord has spoken to me."

Caitlin's heart skipped a beat. She could feel the blood drain from her face.

"And why . . . why would God tell *ye* what He wished for me to do, rather than me?"

"I'd imagine," he said with a smile, "because He knew I'd listen to Him, and ye wouldn't."

She took a moment to digest that pronouncement, then shook her head. "I mean ye no disrespect, but this makes no sense. I can do naught—"

"Darach needs ye, as much as ye need him. He still has much to learn . . . about himself and the real reasons he was banished. There's also the matter of him embracing his true destiny. Ye're the only one who can help him do this, help him weather the pain. Help him find the courage and acceptance he'll need to grow and become all that the Lord wishes him to be."

"Why? Why am I the only one?" Frustration, tinged with anger, roiled within her.

"Because ye're the only one brave enough to stand up to Darach, to give as good as ye get from him. Ye're his light, his inspiration. And he respects ye, cares for ye, and, aye, even loves ye."

"L-loves me?"

It was overwhelming enough to hear such assertions from a man who, by all rights, should hardly know either of them. But to learn she was not only Dar's inspiration, but that he respected and loved her, was more than she could deal with. Panic swallowed her, and she found she could hardly breathe.

It wasn't possible that Dar loved her. It just wasn't!

He but wanted to use her to further his own ends . . . like David Graham had thought to do in making an illustrious alliance with Clan Campbell. David had even imagined he might eventually become clan chief through marriage to her. That was, until Niall had made it abundantly clear his cousin Iain, clan tanist, would be the next chief and, after him, Niall's son Brendan. Shortly thereafter, David had found himself yet another illustrious alliance.

It had to be the same with Dar, if for different reasons. He needed her to obtain his brother's freedom. It didn't matter that he was making a grave mistake in attempting to free Athe. Indeed, his plan might well have a lot to do with his unwillingness—or inability—to envision himself as clan chief.

Goraidh was mistaken. Dar wouldn't listen to her. She couldn't convince him to pursue the chieftainship on his own. And he most certainly didn't love her.

Problem was, she *did* love him. It was perhaps the reason, above all other reasons, she must leave and leave now. If she stayed, he would eventually crush her, heart and soul.

"Nay." Vehemently, Caitlin shook her head. "He doesn't love me. And I don't owe him or his clan aught. All I want is to go home. Go back to the life I used to live."

"Aye, go. Return home then. Return to the life ye used to live." Goraidh leaned on the hoe. "Turn yer back, once and for all, on the love of yer life and yer life's true passion. Turn yer back on the gifts the good Lord has given ye, and don't share them or bring them to their true fulfillment. Run away, and never, ever fully understand the mystery of the Cross."

She frowned. "And pray, what does all this have to do with God?"

"Ye find the Lord in stability, lass. In commitment to the life and persons He has called ye to. As our Lord God has always been faithful to us, so must we be to Him. No matter how hard, how frightening, or sometimes even how mundane it may seem, ye are called to persevere. Ye are called to find Him here and now"—he pointed to his heart—"and not in some other place or at some other time. Here and now . . ."

Goraidh smiled, and the look was filled with such anguished sadness that Caitlin almost went to him and took him into her arms.

"Ye cannot know this, lass," he said, "but it's why I finally came home as well. I was gone for a verra long while. But the Lord, in His own good time, brought me back here. Where He had always intended for me to be, to persevere, no matter how hard and frightening it seemed. Like we all must do. Like ye must do."

It was too much to comprehend, much less make sense of. Caitlin's head spun, and she felt a weight pressing on her chest. It was as if the walls were closing in, trapping her, cutting off her freedom. She couldn't bear it. She had to get away!

"Ye've been kind to both Dar and me," she said hoarsely. "For that I thank ye. But I cannot stay. I just cannot."

Caitlin quickly mounted the gelding. She slipped her feet

into the stirrups, gathered up the reins, then looked down at Goraidh. His image wavered and blurred. Savagely, she blinked away her tears.

"Take good care of Dar, I beg ye. And tell him—"

Suddenly, Caitlin couldn't go on. She nudged the horse in its side, turned his head, and sent the animal galloping back down the hill they had first come.

✝

Dar awoke in the late afternoon. Weakly, he shoved to one elbow and looked around the one-room cottage. In the fading daylight, he noted the little house was simply furnished, with a small hearth at the far end, complete with a "sway" mounted at one of the back corners of the hearth. A cast-iron pot hung from the metal bar that had been swung out to hover over the banked fire of coals. Savory smells emanated from the vessel. Dar found his mouth watering.

Several pottery plates, bowls, mugs, and containers sat on the mantel above the hearth. A series of shelves on the perpendicular wall held a bag of what looked to be oatmeal, a small jar of honey, if the dried amber crystals on one side were any indication, plus several other large, lidded containers of unknown contents. Beneath the window, which through its open shutters Dar noted some sort of flowering fruit tree, were a rough-hewn table and a rickety chair. Upon the table, he recognized his weapons and supplies for his pistol.

Well, *almost* all of the weapons. One knife and the dagg were missing. Unease filling him, he tried to swing his legs out of bed. A sharp pain in his right side caught him up short.

His hand moved to the bandage covering him from his lower right rib cage to the middle of his abdomen. The wound. He had forgotten all about it.

As if it were some gatekeeper of his mind, the wound beckoned a tumultuous parade of memories. He harked back to the tortuous ride with Caitlin, when he had feared that at any moment he might finally lose consciousness and fall from the horse. Or, worse still, simply bleed to death, clinging to her for support.

Vaguely, Dar recalled arriving here, the excruciating pain of the cautery, and then jumbled images of Caitlin and some gray-haired man hovering over him. Finally, as if his dreams had at long last merged with reality, he remembered feeling Caitlin's lips on his, and his hand on her silky, ink black hair.

With a sigh, Dar fell back on the bed. Though all smacked of real events, he wouldn't know which really were true and which were not until he could speak with Caitlin. And she was nowhere to be found, or leastwise nowhere in this diminutive cottage.

The door opened just then. For an instant, anticipation vibrated through him. Then the gray-haired man of Dar's memories walked in.

"Ah, good, good," he said as he headed to a basin of water on the windowsill, washed his hands, then dried them. "I see ye're finally coming out of that deep sleep of yers. Not that it wasn't for the best," he added as he ambled over. "Ye needed a goodly amount of rest to set ye firmly back on the road to health."

The man, blue of eyes, with a wispy gray mustache and beard, pulled the chair at Dar's bedside closer and took a seat. "I'm Goraidh." He held out a work-calloused hand. "And don't tire yerself with introductions. I already know ye're Darach Mac-Naghten."

Dar eyed the man warily. If his calculations were correct, they had reached MacNaghten lands by now. He was likely among friendly folk.

"Goraidh . . ." His brow furrowed in thought. "Aren't ye the old hermit? The one who came back home when his abbey on Iona was destroyed?"

"Aye, one and the same, though not quite as old as some

imagine me to be. And, to clarify things a wee bit, though Iona was destroyed eight years ago, I didn't return home right away." His host grinned. "Now, are ye hungry? I've got an excellent, herb-flavored soup with potatoes and carrots cooking on the fire. If my nose doesn't betray me, it should be ready."

At the reminder of what were the obvious contents of the pot on the fire, Dar realized he was ravenous. "Aye, I'm verra hungry. I don't know, though, how much my stomach can tolerate, being as how it's my first meal in a while." He paused, cocking his head. "Indeed, how long have I been unconscious or sleeping?"

"A day and a half or so." Goraidh rose, walked to the mantel over the hearth, and took down two bowls. "If ye only knew how much better ye're looking, now that the color has returned to yer face," he said, glancing briefly over his shoulder. "Och, but we had a time of it with ye, we did. The Lord's mercy and the lass's refusal to let ye die were the only things that saved ye. Well, that and yer strength and natural good—"

"The lass? Caitlin?" Once again, Dar levered to one elbow. "Where is she? I need . . . need to talk with her."

Goraidh didn't answer immediately but instead ladled up two bowls of soup, paused to take two wooden spoons from a jar on the mantel, then walked over and placed them on the chair by Dar's bed. Next, he pulled over the extra chair from the table and sat down beside him.

"Do ye think ye can eat this without help?" he asked.

Dar nodded. "I'd like to give it a try."

Placing one spoon in a bowl, Goraidh handed it to Dar. When Dar hesitated, he gestured to the soup.

"Eat a bit, and then we'll talk."

Apprehension growing with each spoonful, Dar managed to choke down four swallows before he finally laid the spoon in the bowl. "That was verra tasty, but I don't think I can handle any more for a time," he said. His gaze locked with the hermit's.

"Now, where's Caitlin? I spoke true when I said I'd a need to talk with her."

"Gone." Goraidh expelled a deep breath. "She rode out several hours ago. Took yer horse, a knife, and yer pistol, she did."

Dar looked away and cursed softly. "The little fool! What good's a pistol without shot and powder?" He glanced up then, and his anger flared. "And why did ye allow her to leave? It's dangerous for a lone woman to be riding in these parts. Ye could've stopped her!"

To the other man's credit, he didn't quail in the face of Dar's rising fury. "Aye, I could've stopped her, but then the choice to remain wouldn't have been hers. And she's of no help to ye if she doesn't do so willingly."

"Are ye daft, man?" Dar couldn't believe what he was hearing. "Of course she would've never willingly helped me. That's why I had to abduct her. But at least I intended no harm to come to her. I intended to return her to her brother as safe and untouched as when I took her. But now . . . now Caitlin risks death, if not worse!"

He shoved the bowl of soup into the hermit's hands, tossed back the blankets, and swung his legs over the side of the bed. Immediately, a nauseating dizziness struck him. The room whirled violently.

Dar sat there for a time, willing the spinning to ease. All he got for his efforts was a debilitating wave of weakness that quickly joined forces with the vertigo and queasy stomach. Finally, with a groan, he admitted defeat and lay back on the bed.

He wasn't going anywhere this day, and perhaps not for several days to come. Even if he'd had a horse, which he now didn't, he would never be able to walk to the door, much less mount the animal.

Caitlin had won. She had bided her time and seized her chance at last. But at what eventual cost to her? What cost?

"It's in the Lord's hands now, lad," Goraidh said, leaning over to flip the blankets back to cover him. "Trust Him to set all aright."

"Aye, like He saw to Nara's safety," Dar mumbled, flinging an arm over his eyes.

"Caitlin didn't want to leave ye, lad. But she thought to do ye a greater service. She thought, in reuniting with her brother, to divert his wrath from ye. And also, in the doing, to prevent Athe from gaining his freedom. The lass believes, as do I, that Athe's return to power over the clan would do it greater harm than good."

Dar pulled his arm from his eyes and glared at Goraidh. "And what greater harm could he do than what has already been inflicted on our people? Tell me that, hermit! Tell me—"

Outside, the sound of hoofbeats coming up the hill interrupted Dar. For an instant, he imagined it was Niall Campbell and his men. Then he realized it was but one horse.

A crazed hope flared in him. Once more, he shoved to an elbow.

The door burst open, and there stood Caitlin, wild of hair and eyes red from weeping. Her glance slammed into Dar's.

"I had to come back," she choked out. "I can't run away anymore, or turn my back on my destiny. As frightened as I am to do so, I must persevere."

She ran to Dar and, kneeling beside him, took his hand. "Persevere . . ." she whispered, pressing his hand to her cheek, "with ye and with the Lord."

9

He looked so good, Caitlin thought as she gazed at Dar. True, he had shadows beneath his eyes, his hair was tousled, and his jaw was darkly beard-shadowed. But his color was good. And the sharp intelligence that had been both her bane and source of fascination shone brightly in his eyes.

"Ye . . . ye came back," he said, and the wonder in his voice warmed her heart. "But . . . why?"

Before she could reply, Goraidh, a bowl with spoon in each hand, stood. "There's more hot soup in the pot over the fire," he said. "I've chores to do, so I'll leave ye two to work things out. Then, when all is settled between ye, I suggest ye both have something to eat."

With that, the older man ambled over to the table, set down the bowls, then headed from the cottage.

Caitlin watched him go, grateful for the time he had given her and Dar to talk privately. And it wasn't as if Goraidh even needed to be present. He already knew, she felt certain, what she would say.

"Why did I return?" She inhaled a deep breath. "Because of what Goraidh said to me, just before I left. He accused me of running away from the commitments the Lord has asked of me. And," she added with a wistful smile, "running away from Him as well. It took me a time of riding, though, to mull over his words and see the truth of them."

Caitlin laughed. "Indeed, once I did, I realized that was exactly what I'd been doing my whole life. Seeking and never finding, because I hadn't the insight or courage to face what had always been there, right in front of me."

Dar's brow furrowed in confusion. "I don't understand. Ye're speaking nonsense, lass."

"Aye, it likely seems so," she replied with a chuckle. "It's simple, though, really. I never gave of myself wholeheartedly to aught or, if I did, I chose poorly. Chose what God didn't wish for me to choose. But now I see what He wants, and He wants me to stay the course with ye. He wants me to help ye save yer people."

His eyes widened, and he gently but firmly withdrew his hand from her clasp. "Is this some trick, or have the hardships of the journey and caring for me finally driven ye daft? I know ye, Caitlin Campbell, or leastwise well enough to know ye'd never betray yer own kind."

She smiled sadly. "Aye, I'd never betray my own kind. But what betrayal is there in us returning to my brother and telling him that ye no longer wish for him to give ye Athe? True, Niall will be verra angry at what ye've put him through in taking me, but once I've a chance to speak with him—"

"And what are ye about, to imagine I no longer wish for yer brother not to return Athe to me?" Incredulity, mixed with a rising outrage, tautened Dar's voice. "My intentions haven't changed a whit. Indeed, unless ye hie yerself as fast and far from me as ye can, *while* ye still can, I'll be taking ye hostage again just as soon as I'm able. And we'll be back on the road to Dundarave."

Mild irritation filled her. Why did he have to be so thick-headed?

"Athe isn't the one who must be the MacNaghten chief," she said, trying to remain calm in the face of his heightened emotional state. "Ye are the one who must be chief. Ye are the one who must follow his destiny, a destiny that ye've been running from as fast and far as I have from mine. It's God's will."

"God's will?" Dar laughed and then immediately appeared to regret it as he winced and clutched his right side. "I pray ye, have pity on me and don't say aught more to make me laugh. Have ye already forgotten that I'm outlawed from my own clan, that I'm suspected of murder?"

As if a sudden thought had struck him, he paused. "Indeed, why have ye never asked me if I killed Athe's betrothed or not? I know ye've heard about it. Ye've made too many allusions to the incident not to."

Caitlin shrugged. "At first it didn't seem like a topic safely mentioned. I only hoped ye'd not lose yer temper and murder me as well. Then, later, as I came to know ye better, I knew ye weren't that sort of a man. There seemed no reason to ask ye aught after that."

"Well, I thank ye for seeing past the tales to the man himself," Dar said, his gaze softening. "Nonetheless"—his expression hardened once more—"it changes naught. Most of my clan still consider me a killer and don't wish to have aught more to do with me."

His mouth quirked in grim irony. "And most of the rest will likely never forgive me for the havoc I created in stealing Athe's betrothed from him. If I'd known the effect it would have on my brother, even I might have given more thought to what I was doing."

Dar paused, sighed, then shook his head. "Well, mayhap I would've and mayhap not. I loved Nara so passionately, and she loved me . . . But I couldn't convince my father to change his mind. No matter that Nara wedding either of us would've brought Clan MacNaghten the prestige and influx of additional funds we so desperately needed. The same dowry would've come with

Nara no matter which son she wed. And her own father loved her so deeply that when she confessed to him her love for me, he was willing to give her to me instead."

Again, he shook his head. "But not my father. Not Brochain MacNaghten. Mayhap it was his pride that had been wounded, in the fact that he had, in the end, not been able to control me. And he *had* tried his best to control me all his life." Dar's mouth lifted at one corner. "I still have the scars, and even a few broken bones, to show for all his efforts."

Horror filled Caitlin and she began to understand, if only a little, some of the events that had influenced Dar to do what he had done in abducting her. He had never had many options in life. And it appeared that the only time he *had* chosen to exercise one, it had ended in the loss of the woman he loved and the kinship of his clan. Had his abduction of her, in the failed aftermath of trying to rescue Athe, been his last desperate attempt to regain the acceptance of Clan MacNaghten?

"Yer father was a hard, heartless man," she said at last. "And it sounds as if he didn't spare much love on ye, either."

"Well, it does no good to dwell on what's past. He's dead now. Any hope of him ever forgiving me or taking me back into the clan is gone." Dar scowled. "Besides, none of this has aught to do with yer decision to join with me in trying to save my clan. And it doesn't mean that I've changed my mind about Athe being chief. Or that I care one way or another about what God wishes for me to do. In the end, He's given as much care to me and my welfare as my father did. And that's pretty much near to none."

"The Lord's the only true father ye've ever had, Dar. But whether ye do or don't believe that just now changes naught. If ye'll have me, I want to do what I can to help."

Dar eyed her intently. "Have ye? And in what way? Surely ye haven't at long last succumbed to my irresistible charm, and wish now to bed me?"

"Och, are we back to that again?" Caitlin rolled her eyes, sighing in exasperation. "Though I suppose I should take that as a positive sign ye're well on the mend. But nay, I don't wish to bed ye or any man, save as that man's wife. And, since ye've quite evidently sworn off wedding any woman ever again, pray, let's move on to more practical matters."

The wolfish gleam that had sparked in his eyes as he had spoken of bedding her went out. "I've naught to offer any woman, lass. Indeed, at best, it's all but a guarantee of lifelong hardship to marry into Clan MacNaghten right now. Living as a wife of a clanless man would be even worse."

"Ye could give up yer name and join another clan who'd have ye. After all, ye're only outlawed from the MacNaghtens."

Dar savagely shook his head. "No one, not even a regent and his royal edict, will ever separate me from the clan into which I was born and raised."

She was fast beginning to lose patience with him. "Aye, and do ye enjoy returning to be kicked again and again, like some sniveling cur to its brutal master? When another master might gladly take ye in and treat ye with kindness?" She expelled a disgusted breath. "Truly, Darach MacNaghten, sometimes ye can be the most blind and pigheaded of men!"

He laughed and then quickly clutched his side. "Och, I warned ye not to make me laugh, I did. But mayhap it's just yer way of punishing me for not seeing things as ye do. Not that," he added with a sly grin, "it says aught good for ye, that ye now seem so intent on joining yer fate to such a blind, pigheaded man."

"Give me strength and patience," Caitlin murmured, clasping her hands before her and lifting her gaze heavenward.

"God will need to do more than that," Dar muttered darkly, "to save yer sanity *and* life if ye try to help me."

A sudden realization struck her. "Everything ye do is meant to keep me at arm's length, isn't it?" She leaned toward him, her excitement rising. "It's been that way since the verra beginning. And I think I finally know the reason why."

"Ye don't know aught," he growled and averted his gaze. "And best ye not try to understand further what I'm about. I promise ye. Ye won't like what ye discover."

"And what more would that be? I already know ye're not a murderer, that ye're loyal to a fault, that ye love yer clan even if they seem not to love ye. Also, in yer own way, ye're a verra brave and honorable man and are capable of deeply, passionately loving a woman."

Caitlin knew she was edging toward thin ice. She could tell by Dar's shuttered expression and brittle tone of his voice. But she also knew she was close to getting him to open up to her, to begin to trust her, and perhaps even to share a bit of his heart.

When he didn't respond, she forged on. "I also know ye've been deeply hurt by a father who refused to love ye. That ye feel unworthy because of that, as if the fault had always been in ye rather than in yer father. And that ye bear some guilt over what yer brother has become in the aftermath of Nara choosing to love ye over him. So much guilt, actually, that ye cannot see him for what he is, and are blind to what kind of man ye truly are. And that, if ye persist on this misbegotten course, not only will ye destroy yer clan but ye will likely destroy yerself."

Dar stared at her, dumbfounded. "Ye always did have a shrewish tongue," he muttered at long last.

Caitlin gave a disparaging laugh. "So because ye don't like to hear the truth, ye name me a shrew! Well, I say instead, it's past time ye face what needs facing. It's painful, of that there's no doubt. But if I can do it, then so can ye."

"Can I now?" Dar lay back and closed his eyes. "I fear, lass, that ye've a much higher opinion of what I'm capable of than I do. Even if Athe eventually shows himself to be unable to lead the clan, I've never been one to lead anyone. Indeed, I don't know how. The idea of taking on the chieftainship of Clan MacNaghten fills me with fear. I've failed so many times, in so many things, that if I were also to fail in that . . ."

His voice went hoarse with emotion. On impulse, Caitlin reached over and took his hand. This time, instead of pulling away, Dar clenched it tightly.

"Then there's the matter of my pride. As unworthy as my father always made me feel, I've still got my pride. Clan MacNaghten isn't ever going to come to me and ask me back. I'd have to go to them, humble myself, aye, even beg them to allow me to rejoin the clan. And I don't think I possess the courage for that, or the strength to bear it if they rejected me once again."

"But if ye bring Athe back to them," Caitlin said, beginning to see yet another reason for his unwavering insistence on his brother being the answer to everything, "then ye'll return the victor. Then *they'd* be the ones begging *ye* to come back to them."

He opened his eyes and turned toward her. "A rather hopeless, fantastical plan, wasn't it?" he asked with a sheepish grin. "But desperate men, ye know, are prone to concoct desperate stratagems."

"Well, ye're not so desperate anymore," she said with a determined nod. "Ye've got another ally now. Ye've got me. And ye've got God."

"And ye've got me as well," Goraidh offered from the open doorway.

Caitlin and Dar turned in his direction.

"I thought hermits weren't supposed to get out much, much less take on hopeless quests," Dar said.

The older man's mouth pursed in thought. "Well, I go where the Lord leads, and it's plain enough He wants me to have a hand in this. And besides," he added, a grin spreading across his now rather sunburned features, "when the Lord's involved in aught, it's most certainly not hopeless. Nay, not hopeless at all."

✠

If sheer determination could fuel one's recovery, Dar did so at a rapid pace. By late that day, he was sitting up in bed and even dangling his feet over the side. At first the dizziness and nausea returned again and again, but with rest and additional soup and other fluids, he gradually began to overcome those symptoms.

The next morn, after Caitlin changed his bandages and expressed amazement at how well his wound was healing, Dar was up for a few unsteady steps. By that evening, he was walking with only minimal assistance to sit and eat his supper at the table. Two days later, he pronounced himself ready to resume the journey to Dundarave.

At the table, Caitlin eyed him doubtfully over her bowl of porridge. "That's overly optimistic, don't ye think? Ye're greatly improved, to be sure, but I don't believe—"

"All I'll be doing is riding a horse, lass," Dar said, interrupting her before she turned into the doting healer. "And with ye riding behind me to help support me . . ."

"It'll be a short ride, ye can be sure, *if* ye even manage to mount that big gelding on yer own." Caitlin gave a disgusted snort. "For I tell ye true, I'm not lifting a big oaf like ye up onto that animal."

"So, from being too puny and weak to ride out today, I'm now a big oaf." He grinned. "Best I hear the truth of it, so I know what to expect of ye as an ally. Are ye always this capricious in yer opinions and moods?"

"Only when it comes to ye, it seems," she muttered, digging back into her bowl of porridge. "Ye'd try the patience of a saint, and no mistake."

"Indeed?" Dar arched a dark brow. "The lasses have always seemed to like me well enough. Excepting ye, of course."

Caitlin swallowed her spoonful of porridge. "Likely ye were a sweet one as a wee bairn, and charmed the hearts of all the women. But since ye've become a man . . . well, unless ye weren't quite the rogue ye are now, I can't see what any would've found likeable in ye."

"My braw looks, mayhap?"

"Och, aye, that must be it! How could I have failed to notice?"

They both laughed then and, in a companionable silence, finished their breakfast. The longer he was with Caitlin, the more he enjoyed her—her witty repartee, her lack of fear in confronting him even when she said something she knew he didn't want to hear, and the surprising depth of her generosity.

Her announcement three days ago, when she had unexpectedly returned from the journey Dar had felt certain was her long-anticipated escape, mystified him still. It went against everything a Highlander was and believed in to turn against one's clan. And, though he wagered Caitlin didn't truly consider what she was doing as turning against her own clan, Dar felt fairly certain her brother would view it that way.

Niall Campbell would be livid and likely blame his sister's treachery on him. Instead of a simple hanging, Dar imagined something more painful like drawing and quartering would now be in store for him. Or even burning at the stake as a warlock for having bespelled Caitlin into joining him.

He smiled. If there was anyone bespelled, it was him. He slanted a glance at her. If there was ever a more bonny lass, he had never seen one. Even sweet, gentle Nara with her fair skin and pale blond hair was a wraith in the full glare of Caitlin Campbell's bright and brilliant beauty.

Dar never tired of gazing at her, which of course was only when she wasn't aware of it. She didn't seem to appreciate the lustful offers he occasionally made her, much less the hungry looks. But those weren't the yearnings he feared she would notice at any rate.

He was falling in love with her, if he indeed wasn't already in love. For all too brief, heady moments, he almost imagined she felt something for him as well. At the very least, Caitlin's jibes were almost playful now and, at best, overlaid with a tenderness that touched him deeply.

In the end, though, her belief that she had joined forces with him was an illusion. Whether or not his brother ultimately returned to his position as leader of Clan MacNaghten, Dar had no intention of leaving him in Campbell hands. And Niall Campbell wouldn't turn over Athe unless he received his sister in return.

Despite Caitlin's plan to remain with him, Dar knew that was an impossibility. Once Niall had his sister back, he wouldn't willingly return her, no matter how dearly she wished it.

It was for the best, Dar told himself over and over. She was an innocent and caught up in some religious fervor for which he likely had Goraidh to thank. And that was yet another problem—the hermit's insistence on now involving himself, as well, in Dar's business. His simple plan to rescue his brother was fast becoming far too complicated, and laden with unnecessary assistance. The next thing he knew, the Lord God Himself would also begin to meddle.

There was nothing to be done for it but get on with this journey and see it swiftly to its end. Then he could go his own way, whether it was to resume the life of an outcast or be asked to return to his clan. Come what may, Caitlin Campbell would be gone from his life.

There was no other choice. To attempt anything else would be self-serving on his part, and wouldn't do Caitlin any good. Yet still, *how* Dar wished for it to be otherwise. How he wished never to be parted from her.

Goraidh returned just as they were cleaning the breakfast dishes. A questioning look in his eyes, he glanced down at Dar.

"So, are ye still of a mind to set out this morn?"

"Aye. I cannot spare more time. Even now, I'd wager Campbell and his men are camped outside Dundarave, fuming and making threats, while inside the castle my uncle and his men are beside themselves. We should've been there three days ago, ye know."

"Well, fortunately for ye, it's but another three hours' ride from here," Goraidh said. "And guessing rightly that yer plan hadn't changed, I went ahead and saddled yer horse and my mule. We can be off just as soon as ye two are ready."

Dar looked to Caitlin.

She sighed. "Fine. It'll take me a few minutes to prepare myself. In the meanwhile, why don't ye and Goraidh gather up yer weapons and fill the water flasks? I'm willing to lay odds it'll take *ye* a time to get mounted as well."

He grinned. "And what's the payment for that bet? A wee kiss from ye, mayhap?"

"Only," Caitlin said with a chuckle, "if ye lose, ye vow never again to importune me with yer incessant begging for kisses."

"Done!" Dar walked to the shelf where Goraidh had placed his dagg, powder, shot, and knife and quickly shoved the weapons into his belt and slung the powder horn and shot bag over his shoulder. "I'll be awaiting ye atop the gelding when next I see ye."

✠

It was a wee kiss indeed that Caitlin spared him, once she exited the cottage to find Dar astride the big gelding, a victorious smirk on his face. Still, it was given with a smile, and he secretly suspected she had been glad she had lost that wager. The happiness, however, lasted less than an hour. He soon had other things to occupy himself.

His right side was the first distraction. The jarring canter couldn't help but set it to aching. Too stubborn to admit Caitlin and Goraidh had been correct in suggesting it was too soon for him to be riding, Dar gritted his teeth and suffered in silence.

After the first hour, the ache had evolved into a dull, deep throbbing. Sweat beaded his brow. By the second hour, the effort it took to endure the pain began to weaken him. As surreptitiously as he could, Dar began to lean back against Caitlin for support.

Finally, she reached around him and slipped her hands over his, pulling back on the reins. "Enough of this," Caitlin said. "Whether time is of the essence or not, we're walking the animals from here on out."

"It's not so bad," Dar replied, though even he could hear the strain in his voice.

"Nay, not bad enough for ye to call a halt to this, of that I'm verra certain. But even ye can endure only so much. And since we'll never be able to get ye back up on this horse if ye fall, it's best to err on the side of prudence and slow the pace."

Goraidh drew up alongside them. "She's right, lad. If I do say so myself, ye don't look all that good."

Dar dragged in a shuddering breath, which did nothing to ease the throbbing in his side. "Fine. We'll walk the animals from here on out. But no talking. We'll need to listen for any untoward sounds, as close as we're now getting to Dundarave."

"And how do ye intend to enter yer home if ye're correct, and Niall's already there?" Caitlin asked. "After all, ye're in rather poor shape to hold off my brother and men as ye fight yer way into Dundarave. And, last time I checked, hermits weren't known for their prowess in battle, if they even believed in fighting."

"Which I don't, of course," their companion offered brightly.

"Suffice it to say, there are other ways in," Dar said. "Now, no more talking. Ye'll be made aware of what to do next, when it's the proper time."

With a small snort, Caitlin settled into a disgruntled silence.

In time, with the slower, less jarring pace, Dar's side eased from its throbbing back to a dull, and far more bearable, ache. He began to watch the road for familiar landmarks—the crooked, nearly leafless old rowan tree up on a barren, windswept hill. The rickety, narrow bridge that spanned the now water-clogged burn. The pile of large boulders that marked the descent into a small glen.

With a silent lift of his arm, Dar indicated they should head east down the glen. Ever so gradually, the trees began to thicken until finally they entered a dense, hilly forest. Once in the relative shelter of the trees, Dar finally reined in their horse.

"Here, put this on," he said, withdrawing a length of cloth from where he had tucked it into his shoulder plaid. "Cover yer eyes with it. And make certain ye cannot see."

Caitlin reached around him and took the cloth. "And, pray, why is this necessary?"

"What ye don't know about, ye cannot be constrained to reveal." Dar glanced over his shoulder at her. "Suffice it to say, I'd rather not put ye in the position of risking Dundarave's secrets out of loyalty to yer brother."

"But I already told ye—"

"I know what ye told me," he was quick to interject, "and I believe ye. But we can never anticipate all circumstances, lass, and my first concern must always be for my clan. Please try to understand."

"Fine." Caitlin moved behind him, and Dar could tell she was tying the cloth over her eyes. "I wonder, though, if ye'll ever truly trust me."

He sighed. "I trust yer intentions, lass. I know ye mean well. But these are difficult times. What one believes at one moment can well change in the next. Friendships can die; filial ties can be severed, and trusts can shrivel. And all because of unforeseen events, innocent as they might really be."

Her hands slipped, once more, about his waist. "I know it'll take ye a time fully to trust me. I know, and am trying to be patient."

And I say, Dar thought, *ye try too hard. I'm not worth yer efforts. But, soon enough, it won't matter. Ye'll be back with yer brother, and that'll be the end of it—and us. So dinna fash yerself, lass. And certainly not over the likes of me.*

Granite boulders thrust from the hillside now, some piled into impenetrable masses while others offered small shelters or even the dark mouths of caves. Dar began to count the actual caves and, when he reached the fifth one, he turned the gelding toward it. Tree limbs and low-growing bushes all but obliterated the entrance.

Dar reined in. "We'll be dismounting now."

Caitlin nodded.

He slung his right leg over the horse, freed his left foot from the stirrup, and lowered himself to the ground. He then reached up for Caitlin.

"Come down, lass."

She did so, blindfolded still. Dar took her hand. With the other, he tugged the horse forward, leading them into the cave.

10

From the branches that brushed against her, then the feel of the hard-packed earth beneath her feet, a cool breeze against her cheeks, and the rock walls she touched at times, Caitlin knew they were walking into some sort of cave or tunnel. And the stony corridor seemed to go on for an interminable amount of time, before Dar finally halted her.

"Hold," he said. "We need to leave our mounts here. The door's too small for them to enter."

Obediently, Caitlin waited for the two men to situate the horse and mule in some spot off from the tunnel. Then she felt Dar move past her and heard some door on rusty hinges creak open. Finally, his hand settled back on her arm.

"Come, lass," his deep voice rumbled from out of the stone-muffled darkness. "We're almost there."

She followed where he led, more than a bit miffed that Dar continued to insist on the blindfold. For once at least, though, she kept her opinion to herself. It was but another example of her sincerity that she could offer him, she told herself. He needed to know he could trust her. This was but one more way she could demonstrate it, by respecting his request without complaint or protest.

The door groaned closed behind them. Caitlin guessed Goraidh had been the one to shut it. They walked down several corridors and, though she tried to memorize the number and direction of turns, after a time they all became a jumble in her head. She wondered if Dar wasn't purposely backtracking several times, just to throw her off.

Caitlin smiled. She wouldn't put it past him. He was a very careful, precise man and, if for no other reason, likely had had to become that way just to survive.

At last, they reached what was obviously a flight of stairs.

"Walk beside me," Dar instructed, "and I'll tell ye when each step comes."

She nodded.

They were soon at the top of a long staircase. Dar opened another door, slid a panel of some sort aside, and entered a room. Immediately, warmth assailed Caitlin. The faint scent of wood smoke reached her.

A hearth. They were somewhere within the tower house proper, she realized. But where?

The door closed. Caitlin turned to Dar. "Is it safe to remove the blindfold now?"

"Not quite. It's best ye not know exactly what chamber ye entered into. Besides, we've got to find Kenneth and my uncle. It's past time they be apprised that we've arrived."

Caitlin sighed. "Fine. Suit yerself."

"Now, don't be losing patience just yet, lass," Dar said, amusement tingeing his voice. "Ye've been amazingly tolerant so far. Bear with me but a short while longer."

"I have and I am," she muttered. "Just lead on, if ye will."

He chuckled but did as she requested. After what seemed yet another endless, roundabout trek through countless corridors, they finally entered a large, open area. Shouts of surprise and elation greeted them.

"Dar! Thank the Lord!" Caitlin heard Kenneth cry. "Ye've finally come."

"Ye can remove the blindfold now, lass."

The cloth was off in a flash. For an instant, the glare of the large hearth fire across the room almost blinded her. Then Caitlin's eyes adjusted.

She saw she was in Dundarave's Great Hall. Several men sat on the floor before the fire. A few others stood nearby. The room was completely devoid of furniture, as were the walls, save for one tattered and faded tapestry.

Then she saw Kenneth, accompanied by an older man. Caitlin turned to Dar. He must have seen the uncertainty in her eyes, for he smiled down at her and slipped an arm about her waist.

"Ye're among friends here, lass," he said softly. "Besides Kenneth, the other man's his father and my uncle. And a finer soul never trod this earth."

"Aside from ye, of course," she whispered back, feeling some of her old bravado returning.

Dar threw back his head and roared with laughter. "Right as always, ye are."

The older man drew up just then, Kenneth at his side. His thinning hair was a heavily silvered reddish brown, and he wore a full beard and mustache that was totally gray. Of medium height, the man was solidly built but fit, and his deep blue gaze met hers with a steady, if gentle, interest.

He looked from Caitlin to Dar, then quirked a graying brow. "Considering the circumstances, ye two seem on rather good terms."

"Och, our good terms wax and wane with the pull of the tides or turn of the wind, Uncle." Dar turned to Caitlin. "Lass, this is my uncle, Feandan MacNaghten. And this bonny lassie," he next said, glancing now to the older man, "is Caitlin Campbell."

Feandan MacNaghten bowed. "I'm verra pleased finally to make yer acquaintance, m'lady."

She smiled. "I'm equally pleased to make yer acquaintance.

Though I dearly wish it had been under more pleasant circumstances."

"As do we all, m'lady." Feandan expelled a deep breath and looked to Dar. "Assuming ye came in through the secret passage, ye likely don't know that the Campbell has been camped outside Dundarave for the past three days. The only thing that's kept him from blowing us all up or burning us down was the fear his sister was here. That, and the fact Kenneth was finally able to convince one of the Campbell's men who knew him that ye and the lass had yet to arrive."

"That was likely Jamie," Caitlin volunteered.

Kenneth nodded. "Aye, it was indeed."

Dar turned to Goraidh, who had been waiting quietly the whole time. "Uncle, this is Goraidh, the hermit. He took us in when I was sorely wounded and helped save my life. Which is why," he added with a grim twist of his lips, "we were so long detained from getting here."

"I know Goraidh, the holy priest and hermit of Clachan Hill," Feandan said, casting the other man a shuttered look. "We've met a time or two, we have. What finally brings ye back to Dundarave *and* in such surprising company?"

Goraidh looked to Dar, then back to Feandan, with whom he locked gazes. "The lad's in need of friends, and the Lord decided it was past time I join forces to help him."

"The Lord? The Lord God?" His eyes big and wide, Kenneth stared at Dar. "Have ye at last turned back to God then?"

Dar rolled his eyes and sighed. "Hardly. But Goraidh and Caitlin both seem to think this has become some holy quest. Through no doing of mine, though, ye can be sure."

"Indeed?" Kenneth studied Caitlin intently. "I'd an inkling if anyone could hack through those stone-walled defenses of Dar's, ye could. So tell me, lass, what's this holy quest ye appear to be on?"

"It's clear as day to any who care to see it. Athe's not the right man to be yer chief. Dar is. And the Lord has brought me here to help him accept his true destiny. After that"—she shrugged—"I suppose I'll turn next to helping Dar save yer clan."

If the young bard's eyes had gone wide before, this time they fair to popped out of his head. He looked to his father.

"An interesting proposal, to be sure," Feandan said carefully. "But what about yer brother, lass, fuming outside our castle, with Athe in tow? What do ye suggest we do about them?"

"Well, that's simple enough as well," Caitlin began. "I'll just tell Niall to take Athe back, and then we'll—"

"Enough!" Dar cried. "Does anyone care to hear what *I* think of her outlandish plan? Or am I no longer of any use, now that I've not only brought this wee schemer here but have all but delivered Athe to ye in the bargain?"

Kenneth and his father exchanged wary glances.

"Of course yer thoughts on this matter," Dar's uncle finally replied. "I just assumed, from the way the lass was talking, this was something ye'd both agreed upon."

"Then ye'd be assuming wrong."

"And why would that be?" Her ire rising, Caitlin pulled away and glared up at him. "I thought we'd all this worked out back at Goraidh's cottage."

Dar sighed. "Ye had it worked out to suit yerself, lass. I never agreed to aught."

"But ye know it's for the best! Ye know ye're far more suited to be clan chief!"

"Nay." Dar fiercely shook his head. "I don't know that, and I told ye as much back at the cottage. Indeed, I don't *want* to be chief!"

She had seen that recalcitrant look before. Whether from fear or sheer stubbornness, he wasn't going to budge. Apprehension began to wend itself about her heart.

"So ye're still of a mind to trade me for Athe, are ye?" Caitlin asked, her voice gone low and hoarse. "Is that it?"

"Aye, that's been my plan from the start. I've no intention of changing it now." Dar took her by the arm. "Indeed, the sooner we see an end to this whole miserable experience, the better, I say."

He began to lead her away.

Caitlin dug in her heels, halting him. "And what are ye about? Where are ye taking me?"

Eyes glittering like glacial ice riveted on her. "Where else? To show ye to yer brother and set the exchange at long last into motion."

✝

As he all but dragged Caitlin from the keep, across the courtyard, and up the stairs to the parapet wall, each step Dar took was some of the most painful he had ever taken in his life. Though she said no further word, her gaze spoke volumes. And none of the messages she sent him were either meek *or* mild.

He more than sensed her pain. He felt it to the marrow of his bones, where it throbbed dully with every beat of his heart. And, the closer they came to the moment Dar must give her back to her brother, the greater his dread and despair grew.

Even the thought of never seeing Caitlin again, of her being gone from his life totally and irrevocably, pressed down on him with an ever growing weight. His chest ached. His lungs felt constricted, until he could barely drag in a breath. And he doubted, *how* he doubted, that his courage would be sufficient for the task to come.

A stiff breeze high overhead whipped the flag, flying the Mac-Naghten crest of a stone tower emblazoned with the clan motto of "I Hope in God." The wind caught in Dar's plaid, sending the kilt rippling about his knees and his hair to blowing around his face and into his eyes.

Angrily, he shoved his hair aside and pushed Caitlin to the parapet's crenellated half wall. "Campbell!" he bellowed down to the large encampment about fifty feet away. "Niall Campbell! I've got yer sister. It's past time for an exchange."

"Ye're a pigheaded fool," Caitlin muttered as the camp below them stirred, and three men finally strode out toward them. "Ye're a fool, and ye'll regret this to yer dying day."

"Aye, well I know it," Dar ground out, "but it's for the best. Ye'll see that someday, and thank God that I had the sense to do what had to be done."

"Aye, thank God that He spared me having to remain with the likes of ye! I never could stomach a coward, and ye're one of the lowest, most spineless, most—"

"Wheesht!" Dar hissed as a tall, chestnut-haired man and an equally tall blond man drew up below them, with Athe, hands tied before him, standing between the two. "Ye've made yer point. Ye hate me, and I'm well ready to be rid of ye."

"Caitlin?" the dark-haired Campbell called up to her. "Lass, are ye all right? Has any harm come to ye?"

She shot Dar a furious glare, then turned back to gaze down at the man who was obviously her brother. "Nay, no harm's come to me, Niall. Naught more, at any rate, than the rigors that a hard journey with a vexing, mule-headed man would cause."

As Dar clenched his teeth in silent frustration, Niall Campbell exchanged glances with the blond man, who merely shrugged his shoulders.

"Are ye ready to exchange my brother for yer sister, Campbell?" Dar shouted down to him. "If so, we can do so at the front gate."

Niall nodded. "Aye, I'm ready. No tricks, though, MacNaghten. My patience has worn verra, verra thin."

144

Not as thin as mine, Dar thought, *in dealing with yer wee shrew of a sister.*

"No tricks," he called down instead and, with a tug on Caitlin's arm, turned her and led her back to the stairs.

Five minutes later, with crossbow-armed MacNaghtens placed at several spots on the parapets near the front gate, Feandan Mac-Naghten lifted the heavy crossbeam securing the gate. Goraidh walked over and planted himself before Dar and Caitlin.

"Aye, hermit?" Dar growled. "What is it now?"

"Are ye certain ye wish to do this?" the older man asked. "Knowingly going against the will of God gains ye naught, in the end, but even worse pain and hardship."

Now this, atop everything else!

Dar felt as if he were being assaulted on all fronts at once, and that his defenses were rapidly crumbling. But of all the attacks just now, he couldn't abide the added burden of disappointing an unloving, unforgiving God!

"Then let Him have at it, just as soon as I have my brother back. Once I've done all that I can for my clan, naught else matters to me. Not even," Dar added with a sneer, "God's displeasure."

"Dar!" Caitlin gasped, horrified. "Don't say that! Och, I pray ye, don't say that!"

He turned an agonized gaze on her. "Ye still don't understand, do ye? Once I give ye back, there's naught of value left me in this life. God would be doing me a kindness, He would, if He then smote me where I stood."

"Then don't give me back," she pleaded, taking his hand and pressing it to her. "I don't want to go, Dar. I don't want to leave ye."

For a fleeting instant, he almost relented. Almost ordered his uncle to replace the cross bar. Almost.

But it was too late. Too late . . . ever since he had set the events in motion that had led to Nara's death. Too late. Too late . . .

Dar turned from Goraidh and back to his uncle. "Open the gate if ye will. Let's get this over and done with."

Feandan exchanged a troubled glance with Goraidh but did as he was told. Grasping the stout iron ring, he pulled at the door.

Outside, just ten feet away, were two men in blue, green, and black plaids. Between them, disheveled, a wild look in his eyes, stood Dar's brother.

✝

At long last, she was taking the final steps that would rejoin her with her brother and assure her return home, Caitlin thought as she and Dar walked through the gate and toward the awaiting men. That had been her dream and source of her most fervent prayers for the past several days. Yet why, when the longed-for moment was finally upon her, did she dread it, indeed even feel like someone walking away from happiness rather than toward it?

She had Darach MacNaghten to thank for that. Fury boiled up within her. Just like before, she had yet another manipulative, coldly calculating man to thank for breaking her heart.

Yet, instead of mourning her soon-to-be loss of Dar, she should instead thank God for His intervention. She had tried to be faithful to what she had imagined He asked of her, tried not to run from what seemed to be her commitments and His will. But apparently she had misunderstood. Apparently the Lord really hadn't intended that she stay the course with Dar.

There was a certain peace in the fact she had tried, even if she had ultimately been wrong in what she had thought she must do. A peace in trying to learn and carry out the will of God. Yet still it hurt. How it hurt!

As they drew up before Niall, her cousin Iain, and the auburn-haired Athe, her brother eyed her intently for a long moment. Then he smiled.

"Ye've given me a fright, ye have, lass. But ye seem no worse for the wear."

"Nay"—Caitlin managed a weak smile in return—"I've managed as well as could be expected. But I'm nonetheless verra glad to come back to ye." She shot Dar a seething glance. "Verra, verra glad."

Niall caught the look she sent Dar. "Did he harm ye in any way? Tell me true, lass."

Only my heart. Only my heart . . .

Caitlin shook her head. "I'm fine. Indeed, better than fine." She made a motion toward Dar's brother. "Let's get on with the exchange, shall we? The sooner I'm well rid of these MacNaghtens, the better."

"Go to him, then, lass," Dar growled, placing his hand in the small of her back and giving her a gentle push forward. "I'm equally as eager to be rid of ye and *yer* kind."

Simultaneously, Niall shoved Athe toward Dar. "Ye've gained naught in rescuing this piece of vermin. But take him and be done with it."

Caitlin walked past Athe as he rejoined his brother. *Dar deserves ye, he does,* she thought, casting the unkempt man a contemptuous glance. *If he's so intent on his own and his clan's destruction, he's chosen well in choosing ye.*

As soon as she reached Niall and Iain, her cousin enveloped her in a big hug. "Och, but it's so good to have ye back, lass! If ye only knew the foul mood yer brother's been in, ever since ye were taken . . ."

She grinned up at her handsome cousin. "And that's solely because, with me gone, he only had ye left to vent his spleen upon. But now that I'm soon back home . . ."

"Aye, ye have had a hard time of it these years," Niall said, extricating her from Iain's grasp to take her into his own arms. "Living with the likes of me, I mean."

Och, but it feels so good to be back with Niall and Iain! Caitlin thought, clutching her brother tightly about his waist. If she held him long enough, perhaps she could even blot out the memory of the past days and walk away and never look back. Never look back or wonder . . . wonder what might have been.

"Cut off these bonds and be quick about it!" Caitlin heard Athe snap irritably at his brother. "I'll not stand out here an instant longer, trussed up for all the clan to see. What were ye thinking, ye fool, to allow them to bring me to ye this way?"

So, already it starts.

Caitlin released Niall, pushed away, and wheeled around. She took several steps forward.

"Fine words of gratitude," she cried from the short distance now separating them, "for the only man who cared enough to risk his life and honor for ye. But then, ye've never been worthy of yer brother *or* yer clan!"

"And *ye* are?"

The moment Dar cut through the final bond, Athe grabbed the knife from his brother's hand, spun about, and, before anyone could fathom his intent, much less react, raced up to where Caitlin stood. He grabbed her arm, jerked her about, and laid the knife blade against her throat.

Dar gave a shout of anger. With an outraged cry, Niall leaped forward before Iain was able to pull him back.

"Hold, Cousin," his tanist said. "Ye know he's a madman. Don't push him."

The Campbell stopped, eyeing Athe warily. "What are ye about, MacNaghten?" His glance swung next to Dar. "Was this a part of yer plan as well?"

Dar shook his head. "Nay. Never." He turned to Athe, who still had the blade pressed to Caitlin's throat. "Let her go, Brother. This isn't necessary. Let her go, I say."

Caitlin could feel Athe's hand on her arm clench all the tighter, feel his heart thudding against her back. He was both crazed and terrified. There would be no reasoning with him.

"And when did ye become chief, to order me about?" Athe rasped out the demand. "As usual, ye've failed to consider all aspects of this poorly devised plan. Are ye so simpleminded that ye truly imagined the Campbell would leave without taking his revenge, once he had his sister back? Nay, we need the wench still, if we're to have any hope of making a successful escape."

Dar's gaze slammed into Caitlin's. He knew she hadn't forgotten about the secret passage. He visually begged her not to make mention of it. She blinked once, slowly, trying to assure him she would not betray him.

"I'm sure the Campbell could be convinced to assure us safe passage," Dar said, looking to Niall. "Especially now, with his sister's life in the balance."

"Ye know I would, MacNaghten," Niall snarled, all the while gauging the distance between him and Athe, and his possible options. "I'd grant ye whatever lead ye desired. Just give me back my sister, safe and sound."

"Sticks in yer craw, doesn't it," Athe all but crowed with satisfaction. "To be at another's mercy for the first time in yer life?"

From the corner of her vision, Caitlin saw Dar also begin to eye his brother. He was closer than Niall or Iain, and might hold a bit more element of surprise, considering Athe would likely not suspect him of an attack. But it was still too great a chance to take. Caitlin knew the instant Dar decided the same.

There was nothing she could do or say, though, at such a tense moment. One more voice and opinion in the matter might well be the final tipping point for Athe. So she just closed her eyes and offered up a prayer.

I've tried to do Yer will, Lord, she said, lifting her thoughts heavenward. *And if I've misstepped yet again, I beg Yer forgiveness. But, truly, this is in Yer hands. I cannot do aught more. Just don't,*

I pray Ye, lay any of this at Dar's feet. He never meant for things to take such an ugly turn.

"Aye, it sticks in my craw," Niall said at last. "I don't like begging, but if that's what it takes, I'll do it. Just tell me what ye want, MacNaghten, to let my sister go."

Athe laughed then, a shrill, unsteady sound. "I haven't decided as yet what more I want from ye, Campbell. So, in the meanwhile"—the blade still tight against Caitlin's neck, he began slowly to pull her back toward the gate—"I'll just take the lass with me. Keeping her safe and likely sound as well, until I decide yer fitting punishment."

There was nothing Caitlin could do but back up with him. She shot Dar an imploring look. He gave a slight nod of what she supposed was reassurance. Then he turned to Niall.

"I swear to ye this was never my plan. And I give ye my word no harm will come to Caitlin while she's with us. On my honor as a Highlander!"

"Aye, the same honor ye pledged to Jamie when ye took my sister," Niall replied through gritted teeth. "And I see how well ye've kept to that so far."

"Come along, Dar!" Athe called as he paused at the gate. "Choose now where yer loyalty lies, or I'll choose for ye."

Dar turned, then hesitated and glanced back at Niall. "Ye don't have to believe aught I say, but I will keep her safe or die in the effort."

"See that ye do, MacNaghten," the Campbell chief replied, his gaze hard and full of dire warning. "For I'll hold ye to yer word."

Dar nodded and began to edge away. Then, as he heard the creaking of hinges, he spun around and raced back—arriving just before the gate closed in his face.

II

Dar was furious with his brother, and only the need not to berate him before the men kept his tongue in check. That lasted just long enough, however, for him, Athe—with Caitlin in tow—Feandan, and Kenneth to get to the privacy of the only other room in the tower house that possessed a hearth fire. Then, just as soon as he strode over and removed Caitlin from his brother's all too firm grip, Dar exploded.

"Whatever possessed ye to start all this up again," he demanded, his voice low and taut with anger, "when ye're as aware as the rest of us that we had a safe escape route? If ye'd honored the exchange, the Campbell might have at least been temporarily satisfied and let us be. But now"—he gestured to Caitlin—"not only will he soon be hot on our trail, but there's no hope whatsoever that he'll consider sparing us."

"Aye, what *were* ye thinking, Athe?" their uncle stepped up to ask. "What ye did as yer own man was not only dishonorable but suicidal. Yet, even worse, what ye did as our chief reflects equally as poorly on us."

The red-haired man gave a defiant laugh. "And do ye think I care what Niall Campbell and his ilk consider honorable or not? They're our enemies, in case ye've all suddenly lost the meager sense ye ever had. And enemies don't dictate the terms of conduct.

We dictate our own terms and first and foremost, they're ones of survival. Survival, do ye hear me?"

His glance skittered about the gathering, halting when he saw Goraidh. Athe frowned.

"Who's this?" he demanded, indicating the hermit. "This isn't the time to be adding strangers into what's already a volatile situation."

"Goraidh's a friend," Dar said, deciding further comment on exactly why the situation had suddenly become so volatile was likely unwise. "Ye needn't trouble yerself over him."

Athe laughed. "And I'm supposed to accept the assurances of a broken man, now, am I? Well, it'll take more than yer pledge to allow this man to remain—"

"I know him as well," Feandan offered just then. "He's trustworthy. Indeed, he's as loyal a MacNaghten as any of us, and more so than most."

"Is he now?" An enigmatic smile slowly lifting his lips, Athe considered Goraidh with renewed interest. "Then I suppose he can stay, leastwise for the time being."

As if the hermit no longer held any importance to him, Athe next looked to Caitlin. A feral, calculating gleam flared in his eyes.

Uneasiness stabbed through Dar. He knew that look all too well. His brother was up to something.

"We don't need to drag the lass along to ensure our survival," Dar offered in hopes of diverting whatever Athe was planning for Caitlin. "Indeed, she'll only slow our progress. Why not head out this verra eve and leave her behind? Once the Campbell breaks in and finds her, we'll be long gone."

"Ye mean tie her up and gag her, so he'll waste even more time searching the house before he finds her?" Athe cocked his head and scratched his chin. "Aye, that might work. Especially if we hide her well. He won't dare leave a nook or cranny untouched, will he?"

"Nay, he won't."

That had been almost too easy, Dar thought. In the past, Athe had never given up on any of his ideas so quickly. Whether the weeks in prison had changed him in some manner or not, he would still bear close watching.

"Yer brother's words have merit, Athe," Feandan spoke up just then. "It does my heart good to see ye're finally paying him heed. Dar can serve as a valuable asset. And ye owe him yer thanks, as well, for all he did in procuring yer release. It was his idea, and his alone, to brave Kilchurn itself in attempting yer rescue."

"Indeed, I do owe ye my thanks." Athe walked over and extended his hand to Dar. "I would've never considered ye capable of such cleverness *or* loyalty."

"Hard times bring out heretofore surprising elements of character, don't they, Brother?"

Though Dar knew Athe well enough to discern the true depth of his sincerity—which, in this case, was more for show than anything else—he accepted his brother's hand, gave it a brief clasp, then released it. Whether he liked it or not—and Dar was fast beginning to question his earlier resolve to bring his brother back from captivity—his fate now rested with Athe.

Until he had returned to Dundarave, Dar hadn't fully realized the extent of his need to be rejoined with his clan. But now he did, and was willing to do almost anything to secure that reacceptance. Anything but risk Caitlin in the doing.

"We should assure that the lass doesn't make her escape, though," Athe said, his gaze resting once more on Caitlin, "before we're ready to depart." He turned to Kenneth. "Fetch rope, lad. Best we truss up the wench for the time being. I've no interest in guarding her all eve."

Dar watched the bard head for the door. Then he turned back to Athe.

"I'll guard her, if ye like."

His brother eyed Dar speculatively then, with an enigmatic smile, shook his head. "Nay, she'll be safe enough here in the library once she's well bound. And, with the fire, she'll not lack for warmth. Ye, on the other hand, must attend me while I speak with the men. It's past time I assert my authority as chief. We're in dire need of a leader, we are."

Feandan clapped Athe on the back. "Aye, that we are. Indeed, with yer and Dar's return, I feel a new lightness of heart. Mayhap we can still find some way to salvage a life from the terrible ruins of the past."

Athe's smile thinned. "Aye, mayhap we can, Uncle. Mayhap we can."

✛

After a time, even with hands and feet bound, Caitlin couldn't help but succumb to the fire's warmth. Despite the hard stone floor, she began to doze, finally drifting off to sleep. How long she slept, she didn't know. Some time later, however, hands on her body woke her abruptly.

The fire had died to coals. In the dim light, Caitlin couldn't make out the form above her, or exactly what the person was doing. Then she realized it was a man and he was cutting her feet free.

"D-Dar?" she croaked, excitement tightening her throat. Had he somehow slipped away from the others and come to set her free and help her return to Niall?

"Ye favor him, don't ye, wench?" Athe's harsh voice rose instead from the shadows above her. "Have ye already lain with him? It'd be so like Dar to be the first to plow the field. He can't help but ruin aught that he touches."

As he spoke, Athe pulled away the cut ropes from her ankles. After reaching over to pull first one, then another log from the pile near the hearth, he tossed them onto the bed of coals. In

154

a spray of sparks, the dried wood landed and quickly caught fire.

Next, turning back to Caitlin, he began to run his hands up the insides of her legs. She gasped in horror and kicked at him, managing to roll away when he jumped back.

"It doesn't matter this time, though, ye know." Athe pounced back on her, pinning her legs beneath his. "Indeed, it's even better this way. Better that both MacNaghten brothers have ye, before ye return to yer own brother. Better that ye're doubly ruined. It makes the revenge all the sweeter."

"Let me go, I say!" Caitlin cried as she twisted and turned beneath him. "Dar never touched me. He's too honorable a man for that."

"So ye're still a maiden, are ye?"

Caitlin froze. The embers' glow had caught in Athe's eyes. For a passing instant, he looked almost evil . . . otherworldly.

The note of immense satisfaction in his voice only added to the horrific realization that she was alone and helpless. The thick stone walls would likely muffle her cries to the point no one would hear them.

"More's the better then," her captor said, his unctuous, gloating tone filling Caitlin with revulsion. "For once, I'll have first what Dar wants. And he wants ye, ye know. Wants ye badly."

At any other time, such news would've gladdened Caitlin's heart. But not at this particular moment. If she didn't come up with some plan to thwart Athe MacNaghten in the next few seconds, she would be ravished. No decent man—not even Dar—would want her after that.

"Y-ye're mistaken," she said, fighting the impulse to scream as Athe began to move his hands up her body. "Dar despises me, he does. I've never been aught to him but an object to be traded. Traded for ye!"

His hand settled on the neckline of her bodice. "And do ye think I care, one way or another?"

His fingers clenched in the lace and woolen fabric. With a sharp movement, he tore her dress.

"One way or another," he rasped, "I haven't had a woman in over seven weeks. So ye'll do nicely on all accounts."

Caitlin screamed, struggling as hard as she could against him. For a wild, hopeful instant, Athe was thrown back and fought to keep his balance. Then his legs clamped about hers again. He steadied, leaned down, and pinned her shoulders to the floor.

"Aye," he muttered, lowering his mouth to hers, "ye'll do nicely indeed."

✠

One of the men had managed to find an unbroken bottle of claret in some dark corner of the cellar. Along with a few cups and pottery bowls that had eluded breakage when Dundarave was ransacked by Campbell forces, there were just enough drinking vessels and wine to go around.

Goraidh refused the proffered claret and, instead, stood off to himself in one corner of the Great Hall. As the others gathered before the hearth to toast Athe's successful return, Dar ambled over to join the old hermit.

"Ye don't look particularly pleased at the turn of events. Or are ye just longing for the peace and quiet of Clachan Hill?" Dar asked, his own untouched cup of wine in his hand.

As exhausted as he felt, he didn't dare imbibe in any spirits just now. Not that it might not at least ease the nagging pain in his side. Still, the others seemed surprisingly pleased at his return, and had pressed the claret on him so insistently that Dar had been reluctant to refuse.

The older man managed a wan smile. "A bit of both, I must confess."

They paused to watch as Athe appeared to excuse himself and head across the Great Hall.

"When we leave tonight, ye can take yer mule and head back home," Dar said then, turning back to Goraidh. "Whatever ye thought the Lord had in mind for me, I believe all has nearly been fulfilled. And, just as soon as we depart and Caitlin's left safely behind, there's naught more that needs doing."

"Do ye really think so?" Goraidh quirked a brow. "Och, lad, lad. Ye've got such a limited view of the Lord's far grander scheme for ye, and for the lass!"

Dar shrugged. "I deal best with what I can see and touch. In what *I* do, rather than on waiting for some invisible spirit—*if* He even exists in the first place—to bring about."

The hermit's gaze locked with his. "Ye know as well as I that God exists, lad. Ye don't fool me with all yer protestations and denials."

Irritation filled Dar. "Well, what I do know doesn't inspire me to love or follow."

"Yet ye're inspired to live with compassion and honor. With love."

"Love?" Dar's incredulous laugh was raw and harsh. "Now there ye're truly mistaken. Save for Kenneth and Feandan, I've lived without love for a long while now. And, if the truth were told, I've come to prefer it that way."

"It's safer, to be sure. No chance of betrayal, no pain of rejection or loss, no hopes dashed." Goraidh smiled sadly. "It's why ye've repeatedly pushed Caitlin away, isn't it?" He shook his head. "It's a wonder the lass keeps coming back for more of yer selfish, cowardly treatment."

"Selfish? Cowardly?" Dar nearly choked on his outrage. "I turn her away because to do aught else *would* be selfish and cowardly. She deserves far better than me. Yet a lesser man would lack the strength, the courage, to refuse her."

"But not ye." Goraidh shrugged. "Well, mayhap that's for the best. Ye making all the decisions for the two of ye, I mean. Caitlin is, after all, a wee, weak, indecisive lass. She's never been one to know her own mind, has she?"

The twinkle in the hermit's eye belied his serious demeanor. Dar's mouth twitched at one corner. Caitlin . . . weak, indecisive, and not one to know her own mind. That was the most ludicrous thing he had ever heard. And Goraidh knew it.

"Mayhap I'm being unfair in making the decision for the both of us," Dar said. "But I also know the tragedy that can arise when two people's emotions are high, when passion dictates the course rather than reason. And I tell ye true, I fear my own emotions even more than I fear Caitlin's. Once before, I went against everything safe and sane, defied the strictures of others, and have a dead woman to show for it. What kind of love is that, to destroy the object of one's love?"

"But ye didn't destroy her, lad." His companion laid a hand on his arm. "All ye did was love her and seek to make her happy. And ye would've, if others hadn't intervened for their own selfish, uncaring reasons."

Dar sighed. "I wish I knew what had truly happened to Nara. Mayhap then I could finally avenge her."

"Vengeance is for the Lord. What ye need is to move on with yer life, and not let the past destroy yer future." He smiled. "In the end, that's the true victory and the only one that really matters—that the killer doesn't destroy ye as well."

"So, ye think whoever killed Nara meant to harm me too?" Dar moved closer. "Leastwise, as punishment, if not also in reputation?"

"It's verra possible. It depends on who did the killing."

Just then, a shout came from the gathering by the fire. Dar and Goraidh glanced in that direction. Two of their clansmen had challenged each other to a wrestling match. Amidst much laughter and jovial encouragement, their friends made a circle around the now battling men.

For a time, the two combatants seemed equally matched, each succeeding in throwing the other without either successfully managing the final, definitive pin. The quicker of the two wrestlers, however, was also apparently the more fit. After several more minutes, he caught his companion in a fatigue-induced error. He seized his opportunity, twising about to slam his opponent's shoulder to the floor.

"I've always wondered if it weren't Athe," Dar muttered, turning back to the hermit as the fireside gathering broke up, and men ambled off to seek some corner to sleep in or hunkered down to talk in small groups. Even the mention of his brother's possible involvement in Nara's death caused a sharp pain to slice through him, but the wrestling match had stirred old memories of their own, nearly lifelong rivalry. "He was so enraged when he heard that Nara wanted to break their betrothal and wed me instead. And then, when atop that he learned I'd gotten Nara with child . . ."

At the memory, Dar shuddered. If it hadn't been for their uncle's timely intervention, Athe's unexpected attack would've succeeded in severing Dar's head from his shoulders. Feandan MacNaghten had thought it best to send Dar riding that very day for his own tower house, twenty miles away.

"Well, ye won't be getting any confession from that lad, if he did do it." Goraidh paused and glanced around. "Speaking of Athe, I wonder where he has gone? I don't know about ye, but until we're well and far from Dundarave, I won't feel good not keeping him in my sight."

Dar looked around the Great Hall. Save for the men who had left to relieve the guards on the parapets, the numbers in the room hadn't changed. And, considering the foul turn the weather had taken, he couldn't blame any who chose to remain in the vicinity of the fire.

The day had been overcast, with thick gray clouds lowering over the mountains. Soon after they had returned from the meeting with the Campbell, the skies had opened. Heavy torrents pelted the shake-shingled tower house. Thunder boomed periodically overhead. Indeed, if the rain didn't cease before they made their escape, it would make for a miserable journey this night. The only possible consolation was that the noise of the downpour would cover their departure—and their tracks.

Still, the fact that Athe had been gone from the Great Hall for so long disturbed Dar as well. His brother had plans of his own, ones he wasn't about to share. All they needed was for him to make matters with the Campbells even worse. As if anything could get any—

"Caitlin!"

Even as her name left his lips, Dar was already sprinting across the Great Hall toward the entry area and stairs. There was nothing he could imagine that could make things worse. Nothing but Athe doing something to harm Caitlin.

As he took the stairs two at a time, the weariness of the already long day melted away. The dull ache in his side was of little consequence. All that mattered was Caitlin, her safety.

His brother's hooded looks at Caitlin in the library earlier had set Dar's instincts immediately on edge. But had Athe truly chosen to act on his unsettling if indecipherable plans this quickly? And what exactly were those plans?

Outside, thunder clapped, and the rain only seemed to fall the harder. Water sleeted against the shuttered windows, clattering against the old, rotted wood until the slatted boards shuddered beneath the onslaught. At various spots in the roof, water dripped through. In others, the effect was closer to a steady stream.

As he reached the top of the stairs and raced down the long corridor to the library, he heard the sound of voices and hurried footsteps in the entry. Good. If Athe was up to some nefarious act, Dar might need assistance in overcoming his powerful brother.

A scream, faint but most definitely feminine, suddenly rent the air. Clutching his now fiercely throbbing side, Dar sped down the hallway. He reached the library door and nearly fell against it, gasping for air.

Steady, he told himself. *Just open the door quietly, see what's going on inside, and buy yerself a bit of time to get back yer breath. Athe doesn't know ye've been injured, and ye may well need all the appearance of strength ye possess. If fortune's indeed with ye, it won't be as bad as ye fear.*

Fortune, however, wasn't to be with him. Dar opened the door to a scene that sent ice, then fire, shooting through his veins.

There, on the floor near the hearth, Athe fought with one hand to pin down a bound and struggling Caitlin. With the other hand, he laboriously tugged the skirt up her legs.

She kicked. She threw herself about. She railed at him to let her go, interspersed with casting various other choice if unflattering aspersions on his character. Nonetheless, he doggedly kept on, as if what he intended on doing was more a task to be performed than a pleasure.

"Athe," Dar snarled in between great gulps of air, "get off her. Get off her now!"

For what seemed ploddingly long seconds, Athe didn't appear as if he heard him, or was even aware of another's presence in the room. Then, he glanced indolently back at Dar. He smiled before returning his attention and efforts to Caitlin.

"Get out of here," Athe said, his tone casual, almost bored. "Ye had yer chance at her and didn't take it. Now, it's my turn."

At the utter lack of regard for him and his demand, a familiar trait harking back to their boyhood days, the last of Dar's control shredded. With a growl of sheer, animalistic fury, he launched himself across the room. A few steps and he was at his brother's back, his fingers digging into the thick folds of his plaid to jerk him off and away from Caitlin.

Her eyes wide in surprise, she immediately rolled aside and struggled to her knees, where she flipped her hair from her face to stare up at them. Dar shot her a quick look as he dragged the flailing Athe across the room toward the door. She looked unscathed, save for a slight bruise on one cheekbone and a torn bodice that exposed just the top of her chemise.

His intent was to haul his brother from the library, shove him out the door, and lock it behind him. He knew he couldn't long endure an actual fight before he would weaken and even break open his wound anew. Dar's plan, he soon discovered, wasn't to be.

With an enraged cry, Athe dug in his heels and twisted in Dar's grip, breaking his hold. He scrambled to his feet, his face purpling in anger, a murderous gleam in his eyes.

"Ye d-dare lay hands on yer ch-chief?" he stammered in his infuriated ire. "Banishment wasn't enough for ye, was it? Mayhap a taste of the whip might be more to yer liking? And that's if I'm feeling particularly merciful!"

"Cease with the threats, Athe. They lost their effect a long while ago. But I'll tell ye true. Chief or no, ye'll not harm the lass."

His brother looked him up and down. "And ye think ye're finally man enough to take me on, do ye, little brother?"

"That's a verra good likelihood I am."

As he replied, Dar felt something warm trickle down his right side. Curse it all, he must have broken open his wound in the act of dragging that lumbering ox across the room. So much for all of Caitlin and Goraidh's careful tending of the past few days.

Nothing was served, though, by worrying over what couldn't be helped. All that mattered was protecting Caitlin and backing down his brother—if that would ever be possible with such a hot-tempered, arrogant man.

In the past, Dar had sometimes been able to ease Athe's propensity to solve all issues with battle by reason and, if that didn't succeed, by an abject apology. But he was weary of always being the one to accept the humiliation, if not the beating, without standing up to Athe.

It had never mattered if Dar was right or wrong. Always backing down had won him nothing in the end. Neither his brother's respect nor his father's love.

"Ye've always been spoiling to fight me, haven't ye? Well," Athe said, pulling out his dagger, "let's see how good ye really are, little brother."

Behind Dar, Caitlin gasped as he slowly eased back, withdrawing his own knife. Though he didn't want to hurt his brother, Dar also knew he couldn't endure a prolonged battle of parries and thrusts. There seemed no other options, however. It was evident Athe was determined, at all costs, to maintain his long-held supremacy.

Dagger in hand, Dar circled his brother, his muscles taut with readiness, his weight balanced on the balls of his feet. Athe was the first to strike, and strike he did with lightning swiftness. Only the quickest of reflexes kept Dar from being slashed across the middle. Even so, the passing trail of Athe's knife left a rent in his shoulder plaid.

Dar's eyes narrowed. Evidently, his brother meant not only to draw first blood but to do even worse.

His grip on his own knife tightened. This fight might not end well for one—or both—of them. It might even result in someone's death.

Then there were shouts and footsteps pounding down the corridor. In the next instant, Feandan, Goraidh, Kenneth, and several other men rushed into the room. At sight of the two men, daggers in hand, Feandan, in the forefront, skidded to a stop.

"What is this?" the older man demanded. "Are ye both daft?"

"Athe seems to think he can have whatever he wants, when he wants it," Dar replied calmly, never taking his eyes off his brother. "And he's decided he wants Caitlin."

"Are ye daft, man?" their uncle cried. "Ye ravish the lass, and we're all as good as dead. And I don't mean weeks or months from now!"

"It's also not verra honorable, Cousin," Kenneth offered, moving to his father's side.

"And what's it to any of ye what I choose to do?" Athe snarled, continuing to circle Dar. "After what he's done to me, Campbell deserves whatever humiliation I choose to serve him. And we'll be long gone before he discovers I left his wee sister in a slightly more soiled condition than when she first came to us."

"Ye'll have to first get past me," Dar said. "If ye can."

"And me as well," Goraidh chimed in, slipping around to stand at Dar's side. Kenneth silently joined him.

Though the hermit and bard would be of little added battle support—and likely more hindrance—Dar nonetheless shot them a grateful smile.

"Ye'll have me to deal with as well," Feandan added, "and all these other lads here," he said, gesturing to their compatriots, who looked from Athe to Feandan, then nodded resolutely if reluctantly. "We MacNaghtens have been the cause of far too much injustice and suffering of late. It's got to stop, and stop now, Athe, or we're surely doomed."

The red-haired man gave a harsh, disbelieving laugh. "Haven't ye been paying attention, Uncle? We're already doomed. We've got naught left to lose."

"We still have our honor," Dar said, his voice low but intense. "Would ye take that from us as well?"

"Honor!" Once more Athe laughed. "And aren't ye one to preach to me of honor? Ye, who stole the heart—and body—of a woman never meant for ye! Tell me, little brother. Where was yer honor then?"

"What I did doesn't justify what ye intend to do here."

"And I say it does! Indeed, ye owe me this. One lass in exchange for another."

"I didn't take Nara against her will," Dar said quietly. "What ye mean to do *is* against Caitlin's will. And that's the worst kind of dishonor."

For the first time, uncertainty flashed across Athe's face. He looked from one man to another, as if gauging each one's true intent and loyalty. What he must have found sealed his decision.

"I'll not go against my own clansmen for a wee tumble with the lass," he said finally, sheathing his dagger. "No woman's worth that." He gestured to them all. "Come, let's return to the Great Hall. The lass is safe enough here."

"Aye, safe enough now," Dar growled. "Until we leave this place, I intend personally to guard her."

Athe's expression darkened. Fleetingly, Dar thought he might have yet another fight on his hands. Then his brother shrugged.

"Have it yer way. Though I wonder if someone to chaperone *ye* isn't needed." He leered at Caitlin. "But then, mayhap it wouldn't be hard for Dar to convince ye to bed him, would it, lass? He has a way with the women, he does. And his own, verra special kind of honor."

With that Athe turned and, never looking back, strode from the library. Feandan glanced from Dar to Caitlin, then shook his head. He gestured to the others.

"Come, lads. There's more to all this than my poor head can fathom. Leave Dar and the lass to work it out.

"If aught can indeed ever be worked out," he added, a troubled look in his eyes, "of this sorry, tangled mess we've gotten ourselves into."

12

Once the last man had departed, Dar closed the library door and turned to Caitlin. She still knelt there by the hearth, her hands tied behind her, her face thrown into shadows by the firelight.

He walked over. Grasping her by both arms, Dar pulled her to her feet.

"Turn around. Let me cut yer bonds loose."

She did as he asked. "Are ye certain that's permitted? With both my hands and feet free, I could make my escape back to my brother."

"Aye, and mayhap ye should, after what almost happened to ye," Dar muttered as he withdrew his dagger and began carefully to saw through the ropes on her hands.

Emotion overcame him and he shook his head, his voice going hoarse. "If Goraidh hadn't commented on Athe's absence and I hadn't gotten here when I did . . ."

Dar found he couldn't—indeed didn't dare—go on. Anger combined with an odd mix of anguish and fear, until he didn't know if the next thing out of him would be curses or sobs. All he knew was that he was so very, very grateful that Caitlin was all right.

The ropes fell free. Caitlin tugged the torn piece of bodice up, tucked it in beneath the neckline of her chemise, then turned to face him. Tentatively, she lifted a hand to stroke his face.

"It's fine, Dar," she whispered. "I'm fine. And ye did get here when ye did."

Closing the distance between them, she laid her head on his chest and hugged him. The pressure of her arms around him most painfully reminded Dar of his side. He sucked in a sharp breath.

Immediately, Caitlin leaned back to gaze up at him. "What is it? Did Athe's cut slice more deeply than it seemed?"

"Nay." Dar gently disengaged her arms and stepped back. "But I fear all the physical exertion has caused my wound to break open."

"Let me see." She took his hand and pulled him around until he faced the fire. After releasing the brooch holding his plaid pinned over his left shoulder, Caitlin moved the fabric aside to expose his right side.

The look on her face said it all.

"How bad is it?"

"Ye're bleeding like a stuck pig." She began tugging his shirt free of his belt and kilt.

"Well, that's a reassuring description, if ever I heard one."

She shot him a sharp glance. "I didn't mean it as reassurance *or* to be humorous. If I can't stop the bleeding with pressure, we may well have to use cautery on it again."

That wasn't quite what he wanted to hear. Dar began to feel a little lightheaded.

"Do ye think it might help if I lay down here near the fire?" he asked, already casting about for a spot. "To aid ye in yer examination and care, I mean?"

Caitlin must have grasped his underlying message. "Aye, that'd help me immensely." She took him by the arm. "Here, let me assist ye."

Dar was of a mind to tell her he could get down under his own power. Then, as he began to feel not only dizzy but nauseated, he decided this was definitely not the time to waste energy in a debate. He allowed her to help him to the floor, where he stretched out by the hearth with his right side toward the firelight.

She knelt beside him, flipped up the hem of her skirt, and began to tear free a long strip of petticoat. From that, she ripped off a length, which she then proceeded to fold into a big wad.

"This is likely going to hurt, but I've got to put pressure on the spot that's bleeding. Luckily, it's only about two inches in length."

"Do yer best, lass," Dar said, feeling decidedly better now that he was recumbent. "I'd prefer to avoid the cautery. Most of all, though, I don't want Athe knowing of my condition. He's not above taking every and all advantages."

"Aye, I can well imagine how eagerly he'd seize on any weakness he found in ye." Caitlin paused. "Ready?"

Dar nodded.

She placed the folded cloth over his wound and pressed hard. It hurt. Dar went taut and clenched shut his eyes.

After a time, he opened them. "Is it working?"

Her reply was slow in coming. Too slow.

"Not yet."

He released a pent-up breath. "Then press harder. *Make* it stop."

Caitlin hesitated but an instant, then, leaving the bandage in place, rolled him over to lie atop it. Stars sparkled before Dar's eyes. The pain almost drove him past the brink of consciousness.

And then she leaned on him and pressed down hard on his left side.

✝

Some time later, Dar awoke. He lay there beside the fire, flat on his back, wondering fuzzily why he was on the floor. Then a recollection of intense pain and being swallowed up into utter blackness filled him. The wound . . . the bleeding.

His hand moved to his right side. A thick bandage, bound by several strips of cloth, was fastened there.

"Ah, good. I see that ye've awakened," Caitlin said from the shadows. "Welcome back to the land of the living."

He turned his head in the direction of her voice. She was sitting in the window seat carved from the stone wall.

"I take it ye were able to stop the bleeding without cautery then?"

"Aye, I did, though if I'd needed to do so, ye were in a far better place for the procedure unconscious than otherwise."

Awkwardly, Dar levered to one elbow. "Does anyone know? About my wound, I mean?"

"Nay. But if ye decide to do any more bleeding, I'm going to need to find a new petticoat somewhere."

"Along with yer torn bodice, that might be a difficult thing to explain to yer brother."

"Well, I do recall warning ye this verra morn that it was too soon for ye to be traveling," Caitlin said as she rose and walked over to him, "much less engaging in knife duels with yer brother."

He gazed up at her and smiled. "Aye, that ye did. One of my many failings, however, is that I oft don't listen to good advice."

She sat down beside him. "Aye, one of many. Ye also seem to be doing a lot of bleeding and passing out of late. And that tends to get in the way of accomplishing many of yer grand plans."

"At least all the bleeding and passing out is done in the cause of rescuing ye from fates worse than death." He cocked his head. "Though I'd mightily appreciate it if, from here on out, ye try to avoid any more such occasions. I only have so much blood to spill, ye know."

Caitlin sighed. "Aye, I know. And we've still a long journey ahead of us this night. I can't fathom how ye're going to be able to pull that off, without revealing the truth of yer condition."

"*I've* got a long journey, not *we*." Dar lay back and stared at the wood-slatted ceiling overhead, noting, as if for the first time, how it was encompassed with ornate, carved trim work around the edges. "Naught else has gone right this day, but I intend to at least see ye safely returned to yer brother."

"Suit yerself. Not that it'll do ye any good."

Dar turned to look at her. "Whatever are ye talking about?"

"The longer I'm with ye, the more convinced I become the Lord intends for us to remain together." She scooted closer and touched his arm. "Think on it, Dar. I came back to ye when I could've escaped. Then, no sooner had ye turned me over to Niall, than I was back with ye, albeit thanks to yer brother and a knife at my throat. And now, now ye need me to care for ye and yer wound yet again."

So, Dar thought grumpily, it was back to God again, was it? Well, God, in this case, was but the result of Caitlin's stubborn, and bordering on irrational, determination to remain with him. A braver man might question the source of her resolve, but Dar didn't dare do so.

"Goraidh is quite capable of seeing to my wound," he muttered. "Ye needn't trouble yerself over that."

She didn't reply. Instead, Caitlin climbed to her feet and walked back to sit in the shadowed window seat.

Silently, Dar cursed his clumsy attempt to reassure her that she needn't worry over him. Now, he had gone and hurt her feelings.

"Lass, I'm sorry," he began. "I didn't mean—"

"Aye, ye did!" Caitlin snapped back at him. "Ye always mean

it when ye wish to put me off from ye. And I'm weary of it, I am. I don't know what else to do with ye, to make ye like me, if only but a wee bit."

Like her? Dar closed his eyes. *Like her?*

By mountain and sea, what he felt for Caitlin was far, far more than just a friendly affection! He ached for her down through to the marrow of his bones, the depths of his heart. Ached . . . dreamt of . . . *loved* her!

Tears stung his eyes, and Dar was grateful for the distance she had put between them. Had it come to this then, that another woman had finally penetrated his defenses and turned him into some blethering, weepy idiot? Another woman whom he desired with all his heart but would never have?

He should go to her, comfort her, assure her that he at least liked her. That it wasn't that he didn't wish her to be with him, but that she couldn't. Her brother would never allow it. Dar doubted his own clan would be overly partial to a Campbell in their midst either. And without at least the support of and his inclusion back into his clan, he had nothing, absolutely nothing, to offer her.

As a broken man, Dar had many times barely managed to keep himself alive. He had no coin to speak of. And the times he couldn't prevail on some crofter to give him work to earn his bread, he was forced to rely on the code of Highland hospitality even to eat, much less find decent shelter.

Yet hospitality, for such poverty-stricken folk who frequently lived on the verge of starvation themselves, could only stretch so far. One way or another, he had never been one to beg.

It wasn't, after all, as if he dared appeal to the nobles of the various clans. They would likely soon guess his true kinship. Their hospitality would then swiftly turn to a righteous wrath, to imprisonment if not instantaneous execution.

Nay, Dar thought, he couldn't offer Caitlin any hope, if hope for them was what she was truly seeking. But he also couldn't bear to hurt her.

Gingerly, he pushed himself up. Once he was certain dizziness wouldn't overtake him, he climbed slowly to his feet. He stood there for several seconds until he was assured he wouldn't take but a few steps and topple over. Then he walked to the window seat and settled down beside Caitlin.

"Ye shouldn't be squandering yer strength on the likes of me," she said, her voice tear-choked. "I don't want or need yer pity."

"And when, since the very first instant I laid eyes on ye, have I ever led ye to believe I pitied ye?" Dar asked, taking her hand in his. "Mayhap I had a time or two of quaking in my cuarans, when ye went into one of yer especial rages, but never have I felt even one moment of pity for ye."

"Then why are ye here? Ye owe me naught."

"On the contrary, lass." Dar lifted her hand to his lips, kissed it tenderly, then lowered it back to its place between them. "I owe ye everything. Ye saved my life, twice now. Ye've been loyal and true, and bear far more confidence in me than I've ever had for myself. Atop it all, in yer kindness of heart ye even wish to come to the aid of my clan."

"B-but that's all it is then? A simple case of gratitude?"

Her voice broke, and Dar could tell she was crying. Something within him shattered. He could deal with Caitlin's anger, indeed, most times even reveled in it. But he hadn't the wherewithal to shield his heart from her pain.

"Och, lass, lass," he crooned, taking her in his arms. "It's far more than mere gratitude that I feel for ye. But there's no hope for us. None whatsoever. So let it go at that, I beg of ye. Don't make it any harder than it already is."

Caitlin laid her head on his chest, her arms slipping up to encircle his neck. And she began to weep with great, body-wracking sobs that all but tore open his heart.

172

Yet, all the while they remained like that, clutching each other there on the window seat, she never once protested that his claims were misguided or untrue. And that, more than anything, told Dar all he needed to know.

✠

Still cradled in Dar's arms, Caitlin awoke some time later to the sound of voices in the corridor, then the creak of iron hinges as the door swung open. She straightened from her slumped position and shook him.

"Dar," she said softly. "They've come for ye."

As if from long practice in dangerous situations, he jerked immediately awake. For an instant, he seemed bemused by their position, each so close to the other. Then he quickly disengaged his clasp about Caitlin and scooted away.

"My thanks," he mumbled, his voice still groggy from sleep. "I was caught unawares."

"Aye, and likely because ye were on the verge of exhaustion, not to mention yer recent—"

He put a finger to her lips to silence her. "No more of that, lass. The less they know, the better for the both of us."

She nodded. Dar withdrew his finger and shoved off the stone seat.

Feandan MacNaghten, followed by Kenneth, entered the room. Caitlin watched as Dar hobbled stiffly over to join them.

"Ye don't seem to have weathered yer wee nap all that well," his uncle observed, a concerned look in his eyes.

"A stone seat doesn't lend itself to sweet dreams."

"Not even," Kenneth cut in snidely, "with a soft lass like Caitlin to lie against?"

"Rather," Caitlin said as she rose and hurriedly walked over to them, "Dar most gallantly offered to provide himself as padding from the hard, cold walls while I dozed off. And I'd wager that

173

sort of discomfort would cause anyone at first to move with a bit more difficulty."

"My mistake, m'lady," the bard replied, even as his mischievous smirk belied his true thoughts on the matter.

"Did Athe send ye?" Dar asked, his irritation apparent.

His uncle nodded. "Aye. It's time we depart. And he said to bring Caitlin down with us."

For once, Dar didn't appear to be unduly concerned by that request. He turned, offered her his hand.

"Come, lass. Let's see what my brother next has on his mind."

She placed her hand in his. "It won't matter what ye desire, ye know. I'll be coming with ye on the journey."

He scowled, opened his mouth to most likely contradict her pronouncement, then thought better of it. Instead, he gestured to his uncle.

"Lead on."

The trek through Dundarave's corridors back to the turnpike stairs was a silent affair. The closer they drew to the entry area, however, the faster Caitlin's heart began to beat. She struggled to hold on to her belief that God wouldn't separate them. With each step they took, however, she feared it might be their last together.

What had once seemed the thing to do, because it was the Lord's will, had gradually taken on a stronger and stronger personal need to see it fulfilled. Now, Caitlin feared that if God should suddenly decide it was better for her to separate from Dar, she wouldn't be able to do so. Misery welled within her, pressing hard against her heart.

Grant me wisdom and strength, Lord, she prayed. *Wisdom to recognize Yer will, whatever it may be, and strength to carry it out, no matter how difficult it may seem. And grant Dar the same, for whatever lies ahead.*

Athe, surrounded by the rest of the men, awaited them in the entry. When he first caught sight of his brother, his expression went flinty hard. He was still nursing the humiliation of having to back down to Dar, Caitlin realized. And the humiliation had congealed into a festering abscess of unrequited rancor that could only be lanced with revenge.

A presentiment rippled through her. Sooner or later, the two brothers would again come to blows, and only one would walk away with his life. She looked to Dar to see if he had caught the seething glare Athe had sent him, but it was impossible to tell. Dar wore an expressionless mask.

At the foot of the staircase, Dar halted and turned to her. "Stay here with Kenneth. The less contact ye have with Athe, the better."

It wasn't a request. Caitlin knew better, though, than to waste time disputing his lack of social graces. She nodded and moved to the side with the bard.

Along with his uncle, Dar then strode up to confront his brother. "Feandan said ye wished to depart."

"Aye. It's half past midnight. Likely Campbell and his men are fast asleep and have no desire to venture out in this storm."

"If it's all the same with ye," Dar said, "I'll see to securing Caitlin somewhere for the rest of the night. And I'll make certain she can't escape her bonds."

A slight smile lifted one corner of Athe's mouth. "I'm certain ye're quite to be trusted in such a task. However, yer efforts won't be needed. The lass is coming with us."

Even from several yards away, Caitlin heard Athe's announcement. Her heart gave a great leap.

Thank ye, Lord!

From the sudden rigidity of Dar's shoulders, she was also quick to note his decided lack of enthusiasm for his brother's plan. *Don't do aught foolish, Dar,* she silently pleaded. *Ye'll drain what remaining strength ye have and, from the look on Athe's face, it'll still be for naught.*

"Why this sudden change in plans?" Dar asked, his hands fisting at his sides. "No purpose is served dragging Caitlin over hill and dale. We'll have more than sufficient time to make our escape, before the Campbell realizes on the morrow that we're gone."

"Likely ye're correct, little brother." Athe's shoulders lifted in a negligent shrug. "But the lives of our men are too valuable, just yet to risk losing the advantage of her as hostage. So, we've come to a consensus, all of us have, and the lass will remain with us for a time longer."

Dar turned to his uncle. "Is that true? Did ye, as well, agree to this ill-conceived plan?"

The older man hesitated, then nodded. "I saw no harm in it. The lass is strong and healthy. A wee trek through the hills won't hurt her."

"Nay, it won't. But it'll bring her brother down even hotter and faster on our tails, it will!"

"Mayhap," Feandan conceded reluctantly, "but it's been decided, and there's naught served wasting more time arguing over what ye cannot change. Ye can continue, however, to serve as her guard until we deem it time to set her free."

"Unless ye've finally had yer fill of the lass, of course," Athe volunteered with malicious glee. "Ye *were* alone up in the library for the past four hours, after all. So, if ye're no longer interested . . ."

"Rather, I should've used the time to spirit her away through the tunnel," Dar muttered, "back to her brother."

"Aye, ye could've done so, I suppose. But ye're too loyal for that, aren't ye, little brother? Just as ye also lacked the stomach, didn't ye, to risk what Campbell might've done to us, once he had his sister back?"

Athe made a great show of pretending to study him consider-ingly. "Or mayhap ye did think on it. Play the hero, I mean, and inveigle yerself into the Campbell's good graces by returning his sister all on yer own? Who knows? He might've been so grateful to ye that, with his help, ye might've won a royal pardon for yer efforts."

The other men in the room began to murmur amongst them-selves and send Caitlin angry glances. More concerned for Dar than for herself, an impulse rose to stride over and remind Athe, and all the rest of them, what Dar had already risked in their cause. But caution made her hesitate. To rush too eagerly to his defense might well be more detriment than advantage for Dar.

"If I'd chosen to take Caitlin back," Dar said just then, "it would've been solely to protect her from ye, Brother. Until just now, though, I had no reason to expect not to be leaving her behind this night. I but spoke a moment ago out of frustration and concern for her continued welfare."

"Of course ye did." With an arched brow and mocking smile, Athe looked around at the men.

"Enough, Athe!" Like a knife, Feandan MacNaghten's aggra-vated voice slashed through the rising tension. "Ye already said Dar was as loyal as they came, and that's the end of it. Now, are we going to be on our way before it's morn, or not?"

The red-haired man shot his uncle a seething glance, then nodded. "Aye, best we are and do so posthaste."

He glanced once more to Dar. "Just be sure to keep a good hold on the lass. If she somehow manages to escape on the journey, it won't go well with ye."

"Somehow," Dar muttered, his expression hooded as he turned to gaze over his shoulder at Caitlin, who couldn't quite hide the joy in her eyes, "I'm rather certain that won't be a problem. Nay, not a problem at all."

13

To Dar's surprise, Goraidh chose to continue on with them. Once through the hidden passage, while the others headed out on foot, the hermit mounted his mule and Caitlin was given the gelding. Dar seized the excuse of needing to remain close by her to contain any attempts at escape, and was soon grateful for the lessened strain that riding the horse provided him.

Even with Caitlin seated behind him, her arms securely clasped about his waist, her body offering additional support, he soon found the exertion wearying. As the hours passed in their trek through soggy forest, then water-logged meadows and glens, if not for the horse, Dar knew he would have quickly fallen behind. And his brother would have just as quickly discovered his secret weakness.

As it was, Athe didn't call a halt for a few hours' rest any too soon. It took all of Dar's remaining strength to dismount without blatantly falling off the big animal. Caitlin made a show of pretending to be so saddle sore she needed his help walking over to a tree when, all the while, she was doing more to aid him than he was her.

"My thanks," Dar said softly as he finally lowered himself beside her to lean against the broad base of an ancient oak. "I don't know how much longer I would've lasted." He sighed and closed his eyes.

"Aye, best ye rest while ye can," she murmured. "It looks like they're preparing a midday meal. I'll fetch ye something to eat and drink."

"I don't have much of an appetite—"

"But ye'll force it down nonetheless," she cut him off firmly. "Won't ye?"

Dar cracked open one eye. "Aye, m'lady."

With a disgusted toss of her head, Caitlin turned and headed to where the others were breaking open the parcels of food. No sooner had she departed, though, than Kenneth ambled over and plopped down next to Dar.

"Aye, Cousin?" Dar asked, sending him a sidelong glance. "Ye've something ye wish to say to me, do ye?"

"Have a care with yer brother." The bard settled back against the tree. "I've never seen him so edgy before, like the least little thing would set him off. Set him off into a killing rage."

"Like mayhap the sort he surely went into that night at the MacNabs?"

Kenneth nodded. "Aye, exactly so." He hesitated, glancing covertly around as if attempting to ascertain that no one was within earshot. "Ye worry him, ye do. I fear it wouldn't take much provocation on yer part to bring on yet another battle."

Dar frowned. "Worry him? Why? Because I won't ever let him near Caitlin again?"

"More likely *because* ye stood up to him over her. Ye've never done that before, and he doesn't quite know what to make of it. Or where yer true loyalties lie."

He was too tired to be discussing such a topic, much less trying to discern where his cousin was really going with this. And Kenneth was most definitely headed down some specific path.

"Loyalties other than the intent to protect her from him?"

179

Dar couldn't quite hide the irritation in his voice. "Spit it out, Kenneth. What exactly are ye getting at?"

"It's just not me, Dar. Father thinks the same thing." He paused, inhaled what looked to Dar like a fortifying breath. "Athe fears ye mean to take the chieftainship from him."

If he hadn't been so exhausted and so in need of conserving every ounce of energy he had left, not to mention he didn't need to set his side to aching any worse than it already was, Dar would've laughed out loud. Instead, he just shook his head.

"And how many times must I repeat I've no desire whatsoever to lead the clan? What more do I need to say or do before anyone believes me? Ye or yer father haven't gone and put any ideas in anyone else's heads, have ye? For I can't fathom Athe forming such a daft notion about me on his own."

"It's naught we've said, Dar," Kenneth replied. "It's what others have begun saying *to* us."

Dar turned to look at his cousin. "Others? Some of these men?"

"Aye."

He expelled an exasperated breath. "Then I'm certain ye and yer father are imagining things. I saw their reaction when Athe began to impugn my loyalty. They think I'm smitten with Caitlin, and she has me on the verge of betraying them all for her."

"Well, it's not as if ye hide yer affection for her all that well, ye know."

"By mountain and sea!"

Dar lurched upright and was rewarded by a sharp stab in his side. He caught himself before he grabbed at his wound, but couldn't hide the grimace of pain.

"Ye *have* gone and hurt yerself, haven't ye?" Kenneth eyed him closely. "I wondered as much, when ye could barely walk over to us last night in the library."

"Not a word to anyone. Do ye hear me?" Dar sent him a

furious look. "If Athe should know that I'm not up to full strength . . ."

"He'd waste no time in seizing the chance to bring ye down." His cousin nodded in understanding. "More's the reason not to push him too hard or oft right now."

"I've no intention of doing so," Dar muttered. "Just as long as he keeps his hands off Caitlin . . ."

"Then I suggest ye begin to affect some indifference to the lass, and do so posthaste. Even if Athe fails to act the proper gentleman around her. He may well be casting about for just such an excuse to fight ye again and, in the doing, prove to the others what he's already begun to try to plant in their minds."

Dar turned a blazing gaze to the bard. "Never. I'll never surrender my honor to save my life, and seeing Caitlin safely back to her brother's care is about all the honor left me. Besides, whether he ultimately draws me into another battle or not, Athe's never going to allow me back into the clan. That's as clear as day."

"Well, there's always another sure way to get back into the clan, ye know."

"And exactly what would that be?"

Kenneth didn't immediately answer. "Why don't ye relax a bit? Lean back against the tree and look bored? Yer brother has suddenly taken a wee too much interest in our conversation."

Knowing better than to look in Athe's direction, Dar did as his cousin suggested. He leaned back, crossed one ankle over the other, and closed his eyes.

For a time, the two men didn't speak. Finally, though, Kenneth must have decided it was safe to talk again.

"I don't dare linger here much longer," he said. "Not to mention, the lass even now is heading our way with some food. But I will leave ye with one last thing to consider. The other way to be taken back into the clan is if the clan asks ye to return."

When Dar opened his mouth to protest that Athe wouldn't allow that to happen, Kenneth held up a silencing hand.

"Athe can have naught to say about what the clan wishes, if he's no longer chief," his cousin then continued. "And the only way that can happen is if ye or someone else—if ye stubbornly persist in refusing to consider such a position—is elected chief. Just because we managed to extricate Athe from Kilchurn doesn't mean he deserves to continue being our leader. On the contrary. The more I'm with him, the more convinced I am he's the worst answer to our present dilemma. And that mayhap we erred in bringing him back."

Kenneth pushed to a squatting position beside Dar. "So think on all this, if ye will, and put that clever mind of yers now to solving *this* wee problem. For indeed, if the error's ours, then it's only right and honorable that we be part of the solution. And that what ye desire, in the end, may not be as important as what ye're being called to do."

✝

After the midday meal, they all took an hour's rest, then Athe ordered them to resume the journey. His plan—which he shared only with Dar, Kenneth, and Feandan—was to lose their Campbell pursuers long enough to backtrack a bit, then head to a shieling in a high, verdant meadow near Ben Vorlich, deep in MacFarlane lands. The summer home, where cattle were taken for several months to graze the lush hill grasses, would be one of the last places Niall Campbell would think to look for them, Athe assured Dar and the others.

Dar wasn't certain Niall Campbell would so easily give up, leastwise not when it came to one of his own family. In any case, Dar didn't plan to risk taking Caitlin all the way to the shieling. He didn't trust Athe to release her. Even blindfolded, she might guess their location and eventually reveal it to her brother.

He just needed to buy himself a bit more time in which to gather some additional strength. Another day was about all he could spare, though. After that, they would enter MacFarlane lands. And Dar, like the rest of them, didn't want in any way to betray the clan that had been of such support in these dire times.

In another day's time, he intended to force the matter of Caitlin's release. If Niall Campbell hadn't caught up to them by the time they reached MacFarlane lands, it would be evident they had managed to elude him for at least a time. They were then, in all senses of the word, safely away.

Dar only hoped his brother's reason to continue holding Caitlin *had* truly been just for that purpose. If not, the confrontation he had assiduously been trying to avoid could be avoided no longer. And everything he had striven so hard to achieve, and the danger he had placed Caitlin in, would have been for nothing.

In any event, Dar felt as if everything were already tumbling down around him. Nothing, save that he had managed to extricate Athe from Campbell custody, had gone as planned. Caitlin wasn't back with her brother. Athe was still the same selfish, prideful, uncaring man he had always been. And the long-dreamt brotherly gratitude, which should have resulted in an invitation to rejoin the clan, hadn't—and wouldn't—be forthcoming.

He was tempted to consider his efforts a dismal failure. Indeed, Dar struggled mightily at times not to surrender to despair. But some good had still come out of all of the missteps and poorly resolved plans.

Though he still marveled at the unlikelihood of such an occurrence, he had begun to gather a small group of friends about himself. His uncle and Kenneth had always been there for him, even during the years of his exile. But now he also counted Goraidh and Caitlin as friend. And, atop everything else, Kenneth had mentioned that some of the men in this very group had spoken of him replacing Athe as chief.

No one, save Feandan and Kenneth MacNaghten, had ever before regarded him with interest, much less with caring and respect. He had been the second and last child born to their mother, who had died while he was yet a child. Athe had been the eldest, the heir, their father's pride and joy. And little Dar, who for a time had been sickly and small, hadn't even been expected to live very long.

But now, after all those years of parental abuse and clan disinterest, it seemed others were beginning to gather around him. Why they were doing so mystified Dar, though. Were they at last discovering that Athe wasn't fit to rule them, and were now turning to him by default?

And if they looked to him now for other reasons entirely, what did it all mean? Whatever it meant, should he give it any credence?

They had never wanted him before. What did he owe them now, save what *he* wished to give? To be chosen as the lesser of two evils was hardly a compliment, much less a vote of acceptance and love.

Dar smiled sadly. Acceptance and love . . . He had longed for that ever since he could remember, but perhaps that had never been what truly mattered.

As Kenneth had so recently informed him, what he desired just might not be as important as what he was being called to do. Problem was, though his cousin's words held a ring of truth, Dar wasn't so sure he cared much for the implications of being called. They smacked too much of losing control over one's life, of God and holy quests.

His thoughts traveled back to that day they had departed Goraidh's cottage, when the hermit had stoutly claimed he would be joining them. That he went where the Lord led, and it was evident the Lord wanted him to join what Dar was even then beginning to view as a hopeless undertaking. An undertaking that, convinced as he was that the Lord was involved, Goraidh definitely didn't see as hopeless.

Caitlin seemed equally certain that all of this was God's will. But if God really was in this, why now? God had never seemed particularly interested in Dar before. And what did He expect from him?

With a sigh, Dar closed his eyes for a brief moment. It was too much to comprehend, especially as exhausted as he was. All he knew was he wanted some answers, and that he needed help. As hard as that was to admit, Dar finally faced the fact he couldn't do what he had set out to do alone. Too many things conspired to stop him, one particularly large obstacle being his brother.

He leaned back, felt Caitlin behind him. In response, she clasped him a bit more tightly about his waist and laid her head against him. Bonny, faithful, trusting Caitlin. Dar's heart swelled with love for her.

Dare he hope it was also God's will they remain together? Such a consideration was enough to make a saint out of a sinner. But when had God ever done anything kind or loving for him? And to imagine that now, after all these years, the Almighty might change was beyond comprehension, much less belief. It was but the crowning evidence that Dar had reached the end of his hope—and sanity.

He looked to where Goraidh rode ahead of them. A longing to talk with the hermit filled him. Oh, how he needed explanations, guidance, and a nonjudgmental ear! But such consolations weren't for him. Leastwise, not just now.

What mattered most now was rebuilding his strength, and anticipating from which quarter Athe might next attack. Kenneth was right. His brother was indeed on the edge. Sooner or later, something was going to set him off.

"Are we headed toward MacFarlane lands then?" Caitlin asked later that day, even before they had left the last of former Mac-Naghten holdings.

Dar could barely contain the jolt of dismay her innocent question engendered. "And why would ye be thinking that?" he asked, hiding his rising tension with the greatest effort.

"Well, for one thing, their lands lie in the direction we're heading. I also recognize Ben Vorlich in the distance. And that mountain's most definitely in MacFarlane territory. Besides," she added as he shot a quick glance at her over his shoulder, "ye first introduced yerself as a MacFarlane. It's simple enough to deduce that ye took the name of a clan friendly to ye, when ye didn't dare use yer own."

He cursed his own stupidity. How could he have so easily forgotten the name he had first given her? He knew she was quick of mind. What could he now say to her to divert her from knowledge that could well threaten the safety of this party and, ultimately, the entire clan?

Whatever he did, it was likely already too late. Though Dar doubted Caitlin would knowingly betray them, he couldn't risk the chance that her brother had also learned of his use of the MacFarlane name and had deduced the same likelihood of where they were headed. Niall Campbell, from all reports, was also particularly sharp-witted.

"Aye, that's indeed where we're headed," he said as he urged the gelding forward to a faster pace. "And likely, as well, the chances are strong that yer brother might also be headed that way."

She was quiet for a long moment. "Knowing Niall, that's verra possible. What are ye planning to do about it?"

"What else? I have to tell Athe. We can't risk implicating the MacFarlanes any more than we may already have done, not to mention taking the chance of having yer brother awaiting us somewhere along the way."

"Ye're never going to be able to dispose of me, are ye? Leastwise, not without risking yer clan in the process?"

"*Dispose* is too strong of a word," he replied, not liking at all some of the meanings associated with the term. "But I'll also admit the easiest part of this whole hostage-taking plan has become the most difficult. Who would've thought returning ye to yer brother would've become nigh to impossible?"

"It's almost as unbelievable as the thought of me ever being so torn between being returned and staying with my abductor." Caitlin sighed. "I don't know how I'll ever explain that to Niall."

Dar chuckled softly as they neared the head of the column, with Athe, Feandan, and Kenneth at its lead. "Just tell him I bespelled ye, and ye didn't know yer own mind."

"But that might condemn ye as a warlock, and ye know the penalty for that."

He shrugged. "I'm doomed, one way or another. Though I'll admit burning at the stake wouldn't be my first choice of execution."

She shuddered. "Don't jest about such a fate!"

Then they were pulling even with the three men. "Hold," Dar called, looking over at them. "We need to talk."

Athe glanced up at him. "Do we? It can wait for a few more hours. We'll make camp then."

"A few more hours may be too late. Even now, Campbell and his men could be around the next hill. Call a halt now, Athe, so we can draw aside to speak privately."

Anger flashed in his brother's eyes. He wasn't used to being ordered about, Dar realized, and especially not by him. But there wasn't time for pretty words and pleas. Dar only hoped that once Athe heard what he had to say, he would understand the urgency of the situation.

"This had better be of the utmost import," Athe growled. He turned and signaled the rest of the party to pull aside and wait. Then he looked to Feandan and Kenneth. "Come along. Best ye hear what Dar claims is so vital."

He paused, eyeing Caitlin. "Leave the wench with some of the men. Naught's served with her being privy to our talk."

"There's naught that she doesn't already know." Dar swung off his horse. Before he could lift a hand to assist her, she scrambled down on her own. "Indeed," he then continued, turning to the others, "if not for her, we may have soon ridden into a trap."

Dar's brother arched a brow. "Have a care, Dar, where and when ye involve her in our matters. The more she knows, the more tenuous her position grows."

Was that a veiled threat against Caitlin? Dar chose to let it pass. If all went as he intended, this very day she would be on her way back home.

"And I say, don't be so hasty to judge." He slipped an arm about Caitlin's waist, then gestured to a small burn that ran along the cattle track they had been following. "Over there should be far enough to speak without being overheard."

"Well, get on with it!" Athe demanded impatiently just as soon as they were all gathered by the noisily flowing little stream. "Ye importune us all by yer self-important posturings. I warn ye, I won't tolerate much more of it."

From long experience, Dar hid his own growing anger. "There's a strong likelihood Niall Campbell may have surmised we might be on our way to MacFarlane lands."

Athe's eyes narrowed. "And, pray, why would that be?"

"Because when I first came to Kilchurn, I called myself Darach MacFarlane. And Caitlin just put together that bit of information with the obvious direction we were heading, and arrived at that verra conclusion. Her brother likely also learned of my dual identity soon after he returned home. That, combined with the certitude he's a verra quick-thinking man . . ."

A foul stream of curses erupted from Athe's lips. He lunged at Dar, and only Feandan and Kenneth's quick response managed to prevent him from going for his brother's throat. As it was, Dar took a few steps back to put some distance between them.

"Ye fool!" Athe cried. "Why didn't ye tell me this to begin with?"

"It doesn't matter why I didn't think of it until now," Dar calmly replied. "What matters is, as soon as I did, I came to ye with it."

"And now she knows our plan as well," his brother said, gesturing toward Caitlin. "How much more have ye told her? Indeed, mayhap ye somehow managed to get word to the Campbell of this, even before we left Dundarave!"

"Ye're daft, Athe!" *So, here it began*, Dar thought. "I did no such thing. Indeed, how would I? And, more importantly, *why* would I?"

"How should I know?" The red-haired man's hand slid to the dagger sheathed at his side. "To inveigle yerself with the Campbells, mayhap? I've seen how ye look at the wench. It'd singe the hide off a boar, it would! Mayhap ye fancy taking her to wife, of joining Clan Campbell as a broken man."

Dar's laugh was harsh and disdainful. "Ye'd like that, wouldn't ye? For me to turn my back on the MacNaghtens, once and for all? Well, it'll never be, Brother. Never!"

Athe's smile was malicious and lethal. "But haven't ye? It's been evident for a time now that yer loyalties are divided. On one hand there's the clan and, on the other"—he indicated Caitlin—"there's the lass. It's time to choose, little brother. Choose one or the other."

Dar's hand slid from Caitlin's waist, and he stepped in front of her. "And if I chose the clan, where would that leave the lass?" Even as he spoke, his own hand moved to his dagger.

"That's not for ye to decide." Unflinchingly, Athe met Dar's gaze. "Just give her to me and be done with it."

All the possibilities of what Athe might do to Caitlin roiled in Dar's head. Ravish her, then leave her behind for her brother to find. Kill her. Or just set her free to find her way alone and defenseless, back home to her brother—*if* she even could.

None of the choices were acceptable. Yet the alternative to refusing his brother would surely end in a battle. A battle to the death, if the eager, bloodthirsty look in Athe's eyes were any indication. A battle, in his still-weakened state, Dar could very well lose.

So be it then. Dar shook his head.

"Nay, I won't give ye Caitlin." He withdrew his knife. "It's to be a fight to the finish, is it then?"

A feral smile twisted Athe's mouth. "Aye, so it seems." His own dagger came free of its sheath.

"And what of me?" Caitlin slipped away from Dar to move between the two men. "Before ye two hotheads start slicing at each other, don't ye care to hear of *my* plan? A plan that'll solve all yer problems?"

Dar grabbed at her arm. "Lass, get behind me while ye still may. Athe won't listen to ye. His mind is made."

"Well, then he'd be a fool, he would," she retorted, jerking free of his grip. "And, though he is many other unsavory things, yer brother has never struck me as a fool."

Dar couldn't believe what he was hearing. Did Caitlin imagine Athe wouldn't kill her if it suited him? She was playing a dangerous game, the secrets of which, for some reason, she had deliberately chosen not to share with him.

"She has a mind of her own, that one does," his brother said, surprising Dar with his grin. "Ye may well have taken on more than ye can handle, little brother." He turned his attention then to Caitlin. "Ye're verra perceptive. I'll give ye that." He made a slight wave of his hand. "So speak yer mind and be done with it. What's yer plan?"

"It's simple, really." As if it mattered not to her which option Athe chose, she gave a small, uncaring shrug. "Ye've no way of knowing when and where my brother will turn up. Even now, he could be ahead of ye, lying in wait. But, more likely, he's yet hot on yer trail."

Athe gave an impatient snort. "Aye? How is that of any news to us? And what has any of that to do with yer plan?"

"I'm getting to that." Caitlin waited until the auburn-haired man quieted. "Now, it's also more than apparent ye don't care much for Dar, and he doesn't care much for ye. So send him back to head off Niall, with me as the bait. Then ye and the rest of yer men ride for someplace other than MacFarlane lands. Ye're rid of Dar and me and, if naught else, my brother will slow if not halt his pursuit. Well," she added, "leastwise for a time. I can make no promises for him, of course."

"So," Athe said, cocking his head and eyeing her speculatively, "ye're suggesting I sacrifice Dar to save the rest of us. Leastwise, for a time, of course."

She nodded. "If ye think on it a bit, I'd wager ye'd discover that it solves all yer problems. Being as how ye're hardly a fool, after all."

"And when are either of ye going to include me and my desires in this?" Dar demanded gruffly. "Because mayhap I don't particularly wish to end up imprisoned in Kilchurn's dungeon any more than Athe did."

"But aren't ye also, little brother, the one who's been yammering incessantly about returning the lass to her brother?" Athe smiled. "Well, for my part, I think the lass has a verra fine plan here. It's time ye made a choice. Either give her to me to do with as I see fit, and stop challenging everything I try to accomplish as chief, or choose her and whatever fate that decision leads ye to. Ye can't have it both ways."

On the contrary, Dar thought, *I could have it both ways if ye were no longer chief. For that to happen, however, I'd either have to kill ye or the clan would have to vote ye out. Just now, though, the likelihood of besting ye in a knife battle isn't all that good. And there's no time for a gathering of the clan. Not with Niall Campbell breathing down our necks.*

He wagered Caitlin had come up with this bold scheme in order to save him. She knew how weakened he was. And, in presenting such a brazen offer before Feandan and Kenneth, she also knew it would put Athe on the spot, forcing him to make a decision.

Nothing had been said, however, about Dar's willingness to allow himself to be captured by Niall Campbell. And he most certainly wasn't willing and had no intention of doing so.

In actuality, all he really had to do was get Caitlin within a safe range of her brother. He could then ride away before Campbell could get close enough to apprehend him. It was a simple enough thing, after that, to hide out for a time to heal and regain his strength.

Eventually, if he still wished it, he could then again seek out Athe and the clan. Free finally of the responsibility of Caitlin, Dar could concentrate—because of the indisputable part he had played in freeing his brother—on getting the clan to reinstate him. If Feandan and Kenneth were correct, Dar might well have several men besides them who would back him on that.

On the other hand, how he could get on with his life without Caitlin was a consideration he didn't dare face just now. For the present, all that mattered was her safety and his survival. Later was soon enough to determine where he should go from there.

"When ye present it that way, Brother," Dar finally said, "I've apparently only one option. I gave Niall Campbell my word I'd keep his sister safe. And it has always been part of the bargain that she'd be returned in exchange for ye. It's past time that she was."

"Then get on with ye. Take the lass and ride out now, before I change my mind." Athe sheathed his dagger. "And bring that meddlesome hermit with ye, as well. I've no need of the likes of him."

"Och, ye've a need of him," Dar muttered as he pulled Caitlin back to him. "Ye just don't understand why."

Athe gave a disbelieving laugh. "And ye do? Is it possible? Is my little brother finally going soft in the head and turning his life over to God? I'd believe many things of ye, Dar, but never that."

"Believe what ye want," Dar snarled. "Ye've never known aught about me anyway."

His brother's sneer faded. "Och, I know far, far more about ye than ye know about yerself," Athe said softly. "But that's for another time, little brother. If and when we ever cross paths again, that is."

14

They rode for a time, until twilight shrouded the land. Finally—and none too soon for Caitlin—Dar reined in the gelding and looked over to where Goraidh had pulled up on his mule.

"It's best we make camp for the night," he said. "A cold camp, however. I don't know if or when the Campbell will come upon us, but I'd prefer he not take us unawares."

"And why is that?" Caitlin asked from behind him. "My brother's not likely to fill us with crossbow quarrels before he sees me, so there's no danger of risking our lives if we accidentally come upon him."

"For one thing"—Dar dismounted and held the horse steady while Caitlin climbed down—"it's never wise to accidentally happen upon anyone in the dark. And, for the other," he added as she walked up to him, "be it day *or* night, I don't want to accidentally stumble upon a mess of Campbells. I'd far prefer to find them first, then send ye to yer brother in such a way that I can also safely make my escape."

She didn't move away but continued to stand there, even as the heat of their shared emotions began to far exceed the mutual warmth of their bodies. There wasn't much time left, Caitlin knew, to win Dar over to the idea of remaining with her when they finally found Niall and his men. And, when time was short, a woman had to use every advantage she had.

"Ye'd be safe," she murmured, gazing up at him from beneath her long, dark lashes, "either way. Niall's a reasonable man. And ye are, after all, bringing me back to him."

The effort it took Dar to step back from her was evident. "Aye, he'd likely not kill me on the spot," he replied, his voice husky. "He's the lawful sort, after all. He'd at least first have me tried before he hung me."

There wasn't time to formulate a reply. Dar turned to the right and, pulling the gelding along, headed off the road and into a thick stand of trees. Behind her, she heard Goraidh chuckle.

Caitlin waited until the hermit had drawn up alongside her before she spoke.

"Ye could be a bit more help, ye know," she then muttered, taking care that Dar not overhear them. "He's got a better chance of a decent life with my clan than he ever will with his. And Niall's a godly man. He could be brought to show Dar mercy and extend forgiveness."

"Aye, that he likely could, lass," Goraidh said, keeping his voice low. "Ye usually do get what ye want, don't ye? But what of what Dar wants? Or isn't that what matters most to ye?"

She grabbed his arm and pulled him to a halt. "Of course it's what I want! He's had little enough of happiness in his life. But do ye truly think he'll ever find any happiness with that ill-fated, melancholic clan of his? Why, I've never seen such a cowed, dithering, self-serving bunch of folk in all my life!"

"It wasn't always that way," he said, and Caitlin thought she heard a wistful sadness in the older man's voice. "The bitterness of betrayal, though, can sear clear to the heart of a family and clan."

"Och, aye, and lay that as well at Dar's feet, will ye?" She shook her head. "I would've thought ye, of all people, would understand that it takes more than one misguided if well-intended act to bring down an entire clan."

"And why would ye imagine *I* would understand better than most?" Goraidh asked carefully.

"Why else? Ye're a man of God. I would've thought ye'd possess greater compassion and insight than the rest of them."

"Och, aye. Well, I hope that's true."

The hermit's laugh sounded suspiciously like one of relief. Caitlin eyed him a bit more closely. Was there more to Goraidh's story than he had yet to reveal? If so, holy man or not, he might bear watching.

"Besides," he continued then, "I wasn't speaking of what Dar did when he fell in love with Nara. I was speaking of another betrayal, inflicted before the lad was even born. Another betrayal of brother against brother."

"Indeed?" Her curiosity piqued, Caitlin moved closer. "A Mac-Naghten brother against brother?"

"Are ye two going to lag behind the whole night?" Dar, far ahead now, called softly out to them just then. "We need to get some rest, and it's already later than ye may think. So, if ye would, stop yer blathering back there and catch up with me!"

Further questions would have to wait, Caitlin decided as she picked up the pace along with Goraidh. But, if she had any say in it, not for long.

The misfortunes of Clan MacNaghten apparently went far deeper than she had been led to believe. And, somehow, some way, Caitlin thought with a ripple of presentiment, it all seemed to come full circle back to Dar.

✠

Late the next day, as they made their way across Glen Fyne and then headed northeast up the River Fyne, which Dar hoped to follow until it finally swung west toward Loch Shira, he caught a glimpse of a large party of horsemen cresting a hill north of them. Though still on the other side of the river, the riders headed toward them with a disconcerting speed. At first, Dar couldn't make out from their plaids who they were, but Caitlin soon told him all he needed to know.

With a sharp, inhaled breath and tightening of her arms about his waist, she leaned forward. "It's Niall. I beg ye, stop and let him come to us."

He should do as she asked, Dar thought. Stop and let her down so she could await her brother's arrival. Then ride away while he still had a lead on them. Once the Campbell and his men reached the spot where they currently were, it would still take a time to ford the river. A river that was running heavy and strong from the late spring snow melt.

But now that the moment was finally upon them, Dar found that a strange malaise had settled over him. He didn't seem able to move his limbs, much less turn and help Caitlin dismount. The memory of the press of her body against his back, her light fragrance of heather and fresh air, and her arms about his waist would soon be all he had left.

And he didn't want it to end. Not now. Not ever.

"What do ye intend to do, lad?" Goraidh's voice intruded suddenly on Dar's tortured musings. "They'll be here soon. Verra soon."

The hermit's warning jerked Dar back to action. He turned to Caitlin.

"Ye're safe enough now, lass. Get down. Yer brother will be here for ye in but a short while."

"N-nay." Caitlin's clasp about him tightened. "Stay, Dar. Stay with me. There's naught left for ye with yer clan. Athe will see to that, and well ye know it. Once I speak with Niall, he'll understand. He'll take ye in."

On the contrary, Dar thought. *She* didn't understand. Her

brother had been made to look the fool. No Highlander bore that well, especially not ones as proud as the Campbells. Niall wouldn't forgive, or forget, what Dar had done to him.

"I don't wish to be taken in," he said, hardening himself to her sweet pleas. "I'm a MacNaghten, and that's all I've ever wanted to be. Don't ye understand that? Now, get down before I throw ye down!"

"Have it yer way then, ye pigheaded dolt!" Caitlin cried as she slid from the horse. "It won't matter in the end what ye do or don't want."

Hands fisted at her sides, fire flashing in her eyes, she backed away. "Ye're not rid of me. I'm in yer blood now, Darach Mac-Naghten, and ye'll never get me out. Ye'll see. Ye'll see!"

"Mayhap not," he gritted through clenched teeth, "but ye're *well* rid of me. And, if not now, someday ye'll thank me for that."

Dar looked to Goraidh. "Are ye with me, or will ye stay with her?"

"I'll stay with her until her people arrive." The hermit made a quick motion with his hand. "Go, lad, and be quick about it. Already, they're set to ford the river."

Dar glanced up. About three hundred feet upstream, Niall Campbell, at the head of his men, was already urging his big horse into the river. The animal began to swim strongly, but at mid river the current suddenly proved too powerful. Rather than continue across the surging waters, the horse was slowly pushed downstream.

Niall Campbell fought to remain on the animal's back. He soon apparently decided, though, to lighten the load, slipping from the saddle to swim alongside.

For a few seconds, the horse appeared to gain a few feet toward the other shore, before its forward momentum was once more halted by the onrushing waters. The animal slammed into a large boulder and spun around, wedging Niall between itself and the boulder.

Foaming waves rushed over him. Niall fought desperately to keep his head above the water before finally disappearing beneath the raging torrent.

Caitlin screamed and ran upstream along the rocky embankment toward her brother. Just then, with a great lunge forward, Niall's horse broke free. Carried along by the current, the animal shot past her.

A few seconds later, Niall's limp form broke the water's surface and was also propelled down the river. Caitlin scrambled over the rocks toward the water's edge.

"Lad?"

Goraidh looked to Dar, who had, until that moment, been sitting there transfixed by what had so rapidly been taking place. A question burned in the older man's eyes.

"Caitlin! Nay!" Dar roared, finally galvanized into action. "Stay. I'll do it!"

Caitlin looked up. Their glances met for a brief instant. Joy, gratitude—love—flared in her luminous blue-green eyes.

Then there was no time left to spare. Turning his horse along the shore, Dar headed straight to a spot downstream where he saw that the river narrowed.

He had no choice. He was the only one close enough to reach the Campbell as he came rushing down the river. From the looks of him, Niall had been knocked unconscious while trapped underwater between his horse and the boulder. If Dar didn't get to him, and fast, Niall Campbell would surely drown.

The fact he was risking his life to save his enemy, and would likely be captured in the bargain, wasn't of import. It was Caitlin's brother. If Dar didn't go into the water after him, she surely would. And her woman's strength wouldn't be sufficient to save herself, much less drag an unconscious man back to shore.

He kicked the gelding hard, urging it into a run. He needed to buy some distance downstream before he dove in. He would have only one chance to time his entrance into the water so as to reach the proper spot when Niall floated by. After that, only luck—or heavenly intervention—would get them both back to shore alive.

As he reached the slight narrowing of the river, Dar reined in. He leaped from his horse and scooted down the embankment toward the river. Even then, Niall was barreling toward him.

Dar tossed aside his dagg and slipped from the harness that kept his claymore strapped to his back. He waded out into the shallows until the waters tugged hard around his thighs. Then he dove in.

Just as he broke the surface in the middle of the surging waves, Niall, now on his back, passed him. Dar reached out and grabbed at the other man's arm. He missed. He grabbed again. As Niall shot by, Dar caught him by his ankle.

With a great lurch, Dar twisted about. With one hand, he began swimming toward the shore. Water boiled over him, beating at him like some enraged assailant. He was forced below the surface.

The turbulence blinded him. Suddenly, Dar didn't know if he was up or down. He was flung around and around until he felt dizzy. But not once did Dar release his hold on Niall Campbell's ankle.

Finally, blessedly, his head broke the water's surface. He looked around. A small cove, formed by a stand of boulders jutting from the shore partially into the river, lay just yards ahead. Using his free hand, Dar grabbed Niall by his belt. Then, with the other hand, he pulled over the Campbell until he could grasp him about his waist.

Kicking with all his might, Dar thrust Niall's limp form forward, shoving him ahead of him toward the cove. Just as they passed the boulders, he propelled Niall into the quieter waters.

Then the river caught him, swept him by. A broken tree limb jammed into some hidden rocks snagged Dar at the last moment.

Exhausted, his breath coming in sharp, shallow gasps, Dar held on to the lifesaving wood. Eventually, some of his strength returned. He kicked off, swimming the short distance back upstream toward the cove. Niall floated there.

Dar struggled over to him. Slipping his arm beneath the other man's shoulders, he half-lifted, half-carried him toward shallow waters, toward shore.

There, on a rock-strewn bank, Dar rolled Niall Campbell over and slapped him hard several times on the back. He collapsed then beside the Campbell who, with a grunt, began to cough and retch, expelling the water from his lungs.

In the distance, Dar thought he heard the pounding of hoofbeats and the sound of men's shouts drawing ever near. It didn't matter. His side hurt fiercely. Everything was beginning to go foggy . . . gray. Then Caitlin and Goraidh were there, pulling them both farther up onto the bank and away from the river.

It was the last thing Dar remembered.

✠

Gratefully, Caitlin accepted the blanket her cousin Iain brought over for Dar, and quickly laid it over him. They had already changed him from his own wet shirt and plaid into a spare shirt and plaid that Iain had brought along. Still, even in dry clothes and yet unconscious, Dar shivered uncontrollably.

"Niall's decided we'll make camp for the night here," the dark blond-haired man said as he squatted beside Caitlin. "We've got a few men out hunting us some supper, and others gathering wood. We'll soon have two fires going, and place one here to help warm him. He should be much improved soon enough."

"I hope so." Caitlin glanced at Dar, worried. "He's been

through so much in the past week. And now to take a dousing in such frigid water . . ."

"He's young and strong enough, lass. He should come through this as well."

Iain's gaze strayed to Goraidh, who sat on Dar's other side. Like Dar, the hermit had his hands bound behind him.

"Ye can keep watch over him, can't ye? Caitlin's brother is recovered enough that he's now wondering where his sister is."

"Aye." Goraidh nodded. "I'll watch Darach, and gladly." He looked to Caitlin. "Best ye pay yer brother a visit. This wouldn't be the time to anger him, not after all he's gone through himself in trying to get ye back."

Caitlin felt as if she were being pulled in two different directions at the same time. She didn't want to leave Dar just yet. Leastwise not until his shivering abated and he regained consciousness.

She knew his wound hadn't torn apart again, though how he had done what he had done in rescuing Niall from the river and not ripped it open once more was nothing short of miraculous. But what if he had suffered some internal injury in the river? If that had occurred, there wasn't much she could do for him.

Still, leaving his side right now felt as if to do so would be never to return. She simply must, though, Caitlin resolved, learn how better to place all her trust in God. Once again, and despite all of Dar's intentions to the contrary, the Lord had prevented them from parting. What further proof did she need that she and Dar were meant to be together?

Besides, Goraidh was right. Niall equally deserved her presence. And she did have a few choice words to share with him about his foolhardy foray into what had, in retrospect, been the worst section of the river to ford.

With a sigh, Caitlin rose. "I was but waiting for all of ye to cease yer fawning over Niall. Indeed, I've never seen so many men in such a dither."

Iain grinned. "Well, he is the Campbell, ye know."

"To ye, mayhap," she replied, smiling. "To me, he's just my big brother."

"Aye, and somehow I'm wagering ye'll have a few less-than-flattering thoughts for him, ye will." Her cousin gestured ahead of him. "Shall we be going then?"

Caitlin cast one more glance down at Dar, then nodded. "Aye, I suppose we'd better. Ye know how imperious Niall can get when he's kept waiting."

"Indeed?" Iain feigned mock surprise. "And I've never seen that in him. Surely ye're mistaken, lass."

She laughed then. She couldn't help it. They shared a special bond, she and Iain, and while growing up had frequently teased each other over their frustration with the strong-willed Niall. Not that Niall, in the end, hadn't usually been right. They both just wished, at least once in a while, *they* could be right instead.

Some of the clansmen were already stacking wood for a big fire close to Niall when she and Iain arrived. Save for a bruised cheek and a scrape on his chin, her brother looked surprisingly well for his recent, near fatal experience in the river. He, too, was dressed in dry clothes and had a blanket slung over his shoulders, which he had pulled tightly to him. He was also shivering and his lips were tinged with blue.

"Let's get that fire burning, will ye?" he muttered irritably as Caitlin came around to sit beside him, and Iain ambled off. "Then start preparing the other for the MacNaghtens. None of *ye* are stiff with cold, and should be able to move far more quickly than ye are."

"Well, ye must be feeling a lot better," she observed dryly when he finally turned to her. "I can always tell when a man's on the mend. He gets verra testy, he does."

"And aren't I allowed a bit of testiness," her brother asked, "after nearly drowning on yer behalf?"

"The intent was most appreciated—not the drowning, mind ye, but the rescue attempt. Whatever possessed ye, though, to leap into the river like that?" She glanced at him, a quizzical look on her face. "Ye're usually the first to slow the pace and assess the situation, rather than rushing in as impulsively as ye did."

Niall shrugged. "I was rapidly tiring of getting so close only to lose ye. And, leastwise to me, MacNaghten looked as if he wasn't sure he really wanted to return ye or not. I but thought to distract him from his decision."

"A clever move." Caitlin chuckled. "Of course, if he hadn't instead chosen to save ye, rather than rush off with me, yer fine plan may have come to naught."

He paused to nod his approval as one of the men lit tinder and stuffed it in between the stacked logs. "Aye, I'll admit I didn't think it through all that well. I'll tell ye true. I never would've imagined he'd come in after me. Not with the men bearing down on him from the other side of the river, to ford that verra spot where he pulled me over to the shore."

Caitlin bit her lip, searching her mind for the right words. "He's not like his brother, ye know. Naught like Athe at all. Dar has honor. He's a good man, Niall."

"Is he now?" As the logs began to take flame and fire leapt high into the red gold sky, her brother lifted his hands to warm them. "Mayhap he is. That's hard to conceive, though, when he abducted my sister, dragged her on a merry chase around Perthshire, and then villainously took her back after she was traded for his brother."

"Athe was the villain in that, not Dar. Ye didn't expect him to leap on his own brother while the fool had a dagger at my throat, did ye?"

"Nay, but I still cannot help but suspect the two of them had planned it to happen that way."

"Well, I can assure ye, Dar almost never left my side from the moment we arrived at Dundarave, and he never got close to Athe in Kilchurn, so there was little if any opportunity for him ever to plot aught with his brother."

"Almost never left yer side, did he?" Niall eyed her closely. "And that's yet another bone I have to pick with him."

She sighed and lifted her gaze heavenward in an entreaty for patience. "And what might that bone be?"

"Whether he treated ye honorably. Tell me true, lass. Did he?"

He treated me far more honorably than I at times wished to be treated, Caitlin thought. Too oft to count, she had secretly longed for his kisses, or to be held in his arms. But that wasn't what Niall was asking.

"Aye," she softly replied. "Dar always treated me honorably. Always."

Her brother took her hand. "Truly, lass?"

She met his worried gaze with a steady, honest one of her own. "Truly."

"Good." He released her hand and sat back. "Then I suppose I won't hang him just as soon as he wakens, like I'd originally intended to."

"Niall!"

"What?" He grinned. "And have ye so little confidence in me, that ye'd believe I've turned into a blood-crazed lunatic in the short time we've been parted? Nay"—he shook his head—"Darach MacNaghten has earned punishment. I just haven't decided what that punishment will be."

"So, ye'll take him back with us to Kilchurn, will ye?"

"Aye. He can stew a bit in our dungeon. Until I decide what to do with him."

"But he saved yer life, Niall."

"Nonetheless, thanks to him, his MacNab-murdering brother

is free once again. And, since I was responsible for holding him until he went to trial, and instead lost him, I'm now the laughingstock of the clans."

Caitlin made a small, disdainful sound. "I hardly think the other clans would dare laugh at ye."

"Well, then suffice it to say I failed in my duty, and have Darach MacNaghten to thank for it. Now I've two unpleasant tasks to complete—recapture Athe MacNaghten and punish his brother. And, these days, I far prefer spending my time in the company of my bonny wife and wee bairn than traipsing around the Highlands or meting out punishment."

He turned to her then and took her in his arms. "Leastwise, though, I've got my sweet sister back, safe and sound," he said, his voice taut with emotion. "And that's more blessing than I'd hoped for. The Lord has been good to both of us, He has!"

Aye, He has, Caitlin thought as she slipped her arms about her brother and hugged him in turn. *He has given me a worthy man to love. He has given me Dar. And, though the future is yet unclear and the road ahead may yet be fraught with difficulty, I must place all my trust in Him.*

Trust that everything will turn out well for both Dar and myself. And for his clan, because he loves them, as undeserving of him as they truly seem to be.

15

Not long thereafter, Dar finally awoke. The warmth of a nearby fire soon helped him feel almost recovered from the chill immersion in the river. The fact that he was now a captive, with his hands tied behind him, however, wasn't the most pleasant of discoveries.

By and large, the Campbell clansmen left him and Goraidh alone, coming by only from time to time to add a log or two to the fire. From across the camp, though, Dar could see Caitlin sitting with her brother, who looked decently recovered as well. Though Dar knew that had been the plan all along—to return her to her own kind—the realization that the deed had finally been accomplished nonetheless grated on him.

He no longer had any claim on Caitlin. Which was, in any case, ludicrous even to contemplate. In truth, he had never had any claim on her to begin with. At best, the time they had spent together had been a stolen time. It had never been real or possessed any lasting significance.

"Don't look so glum, lad," Goraidh said, gently intruding on Dar's dismal thoughts. "Ye haven't lost the lass. Far from it, I'd say."

"Aye," Dar muttered, not even bothering to look his way. "Ye can't lose what ye never had."

"That's what ye imagine, do ye? That Caitlin doesn't care a

whit for ye?" The hermit sighed and shook his head. "And ye wonder why the lass loses patience with ye. What a dunderhead ye are!"

"A dunderhead, am I?" Dar gave a harsh laugh. "Well, if I am, what does it matter? If the Campbell doesn't soon hang me, it won't be long before I'm moldering in Kilchurn's dungeon."

"And Caitlin, being the shallow lass that she is, will of course soon forget all about ye."

Dar shot his companion a searing glance. "She's not shallow. But for her own good, she *should* forget me, and I'll be glad when she does."

"Well, be that as it may, ye won't be getting rid of me quite so easily."

"And why not? Ye've committed no crime against the Campbell. Ask Caitlin to vouch for ye. Ye could likely be on yer way home to Clachan Hill on the morrow."

"And are ye also deaf as well as thick of skull?" Goraidh released a frustrated breath and shook his head. "I just told ye, in so many words, that I'm staying with ye. It's where I should've been long ago—at yer side—but only of late have I finally begun to see what the Lord always wished of me."

Confusion filled Dar. Goraidh should've been with him long ago? But why?

"Ye're making no sense," he began when he saw Caitlin rise.

Immediately distracted, he watched her walk over to where the men were beginning to carve the stag, which had been roasting for some time now, and hold out a plate. Drinking in the sight of her like one long starved, Dar memorized every feminine curve, the ebony sheen of her hair, the fair skin, full, pink lips, and beloved countenance. His heart ached seeing her, wanting, if just one time more, to hold her in his arms, to kiss her sweet mouth.

But that was never to be again. Never to be, and he must be a man and accept that.

Finally, her plate laden with several thick slices of venison, she paused to pick up two freshly baked bannocks, a water flask, and two cups. Then, making her way around the fire, she headed straight for them.

Dar's heart commenced a pounding in his chest. His mouth went dry.

"Hmm, so ye can't lose what ye never had, can ye?" Goraidh asked, his tone amused but chiding. "But likely she's just coming to ye out of a sense of Christian duty. She is a devout lass, after all."

"Enough, Goraidh!" Dar growled. "If ye don't have a care, she'll hear ye."

"As if she hasn't already discerned yer true feelings—*and* motives!"

Caitlin was drawing too close by then for Dar to reply to the hermit's mocking comment. Instead, he chose to look up as she approached, and manage a taut little smile.

"I thought ye two might be hungry," Caitlin said as she sat before them and placed the plate of food on her lap. "Unfortunately, I was unable to convince my brother to have ye untied so ye might eat."

She began to slice the meat into bite-sized pieces. "As a consequence, I'm afraid I'm going to have to feed ye both."

Rage filled Dar. Atop it all, he must also be publicly humiliated!

"I'm not so hungry that I'll be fed like some bairn." He jerked his head in Goraidh's direction. "Feed him, if he'll accept it. But don't trouble yerself over me."

Caitlin glanced up then, and angry tears gleamed in her eyes. "Do ye think I enjoy shaming ye like this? But it's the only option, and ye *will* eat, Darach MacNaghten! I haven't repeatedly nursed ye back to health now to have ye toss it all aside because of some misguided, masculine pride."

"Misguided? And what man would tolerate being fed by a . . . a woman?" He was so furious he could hardly manage a coherent thought, much less word.

"Well, ye're not much good to yer clan frail and half-starved, lad," Goraidh ventured softly. "And what do ye care what the Campbells think? Indeed, they're the fools for even offering to feed ye. They'll rue that moment of weakness, they will. Won't they?"

Dar glared over at the older man. "Aye, they will. Not that I needed yer sly needling to figure that out." He turned back to Caitlin. "Fine. I'll eat, if only not to have to endure further insults from the likes of ye."

Caitlin bit her lip, Dar sensed, to keep from smiling. He didn't mind. Since she had first met him, he had given her little enough to smile about. Let the lass enjoy her one, wee victory. And, as the savory scent of roast venison rose to mingle with that of the fresh-baked bannock, he had to admit he was famished.

After a time of taking bits of meat and bread from Caitlin's fingers, Dar decided there were some definite advantages to being fed by a bonny lass. Her fingers were soft, gentle, and the touch of them on his lips was most pleasing. Too pleasing, he began to realize, and finally turned away when she offered him yet another bit of venison.

"That's enough, lass," he said, surprised at how husky and strained his voice sounded. "Some water would be most appreciated to wash it all down, but I think I've had all I can handle of the food."

"As ye wish," she replied, her cheeks most becomingly flushed, her gaze unnaturally bright.

She's as moved as I am, Dar realized with a start as Caitlin held a cup of water to his lips. The realization filled him with a savage joy, and he yearned, how he yearned, for his hands to be free. More than anything he had ever wanted in his life, he wanted to take her in his arms, hold and kiss her.

Instead, Dar silently accepted the cup and drank deeply. In that moment, their glances met and melded. Something strong and deep arced between them. Bound as he was, Dar nonetheless felt an almost physical union, as if they touched without touching.

Beside them, Goraidh loudly cleared his throat. Dar wrenched his passion-glazed glance from Caitlin to meet that of the hermit.

"As pleasant a time as ye two have been having," Goraidh said, "it hasn't been quite as private an interlude as ye might have imagined." With a subtle but definite motion of his head, he indicated some spot across the camp.

Dar looked up. There, his tawny brown gaze smoldering with rage, sat Niall Campbell, glaring back at him.

✠

The next morn, Niall had the camp roused at dawn. After a quick breakfast of leftover bannocks and cheese, they packed up and set out on the journey back to Kilchurn. Caitlin rode with her brother, while Dar was put on the gelding. Both his and Goraidh's beasts were then led by Campbell clansmen. Niall wasn't about to risk an escape, and insisted on keeping both men's hands bound.

By early evening, the party reached Loch Awe and soon rode through Kilchurn's gates. Dar and Goraidh were immediately escorted to the dungeon, while Anne took charge of an exhausted Caitlin. Though a hasty meal was prepared for her, Caitlin ate only a little before beginning to doze off. She was soon hustled off to bed.

She awoke late the next morn. Sunlight streamed in past shutters apparently thrown open by one of the servants some time earlier. For a while, Caitlin lay in her big bed, reveling in the utter luxury of it. Never before had she realized how wonderful a bed could feel, the soft pillow beneath her cheek, the smooth feel of the sheets, the light weight of the warm down comforter. She resolved never to take even the simple pleasure of a good bed for granted again.

Her thoughts soon turned to Dar, to his whereabouts and comfort. She hoped Niall had been merciful and not sent him to the pit. Reserved for the most wicked of criminals, the pit was little more than a hole in the earth, with straw strewn on the floor for a bed. Though not significantly better, at least the cells had a slit of a window and a raised stone platform on which lay a straw-stuffed mattress.

Shoving to a seated position, Caitlin swung her legs over the side of the bed. As she did, a movement in the corner caught her attention. It was old Agnes, Anne's serving maid.

"And where's Fia?" Caitlin asked, inquiring about her own serving maid.

"She tripped down the stairs yesterday and twisted her ankle. The Lady Anne thought it best she rest herself for the next few days, with an ointment of elder leaves applied to her poor, swollen limb to soothe the sprain." Agnes smiled. "So, here am I to aid ye this morn."

"A bath would be nice," Caitlin said after a moment's consideration. "I haven't had a very thorough one since the day I was abducted."

"I thought ye might be wanting one when ye awoke, so I already have water heating for ye in the kitchen."

The old woman rose and walked to the door. She opened it and gave directions to someone waiting out in the hall.

A half hour later, Caitlin was luxuriating in a hot bath, her head being gently scrubbed by Agnes. The scent of lavender and other aromatic herbs wafted up from the steaming water. She must add hot baths, Caitlin mused, to her list of simple pleasures.

"Did he treat ye harshly, lass?"

"Who?" Caitlin glanced over her shoulder at the old servant.

"The young MacNaghten, of course."

"Och, nay." She shook her head. "He was kind and verra honorable."

"We all worried about ye, we did. And Janet was beside herself, insisting there was a strong likelihood that he'd ravish ye. But the Lady Anne assured us she didn't think the lad was that sort. Which was a good thing," Agnes babbled on, "as yer brother was beside himself with rage and worry."

So, even in the short time Anne had had to talk with Dar, Caitlin thought, she had been able to take his true measure. It might well be to Dar's advantage. If anyone could convince Niall to treat him mercifully, it would be Anne.

She scooted up in the tub. "Please, rinse my hair now, if ye will, Agnes. I need to be done with this bath and dressed. There's much I must do this day."

"As ye wish, m'lady," the old woman said, clearly mystified by Caitlin's sudden change of mood. "Not that there's aught ye need to concern yerself over. The Lady Anne gave orders that ye be allowed to rest and recuperate today, in whatever way ye wished."

As if I can rest until I know Dar and Goraidh are being well treated, Caitlin thought, closing her eyes while Agnes began pouring water over her soapy hair. *Then there's also the matter of what Niall intends to do to Dar.*

Nay, there'll be no rest for me this day, she resolved. *Though Dar has yet to be parted from me, there's much to be done. For surely the Lord didn't intend us to spend the rest of our lives separated by the iron bars of a dungeon.*

✠

"What do ye mean, I can't see him?" Caitlin demanded an hour later as she confronted her brother in the library. "Ye've no right to—"

"On the contrary," Niall cut her off, glancing up from the papers strewn on the large, oak table where he was sitting. "I've the right to do whatever I wish. And if I don't want ye seeing aught of that man ever again, then that's how it'll be."

"But why?" She came around and pulled up the chair nearest his and took a seat. "He's in the dungeon and not going anywhere. And I need to see to his wound, make certain it's healing well."

"Anne can take over the care of his wound." Niall looked back down at the scroll he was reading. "So, ye see, there's no further reason for ye to trouble yerself over him."

Caitlin knew when she was being dismissed, but she wasn't having any of it. "He's my friend, Niall. That's reason enough."

"Yer friend?" Ever so slowly, her brother lifted his gaze to hers, a gaze that was hard and disbelieving. "The man abducts ye against yer will. Then, once at the verra least, ye were in danger of yer life when Athe MacNaghten had that knife to yer throat. Not to mention I was forced to ride for days in order to get ye back. And a dangerous lunatic is once more free, thanks to yer *friend*." His eyes narrowing, Niall cocked his head. "Now, tell me exactly how this man has managed to become yer friend?"

How indeed? Caitlin wondered. She wet her lips.

"He was kind to me, as kind as he could be, considering the circumstances. And we talked, came to know each other." She could see she wasn't making much headway with her brother but forced herself to continue. "He did it for his clan, Niall. They're sore beset right now, and Dar imagined the return of their chief might help them. But even he finally came to realize that Athe's return was worse than no help at all."

"A true consolation to me," Niall muttered. "I let Athe Mac-Naghten go, and the man who forced me to do so now regrets what he did. It surely makes up for all the havoc the MacNaghten chief will now wreak. And mark my words, he will wreak havoc."

"If ye let Dar go, he could return to his clan and try to wrest the chieftainship from his brother."

"Let him go?" Niall gave an incredulous laugh. "Are ye daft, lass? The odds are just as strong the two would join forces, and that'd be double the strife and tribulation."

"Dar would never join with his brother!" Caitlin said hotly. "He's naught like Athe. Naught at all!"

Niall slammed his fist down on the table. She jumped.

"Enough, Caitlin!" he roared. "It disturbs me greatly how enamored ye've become with this man. Ye've always followed yer heart more than yer head. This incident, however, makes me begin seriously to doubt yer judgment. Despite the fact he saved my life, he's our enemy, lass. Our enemy!"

"No enemy would save yer life, Niall."

"Well, I don't trust him. And he's as much a murderer as his brother, or have ye forgotten that? His own clan cast him out. His own clan!"

Tears of frustration filled her eyes. How was she to explain, convince Niall that none of those tales about Dar were true? He didn't even seem to think she possessed common sense anymore, and how could she defend against that? It *was* daft that a captive would become friends with her captor. And if Niall ever guessed the true extent of her feelings for Dar . . .

"I know it all seems illogical to ye," she began hoarsely, struggling to contain her tears. "But I know Dar. He's not the bane of his clan; he's its only hope. Its savior. But he needs to be given a chance. He needs friends, people who believe in him."

"Rather, he needs a good, long time to stew in the dungeon," her brother growled, "and I'm going to be the one to give it to him."

"Niall, nay!" All the pent-up emotions of the past days broke through just then, and the tears coursed down Caitlin's face. "Don't do this. I beg of ye. Don't do this!"

"Leave it be, Sister." His voice was dark with warning. "Push much harder, and I'll send him off to Edinburgh and the Tollbooth. And the chances of him living verra long there aren't good. So, take yer choice. Stay away from him and let me punish him in my own way and time. Or see him soon on his way to Edinburgh."

She couldn't bear to spend another moment in the same room with her brother. "Ye're a cruel, heartless, uncaring man, Niall Campbell!" Caitlin cried as she began to back toward the door. "And ye're wrong. Wrong about me, wrong about Dar."

"And ye, sweet little sister," he said, "need to decide where yer loyalties lie. I am yer chief, above even being yer brother. If I must command ye to leave that man be, then I do so. Will or won't ye obey me?"

Her back collided with the door. For a horrified instant, Caitlin just stared at her brother. That he would ask such a thing of her, in such a way, was almost beyond bearing. Almost as unbearable as turning her back on Dar, of promising never to see him again.

To be cast out from one's clan, to be shunned by one's family . . . Caitlin at last understood at least some of the pain Dar must have felt when he was outlawed. How had he survived such a heartbreaking, excruciatingly painful event? She knew she couldn't. She hadn't his strength or courage.

And so Caitlin did what she had to. She nodded her acquiescence.

"Aye," she whispered with downcast eyes, "I'll obey ye." Then anger surged through her, and she looked up, her furious gaze slamming straight into her brother's. "But I'll never forgive ye for this. Mark my words, Niall Campbell. I'll never, ever forgive ye!"

✠

He should be thankful, Dar supposed, that he had a whole cell to walk about in, a wee window to peer out of, and a mattress of sorts to lie upon. It could have been far worse. He could be dead or, worse still, down in that foul hole in the ground.

His mouth quirked wryly. And so it had come to this, then, that he was forced to count his blessings in such poor terms. Count his meager blessings, and wait and wonder when even those might be taken from him.

He had yet to be here a whole day, and already the confines of his prison cell were beginning to eat at him, nibbling away at his confidence and peace of mind. The doubts, the frustrations, the questions . . . He could well understand why men frequently went mad in prison, even before their bodies failed them.

Already, he dearly missed Caitlin. How he yearned to hear her voice, even if it were raised in anger as she berated him for being a pigheaded lout. Indeed, he would even welcome Goraidh's endless prattling about God.

In the past days, Dar had discovered how much he had missed human companionship, and the company of those who cared about him, who he could call friend. He wasn't a solitary man by nature. He had only tried to convince himself he was because he'd had no other choice.

Dar sighed and shook his head. A fine time to be discovering he craved human companionship, when he would likely never have it again. And yet both Caitlin and Goraidh claimed that God was not only merciful, but loving!

In the guard's chamber outside the cell there came a creaking of the dungeon's main door as it swung open. Then Dar thought he heard the soft murmur of a woman's voice. For a wild instant, hope flared that it might be Caitlin.

Then he realized it wasn't her voice. Likely a servant bringing the guards the evening meal, he thought. Whatever her purpose, he didn't care.

A key jammed into the lock of his cell door. The door opened, and three guards, one holding a loaded crossbow, stood there. Dar rose.

"Aye?"

"Sit down, MacNaghten," Dougal, the head guard, said. "And, if ye've got a shred of sense left in ye, don't cause us any trouble."

Dar decided it was the better part of wisdom to comply, and he did.

With that, the head guard and one other walked across the cell. Each grabbed Dar by an arm and shoved him back until he was up against the wall. The shackles and chains, attached by rings to the wall, were then fastened about Dar's wrists.

"Is this really necessary?" he asked. "It's not like I'm going to go far. Leastwise, not with a crossbow quarrel pointed straight at my heart."

"It is if we're to let the Lady Anne near ye," Dougal said. "Her husband isn't all that inclined to trust that ye wouldn't otherwise attempt another abduction."

"Och, aye. And with a bit more practice," Dar drawled, "this time I might just make a success of it."

The head guard backhanded him. "Have a care what ye jest about, MacNaghten! We don't take kindly to yer sort running off with our women."

With a black look at the guard, Dar wiped the blood from his mouth.

"Enough, Dougal!" Anne Campbell hurried into the cell. "Ye've no call to abuse a prisoner, especially one who's chained to the wall."

The head guard backed away, rendering the Campbell's auburn-haired wife an apologetic half bow. "Aye, m'lady. Forgive me, but I just don't find any humor in his flippant manner. He needs a lesson in respect, he does."

"Well, mayhap he'll eventually learn it while at Kilchurn." Anne walked over to where Dar sat on the bed and placed her box of healing supplies beside him. "It won't be today, though, I'm sure."

She turned to the three men. "Ye can leave us now. I'm quite certain he can't harm me, as firmly chained as ye've made him."

"But, m'lady—"

With a smile, Anne held up a hand. "I'll be fine, Dougal. And, besides, ye're just a summons away, aren't ye?"

"Aye, m'lady."

The head guard bowed once more, then motioned for the other two men to leave the cell. He followed in their wake.

"Dougal?"

The guard turned. "Aye, m'lady?"

"Please shut the door behind ye, if ye will."

His mouth opened, and for a moment it looked as if he were about to protest such a request. Then he clamped it shut, nodded, and walked out, closing the door behind him.

Anne turned back to Dar. "I'm sorry that he struck ye. Ye really must have a care, though, with that clever tongue of yers. Naught's served jesting about another abduction, ye know."

"Aye, I suppose ye're right." Dar angled his head to stare up at her. "And may I at least ask why ye're here, Lady?"

She chuckled. "It seems that I end up tending to all of Caitlin's new acquaintances of late. First yer friend the bard, and now ye."

"Ah, my wound. She worries overmuch about it, she does."

"Well, mayhap once I have a look at it, I can allay her concerns." Anne made a move toward him, then hesitated. "With yer permission, of course."

Dar's reach with the shackles was just sufficient to tug his shirt free of his plaid. He pulled the linen fabric up and back to reveal a rather sorry-looking bandage wrapped around his middle.

"It was in a lot better condition—the bandage was—when Caitlin first put it on." He smiled ruefully. "I'm just not one to take care of it, or myself, of late."

"Ye saved my husband's life and saw Caitlin safely back to us," she said as she opened her box and extracted a small pair of scissors. "I'd say, in the doing, ye didn't have much opportunity to consider yerself overmuch."

He shrugged. "I did what I had to do. I'll tell ye true, though. I didn't save yer husband out of any concern for him. I did it for Caitlin. If I hadn't gone into the river, she would have."

"Niall mentioned he suspected that was yer true motive." As she talked, Anne clipped the bandage binding his middle free. "Nonetheless, I thank ye, from the bottom of my heart, for how well ye did what ye did and for whatever reason."

As the main bandage fell away, Dar looked down at his wound. For all he had put it through of late, it appeared surprisingly good. The edges were well-joined; there was no sign of festering and very little drainage on the bandage.

"I think I might live," he said, looking up at her with a grin.

"Aye, indeed ye just may," she replied with an answering smile. "Caitlin will be happy to hear that ye're on the mend."

Dar's grin faded. "How is she?"

Anne looked up. "She's faring well. She's verra angry with Niall right now, though."

A frown puckered Dar's brow. "Why is that?"

She turned to her box, pulled out fresh bandages, a bowl, a clean rag, and a flask of water. "He forbade her from having further contact with ye. Seems he's a bit concerned over the extent of yer friendship."

For a long moment, Dar didn't reply. Indeed, how was he supposed to respond to such a statement? Lie and say they weren't friends, or tell the truth?

Och, aye, he thought. *And wouldn't the truth go over well with Caitlin's brother?*

After the look Niall had sent him across the fire the night before last, Dar was afraid the other man had surmised far more than

Dar would've ever wished him to. It was getting to the point he wasn't hiding his true feelings for Caitlin very well anymore.

"We were together for a time, a verra intense time," Dar said at last. "But that's over now. Yer husband needn't worry about me."

"And what of Caitlin?" Anne asked as she began gently to cleanse his wound. "What do I tell her?"

He needed to tread carefully with this woman. She was a clever one, and Dar's instincts warned she was after something. But what?

"I don't understand what ye're wanting from me, Lady. Did Caitlin truly ask ye to speak to me?"

"Nay." Rag in hand, Anne looked up. "Have ye already forgotten? She's not permitted to have aught to do with ye anymore."

"Then why do ye wish to know what ye should tell her?"

Niall Campbell's wife smiled. Dar had a sudden suspicion he was about to hear an answer to a question he might very well regret asking.

"It's quite simple, really," the auburn-haired woman said. "She's in love with ye, lad. And, as her sister-in-law, I'd verra much like to know what yer intentions are regarding her."

16

She spoke as if he were a man asking leave to pay court to Caitlin. But such a possibility was beyond ridiculous. It was a farce.

Pain seized him, twisting his heart in a cruel grip. And after the pain came anger. Anger that, atop everything else that had happened, he must now endure this humiliation as well.

"I know I've done ye and yer clan a grave injustice," Dar ground out through clenched teeth, "and that we cannot ever be aught but enemies, but I'd never have thought ye the kind to mock a man and his honest affection. Be that as it may, I'll set yer mind at ease so ye can finish what ye came for and leave me in peace."

He met her gentle gaze with a brittle one of his own. "I've no intentions toward Caitlin. I may be a fool, but I'm not so big a fool as to imagine there's any chance for us. Besides, as I've told her time and again, I've naught to offer her or any lass."

Dar laughed sardonically. "Indeed, I learned my lesson the first time, when I dared to love a woman who could never be mine. And she died for my arrogance."

Anne stared at him, silent for a long moment. "But ye do love her, do ye?" she finally asked.

He couldn't believe she would persist in this. Confusion filled him. Her seemingly compassionate mien belied her callous persistence on such a distressing subject.

"Unworthy as I may be, what I feel for Caitlin is honorable and true, and not aught to be ridiculed by the likes of ye and yer kind," Dar said softly, glancing down. "So, leave me, if ye will. Please."

"Nay. I'll not do that."

He looked up, surprised. There was no anger or malice in her gaze.

"And what more is there to say? I already told ye I won't speak further of this."

"Well, for one thing," Anne said as she laid aside the rag and turned to pull a small jar from her box, "I'm not finished tending to yer wound. There's yet some marigold ointment to apply, then a new bandaging needed. And, for another, there's indeed far more yet to say."

He held out no hope Caitlin would ever be his, but this silver-eyed woman was most persistent in whatever she intended. Dar couldn't help but be intrigued. If nothing else, as long as he kept his emotions in tight check from here on out, she would at least be entertaining. And it wasn't as if he had anywhere else to go, or anything else to do, especially chained as he now was to the wall.

"Then have at it," he said, gesturing to his side. "And say what ye will. Ye've made certain that ye have a most captive audience."

Anne grinned then. "Aye, I have, haven't I? I must consider such a technique to use on Niall, the next time he gets into one of his mule-headed rants and won't pause long enough to listen to me."

She bent then to begin applying a thin coating of ointment to his wound. Her touch was light, almost imperceptible. Dar found himself wondering how an apparently kind and intelligent woman could have found it in her heart to love a man such as Niall Campbell.

"How came a MacGregor lass to wed a Campbell?" he asked. "From what I've always heard, it's not like the two clans have ever been the closest of friends."

"Och, and that's a wee understatement," she replied with a laugh. "Truth was, I was given to Niall in a handfasting, in hopes of bringing peace between the Campbells and MacGregors. It was my father's idea. He knew we couldn't long withstand Campbell might."

"And did ye wish it so, the trial marriage for a year?"

"Nay." Anne shook her head, leaned back, and stoppered the jar. "Far from it. And, with my reputation as a witch, not to mention being a MacGregor, I wasn't well-received at Kilchurn. Niall had his own problems as well, what with soon having to fight for the chieftainship and someone wishing him dead. He wasn't any happier to have me here than I was to be here."

"Yet ye both seem happy enough now. With yer marriage, I mean."

She put the jar away and turned back to him with a folded bandage. "Aye, verra happy. He's a good man, and a fair one. Give him a chance. Ye'll see."

Dar's mouth quirked. "He has all the chance he desires. I'm not going anywhere anytime soon."

"I suppose ye're not." Anne handed him the bandage. "If ye will, hold that over yer wound while I wind the strip of cloth around ye."

He did as requested and she was soon finished.

"All done." The auburn-haired woman paused to put the supplies back in her box. "Now that we've pretty much settled my past, I've a few questions for ye. If ye don't mind, of course."

Dar shrugged. "I can't say until I hear what ye wish to know. But ask away. The company of a fair lady is far more pleasant than staring at these four walls."

"My, how swiftly yer mood changes," she said with a chuckle. "And only a few minutes ago, ye were bidding me leave."

He smiled. "As long as we stay off the subject of Caitlin, I can't think of much that I won't discuss."

"That particular subject has been addressed and my questions well answered." Anne grinned. "So ye needn't worry I'll return to that—leastwise not today." She paused. "I'm curious, though, about the older man who came with ye. Goraidh's his name, I believe."

Dar nodded. "Aye. He's a hermit now, but once was a monk on the Isle of Iona. I know verra little else about him, save that he took me in when I was sorely wounded. Between Caitlin's fine healing skills and likely his prayers, I survived what would've otherwise surely been the end of me."

"And what is he to ye in all of this? Caitlin claims he wasn't involved in the abduction in any way."

"She speaks true, Lady. There's no reason for yer husband to continue to hold him. Goraidh's no threat to anyone."

"So Niall was convinced to believe. Still"—Anne angled her head to study him closely—"when the offer was made to the man to be set free, he refused. He informed Niall, and very passionately, that he, even more than ye, deserved this punishment. And that he wouldn't leave until ye were also able to do so."

Dar's brow furrowed in puzzlement. "But how is that possible? That he deserves this even more than me? It makes no sense!"

"Would ye like to see him, speak with him for a time?" she asked. "Mayhap ye could tease out the answers. One way or another, ye're the one all this seems to revolve about."

"Aye, so it seems," he replied, an uneasy presentiment beginning to coil within him.

As the silence between them lengthened, Dar realized Anne was still awaiting his response. He met her questioning gaze.

"If it's permissible, I'd verra much like to speak with him."

She rose and took up the box of healing supplies. "Niall's already given his permission. I'll have him brought to ye now."

He lifted his hands, and the chain clanked. "Is it necessary I be chained in Goraidh's presence? He's hardly in any danger of attack or abduction from me, ye know."

"I'll have the guards remove yer shackles. I wouldn't have had them on ye even for my visit, but Niall wouldn't let me see ye any other way."

"Considering my reputation and recent actions, if ye'd been my wife I would've done the same."

"Well," Anne said with a laugh, "and mayhap that's because ye men aren't always as good a judge of character as we women."

"Mayhap, Lady. Mayhap."

✝

Ten minutes later, the guards led Goraidh into Dar's cell. The hermit looked no worse for his own incarceration, but a troubled expression, nonetheless, gleamed in his eyes. Dar waited until the cell door was shut and locked behind them, then rose and walked over to the other man.

"Come, sit with me on my bed," he said, turning to gesture back the way he had come. "There are things we need to speak of. And the farther from prying ears, the better, I say."

"Aye." The hermit nodded solemnly. "There are indeed things, long unspoken, that must at last be shared."

Dar walked back to his bed and sat. For a moment, Goraidh seemed to hesitate then, with a squaring of his shoulders, followed.

Once he was seated, Dar lost no time in striking to the heart of the matter. "The night at the campfire. Ye said a strange thing. When I suggested ye return to Clachan Hill, ye insisted that ye were staying with me. That it's where ye should've been long ago. And then the Lady Anne just told me ye were offered yer freedom and refused it. That ye deserved to be punished even more than I."

Dar impaled him with a steely glance. "What did ye mean? Ye owe me naught. Indeed, until that morn we arrived at yer cottage, I'd never even met ye."

Goraidh couldn't quite seem to meet his gaze, and instead lifted it heavenward. Dar had the distinct impression the man was offering up a quick prayer, but for what, he didn't know.

"What I'm about to tell ye, I beg ye listen to its end," the older man finally replied. "Hear the entire tale, whether ye like what I tell ye or not. That's all I ask. Can ye do that for me?"

"Aye," Dar said carefully. "I suppose that's not too onerous a task."

The hermit smiled sadly. "Just remember that, if ye will." He paused, inhaled a deep breath, then began. "I'm related to ye by more than simple clan kinship. I'm the eldest of three sons, and my two younger brothers were Feandan and Brochain. I am uncle to yer cousin Kenneth."

"And so my uncle, as well." Dar stared at him in surprise. "But why was I never told I had another uncle? Choosing a life at Iona is hardly a reason never to speak of ye again."

"My wife died in childbearing." Goraidh looked away once more. "I mourned her for a long while, a verra long while. But when the time came to consider that, as clan tanist with an ailing sire, I must father children of my own, there was only one lass for me. Unfortunately, she was the wife of my brother, Brochain."

A sinking feeling forming in his gut, Dar stared at him. "Ye . . . ye lusted after yer own brother's wife?"

"I had almost wed her the first time, but my father decided her dowry was too meager and she was better suited for the second son. So I instead accepted his choice of a bride. And we were happy, we were. God blessed our union." He sighed. "But once she died, my heart turned once more to wee Muira. And it didn't help matters that she was verra unhappily wed to Brochain."

"Pray, continue," Dar prodded, his mouth going dry with anticipation of what was to come.

"Suffice it to say, I got her with child. And ye were that child." Goraidh looked back to Dar. "For a time, Muira and I considered letting Brochain imagine ye were his, but I couldn't add further lies and deceit atop the cuckolding of my own brother. When I told Brochain, he was verra angry, as well he should have been. Even more than the betrayal of his wife and his brother, though, he was concerned with his reputation—and he likely also soon saw the affront against him as a chance to gain the chieftainship he'd always coveted. So Brochain offered to claim and raise ye as his own, in return for my word to forfeit the tanistry and leave MacNaghten lands forever."

"And if ye didn't?"

"He'd not only tell our father—which would've likely been the death of the old man—but also demand I be punished. And he refused to divorce Muira. So, one way or another, he would've still had ye."

"That's when ye left for Iona, isn't it? To seek forgiveness for yer sins by living a life of prayer and penance?"

"Aye." The hermit nodded. "And I stayed there for twenty years, until the abbey was dissolved. By then, my father and Muira were long dead. Still, though I was heartsick for home, I thought at first to keep to my vow. So, I journeyed to Ireland, where I remained at another monastery for six more years. In time, though, I could no longer ignore the truth of the matter. The Lord wanted me to return home, to face the consequences of my actions. So I came back here, to Clachan Hill, two years ago this summer."

As Dar listened to the tale unfold, he found his anger beginning to rise. His true father had returned home six or seven months after Dar was banished. Yet, as difficult as it might have been for Goraidh to find him, it wouldn't have been impossible.

Things began to fall into place. Feandan's strange expression when they had arrived at Dundarave. His swift endorsement of Goraidh when Athe had challenged the hermit's presence. Goraidh's myriad cryptic comments.

"So, in the two years since," Dar said, "ye never once troubled yerself to discover how yer own son fared!"

"Och, I troubled myself," the older man said with a bitter laugh. "From time to time, Feandan came to visit, and I plied him with questions about ye. But I'd also given my word. As paltry a thing as it was, after what I'd done, I felt I should at least abide by it.

"And I felt so guilty, such a sinner, that the rest of my life would never be enough time to repair what I had done anyway. Why, indeed, I asked myself, would ye ever want to know me, much less ever call me father?"

"Ye could've at least given me the chance to decide, when ye finally did meet me. Yet, even then, ye didn't."

"Aye, I could've. But, once ye began to recover, I didn't know how ye might take such news. And then the time never seemed right. Ye had the lass to think of, and then yer brother . . ."

He sighed. "Ye had enough burdens laid on yer shoulders. I didn't wish to add yet more. So I prayed to God to show me the proper time and place. And it seems finally to be now, here in Kilchurn."

"He hated me, ye know. Yer brother," Dar ground out. "I always wondered what was wrong with me, that I could never seem to please him. I tried so hard to please him, over and over and over, and it never mattered. I never won his love. And then, when I met Nara . . ."

Goraidh smiled sadly. "Things came full circle then, didn't they? The sins of the father were laid on the son and, in similar ways, we both became outlawed from our own clan."

"Aye," Dar said, his fury burning now like acrid fire in his belly. "But *ye* might have prevented my fate from mirroring yers, if ye'd had the courage to come back for me. I hardly knew my mither. She died of a fever when I was but five. Mayhap if she had lived . . ."

He shook his head, bitterness at what might have been filling him. "Well, it doesn't matter now, does it?"

"It does, if ye have it in yer heart to forgive a foolish old coward. A man who'd now gladly be a father to ye, if ye'd have him."

Dar saw the pain, the entreaty, the hope burning in Goraidh's eyes, but there was no forgiveness in him. He'd had that beaten out of him years ago. He hadn't any left to give.

"Ye had many times in which to redeem yerself," he said, his voice gone low and hard. "But the longer ye stayed away . . ."

For a moment, he couldn't go on. He looked down, his throat constricting with emotion.

Finally, Dar met the glittering gaze of the other man with an equally tear-filled one of his own. "Leave me. I cannot forgive ye. Not now. Not ever."

Goraidh opened his mouth to protest. Dar grabbed him by the front of his tunic, jerked him to his feet, and shoved him toward the door.

"Guards!" he shouted, his voice so hoarse he hardly recognized it. "Take this man away. We're finished with our visit. Finished!"

✠

An hour later, Caitlin found Anne in the healer storeroom. The auburn-haired woman was busy making some additional decoctions from recently harvested herbs and flowers and, at first, didn't notice Caitlin's presence. A loud clearing of a throat, however, finally gained her attention.

"Och, just in time to assist me," Anne said, glancing up. "Come here, if ye would, and hold the strainer steady over the jar while I pour in this boiling water."

Caitlin had more pressing matters at hand than preparing healing potions, but she obediently did as requested. Just as soon as Anne finished and put aside the hot pot, though, Caitlin launched into her questions.

"The wound. How did Dar's wound appear? Is he finally on the mend?"

Her sister-in-law shot her a slanting glance. "Aye. It's healing verra well. No festering, no reopening of the cut, and only the most minimal of tenderness now and mainly just with movement."

With that, Anne went back to her work, measuring out additional amounts of ground herbs into several other small jars. Caitlin waited, her impatience growing, hoping for further news about Dar without having actually to ask it, but her efforts were to no avail. It was evident that if she wanted information, she was going to have to come right out and demand it.

"So, aside from his wound—which I'm verra glad to hear is finally healing—how is he doing?" she asked at last. "Does he appear to be handling his incarceration well? Did he say aught of . . . of what he hoped would become of him?"

Caitlin stopped, realizing how silly and pointless this was all sounding. How well would any Highlander, born and bred to the unfettered freedom of mountain and glen, tolerate being confined to a dark, dank hole in the ground?

"Och," she cried in frustration, "just tell me what he said and how he looked! I'm beside myself with worry over him and . . . and I miss him so!"

Anne stopped her work, reached over, and took Caitlin's hand. "He misses ye too, lass. I could tell, though getting him to admit aught of his feelings for ye was harder than pulling a thorn from an injured wildcat. He guards his heart verra closely, especially things most close to his heart."

Tears stung Caitlin's eyes. "H-he misses me? He said that?"

"Nay." Anne smiled and shook her head. "Not in so many words, but a woman can tell." She paused, her smile widening to a grin. "He's also a verra charming man. Once he lets his guard down a bit. I can see why ye're so attracted to him."

"I never said I was attracted to him."

Even as Caitlin uttered the denial, a telltale flush warmed her cheeks. And it only worsened at the knowing look her friend shot her.

Och, what was the use? She had always been a poor liar. And she had never been able to fool Anne for a minute.

"Aye, I'm attracted to him," she murmured, looking down. "More than attracted to him, if the truth were told." She glanced up. "Ye must think me a fool, once again to give my heart to a man so unsuited to me."

"And is that what ye think? That he's unsuited to ye?"

Sadness swelled within Caitlin. "Not in the ways that truly matter. Nay, never in that. But he's a broken man from a proscribed clan. Can ye think of aught more unsuitable for any lass, much less the sister of a chief of Clan Campbell?"

"When first I came to Kilchurn, there were many who thought me unsuited to the clan tanist—a lowly MacGregor and suspected witch, no less. And ye, if I recall, were one of those."

Caitlin inhaled a deep breath. "Aye, I was one of those, leastwise for a time. But what fools we all were."

"Mayhap, in time, the same might be said for Darach. Perceptions can change, if given time and the right opportunities."

"He's a good man, Anne." Caitlin gazed deep into her sister-in-law's eyes. "He's honest and true, and pretends to naught that he really isn't. Indeed, he doesn't even realize how wonderful he is, or that he has friends who not only care about him but respect him."

Something flickered in Anne's silver gaze. "Speaking of friends, that older man Goraidh. Did ye know Niall offered him his freedom, and he refused it unless Darach was freed as well?"

Caitlin frowned. "Nay, I didn't. But that proves my point. Dar's friends, however few they may yet be, are verra loyal to him."

"Well, I gave them leave to visit with each other for a time. Hopefully, that'll improve both their moods a bit, not to mention answer some of Darach's questions about his friend." Anne picked up the pot. "I need to fetch more hot water from the kitchen. Do ye want to come along?"

"And what questions might they be?" Caitlin fell into step behind the auburn-haired woman as she walked from the room.

"The fact that Goraidh not only refused to leave until Darach was freed, but also claimed he was even more deserving of punishment than Darach."

"What a strange thing for a holy man to say."

"Aye, I thought so as well."

Her thoughts racing, Caitlin followed Anne into the kitchen. Maudie was busy overseeing the final preparations for the evening meal. Servants bustled to and fro, filling bowls with steaming vegetables and platters with countless halves of roasted chickens before handing them to other servants to carry to the Great Hall. As Anne made her way to the large pot of water always kept hot on the hearth, another servant hurried in, a tray of covered dishes in her hands.

"What a waste of time that wee trip was," the girl exclaimed to Maudie as she set the tray on the big worktable beside her. "Neither of them wanted to eat aught of yer fine meal. Ye'd think they were both royalty, rather than the verminous villains they really are!"

The head cook looked up from the loaf of fresh-baked bread she was slicing. "Well, I'm sure being locked in a dungeon would eventually take the edge off anyone's appetite."

The servant laughed. "Och, that's not the half of it! Dougal told me they'd all but ended up in a fight earlier, with the younger one demanding that the older one be escorted from his cell. Just like he was some noble, I tell ye, putting on airs and ordering the guards about."

Caitlin's and Anne's gazes locked. Concern gleamed in Anne's eyes. More than concern, however, burned beneath Caitlin's breast.

Dar and Goraidh had almost gotten into a fight? That didn't sound like either of them. Something was terribly wrong.

She turned and headed for the door, ignoring Anne's call to wait. Though Niall may have banned her from contact with Dar, he hadn't said she couldn't visit the hermit. One way or another, before this day was done, Caitlin meant to find out what had happened to drive such a wedge of animosity between the two men.

17

Dougal eyed Caitlin with misgiving. "Begging yer pardon, m'lady, but I'm not certain yer brother would be wanting ye down here, much less visiting the prisoners."

"Niall doesn't want me visiting Darach MacNaghten," she replied, struggling to hide the exasperation that threatened to spill over into her voice. "He said naught about visiting the hermit."

"Aye, but—"

"And, since Niall has already offered to free the man," Caitlin hurried to press her point, "it's not as if he poses any danger to any of us."

"Aye, but—"

"Enough, Dougal." She gestured toward Goraidh's cell door. "If Niall tries to lay blame upon ye, I'll vouch for yer numerous and most hearty protests. Not that he will."

The head guard expelled a long-suffering sigh. "Fine. Have it yer way. But, just to be safe, I'm going to shackle him, just like I always do with the younger one. I'll take no chances on either of them laying hands on ye."

"He's a holy man, Dougal! Ye needn't—"

The guard held up a silencing hand. "Those are my terms.

If ye don't like them, then ye'll just have to take it up with yer brother."

It was Caitlin's turn to sigh. "Suit yerself. Just go gently with him, if ye will."

Dougal picked up the large ring of keys and headed for Goraidh's cell door. "Och, and I'm always the soul of gentleness, m'lady. Ask any of the prisoners who spend time down here."

Five minutes later, Caitlin entered the cell to find the hermit chained to the wall beside his bed. She waited until the head guard left the room, then firmly closed the door in his face.

Though Dougal may have construed the act as one of rudeness, Caitlin knew of his tendency to eavesdrop and then spread the gossip throughout Kilchurn. And what she had to say to Goraidh and he, most likely, to her, surely involved Dar. None of which was anyone else's business.

The older man sat in the far corner of his bed, or leastwise as far as the length of chain would allow him. It was enough, however, to hide his face in shadow.

"So, what have ye heard?" His somber voice rose from the darkness. "I assume the tale of what happened between Darach and I has already spread throughout Kilchurn?"

Caitlin walked over to stand before him. Even in the dimness of the corner, Goraidh's blue eyes glinted unnaturally bright. Whatever had transpired earlier, she realized, had been painful.

"I can't say how far the news has spread, but I overheard the maid who brought back both yer uneaten suppers complaining about it. And that ye and Dar had some sort of falling-out."

"Falling-out?" Goraidh gave an unsteady laugh. "Well, I suppose that's one way of naming it. He hates me now, lass, and never wants aught to do with m-me." His voice broke. "Och, dear Lord, dear Lord! When it comes to Darach, what more can I possibly do wrong?"

Dread rose to entwine about Caitlin's heart. Her hands fisted at her side. Och, what had he done?

"Might I sit beside ye?" she asked instead, indicating the bed. "Whatever has happened, I'd prefer it go no further than ye and I."

He nodded. "Suit yerself."

She climbed up on the bed to sit close, but facing him. "Now, tell me all," Caitlin demanded softly. "I cannot help either of ye if I don't know what happened."

"Nay, ye can't, to be sure," Goraidh mumbled, looking down at his shackled hands. "Though there's no hope of help for me, mayhap ye can still help Darach. Indeed, ye're likely the only one who can, if any can."

"Ye know I'll do whatever possible." She reached over and took one of his shackled hands. "Now, tell me. What happened?"

He squeezed her hand, then sighed. "I finally told him the truth. That Brochain was never his true father. That, instead, I was . . ."

As Caitlin listened to Goraidh's agonized tale, her emotions swung from shock to anger to compassion for the older man. At the same time, her concern for Dar grew by the minute. Would he never find some peace and resolution in his life, some happiness?

"Ye must find a way to see him, speak with him, lass," the hermit finished at last, the tears coursing now down his cheeks. "I didn't want to leave him or Muira. I swear to ye that I didn't. But I s-saw no other w-way . . ."

He buried his face in his hands and began to sob.

There was always another way, Caitlin thought, her anger rising anew. But it was so like some men to run when things got unpleasant, rather than stay and fight. David Graham had done that, as well, when the time had come for him to make a commitment. Goraidh had done the same and left Muira, and eventually

Dar, to bear the consequences alone. Dar, alone, had tried to stay and fight for his Nara, until he was cast out of his clan.

But none of this was of any help to Goraidh. It was evident he had paid a terrible price for his desertion, however honorable he may have convinced himself it was at the time. Now, all that was left him—and Dar—was to find some way to repair the damage. If there *was* any hope of repairing such a chasm of pain, misguided intentions, and now long-dead opportunities.

After a time, Goraidh finally regained control of himself. "I've failed him, I have, at every turn," he managed to choke out. "Mayhap I should never have told him the truth, but I'd carried the secret for so long. And I needed to make amends, if I could. If he would let me. Yet, instead, all I did was hurt him even more deeply than if I'd never told him the truth at all."

"Aye, ye caused Dar great pain. Ye failed to be the father he always needed, a far better father than the one Dar had forced on him instead. And ye ran away when it would've been more difficult to stay." Caitlin dug a handkerchief from a pocket of her gown and handed it to Goraidh. "Nonetheless, at long last ye did the right thing. And, as distressing a revelation as it was to hear, Dar needed to hear it."

Goraidh blew his nose and wiped away his tears, then smiled wryly at her. "Ye aren't the sort to soften yer words, are ye, when hard things must be said?"

"Nay, I'm not, and it's oft been my undoing." She smiled back. "Mayhap I feel I can say this because, in these past weeks, I've learned about running away myself, and how easy it is to do so instead of seeing the Lord's hand in the life and people we're given. Sometimes, staying is so verra much harder than leaving. But sometimes, when we flee the pain or unpleasantness, in the doing we sacrifice the opportunity to grow closer to God. We forfeit the cross that is and has always been our verra own."

"As I fooled myself into imagining I was doing the better thing by leaving them," the hermit said with a rueful nod. "And, though I tried in the time I spent on Iona to be a good and holy monk, it was never what the Lord truly wished of me. It was but my own fear and pride that drew me away from where I was really meant to be. I chose the easier—and far less holy—path."

"Ye were young. Ye thought ye were doing the best for Dar when yer brother told ye he'd raise him as his own," Caitlin said, the certainty—and understanding for the youthful, inexperienced Goraidh—growing within her. It wasn't such a hard leap, after all. She had done the same so many times herself.

"Ye thought ye were saving Muira from the shame of others knowing of her infidelity. To walk away, when yer heart was surely begging ye to stay, must have been the hardest thing ye ever did. But ye did it out of love, and from a hope for a better life for the two people ye loved the most."

"Aye, I thought all those things," the hermit said glumly. "I meant well. But I was still wrong. I was still weak and foolish and, ultimately, a coward."

"But now ye're neither weak, nor a fool, nor a coward. And there's naught any of us can change about what has passed. There's only today, and the next, and the next to deal with. And there's always hope. Hope in God. Hope that He will bring a fire within us all, to cleanse away the pride and sin and fill us anew with wisdom. With forgiveness . . ."

"Aye . . . hope. It *is* the MacNaghten clan motto, after all." Goraidh sighed. "Tell me what to do, lass. Ye know Darach better than anyone. What can I do to make amends, to win his forgiveness, if the chance ever to win his love isn't already forever gone?"

I know him better than anyone?

At the irony of that pronouncement, Caitlin almost laughed out loud. If only Goraidh knew the truth. For the most part, Dar was a closed book, a fiercely guarded fortress. Indeed, even now, Caitlin wasn't certain where she really stood with him.

239

All she did know was that she loved him, and his pain was hers. If there were any way she could bring him solace and a willing ear to listen to his frustration and suffering, she would. But even that bit of succor might not be hers. Not if her brother continued in his adamant refusal to allow her to see Dar.

Aye, there was irony indeed, Caitlin thought, in the fact the man who *was* permitted to speak with Dar had only caused him further pain, and the one who might be able to assuage it, if only a little, wasn't allowed within a hundred feet of him. But that wasn't of much consolation to Goraidh, whose heart was broken over failing both his son and his God. It also solved nothing of Caitlin's own frustration over being kept from the man she loved.

She climbed from the bed to stand beside it. "There's naught ye can do just now," she said, her resolve growing. "For a time, at least, the responsibility is mine. All ye can do, for the both of us, is pray. Pray hard that the Lord clears the way, because"—her mouth twisted in a grim smile—"that's what it'll take to convince my brother to let me see Dar."

✠

For some reason, Caitlin wasn't surprised to find Niall and Anne awaiting her in the guardroom outside Goraidh's cell. She took one look at them, then headed for the dungeon's main door.

"We need to talk," she said over her shoulder as she hurried past them, "and it needs to be in private."

Her brother cast her a quizzical glance, then shrugged and fell into step behind her, Anne at his side. They followed Caitlin down the corridor until she found an empty servant's room, walked in, and turned to await them. Anne entered last, then discreetly closed the door.

There wasn't any point, Caitlin decided, in working her way around to the topic at hand, so she didn't. "I assume Anne has already informed ye of why I came down here," she said. At her brother's affirmative nod, she continued. "A short time ago, Goraidh informed Dar that he was Dar's true father, not Brochain MacNaghten."

Niall arched a dark brow. "Indeed? So, Athe's only Darach's half-brother, is he?"

"Aye." Caitlin's nod was curt. "The news was, quite understandably, verra upsetting to Dar. Hence, why he now wants naught to do with Goraidh."

"Aye, it's understandable enough." Niall paused, eyeing her carefully. "But what's all that to me, or ye, for that matter?"

"I was about to get to that."

"I'm sure ye were," he muttered sardonically.

Anne put a hand on her husband's arm. "Hear her out, Niall. This is verra important to Caitlin."

Caitlin shot her sister-in-law a grateful glance, then riveted her gaze back on her brother. "Dar's my friend. Above everything else and despite yer reservations to the contrary, he's my friend, Niall. And, right now, he's suffering great pain and confusion. I want—"

"Ye cannot see him. And that's my final word on it!"

At his gruff interruption, Caitlin ground her teeth in frustration. *Dear Lord*, she thought, *help me make him understand. Help me!*

"Then ye need to reconsider yer final word," she said, a sudden, peaceful conviction filling her. "Though ye'll always be my older brother, and I yer little sister, I'm not little anymore. I'm a grown woman and deserve to be treated that way."

"Ye've yet to prove to me—leastwise in yer unerringly poor choice of men—that ye've the maturity I expect in a grown woman."

"Niall!" Anne said in soft protest.

He held up a hand in warning to his wife. "Annie, it's past

time ye stop coming to her defense. A grown woman can defend herself," he said, turning back to Caitlin. "Can't she, lass?"

She felt her face grow hot. Her pride stung, Caitlin opened her mouth to name him the arrogant, pigheaded lout that he was, when something caught her up short. She had asked the Lord for aid. Berating her brother was hardly the way to allow Him to work through her.

"Aye, a grown woman can defend herself," she replied, forcing a calm surety into her voice. "And ye're right. In the past, I have made poor choices in men, David Graham being mayhap the prime example of them all. He was naught more than false flattery and empty intentions. He had a fine name and manner about him, but there wasn't a shred of honor in him. Indeed, he was everything I didn't need in a man."

"Then what do ye need, lass? Or do ye even know?"

"Och, I know." Caitlin smiled, the certitude of her knowledge filling her with a profound joy and satisfaction. "At long last, I know. I need a man of deep feelings, of courage, honesty, and, above all, honor."

She paused to draw in a fortifying breath. "In the most unexpected place and unlikely of ways, I've finally found such a man. Though everything about Dar might lead one to imagine the contrary, he's naught like the others. Coming to know him has opened my eyes to what truly matters in a man—or anyone, for that matter. Being with him has taught me more of God and His will for my life than all the fine sermons I've ever heard on Sunday. And loving him has finally made me a woman. A woman who knows now what she really wants and needs."

Niall looked at her as if she had suddenly grown two horns on her head and a large wart on her nose. Heart pounding, Caitlin stared back at him, refusing to quail before his daunting gaze and intimidating presence. She loved her brother with all her heart but, always before, she had held him in such high regard she sooner or later bowed to his will.

But not this time. This time, all that mattered was Dar. Dar, the man she loved, and who was surely hurting and needed her.

"Caitlin," he said at last, "I don't wish to control ye or yer life. I but love ye and want the best for ye. And, despite all yer fine words in his defense, I cannot help but think ye're making a verra big mistake—"

"Then let me make it, Brother!" she cried. "Ye can't protect me all my life, nor should ye. And if I do make a mistake, then so be it. It's my right as a woman, an adult, to do so. But I don't think I am making a mistake. No matter what ultimately happens between us, I'm not ever going to regret having been Dar's friend. He has given me so much. It's past time I give him something in return."

Niall looked to Anne. She smiled and nodded. He turned back to Caitlin.

"Just this once, then," he growled, "for I haven't yet decided what I'm going to do with him. Just this once, Caitlin, and then ye must vow not to badger me about him again."

Happiness flooded her. She ran to her brother and threw her arms about him, giving him an exuberant hug.

"Well, I won't give up on finally being able to visit Dar whenever I wish," she said, leaning back to gaze up at him. "I cannot vow ye that. But I will give ye time to make yer decision about him. For I know that, sooner or later, ye will see Dar for the good man he truly is!"

Gently, Niall brushed back a lock of hair that had fallen into her face. "I hope ye're right, lass. Enemy though he be, I honestly hope ye're right."

She grinned up at him. "I am, Niall. I know I am."

✝

Even as the light from the meager slit of a window began to dim into darkness, Dougal, muttering something about how all he did nowadays was prepare prisoners to pay court to visitors, stomped into Dar's cell and quickly jerked his arms back into the shackles and locked them. Dar gave a passing thought to informing the head guard he didn't much care to pay court to anymore visitors this day, then just as quickly discarded the idea. All he would likely get for his impertinence, after all, was the back side of the burly guard's hand.

Besides, there was no reason he had to talk to anyone if he didn't wish to. Which, in the foul mood he was currently in, he certainly didn't. So, with a sigh, Dar instead scooted back to lean against the rough wall, rested his iron-bound arms beside him, and closed his eyes.

Even before she spoke, he knew it was Caitlin. There was just something about the air around her as she moved toward him. As if it were charged, weighted with her presence. He felt as if his heart were being drawn from him toward her, to its rightful other half, its soul mate.

Yet, if there were any time that he didn't wish to see her, it was now. He hurt. He felt ripped asunder. He wasn't certain who he was or what he wanted anymore. Or even what he should want or deserved to expect.

"If ye've a shred of compassion for me," he muttered, not daring to open his eyes, "ye'll turn around and walk out the way ye came. I'm not . . . not in a good way right now. Ye won't find me verra entertaining company."

She drew up before him and softly chuckled. "And how is that much different from most other times we were together? Answer me that, Darach MacNaghten."

Ah, but it's so good to hear her sweet voice! Dar thought. Even now. Even when he was yet less than what he had always imagined himself to be.

Still, this brief moment with her, before he sent her on her way, was surely a foretaste of heaven. Until this very instant, he hadn't realized how deeply, how intensely, he had missed her.

He exhaled a weary breath and opened his eyes. Caitlin stood there, her slender form backlit by the single, sputtering torch shoved into its iron holder across the room. A yearning to touch her, hold her, seized his heart and twisted it cruelly.

"How is that different . . . ?" As Dar began to repeat her question, he found he could barely keep his thoughts coherent. "Och, I haven't the strength to bandy words with ye, lass! Ye've already won. Just leave me be, I beg of ye!"

"Nay. I won't leave ye, not after fighting so hard to come to ye!"

She took two quick steps and was on the bed beside him. In the next instant, she had snuggled up against him and was slipping her arms about his waist. With a contented sigh, Caitlin laid her head on his chest.

"Do ye know how oft, in the past days since we came to Kilchurn," she asked, "that I've dreamt, ached, for this moment? Och, but I've missed ye, Dar. Missed ye so verra, verra much!"

He couldn't help it. He had missed her, ached for her, as much, if not more. Though the length of the chain binding him limited much movement, it was enough he could bring one arm up to clasp about her waist.

"And didn't I tell ye to forget me?" he asked huskily. "No good will come of ye pining after what ye can never have."

"Aye, no good would come of such futile longings," she murmured back. "But they aren't futile, Dar. We must but trust in the Lord and allow Him to do what He wishes."

"What He wishes!" He couldn't help a harsh laugh. "And did ye know that my true father is a holy man, a man who claims to follow the will of God? A lot of good that did for him or me—an illegitimate son whom he gave over to his brutal, half-

245

mad brother. And now he desires absolution. Well, let him ask for all the absolution he can get from his God, for he'll never receive aught from me!"

"I know, I know," she crooned, pressing yet closer to him. "Ye must just trust in the Lord a while longer, Dar, and all will be made clear. All will come to fruition and ye'll finally have the happiness ye've so long sought and always, always deserved."

"And what happiness is that, lass?" Tears welled in his eyes, and Dar fiercely blinked them away. "I'll never be able to return to my clan, and instead will rot in this cell or be tried and executed. And now I cannot even claim my mither's husband, poor sire that he was, as my true father!"

"Well, the fact that he wasn't the son of *his* mither's husband, but rather that of the king of Scotland, doesn't seem to have been much of an obstacle in the Regent's rise to the most powerful position of the land," she offered dryly. "And it matters not to me, either. What yer mither and real father chose to do doesn't make ye less of the man ye've always wished to be. And it also doesn't lessen ye a whit in my eyes."

Dar couldn't help a tiny twitch of one corner of his mouth. "Well, then ye've never been as fine a judge of character as I first imagined ye to be."

"And ye're just as rude as ye've always been, to disparage my judgment so!" Caitlin pushed back to glare up at him.

"I warned ye, did I not, that I wasn't going to be verra good company. Or did ye happen to miss that wee caution?"

"Feeble excuses, one and all! Ye always were an ungrateful lout!"

Compunction filled him. She had come here to offer him comfort, because she cared, and he was indeed being an ungrateful lout.

"Aye, that I am," Dar said sadly. "Please forgive me. Ye, of all people, deserve better than that."

With what sounded like a satisfied sigh, Caitlin snuggled once more against him. "Aye, that I do."

She felt so good, so soft and warm and womanly, Dar thought. For a time, neither spoke, and he was quite content just to be with her. Likely, he would never have a time with her like this again.

He must soak up every sensation, every emotion, and every word that fell from her lips to keep him for whatever lifetime was left him. To stave away the long loneliness to come. To assuage the darkness and despair. To fortify him with the memory of what it had felt like, for even this brief time, again to be loved.

Once more, tears stung his eyes. This time, however, he couldn't staunch them. What did it matter? He had no pride to speak of left him. The sooner Caitlin saw him for the man he now was, the better for her.

Dar couldn't hide the tears for long. Likely some woman's instinct, he thought ruefully, as she leaned back and touched his face. Ever so tenderly, she wiped his tears away then, with a sigh, went back to holding him. He gripped her tightly.

"Do ye know that I love ye, lass?" he asked after a time, his voice raw, rasping. "For what that'll ever be worth."

"Aye," she breathed, "I believe I do. And, in turn, for what it'll ever be worth, I love ye too."

It had to be enough, Dar told himself, this wild, soaring joy he felt. Had to be enough to last a lifetime. Had to be enough . . . and it was.

They sat there for a long while, as darkness, save for that lone, sputtering torch, slowly enveloped them in a peaceful, perfect little world of their own.

18

Dar slept well that night, the first good night's sleep he'd had since coming to Kilchurn. He awoke with a smile on his lips, immediately thinking of Caitlin as soon as his mind turned from dreaming of her to full consciousness. Stubbornly, hungrily, he allowed himself to linger in that soft, warm, pleasant state for as long as he could. Which didn't end up being nearly long enough.

First, the current guard of the day stomped in with a bucket of water to aid Dar in the performance of his morning ablutions. Soon thereafter, a kitchen maid brought down a tray of bannocks, cheese, and a mug of cider. Dar found he was famished and finished the tasty offerings in record time.

A few hours later, Dougal's particularly loud and grating voice could be heard in the guardroom outside. Though Dar couldn't quite make out his words, he could tell the man was annoyed. That perception was only further reinforced when a key was slammed into his cell's lock and the door was shoved open.

In the man's hands were two pairs of shackles connected by a short span of chain. One set was obviously meant for hands, the other for ankles. The second guard followed closely behind.

Dar rose to his feet. "Am I going somewhere this morn?" he asked, eyeing the ironware in Dougal's hands.

"Aye, that ye are." The head guard motioned to the bed. "So sit yerself back down and, if ye've a shred of sense in that thick skull of yers, don't make any sudden moves."

"I've no intention of causing trouble," Dar said as he took his seat once more. "Would ye care to share with me, though, where I might be going?"

"To the gallows would be *my* choice, if anyone cared to ask me," the man snarled as he roughly took one of Dar's hands and clamped and locked a shackle about his wrist, then did the same with the other. "But ye've a wee reprieve, it seems. The Campbell wishes to speak with ye in the library."

Though Dar was well aware Caitlin's visit last eve had to be sanctioned by her brother, it was nonetheless surprising that Niall Campbell now wished to see and speak with him. Foreboding filled him. Surely no good would come from this meeting. Leastwise, no good for him and Caitlin.

There was nothing to be done for it, though, but face the inevitable, as unpleasant as that might be. It was, after all, part and parcel of his life of late. Last eve had never been anything more than a brief, stolen moment in a forbidden love.

The shackles about his ankles severely limited his movement to an awkward, humiliating shuffle. That pleased Dougal greatly, if the wide grin that split his face at Dar's first few steps were any indication. Refusing to give the man further satisfaction, Dar schooled his face into an expressionless mask.

"Lead on," he said calmly. "I'll try my best not to walk off and leave ye in my eagerness to meet with the Campbell."

Dougal gave a shout of laughter, then motioned for Dar to head out the door. "And I'll try my best not to 'accidentally' trip ye on the stairs. Not that I'm making any promises, mind ye."

Though there were more than a few times when the head guard, accompanied by two others, almost jerked Dar off his feet when it came time to turn down a certain corridor or climb up a particular flight of stairs, they made it to the library door without mishap. A muffled "enter" came in response to Dougal's ham-fisted knock on the thick oak door. A few minutes later, after a stumbling shuffle across a large library lined with books, Dar was pulled to a halt before an enormous, inlaid oak table.

Niall Campbell sat at its head, a quill pen in an inkwell, several rolled scrolls, and one open one laid before him. At sight of the shackles, he frowned.

"I gave no order for him to be brought to me in chains." He shoved back his chair and stood, riveting a hard gaze on the head guard. "Was this yer doing, Dougal?"

The man went a few shades paler than he already was. "He's a hardened criminal, m'lord. I didn't feel it wise to risk endangering anyone just to spare the knave's pride."

"Well, there's no danger now. Pray, remove his shackles. Then leave us."

"But m'lord," the other man protested, "is it wise to—"

"Are ye implying I'm incapable of protecting myself?" Niall snapped. "Or do I just appear to ye to have gone soft since I became chief?"

"Och, nay, m'lord." Dougal immediately slipped the key ring off his belt. "Ye're still the match—and more—of any man in Kilchurn, ye are. I just don't trust this one. He's sly and conniving, he is."

"Well, post two guards outside then," Niall said, amusement now glinting in his eyes, "to appease yer concerns. And if this man chooses to attack me, I'll be sure to scream loudly enough for them to hear and come to my aid."

"A-aye, m'lord," the guard said as he knelt and swiftly unlocked and removed Dar's ankle irons, then stood and did the same for those about his wrists.

"Ye can go now, Dougal," Niall said when the head guard continued to stand there. "And take the irons with ye, if ye please."

Dar had never seen the burly man move so quickly in crossing the room and exiting through a door. Once the wooden portal shut soundly behind him, Dar turned back to Niall Campbell.

They were of similar height. Dar found himself staring into tawny brown eyes that, in turn, steadily regarded him. For a long moment, both men took each other's measure. Then Niall motioned to the chair at his right.

"Sit, if ye will." He took his own seat. "We've much to discuss."

"I'd prefer to stand."

"Well, I'd prefer ye didn't." Once more, the Campbell's gaze hardened. "And I'm sure ye can understand my lack of favor with another man towering over me. So, sit, please."

Dar didn't see the point in sitting down to table as if the two of them were equals. At the very least, it was a farce of the grandest order. But he also supposed it was better than standing or—even worse—being forced to kneel before one of his direst enemies while in shackles. And Niall Campbell *was* making an effort of sorts to treat him respectfully.

"Suit yerself," he muttered and, pulling out the chair, took his seat.

They remained there for a time, Dar silent and sullen, Niall silent and considering, the only sound in the room the ticking of the clock hanging over the mantel. Finally, though, the Campbell released a long, slow breath.

"My sister appears to hold ye in verra high regard," he said, making a steeple of his fingers beneath his chin. "She claims ye're innocent of the murder charges laid against ye over two and a half years ago. And, since ye were never implicated in the MacNab slaughter . . ."

He paused, his gaze narrowing. "There's still the matter of yer abduction of my sister, and my unwilling coercion to free that bloodthirsty madman of a brother, though. Or, pardon me, yer half-brother now, isn't it?"

The reminder of who his true father was pierced clear through Dar's heart. He couldn't help a grimace.

"Aye, my half-brother. But it changes naught. One way or another, I'm still a MacNaghten. I'm still, leastwise in yer eyes, verminous scum."

"Yet my sister loves ye. And ye apparently, leastwise according to Caitlin, love her. Which puts me in the middle of a verra sticky situation."

Dar felt the blood warm his face. Curse Caitlin for telling her brother what had been, for him, a deeply personal admission. An admission not meant for the ears of anyone else, and especially not for the chief of Clan Campbell.

"There's no sticky situation," he growled, glaring over at the other man. "Indeed, I never intended for her to know. I just wasn't myself yestereve, and then she came to me . . ."

"Aye, mayhap I erred in allowing her to do so." Niall dropped his hands to the table and leaned forward. "Mayhap I err now, as well. But on the strength of her conviction about ye, and the fact ye never seemed to be involved in all the stupid, poorly considered acts that led yer clan to its present fortunes, I'm willing to give ye a chance to redeem yerself."

He smiled wryly. "Well, there's also the fact that my wife reminded me of a thing called forgiveness. And that I've a few failings of my own that I frequently have to ask the Lord to forgive, and then make reparations for. As ye must now make reparation for yer audacity in abducting Caitlin, and yer insult to me in the doing."

Listening to Niall Campbell, Dar felt as if, once again, he was in some waking dream. Last eve with Caitlin had possessed a fantastical quality of its own. Now, however, it seemed as though her brother were offering him not only forgiveness but also an opportunity to make amends. Offering him life instead of death.

"What are ye about, Campbell?" he demanded hoarsely. "Is this some trick, or but a cruel jest to break my spirit? For what I've done to ye and Caitlin, I deserve imprisonment, if not certainly execution. I'm a MacNaghten, after all. By decree of the Regent himself, ye're expected, nay, bound to put me to the sword if ever ye happen upon me!"

"True enough, if ye really *were* a MacNaghten," the other man said with a nod. "But as a broken man, ye're not truly part of clan MacNaghten anymore, are ye? That was the intent in outlawing ye, was it not?"

He supposed he should find some consolation in that, Dar thought. As a broken man, he *was* technically outside the Regent's proscribement. But, in his heart of hearts, he still considered himself a MacNaghten and always would.

Nonetheless, what was the harm in accepting Niall Campbell's loophole? Shameful as whatever reparation one's enemy might additionally demand, it would also give him the chance to live to fight another day. A chance the man sitting across from him might well rue.

"Aye, that was my father—my stepfather's—intent," he said. "I fail to see, though, how that changes aught. What price could I possibly pay—save that of my life—that would appease yer anger at what I've done?"

"Swear allegiance to me for the span of a year. Agree to serve me in whatever manner I ask of ye. And, in the doing, prove to me ye're truly the man my sister seems to think ye are."

Dar's eyes widened in disbelief. "Serve ye? How? In betraying my people?"

Niall chuckled softly. "Och, now there's a thought. Since ye know a secret way in and out of Dundarave, don't ye?"

"Athe may be mad, but he's no fool. With me in yer custody, do ye seriously imagine he'd risk holing up in Dundarave again?"

The Campbell shrugged. "Mayhap not. It's not an issue at

any rate. I'd never ask ye to betray yer own. I want yer loyalty given honestly. I want ye to prove to me ye're worthy of my sister."

Dar's mouth dropped. "And why does that matter? Ye'll never give Caitlin to me as wife. Indeed, if *I* were ye, I'd never give her to me as wife!"

His arms settling on the armrests, Niall leaned back in his chair. "And why is that? Would ye beat her or be unfaithful to her?"

"Would I beat—of course not! What kind of man do ye think I am?"

Dar caught himself up short. This discussion was beyond pointless. Niall Campbell was toying with him, and that was the simple truth of the matter.

"Ye wish for me to make reparation," he said through gritted teeth, "and that's fair enough. I've naught to lose—save mayhap my pride—in swearing fealty to ye or in working for ye for a year. Indeed, as long as ye give me shelter from foul weather, adequate food to fill my belly, and in time mayhap a new plaid to use as clothing and bedding, I'm better off in your employ than wandering the hills without clan or home to call my own. But don't pretend to dangle the hope of ever having Caitlin as wife before me. Ye know as well as I that's an impossibility."

"Aye, mayhap ye're right." Niall shrugged again and, glancing down, fingered the edge of the parchment document. "So many things can happen in the course of a year. Caitlin might lose interest in ye, or ye in her. Another far more suitable man might ask leave to court her . . .

"Ye're right," Niall said of a sudden, looking back up. "It's hardly worth discussing."

Dar gave a sharp nod. "Then we're in agreement, are we? I owe ye my allegiance for the span of a year, and then I'm free to go my own way?"

"That's what I said. In that year, though, ye're to remain here and go no further than the borders of Kilchurn's lands, unless otherwise given leave personally by me."

If there were ever to be a better time to negotiate all aspects of this pact, Dar knew it was now. "The hermit Goraidh."

Niall arched a brow. "Aye, what of him?"

"I want him gone from here. Set him free, send him on his way, but get him gone from here. I don't want ever to cross paths with him again."

"That sounds a mite severe. He may have erred greatly in his past treatment of ye, but he is yer father."

The word grated on Dar like the irksome creaking of a rusty hinge. "He's no father to me. One way or another, I wish to be well rid of all my fathers."

The Campbell appeared to consider Dar's request, then shook his head. "Nay. He stays or goes as he wishes. That cannot be part of the terms of our agreement. And if he does decide to stay, and there's a need for him to work with ye, then work with him ye must."

He slid the parchment that had been spread out before him across to Dar, then offered him a quill dipped in ink. "So, are ye of a mind to put yer mark on this agreement or not? It's the best ye'll get from me, or anyone for that matter. If the truth be told, it's likely far better than ye deserve."

Dar eyed the document. "So my word that I'll honor this pact isn't enough?"

"Nay, not in this particular case. If ye fail to keep to our agreement, I want irrefutable proof of all that I offered ye."

Irrefutable proof for whom? Caitlin? Proof that her brother had done all in his power to treat the man she loved fairly, honorably?

Was this part of some bargain Caitlin had worked out with her brother? It smacked of her touch, it did. Fury and frustration filled Dar, and he was of half a mind to toss Niall Campbell's offer back in his face. But that would be the work of a fool. And he wasn't a fool.

After all but giving up hope even of survival, his heretofore dismal existence had suddenly taken a turn for the better. Dar now had a chance at life, at freedom. No one, not even some sorry excuse for a father, was going to take that away.

Then there was the possible opportunity to see Caitlin from time to time. A year more of being near the woman he loved, even if from a distance. If the truth were told, that was the sweetest inducement of all . . .

It didn't matter that her brother expected Caitlin, in time, to lose interest in him. Dar couldn't blame him for seeking a gentler, kinder way of denying his sister what she imagined she wanted but would soon realize she didn't. Time, after all, was the healer of most wounds—especially wounds of the heart.

Time was also the mirror in which one, if one was permitted to gaze long enough, would finally see the reality of an ill-fated, hopeless love.

Dar took the quill, flipped the parchment around, and quickly read it. Then, satisfied the terms contained nothing they hadn't already discussed, he signed his name.

✛

For the first two weeks, per both Anne's and Caitlin's suggestions, Niall had Dar assigned to gradually more strenuous work. Initially, along with Goraidh, he assisted the castle clerk, spending most of his time copying documents. After just a few days in close quarters with the hermit, who, from his years on Iona, possessed breathtaking skills in calligraphy and book illumination, the increasingly harried clerk begged Niall to separate the two men before the tension between them drove all of them mad.

By the middle of the first week, Dar was sent to the kitchen. There, he filled cauldrons with countless buckets of water drawn from the well, carried countless other buckets of kitchen waste out to the kitchen midden, butchered chickens then scalded and plucked them, brought up baskets of potatoes and other root vegetables from the cellar, and washed what seemed like mountains of dishes. The humiliation of doing such work he kept tightly locked in a back corner of his mind. It was his punishment, and punishment, Dar repeatedly reminded himself, was supposed to be unpleasant.

He was nonetheless eager, by the end of his second week, to leave kitchen duty and move to light work in the stables. Feeding and grooming horses, then mucking stalls, was far more to his liking. And the company of other men, though they regarded him with cool disdain, was preferable to the constant giggles and whispering, not to mention the shy, hungry looks, of the kitchen maids.

There was also less opportunity to cross paths with Caitlin in the stables. That, he quickly realized, was both a blessing and a curse. She was the bright spot in his day. She also triggered such intense yearning that even one unexpected encounter left him aching hours later. Aching to speak with her, to touch her, to hold and kiss her.

It didn't help that Caitlin's expression, whenever their glances met, was equally full of longing. She rarely spoke or overtly acknowledged him, though. Dar soon surmised that her restrained conduct must have been part of the pact she had made with her brother, in order to win Dar the chance to repay his offenses.

A year . . .

At first that span of time had seemed of little consequence. The days passed swiftly enough, filled as they were with almost constant work until he finally fell, satisfyingly exhausted, into bed each night. However, when it came to his unrequited need to have, yet again, the same closeness he had shared with Caitlin on the journey to Dundarave, the minutes turned to hours, and the hours to months. Well, whenever he *allowed* himself to dwell on it.

It was likely but another aspect of his punishment, Dar thought wryly one afternoon, a month after he had returned to Kilchurn, as he used a wooden pitchfork to distribute clean straw into the freshly mucked-out stalls. Niall Campbell was a clever one. He surely knew many ways to break a proud man down.

Menial tasks, women's work, submission to a master one not only hated but feared for what he could do to a far weaker, beleaguered people were but a few of the methods. Unrequited longing for a woman Dar knew he could never have, but who was constantly dangled in his face, also ate away at his pride and sense of manhood. It made him feel frustrated, impotent, and a fool.

"Once ye're quite done contemplating the consistency of the straw," a familiar feminine voice rose just then from behind him, "and ye're finished with yer stable chores, Anne would like yer assistance in the herb garden. Preferably before sunset, if ye will."

Dar wheeled around. Caitlin stood in the doorway to the stall, a smile tugging at the corners of a mouth that she struggled to keep stern. He swallowed hard. For the first time in his life, Dar found himself without words.

Not that words were precisely the first thing on his mind. He drank in the sight of her like a man dying of thirst. Her ebony hair flowed like thick silk over her shoulders and down her back. Her brilliant eyes sparkled like gems. And the emerald green gown she wore, simple and flowing, save for the lace at the neckline and trimming the cuffs of her sleeves, enhanced her slender figure to perfection.

"I . . . I've missed ye," Dar finally managed to croak out. "Missed that shrewish little tongue of yers and that canny wit. But, most of all, I've missed ye at my side. Though I didn't realize it at the time, those days when ye were my captive were the sweetest days of my life."

She smiled sadly. "Aye, so they were for me. And I've missed ye, Darach MacNaghten. Missed ye more than I can say."

They fell into silence then, content just to gaze at each other. At long last, though, Dar cleared his throat.

"Er, so the Lady Anne sent ye to fetch me, did she? Was that intentional, or did she merely lack anyone else readily available to send?"

Caitlin laughed. "And what do ye think? Of course she intended to send me, especially after I begged her to do so. I just had to have a moment alone to talk with ye."

"Then I'm glad she did." Dar hesitated. "How have ye been, lass?"

"All but pining away with love for ye, but otherwise, I'm doing well. And ye? How are ye?"

"My wound's all but healed and my strength's returning with each passing day. The work's hard, but the food's good, and I've a warm place to sleep at night. I can't complain." He grinned. "Well, not much, anyway."

"Have ye had much opportunity to speak with Goraidh or made yer peace with him? He refuses to leave here until ye do."

At the unwelcome reminder of the hermit, bitter anger filled Dar. "He'll die and be buried here before I ever speak again with the likes of him!"

"Dar, ye need to find some way to forgive him. It'll eat ye alive if ye don't."

He went back to spreading the remainder of the straw around the stall. "Leave it be, lass. As far as I'm concerned, the man's already dead to me."

"Goraidh made a mistake. A terrible mistake. But he deserves a second chance."

Dar's laugh was disparaging. "A second chance? And pray, when was I ever given a second chance? When, Caitlin?"

"When?" Her eyes flashed with rising anger. "How about

right now? Isn't that exactly what my brother's giving ye right now? But that's different, isn't it? Ye deserve a second chance, and Goraidh doesn't!"

With that, she grabbed her skirts, turned, and stalked away.

Caught by surprise at her sudden departure, for a moment Dar just stared after her. Then, in a rush of renewed energy, his faculties returned.

He threw aside the pitchfork and hurried after her. He only made it halfway down the aisle, however, before another voice—this time a man's voice—called to him softly from a shadowed corner of the stables.

"Dar, hold up, will ye? We need to talk, and talk now!"

Dar slid to a halt and turned in the direction from which the voice had come. Out of the darkness beneath the loft and from behind stacked bales of hay, a man stepped out. It was his cousin, Kenneth.

19

Kenneth's eyes were burning pits in a pale, haggard face. His left cheekbone was severely bruised, and his lower lip was split and swollen. He looked exhausted, wrung out, and Dar instinctively knew something very bad had happened.

He hurried to his cousin, took him by the arm, and pulled him back into the sheltering overhang of the loft. "Why are ye here? Do ye know the danger ye risked in coming back to Kilchurn?"

"Indeed?" The bard's laugh was shaky and tinged with hysteria. "Well, ye don't look either in danger *or* a prisoner. And it seems things are going quite splendidly between ye and Caitlin."

If Dar had had his way, he would've preferred not to have to explain the provisions of his and Niall Campbell's agreement with his cousin. Though he was gradually coming to terms with the conditions of his servitude, there was still a part of him that felt guilty, as if, in the doing, he had betrayed his clan. It didn't matter that his clan had turned its back on him and no longer cared if he lived or died. He still had his pride.

"What's between me and Caitlin, or why I'm no longer confined to the dungeon," he ground out instead, "isn't the issue just now. Ye wouldn't be here unless ye had a reason. And I'm willing to wager that reason isn't to bring me happy news." Dar's grasp on Kenneth's arm tightened. "So, go ahead. Spit it out and be done with it."

Shoulders slumping, his cousin looked away. "Father's dead."

"Dead?"

Feandan, the only brother of all the three brothers who had truly been like a father to him? Pain stabbed through Dar, gouging clear to his heart. His breath caught in his throat. He fought to breathe, and it took a time before he could continue.

"How?" he demanded hoarsely at last, dreading the answer even before he heard the reply. "How did he die?"

"How else?" Kenneth riveted a furious gaze on him. "Athe killed him."

"N-nay. Och, nay!"

In a rush, all the strength drained from Dar. He stumbled to the nearest hay bale and sank down onto it, his limbs trembling, his gut churning. His hands clenched into fists.

"Why?" Dar shot his cousin an anguished glance. "Why would Athe do such a thing? Yer father was no threat to him. All he wanted—"

"All he wanted was a worthy chief to lead the clan," Kenneth savagely said. "All he wanted was for ye to come home and assume yer rightful position. But ye wouldn't, would ye? Ye hadn't the heart to fight for us. Indeed, once ye laid eyes on Caitlin, ye didn't care for aught anymore but having her. So ye turned yer back on us, deserted yer clan!"

As the other man threw accusation after accusation against him, Dar winced as if struck by repeated blows. Everything Kenneth said was truth. He hadn't wanted to be chief and all but fled from even the consideration of such a task. And, though Kenneth was wrong in claiming he lacked the heart to fight for his clan, it was also reality that he hadn't fought too hard against the Campbell's offer to remain at Kilchurn for a year. In one sense, it had come as a reprieve from the heavy responsibility of trying to save a people who seemed almost not to want to be saved.

In another sense, his pact with Caitlin's brother also gained him time to be with her yet a while longer. He just wasn't ready to leave her totally, or forever. Not, he realized of a sudden, even for the sake of his clan.

Shame swallowed him. Shame and despair. Dar leaned over and buried his face in his hands.

"I'm sorry, Kenneth," he said, groaning out the words. "Och, I didn't think . . . Och, I'm so verra, verra sorry!"

"Since ye left us, Athe's gotten increasingly worse. He suspects most of us of plotting against him. He has taken to gathering a small group of men around him as guards. He hardly sleeps, paces constantly, and spends hours at a time scheming with his guards, when he isn't sending out spies to places unknown.

"Two nights ago, it all came to a head. He announced he'd news that the Regent was coming to pay the Earl of Argyll a visit. He announced he planned to lay in ambush along the Regent's proposed route as he passed through Hell's Glen and, when he and his entourage rode by, kill him."

Dar looked up and turned to stare at his cousin. "Kill the Regent? But that'd surely be the final nail in our coffin."

"Aye," Kenneth said, nodding. "Exactly what Father told him. But Athe refused to be deterred. In Athe's increasingly disturbed mind, the Regent is solely to blame for laying the proscription on us, and must be punished. Father and Athe ended up in an argument which, before anyone could stop him, Athe suddenly ended by drawing his dagg and shooting Father.

"I went mad then and tried to get to Athe. For my efforts, I only managed to receive a sound beating from his men. When they were done with me, they all laughed as I crawled back to Father. And, as Father lay dying in my arms, yer brother calmly c-called his guards to him and w-walked away."

The bard's voice broke and he began to sob. Dar rose, walked to his cousin, and wrapped his arms about him. After a time, Kenneth appeared to regain control. He pushed Dar back.

"He didn't live verra long," his cousin said, angrily swiping aside his tears. "There was just enough time for one request. And that request was for me to bring ye back. Bring ye back, because ye're now our only hope."

Our only hope . . .

Once, Dar would've been overjoyed to be asked to return to the clan. To be considered not only a person of value but the clan's only hope.

But not now. Now, his only value lay in ridding them of an even greater scourge. If he could. And, if he couldn't, what would it ultimately matter? He had been dead to them all along as it was.

"If Athe's surrounded himself with guards," Dar said finally, "he'll be even harder to deal with than he was before. And if he'd shoot his own uncle, he'll likely be even quicker to shoot his hated half brother, who he fears has returned to take the chieftainship from him."

"Half brother?" Kenneth smiled sadly. "So ye finally know, do ye?"

"Aye. Goraidh at last found the courage to tell me the truth." A sudden thought striking him, Dar paused. "And how long have ye known the truth and not chosen to tell me?"

"Father told me shortly after ye left to take Caitlin back. Until then, at the request of his two older brothers, he kept the secret. But once he saw ye with Goraidh, he knew it was but a matter of time until yer true father told ye. He also didn't want the secret dying with him. The secret that ye, even more than Athe, have as much, if not more, right to be chief."

"Actually," Dar replied dryly, "if we're talking about greater right, Goraidh long ago relinquished his claim to the chieftainship. So, short of a successful challenge by any of his relatives, Athe is his father's—the last chief's—appointed successor."

"Well, then that leaves only ye left to challenge him. A former monk and a bard are hardly chieftain material. Especially now, when it'll take a true warrior to wrest the position from Athe."

Dar's laugh was mirthless. "Then we've a problem, Cousin. For this warrior still doesn't wish to be chief, much less risk his life in a lost cause."

"Aye, I suppose we are a lost cause, aren't we?" Kenneth demanded, his voice going taut with fury. "What's the point of attempting to rejoin a proscribed clan, when one may well now have opportunity to gain admittance into powerful Clan Campbell? And, in the doing, also mayhap win the hand of the bonny Caitlin?"

"I don't hesitate because of aught Niall Campbell has offered me—and he most certainly hasn't offered me Caitlin's hand, ye can be sure!"

Frustration filled Dar. How could he make his cousin understand, when he wasn't so certain *he* even understood the emotions roiling within him. All he did know was that he deeply resented being expected to sacrifice his life for a clan that had never—save for a very few—cared if he lived or died. And those few—with Feandan's death—had now dwindled to just Kenneth.

"There's naught left for me with Clan MacNaghten," Dar said, knowing it was truth even as shameful an admission as it was. "The clan has never sought to censure either Brochain or Athe, and it's a power they've always had. So, it matters not to me if Athe finishes the destruction his father began. I'm free of it at long last."

"Ye only imagine ye're free," the bard said, his eyes blazing with a strength and certitude Dar had never before seen in him. "All ye're doing, though, is fooling yerself. As I, when I finally realized what we were about, fooled myself that night at the MacNabs into thinking what we were doing was justified for the insult they had done us. And that, because I didn't lift a hand to harm any of them, I wasn't as guilty as the rest of the clan.

"But I was, Dar. I played the part I was given. In the doing, I lured them into the trap that was their destruction. I killed by omission, just as ye surely will."

Dar wanted to look away. It was almost more than he could bear to see the disappointment in his cousin's eyes.

They had been friends since childhood. Kenneth had been one of a very few children who would dare risk their chief's displeasure by befriending the despised son. And, after he was banished, Kenneth had been the one link still joining him to the clan, periodically meeting with him at a secret place, to bring him news, food, and whatever money Feandan could spare.

For all those acts, and more, Dar would always be grateful to him. Would always love him.

But, despite Kenneth's friendship and Feandan's attempts to protect him as best he could from his brother's cruel ways all those years of his growing up, they hadn't been enough. He had always wanted—needed—more. And here, as unexpected and illogical as it might seem, Dar had begun to find what he had been seeking his whole life—peace, love, and even a strange acceptance.

"Mayhap ye're right, Cousin," he said at last. "Mayhap I'm wrong and will regret my decision. But, for the first time in my life, I've the ability to choose. And I'm not so willing to toss that aside for some nebulous chance at besting Athe, for a position I'm not so certain I even want.

"There's no reason, though, for ye to return to that hornet's nest, either. Yer father's gone, and few if any brave enough left there are likely to support ye. Stay here. The Campbell's still in need of a bard. Once he hears ye play and sing, he'll quickly forget ye're a MacNaghten. Stay, Kenneth. It's a chance at a new, better life for the both of us."

For a fleeting moment, indecision flickered in the younger man's eyes. Then he shook his head.

"Nay. Someone has to return to challenge Athe. Someone has to make the others finally face the truth."

"But he'll kill ye, Cousin," Dar cried, dismay flooding him. "Ye're no match for him. One way or another, he'll kill ye!"

"Mayhap he will." Kenneth shrugged. "I'll take my chances. But at least I'll have tried."

Dar didn't know what to say. Indeed, everything had been said. They had reached an impasse.

"I'll wait down by those oak trees on Loch Awe for ye until midnight. In case ye've a change of heart," Kenneth said. "But no longer than midnight, Dar. Athe plans to ambush the Regent in two days' time. And it'll take over a day's travel to reach his new hideout."

"It won't matter, Kenneth." Dar managed a weak smile. "I'm not coming with ye. I'm done with them. Done."

"Aye, mayhap ye are." His cousin gripped his arm. "And, if ye are, then so be it. But I'll wait, nonetheless."

Dar placed his hand over Kenneth's. "Have a care, Cousin."

His throat closed, and he couldn't say more. Instead, Dar released his hold on the other man's hand and, disengaging from his clasp, stepped back.

Kenneth eyed him for an instant longer, then turned and walked from the stables.

✝

After the supper meal that evening, Dar was assigned to feed the horses, then see they were all secured in their stalls for the night. He lingered there for a time once his chores were done, knowing there was nothing left him but to retire to his subterranean room. And he wasn't ready to lie there in the silent darkness, alone with only his thoughts.

He knew the time would pass with interminable slowness as he counted down the hours until midnight came and went. Until it was too late for him to reach Kenneth before he rode out for places unknown. Until it was too late . . . too late to change his mind.

The fact he was all but condemning his cousin to certain death wasn't the issue. Dar didn't dare let it be that. Kenneth must make his choice, just as he must.

And who could really blame him for choosing life? After all this time, he deserved what he had fought so hard for all these years. Life and some small shred of happiness.

There was no shame in turning his back on his clan. No one would know, save Kenneth, if his cousin even lived much longer. Indeed, Dar thought with a bitter smile, once Kenneth was gone, no one in his clan would even miss him.

They had all been misled in any event—Kenneth, Feandan, and even Caitlin—into believing it was his destiny to be the MacNaghten chief. From birth, Athe had been groomed to assume that role. Yet look how far he had fallen short. How could they possibly expect a man who lacked even the most minimal guidance and encouragement to do what a man minutely trained couldn't do?

Yet, with an instinct strong and sure, Dar also knew it took more than training to be a good chief. Instead of pride, it required a humility to admit one's shortcomings and strive always to better oneself. It required a wisdom not gained with words but by hard experience, by suffering. And, instead of an inbred sense of entitlement, it required unrelenting perseverance and endurance. Perseverance to go the extra mile, to inspire rather than intimidate, and never to give up trying.

All traits Athe lacked. Yet traits Dar had learned in order to survive. Survive . . . and transcend what might have turned him into the same kind of man his brother had indeed become.

Niall Campbell, Dar realized, possessed all the traits that made for a good chief. He had never imagined he would admit such a thing about a man whom he had once considered his direst enemy, but his opinion had suffered a major upheaval the day the Campbell had offered him that document to sign. He had admitted not only to failings of his own but to a faith in God that helped him be a better man. He had offered Dar not only forgiveness but also a chance at a better life.

He had gone the extra mile when no one would have expected he should. Indeed, Dar thought, there were likely many who questioned if not actually derided his decision. Yet his love for his sister and for the Lord had compelled him to do it anyway.

Dar's grudging respect for Niall Campbell was but another reason he didn't want to ride out with Kenneth this night. He had given Caitlin's brother his word that he wouldn't leave Kilchurn's environs without his permission.

Yet what Kenneth was asking him to do wasn't Campbell business or responsibility. It was MacNaghtens', and only Mac-Naghtens'.

Besides, if Dar were to ask permission to return to his clan, he would be stepping outside the protective realm of a broken man. That might well place Niall Campbell in a very difficult, if not outright dangerous, position.

On many levels, there was no turning back if he left Kilchurn this night. Though Kenneth couldn't fully understand the extent of the sacrifice he asked, it was far, far more than just the risking of Dar's life. Yet Dar also knew his cousin asked it because it was important. He asked it because they were of the same blood and, in the Highlands, the love of and commitment to one's clan ran deep. Very deep.

Ye only imagine ye're free . . .

At the time Kenneth had first uttered them, the words had rammed home, sharp and piercing. As they also did now, in the remembering. His cousin was right. Someone had to challenge Athe, make the others finally face the truth. Someone had to try, and keep on trying.

It didn't matter that it might well be a hopeless cause. It didn't matter that he felt woefully inadequate to assume the mantle of chieftainship, if he somehow did succeed in winning it. All he could do was his best, until a better man stepped forward. And if that better man never did, then so be it. All he could do was try and, like Niall Campbell, when he faltered and failed, ask for forgiveness.

His heart heavy, Dar walked from the stable and out into a warm, starlit, late June night. It was yet several hours until midnight. There were things to do and say, however, before he could at last depart. And, likely far sooner than Caitlin had expected, he would now fulfill her request this day.

He needed to speak with Goraidh.

✠

In his concerted efforts to avoid anything to do with the hermit, Dar hadn't learned which room Goraidh had taken in the servant's sleeping area. Fortunately, he finally found one of the servants who knew where the older man was quartered. The actual act of knocking on his door, however, was harder than Dar had imagined it would be.

Several times, he lifted his fist to Goraidh's door, only to lower it. At long last, though, disgusted with his cowardice, Dar forced himself to rap softly on the door. The look on Goraidh's face when he opened the door almost made Dar's own apprehension seem comical.

The older man paled. His mouth dropped open and he stood there, speechless.

They stared at each other for so long Dar's rising impatience finally overcame his own reticence. "Are ye going to ask me in, or would ye prefer I discuss MacNaghten business out here in the hall?" he growled.

"Och, aye." The hermit all but jumped back and motioned him in. "Please, enter, if ye will."

Dar stalked in and turned. Just as soon as Goraidh shut the door, he indicated that they should both retire to the farthest corner of his small chamber. The older man hurried over.

"I'll get right to the point," Dar then said, pitching his voice low. "I need yer help."

Goraidh's eyes widened, but he nodded. "I'll do aught ye want. Aught, of course, save leave ye."

"Well, in a sense, that's exactly what I'm asking." Dar paused, struggling with how best to break the news of Feandan's death to his brother. "Yer brother's dead, murdered by Athe," he finally blurted out, knowing there wasn't any tactful way to broach such a painful subject.

The blood drained once more from Goraidh's face. "How? And, more importantly, why?"

Dar dragged in a deep breath, then proceeded to recount Kenneth's tale of the events. "Suffice it to say," he finished at last, "I'm going back with Kenneth. And that's where yer assistance is needed."

"In accompanying ye two." The hermit nodded his assent. "Ye know I'll help in whatever way I can."

"On the contrary. I need ye to remain here. At least one of our family must survive, in case the clan ever regains the sense it apparently long ago lost. Moreover, I cannot risk informing Niall Campbell of my intentions to leave Kilchurn this night. It would . . . complicate too many things."

"But he might help ye overcome Athe," Goraidh said. "Indeed, it'd likely please him to no end to recapture the lad. And that could solve both of yer problems—Athe removed from the chieftainship once and for all, and yer assurance of surviving."

"Aye, that it would. But it'd also leave Clan MacNaghten without a chief again. For do ye seriously believe they'd have me as chief, if I betrayed them by dragging the Campbell into this?"

The hermit's shoulders slumped. "Nay, I suppose not. Our cursed pride would never bear such a humiliation, would it?"

"Nay, it likely wouldn't. Leastwise, not atop all the other humiliations the clan has suffered in the past year."

"I just don't like the idea of ye and Kenneth facing Athe alone." Goraidh shook his head. "Mayhap if I was there with ye, though . . ."

"There's naught that can be done for it. In case we fail, and Athe decides to carry out his assassination attempt, the Campbell must be made aware of the plot and be at Hell's Glen to foil it. It may well be the last service Kenneth and I can do for the clan—save them from that final and most fatal of all mistakes. But, to do so, we need yer help."

Goraidh sighed. "Aye, I suppose the Lord has indeed given each of us the task we're most suited to carry out."

"Fear not," Dar said. "Yers isn't as easy as it may sound. Ye have to convince Niall Campbell that my unexpected departure isn't part of some scheme to lure *him* into an ambush, instead of the Regent. Any man who breaks his word, like I'm being forced to do, isn't one most would risk their life on." He expelled a frustrated breath. "Och, I fear, in the end, all our efforts—and lives—might yet be wasted."

"Caitlin will believe me. I'll first enlist her aid in convincing her brother."

Dar considered that a moment, then nodded. "Aye, that might be the best way." He hesitated. "Would ye tell her something for me?"

"Aught that ye wish."

Dar hated revealing things of such a personal nature, especially to a man he still couldn't find it in his heart to forgive. But Goraidh was all he had. And he didn't want Caitlin imagining he had used her to gain his freedom, or had willingly deserted her.

"Tell her, if ye would, that I'd never leave her save for such a dire situation. And tell her I was tempted—sorely tempted—not to do so at any rate. And that I love her and always will."

"I think, in her heart of hearts, she'll know that without me even having to tell her," the hermit said. "Still, I'll carry yer message to her. I also thank ye for entrusting such a vital thing to me. I know that if there had been anyone else ye could've picked for the task, ye would have."

"Mayhap. But I also know, no matter my personal feelings toward ye, ye'll do yer best for the clan."

A pained disappointment glimmered in the other man's eyes. "Aye, that I will. I give ye my word."

"Well, it's likely time I was going. I don't want to risk missing Kenneth." Dar turned, then hesitated as a thought struck him. "If I succeed in ousting Athe, the Campbell will know by the lack of MacNaghtens in Hell's Glen two days hence. If so, tell him I'll be awaiting him at Dundarave. And that, chief or not, I'll gladly return to Kilchurn to serve out the remaining year I swore to give him."

Some emotion flared in the hermit's eyes. "I'll tell him. And I'll tell him, as well, that no matter what the outcome, my son is a man among men. And that I'm verra, verra proud of him."

Dar looked Goraidh straight in the eye. "Thank ye for that," he said at last, fearing that to say more would open the long-held bastions of his heart.

Instead, without another word, he turned on his heel and strode from the room.

20

Caitlin had just finished her breakfast when a knock sounded on her bedchamber door. As she swallowed the last bite of her bannock and cheese, then drained her cup of tea, her maidservant hurried to answer the door. There was a moment of indistinct conversation, then the woman turned.

"It's the hermit, m'lady," she said, glancing back at Caitlin, who sat on the window seat, her breakfast tray on her lap. "He says it's most urgent that he speak with ye. And speak with ye now."

A ripple of premonition passed through Caitlin. *Dar. Something had happened with Dar.*

"Then show him in, please." As she spoke, Caitlin set the tray aside and rose.

Goraidh walked in and over to stand before her. "I need to speak with yer brother, m'lady, and would like ye there when I do. Will ye come?"

"Now?"

"Aye, now. Time's of the essence."

She eyed him carefully. "This has to do with Dar, doesn't it?"

He nodded. "With Darach and so much more."

The urgent look in his eyes said it all.

"He's gone, isn't he?"

The answer she dreaded was reluctant but honest. "Aye."

Pain lanced through her. Dar had left without telling her or taking her with him? How could that be? Time and again, no matter how hard either of them had tried to the contrary, the Lord had always brought them back together.

"He'll come back," she said, struggling to believe that herself. "Ye'll see. He'll come back."

A compassionate understanding gleamed in the older man's eyes. "If it's the Lord's will, if Darach lives, aye, I too believe he'll come back. Come back because of ye."

Dar's father touched her cheek. "He told me to tell ye that he'd have never left ye save for such a dire situation. And even so, he was sorely tempted not to. And that he loves ye, and always will."

Tears flooded Caitlin's eyes. "I should've gone with him. Things have always turned out better when we were together."

"Not this time, lass. This time, Darach goes to confront Athe and will need all his faculties concentrated on that onerous task. This time, ye would've been a distraction he couldn't afford." Goraidh managed a wan smile. "He would've been overly concerned with ye and yer safety, instead of with Athe."

She knew Goraidh spoke true, but it was still so hard to let Dar go alone. If he should die, and the last thing she had ever said to him had been said in anger . . .

Caitlin expelled a small, resigned breath and nodded. "Let's be on our way then."

Gathering her skirts, she headed for the door, Goraidh following. As they walked the corridor, Caitlin turned to her companion.

"Though Niall leaves early most morns to see to the day's tasks," she said, "usually on Sundays, before church, he spends an extra hour or two with his family in the privacy of their bedchamber. Let's hope he's yet there. If not, it may take us a time to scour Kilchurn for him."

"I pray that it'll be so this day, m'lady."

They reached the door to Niall and Anne's bedchamber. Caitlin rapped on the door, hard and urgently. Her impatience grew by leaps and bounds as she waited for someone to answer, and the seconds seemed to plod by with maddening slowness. At long last, though, the door opened. It was Niall.

A quizzical look in his eyes, he stared at them. "And what, pray tell, is the reason for a visit from the two of ye?" Even as he asked, something appeared to change in his gaze. "It's Darach, isn't it? What has he gone and done?"

"What I have to tell ye, m'lord," Goraidh spoke up before Caitlin could respond, "is best discussed in private. And as soon as possible."

Niall hesitated, then stood back and swung the door wide open. "Come in then. Anne's here, but there's naught ye can't say in her presence."

Caitlin and Goraidh hurried in. Niall closed the door behind them.

"Annie, we've guests," he called out to his wife.

Brendan in her arms, she stepped from around a dressing screen. At the sight of the solemn expressions on both Caitlin and Goraidh's faces, her smile faded.

"What's wrong?" She looked from Caitlin to Goraidh, and back again. "It's Darach, isn't it?"

Caitlin glanced over at the hermit. "Best ye tell them and be done with it."

Goraidh drew in a deep breath. "Athe killed his uncle—my brother—and intends to ambush the Regent on his trip to visit Argyll in less than two days' time. Dar left to try and stop Athe."

"Och, nay," Caitlin whispered. "Athe's surely gone mad, to plan such a terrible deed. Dar's in even worse straits than first I imagined."

Anne walked over to join Caitlin. "Come, lass," she said, slipping her free arm around Caitlin's waist. "Ye look as pale as a ghost. Come, let's sit down."

She allowed herself to be led to the bench at the foot of her brother and sister-in-law's bed, where she sank gratefully down upon it. She indeed felt dizzy. Dizzy with fear for Dar.

"So, he barely managed a month," she heard Niall say, fury in his voice, "before he no longer could bear it here. Just time enough for us to lower our guard and cease to watch him as closely."

"He had to go, m'lord. Athe must be stopped. Darach's the only one who can do it, if anyone can."

"He broke his word. There's naught more to be said."

Exasperation, tinged with anger, cleared Caitlin's head in record time. She leaped to her feet and strode over to stand before her brother.

"Are ye deaf as well as pigheadedly determined to find fault where there's none?" she demanded, grabbing her brother's arm. "Dar went back to stop Athe from assassinating the Regent! And the only way he could do that was by fighting him for the chieftainship, a chieftainship he has never even wanted."

"He could've—should've—come to me first," Niall growled. "He gave me his word that he'd not leave Kilchurn without my permission. My permission, Caitlin. Not yers, not Goraidh's, not anyone else's. Mine, and only mine!"

"Aye, that he did, m'lord," Goraidh interjected. "But what's between he and Athe is MacNaghten business, not Campbell. He didn't need or want yer help. Indeed, it would've only made things worse."

"Not as worse as it will now be." A grim look on his face, Niall shook his head. "I never should've trusted him. And I never will again."

"Well, that's another matter entirely, and best saved for later." Unflinchingly, Goraidh met Niall's blazing glance. "What's needed now is for ye and yer men to hie yerself to Hell's Glen to ensure the Regent's safety. For if Dar fails to stop Athe, there'll then be only ye who can foil the ambush."

"And who's to say that the ambush won't be meant for us instead?" Niall demanded. "Mayhap this is all but part of some plot Darach concocted to avenge himself on me. Did ye think of that, MacNaghten?"

"Aye, both Darach and I thought ye might suspect that. But it isn't true. My son would've never left here save for the most dire of reasons." Goraidh glanced at Caitlin. "He had too much to lose to leave here otherwise."

At the look of understanding in the hermit's eyes, Caitlin's eyes again filled with tears. "I left him yesterday, furious and accusing him of having been given a second chance, yet unwilling to give ye a second chance. But he has done so, hasn't he, Goraidh? He came to ye, spoke with ye, and entrusted this terrible responsibility to ye. The responsibility of convincing my brother that Dar spoke the truth, and that Niall now needs to heed and act on his words."

The older man smiled sadly. "Aye, he did. And I told him I was proud of him. So verra, verra proud."

"That doesn't make me inclined to risk my life or those of my men. Proud ye may be of yer son," Niall said, "but to me he's naught more than a liar and deceiver."

"Niall, that's not fair."

At his wife's unexpected intrusion into the conversation, Niall turned now to her. "Fair? I've been more than fair to that man, Annie. And this is how he repays me!"

"And what exactly would ye have done, if it had been ye instead of him in such straits?" she asked, moving to his side. "Would ye have involved another clan in what was Campbell business? I don't recall ye asking for aid when ye were struggling so hard to keep *yer* position as chief."

High color flushed her husband's cheeks. "It wasn't anyone else's business. Besides, I had things under control."

Anne chuckled. "Aye, that ye did, save when ye nearly died from poisoning and, in the interim, I was almost burned at the stake. But, be that as it may, ye never once asked for help, either from within the clan or from outside it. And Darach's as proud and resourceful a man as ye."

"He also isn't a liar or deceiver," Goraidh added heatedly. "He said to tell ye that if he succeeded in ousting Athe, ye'd know by the lack of MacNaghtens in Hell's Glen in two days' time. And, if so, Darach would await ye at Dundarave to surrender himself back into yer control for the remaining year he owed ye."

"Och, aye." Niall's laugh was disparaging. "I can just see him surrendering to me if he is, by then, the MacNaghten. Under the terms of the proscribement, that would likely be a death sentence for him, and well he knows it."

"Nonetheless, he told me to tell ye that."

For the first time, indecision flickered in Niall's eyes. Hope swelled in Caitlin.

"Ye can't do aught to aid Dar in his quest to remove Athe from power," she said, gazing up at her brother. "Which he's at least finally trying to remedy, after causing the unfortunate situation that all began when first he abducted me. Ye can, though, believe Dar when he warns ye of what might happen to the Regent if he fails to stop Athe. And ye can do something about that.

"I may well lose him in this brave but likely futile sacrifice of his," Caitlin continued, squeezing Niall's arm. "At least honor him—and me in my choice of this good, noble man—by doing as he asks. Please, Niall. Please!"

He looked down at her. "Ye can still ask this, knowing ye risk my life and the lives of our men in the doing? Are ye certain there's not the tiniest bit of doubt about this plan in yer mind?"

She met his piercing gaze with a joyous one of her own. She couldn't be with Dar to fight at his side. But she could fight for him nonetheless.

"I trust Dar with not only my life," Caitlin said, her conviction shining in her eyes and resonating in her voice, "but with *all* our lives. There's no doubt in my mind that what he says is true. No doubt whatsoever."

✝

This time, Athe did decide to take refuge in the summer shielings on Ben Vorlich, deep and safe in MacFarlane lands. It was the perfect staging area from which to make but a half day's ride to Hell's Glen, Dar thought as they urged their mounts up the ever rising terrain. It was also a good place to hide among MacFarlanes who were already beginning to bring their gentle, shaggy cattle up to graze on the lush summer grasses.

The presence of another clan, however, Dar well knew, wouldn't deter Athe from fighting or killing him. That was MacNaghten business, and nothing in which another clan would care to involve itself.

Besides, he reminded himself as he and Kenneth rode past the cattle folds and small, sod-covered houses, the summer community consisted mainly of women and girls who milked the cows and made cheese and butter, and boys who were responsible for herding the cattle out each day to fresh patches of grass, then bringing them back to the cattle folds each eve. Adult MacFarlane men were in short supply, there primarily as protection, to do repairs, hunt, and help with some of the more difficult cattle.

Even though they were dressed in nondescript plaids, it didn't take long to find his clansmen. Indeed, holed up in the huts on the farthest side of the temporary village, from their vantage halfway up the glen, his clansmen noticed the new arrivals before Dar and Kenneth discovered them. A group of about ten men immediately set out in their direction.

"I suppose there's no turning back now," Dar said.

"Nor do I want to," muttered his companion riding beside

him. "It's past time Athe relinquish his position as chief. Not once has he used it for the betterment of the clan. Nor did his father before him."

"If events don't go in my favor"—Dar shot his cousin a quick glance—"and ye can get away, do so. Naught's served in both of us dying this day."

Kenneth gave a sharp laugh. "And where would I go? To beg shelter from Niall Campbell?"

"He's a merciful man, Cousin. And, for all practical purposes, ye'd be an outlaw from the clan." Dar paused. "Ye could also help him track down Athe. Ye'd know, better than anyone would, where he'd be likely to go next."

"Ye're asking me to turn traitor against my own clan, Dar."

"Aye, in a sense I am." He sighed. "But we were the cause of Athe's return to power. It seems only just that we also be part of taking that power away from him. If I fail, there's only ye left. And ye can't do it without help. Powerful help."

"Best ye don't think of failing," Kenneth said through gritted teeth as their clansmen drew near. "Best ye face them all as the man of the hour, come to save them from their madman of a chief."

Dar smiled and reined in his horse. "That I will. Still, it's always best to have a backup plan."

Geordie MacNaghten, a big, blustering hulk of a man and their distant cousin, halted before them just then. "So, ye decided to pay us a wee visit, did ye, Dar? Yer brother isn't at all pleased, ye can be sure."

"No more pleased than I was," Dar replied calmly, "when I heard he'd shot our uncle in cold blood."

"So, the wee Kenneth went bawling to ye, did he?" Geordie's lip curled in derision. "Well, it'll go poorly for him that he did."

"And is that what our clan has become in my absence?" Dar swung his leg over his horse, jumped down, and walked up to meet Geordie eye to eye. "Cowardly bullies who shoot unarmed men and beat those not trained in the warrior arts? If so, I've stayed away far too long, and shirked what has always been my destiny."

The other man stared at Dar for a moment longer, then averted his gaze. "Well, we'll see what destiny truly has in store for ye. Come along. Athe doesn't like to be kept waiting."

Dar motioned in the direction of the hill. "Lead on, then. I'm as eager to meet with him as he seems to be with me."

They set out, the other clansmen falling into step around them. As they passed, women and children paused in their work to stare.

Dar kept his gaze riveted straight ahead. Now that the moment he had so long avoided was almost here, his emotions churned within him. Perhaps the path to this day had been laid out for him long ago, in the boyhood rivalry Dar had always wondered at, and of which he had always come out on the losing end. But that past submission had been of his choice, because he had seen no other option.

Today, though, the time had come to confront his brother. There was no father left to please, leastwise no reluctant, stand-in father, and no reason to yield to an older brother in the futile hope of doing so.

There was only the hope of saving his clan from far worse retribution. Yet, even if he did manage to kill Athe and gain command of the clan, Dar didn't know what more he could do for them. In the end, perhaps all that was left was to help them live out the remainder of their days with honor.

His mouth quirked in irony. Was it even possible? Could the man most thought to be a despicable killer, no matter if he bested Athe this day, ever be permitted to lead the clan?

Such a consideration seemed so impossible, so inconceivable, that it would surely require some sort of Divine intervention even to succeed. A Divine intervention that both Caitlin and Goraidh had long claimed was the reason he had finally arrived at this moment. Perhaps it *was* the will of God. In the end, God was surely his only hope.

He was no longer so proud that he wouldn't accept the Lord's help. He hoped he had gained a bit of wisdom in the time of his banishment, and especially in the past weeks he had spent with Caitlin . . . and even Goraidh.

Regret flooded him. Now, when it was too late, Dar regretted not offering his father his forgiveness. Now, he might never have the chance to correct that omission.

As hard as it was to admit, Dar had been inexpressibly touched by the hermit's declaration that he was proud of him. At long last, he had finally heard the words he had so yearned to hear.

At least, Dar had loved and been loved by Caitlin. Too much had happened to truly savor their time together, and most certainly since they had finally spoken of their love. Still, there was comfort—and a certain peace—in remembering what they had shared.

She had helped him to feel worthwhile again, to feel like a man. He had never been more vibrantly alive than he was when he was with her. But, most of all, she had helped him to see that true honor, despite any and all opposition, lay in doing what one felt in one's heart to be right.

I know I've turned my back on Ye for a long while, Lord, Dar couldn't help but silently pray. *I know I've no right to be asking Ye for Yer help now. I don't ask so much for myself, though, as for my people. They're so lost, following a leader who's so verra unworthy of them. Bring them, at last, a leader they deserve. And if it isn't me, at least bring forth someone who* is *worthy.*

I ask, as well, for a chance to see and speak with my father again. Or else give him the gift of knowing, leastwise in his heart, that I forgave him. And, just a wee bit more for me, too, if Ye will, that

I might be able to be with Caitlin one last time and thank her for all she has done for me. But if none of this is Yer will, then so be it. Just let me at least die clothed in Yer mercy and forgiveness. In Yer love . . .

From a hut in the center of the little circle of dwellings up the hill, Athe stepped out just then. His eyes gleamed with a wild, crazed light. A dagg was shoved in his belt, and in his hand he gripped a claymore. Armed as he was with only his knife, Dar wondered whether a pistol ball or a sword would soon be piercing his heart.

"Ye've come back for no good, haven't ye, Brother?" Athe cried when Dar was still several yards away. "Well, yer chance to run is over and done with. Ye've been pushing to fight me all these years. Today, ye'll do it, or die." He laughed. "Indeed, ye'll die whether ye do or don't fight me."

Dar halted a few feet from him. "I'll fight ye, and gladly. It's past time ye were challenged to a battle for clan chief. Ye've been at it overlong and have done a poor job of it in the bargain."

He spread his hands wide for all to see. "I need a more suitable weapon, though, than my wee dagger. Unless ye plan to shoot me straightaway with that pistol, which would go against clan tradition in a fight for the chieftainship, might I suggest ye put it aside? Instead, let's settle this with the sword."

Athe pulled his dagg free and handed it to one of his guards who had come up to stand beside him. "A pistol shot would be far too merciful for the likes of ye. I much prefer slicing ye up bit by bit until I've slowly and verra painfully killed ye. Ye need yer pride whittled away, at the same time as I whittle away at yer flesh.

"Give him yer sword," Athe spat at another guard who wore a claymore on his back. "I've allowed this sniveling coward to live far too long as it is."

The claymore's handle felt good and solid when the man

slapped it into Dar's hand. He hefted it and knew it was a well-balanced weapon. It was also long and heavy, nearly the length of the height of the man who had given it to him.

Wrapping his other hand around the handle to use it in the traditional two-handed grip, Dar took a few steps back and settled into a fighting stance. "Kill me if ye can, Brother," he said. "Or give over the leadership now and I'll spare yer life."

"No quarter, Dar," Athe snarled, a feral grin on his face. "No quarter."

With that, the claymore raised in a high, slicing position, he leaped forward. Dar nimbly dodged him and left a carefully controlled cut on Athe's arm in the passing. With an enraged roar that was part pain and part surprise, his brother slid to a halt, wheeled about, and charged again.

This time, Dar met the attack head on. Blades clanged together, skittering down until each rested on the other's quillon guard. Muscles strained as both pushed hard.

The month of increasingly strenuous work had served Dar well. With a sudden shove, he sent Athe stumbling backward.

His face red with anger and sword held high, his brother charged yet again. Dar could've easily thrust his own weapon straight into Athe's unguarded belly. At the last second, however, he hesitated. With the moment finally upon him, Dar found he had no taste for taking his own brother's life.

He parried Athe's downward swing and they slammed back together. Their gazes locked. Something passed across Athe's face. His mouth lifted in a malicious smile.

"I knew about yer real father. I also knew ye didn't kill Nara," he whispered. "I knew because I found her dead before ye did. Dead at the bottom of that cliff, with Father standing there at the edge, gazing down at her."

"F-father?" Dar asked, the unexpectedness of the revelation like a blow to his gut. "But why?"

With a laugh, Athe shoved Dar away and attacked again. This time, Dar staggered back beneath a furious onslaught of crosscuts and thrusts, barely able to defend himself. He cursed his passing inattention. His brother had succeeded in momentarily distracting him. With a ferocious effort, Dar forced his thoughts to return to the task at hand.

He surged forward, fighting back with powerful parries and thrusts. For a time, both seemed equally matched.

The repeated clang of steel upon steel began to gather an even larger audience—one now of MacFarlane men and even some women. At last, though, Dar and Athe came together once again. Quillon guard met quillon guard as both pushed and shoved and struggled to catch their breaths.

"He k-killed her, ye know," Athe panted in a low voice. "Killed her because she wouldn't agree to wed me, even as sh-she carried yer spawn in her belly. When I came upon him afterward, having heard she was to meet ye there near the cliffs, he told me that we'd blame it all on ye. Ye were, after all, the one who had set her death into motion, in daring to take what wasn't yers."

With a cry of fury, Dar crashed into his brother. Athe was sent flying back, lost his footing, and fell to one knee. This time, however, Dar was in no mood to pull back or spare him. He surged forward, sword upraised to deliver the killing blow.

Athe, stretching out toward him, reached Dar before Dar reached him. He thrust his sword deep into Dar's lower leg, then twisted it to scrape steel against bone.

Excruciating pain exploded in Dar. Bright lights sparkled before his eyes. For an instant, everything began to gray. With a superhuman effort, he fought past it because he had to. Had to, or die. Fought to see clearly enough to bring his blade down, aiming it straight at Athe.

The claymore sliced into sinew and flesh, all but severing Athe's left arm from his body. His brother screamed, a shrill, fearful sound, and fell back. Fell back to writhe in agony while his life's blood spurted away.

Dar sank to his knees, his own breathing harsh and labored, his leg burning like fire. And, as Athe's guards rushed over to their former leader, Dar felt other hands on him, bearing him up. He turned, saw Kenneth's face, then looked to the opposite side and saw the faces of several others.

"Is . . . is it f-finally finished?" he mumbled, feeling as if he were simultaneously going to be sick and black out.

"Aye, that it is, Cousin," Kenneth said, a grim smile on his face. "Ye're now the MacNaghten."

Relief swamped him. Dar sagged back.

"A dubious distinction . . . considering I never wanted the job in the first place," he whispered, managing a weak grin.

"Well, no matter how ye feel about it, ye're stuck with us now."

Dar looked down and saw the blood pouring from his leg. "Then ye'd better get this cauterized straight away," he said, the pain only intensifying the ever spiraling dizziness, "or ye might not have me for long."

"Aye, that we should." His cousin sighed. "And where is Caitlin when ye need her?"

It was a meager victory, but one Dar clung to for a long while thereafter. This time, when they finally pressed the hot iron to his flesh, at least he managed not to pass out.

21

Caitlin waited until after Niall and fifty of his clansmen had ridden out late that afternoon. Then she sought and found Goraidh in the castle's small herb and vegetable garden.

"I'm going to Dundarave," she promptly informed him once she'd made certain there was no one near to overhear them. "Will ye come with me?"

The older man rose slowly from the row of rosemary bushes he was trimming, set the shears back in its wooden tool box, and dusted off his hands. Only then did he meet her gaze.

"And ye've procured yer brother's approval for this wee trip, have ye?"

"Of course not." She sighed in exasperation. "Ye know as well as I Niall wouldn't allow it. Right now, he likely wants me as far from Dar as he can get me. But I can't stand passively by while Dar's in danger. I need to be close enough so that, if he needs me, I can be there for him."

"To do what? Help him fight Athe? Aid him in convincing the clan they should take him as their chief?" Goraidh shook his head. "Lass, lass, ye'd be no help. Indeed, ye'd be worse than a hindrance. Ye might even be the distraction that'd be Darach's undoing."

"Don't ye think I know that?" In spite of her efforts to the contrary, impatience threaded her voice. "But if he succeeds in unseating Athe, Dar told Niall he'd await him at Dundarave. And I want to be there first, so I can speak with Dar."

The hermit eyed her warily. "Talk to him about what?"

"What else? About his noble if foolhardy offer to turn himself back over to Niall." Caitlin paused to point to a rose bower that was finally beginning to bloom with fragrant, single-petaled, pink flowers. "Come, let's talk over there, away from prying eyes."

"So, ye mean to convince Darach not to honor his word to yer brother, do ye?" Goraidh asked once they were seated on the bower's stone bench.

"It's the only option. If Dar becomes clan chief, he's back in the fold and will be equally subject to the proscription. And that puts both him and Niall in a difficult position. By law, Niall will be obligated either to execute him or turn him over to be jailed and tried, and then likely executed anyway. Yet, if we can just buy some time, it's possible the proscription might eventually be lifted, especially if Dar, as clan chief, can keep his people alive and out of further trouble. But he has to live to do so."

"Aye, all that's verra true." The hermit clasped his hands in his lap and, for a moment, looked down. "Still, I'm not so certain he'll do that," he then said, glancing back up.

"If anyone can convince him, I can."

Goraidh chuckled. "Aye, that ye can." He cocked his head. "It'll be dangerous, ye and I traveling alone. I'm not the best with a sword, ye know."

"I can handle a small sword passably well, in addition to a dagger." Caitlin smiled. "And I intend to travel as a lad, which should simplify things a wee bit. We'll just dress verra poorly. That way, few will be tempted to try and rob us."

"And what of the Lady Anne? Will ye tell her of yer plans, or not?"

Caitlin hesitated, torn between her inclination to keep the plan secret or share it with her best friend and confidante. Try as she might, though, she couldn't find it in her heart to leave without any explanation. Besides, once Anne understood her reasons, Caitlin knew she wouldn't stop her.

"I think I owe her that much and, through her, Niall. After all, if Dar will have me as his wife, I'll not be returning to Kilchurn anytime soon."

"He loves ye and no mistake. Still, I'm not certain he'll agree to wed ye. Campbell though ye be, to become a MacNaghten makes ye as subject to the proscription as the rest of us. And Dar already feels at least partly responsible for the death of the first lass he loved."

"Well, let's deal with one problem at a time, shall we?" She stood. "I'd like to depart in two hours. Can ye be ready by then?"

"Aye."

"Good. Then I'll meet ye at the stables. In the meanwhile, please see to some food for our journey. Tell the kitchen staff that ye've a verra large appetite when ye travel, and I'm sure it'll be enough for the two of us. Fortunately, there's a full moon tonight. If we ride hard and fast, we should be at Dundarave by dawn."

"As ye wish, lass. Best ye see to the Lady Anne then."

Caitlin nodded. Despite her earlier optimism, it wasn't going to be easy to convince Anne to let her leave. But Anne at least understood a woman's heart. And it was past time, Caitlin thought, she be allowed to follow it—wherever it led.

✞

Dressed in nondescript trews, shirt, and a threadbare jacket, her hair tucked up beneath a soft, woolen Highland bonnet, and her face smudged a bit with dirt, Caitlin managed to transform herself into a slender but passable-looking lad. They both obtained swift horses, capable of outrunning any sent out to overtake them. Short swords were stashed in their packs, and they wore daggers at their sides. Nothing identified them as from any specific clan, and especially not of Clan Campbell.

Reluctantly, Anne gave Caitlin leave to go to Dar only after Goraidh assured Anne that if Dar didn't live to reach Dundarave, or Athe came there, he would immediately use the secret passage to bring Caitlin back to Kilchurn. Their parting, however, was still emotional and tear-filled.

"Niall's going to be verra angry with me," the auburn-haired woman said as she clung, weeping, to Caitlin. "As it is, he's already furious with Darach for breaking his word to him. And now to send ye out to all but elope . . ."

Caitlin managed a shaky laugh. "Ye might yet see me back here in record time. Goraidh's convinced Dar won't wed me."

"Knowing the predicament he and his clan are in," Anne replied, smiling bravely through her tears, "I wouldn't put it past him. Which is the only reason I'm letting ye go to him."

"Why?" Caitlin frowned. "Because ye're certain he'll send me back here posthaste?"

"Nay, because he's too honorable to wed ye only, in the doing, to put yer life in danger."

"Well, one way or another, if he still lives I'll be able to see and speak with him one last time. And that's more than worth the risk." Gently, Caitlin disengaged herself from her sister-in-law's arms. "It's time we were going, Anne."

"Aye, that it is," the other woman said, stepping back. "Ye've grown up, lass. I'm so happy for ye."

"Growing up isn't as easy as I once imagined it to be." Caitlin grimaced. "Indeed, it's verra hard and, at times, verra scary. There are no guarantees that things will turn out like ye hope they should."

"We're here for ye, should ye need to return. Kilchurn will always be yer home—and sanctuary—if ever ye should need it."

Caitlin's eyes filled anew with tears. "I know, Anne," she whispered.

Turning, she strode over to her horse and mounted. Then, glancing down at the woman who had become her dearest friend, she smiled.

"Tell Niall I love him, will ye? If I don't see him anytime soon, I mean. And that I had to follow my destiny, follow the path the Lord has called me to."

"I'll tell him, lass."

"Farewell then, Anne." Caitlin reined in her horse. "I pray we meet again someday."

"We will, Caitlin." Her sister-in-law smiled through her tears. "I know we will."

With that, Caitlin looked to Goraidh. He nodded. They nudged their horses in the side. As one, the animals set out at a fast walk. Once clear of the drawbridge and back on solid land, Caitlin urged her mount into a trot and then a rocking canter. Goraidh did the same.

With the sun beginning its descent into the west, they made their way along the northernmost edge of Loch Awe. Behind them, mighty Ben Cruachan glinted in the sunlight, its craggy twin peaks now bare granite in the summer warmth. Bright yellow broom covered the hills, and the hawthorn trees had finally bloomed, garbing themselves in delicate white flowers.

Caitlin didn't dare look back to Kilchurn's massive, stone towers. The enormity of what she was doing had finally struck her and she knew, if she looked back, her resolve might waver. Waver, then crumble away, leaving her powerless to resist the seductive call of home, of all she had heretofore known and loved.

As much as she loved Dar, as much as she truly believed this was the path the Lord was calling her to follow, she was also riding toward a frightful unknown. The journey to Dundarave was dangerous. They might not make it there alive, or leastwise unharmed. Even if they did arrive safely, Dar might never come. Indeed, he could already be dead.

Yet if he did live and did come, there was also no surety he would allow her to stay with him or take her to wife. And that was the best that might happen.

After several hours on the road, they decided it prudent to rest the horses for a bit. The sun had set, and the only light now was that of the full moon. After walking the horses for a while to cool them, they found a small burn sheltered by trees. As the animals drank their fill, Caitlin and Goraidh settled down onto a fallen log and ate some of the food Maudie had so hastily prepared for them.

"Yer courage, lass," Goraidh said finally, after he had finished his bread and roast chicken, "puts mine to shame. Yet even more may be required of ye in the days to come."

Caitlin lowered the water bag and swallowed before answering. "I've been thinking a lot about that."

"What will ye do, if he sends ye back home?"

She looked down. "I don't know. I don't even want to imagine such a thing."

"All along, ye've been so certain ye and Dar were meant to be together. That it was the Lord's will for the both of ye." He leaned toward her. "But have ye ever considered that, instead, it's been the Lord's will for the both of ye to be together for a time only? For ye to teach and learn from the other, in order to bring ye both closer to God? And that, finally, when ye've learned what He intended for ye to learn, the time may be past for ye to share yer lives?"

His questions put words to Caitlin's deepest fears, fears that had heretofore been little more than a roiling, nameless mass of confused thoughts and feelings. She forced her gaze to lift and meet his.

"If that truly is God's will," she softly replied, "I don't know if I'll have the strength to bear it. I keep telling myself it's enough if Dar lives and is accepted back into his clan. That he's finally happy and has found fulfillment in doing something worthwhile. But . . . but I don't know if my love's equal to that. And I don't know if I can accept it, even if it's indeed the Lord's will."

"Sometimes," her companion said, "we aren't so verra good at separating what God wants from what we want. And, more times than we'd care to admit, in our minds—and hearts—we fashion things to appear as if they're from the Lord when they truly aren't." He smiled sadly. "I've certainly learned that in a verra hard and painful way. Other times, though, we cling overlong to the old, familiar path, when God's now beckoning us to take a new one. One that will lead us even closer to Him, if we can surrender our own desires, our hopes and dreams. If we can but follow Him into something that, leastwise initially, appears dark, fearsome, and even heartbreaking."

His gaze softened then, filled with a compassionate understanding. "Have ye the courage if need be, if the Lord asks it of ye, now to sacrifice Dar to a different path than yers? If God *does* ask it of ye? Even if the consequences to Dar might seem dire?"

Caitlin laughed, the sound brittle, unsteady. "Now that would *really* present a problem if, atop everything else, Dar wants me and somehow God still makes it clear that I must not stay with him!"

"I was thinking more of the possibility that if Dar, despite the danger, was set on surrendering himself back to yer brother's custody. And that, in the doing, it led to his death. Could ye accept that? And could ye forgive yer brother for the eventual outcome?"

"Niall would never kill Dar." Fiercely, she shook her head. "He's not that kind of man."

"But he might be forced to turn him over to someone who would."

A savage fury engulfed her. For a long moment, Caitlin didn't trust herself to speak. Both Niall and Dar were men of honor. That honor, though, might compel them to do things that ultimately could result in Dar's death.

As much as she sometimes bemoaned the consequences of such high ideals, Caitlin also knew honor was an issue from which she would never be able to sway them. Nor, if the truth were told, would she want to. Honor was what made them the men they were. The men she loved.

She fought back against the sudden swell of despair, shoving it into the furthest recesses of her mind. "There's naught I can do if Dar chooses to return to Niall's custody," she said at last. "All I can do is fight my hardest to save him. And I will. Still, though I know the Lord will sooner or later have His way, I'm not yet certain what that way must be. When I do know it, then, and only then, I'll try to accept it."

"That's all any of us can do, lass. Just try and listen. Listen to Him with the ear of our heart."

There was nothing more to be said after that. Her appetite gone, Caitlin wrapped up what she hadn't finished of her meal. They packed away the food, refilled their water bags, and climbed back on their horses.

Save for one more rest stop to cool and water the horses, they rode through the remainder of the night. By the first light of dawn, Dundarave came into view. The front gate was wide open, and no one moved within. Whatever the eventual outcome, they had reached it before anyone else had.

Goraidh, in case Athe lived and decided to seek sanctuary here, took the horses around to the forest entrance to the secret passage into the tower house. Caitlin locked the gate behind him, knowing, if the need arose, a Dundarave secured from the inside would buy them time to escape. Then she made a bed on the parapet with the woolen plaid she had brought with her, and lay down to rest and await Goraidh's return.

Any sounds of an approaching force of men, she well knew, would awaken her. A force of men that might be those of Athe, Niall, or, if all went as she prayed, Dar. Until that time came, however, she needed to sleep and rebuild her strength.

Strength for what was to come . . . as the Lord willed.

✠

Despite everyone's pleas to rest at least another day before setting out for Dundarave, Dar couldn't be swayed. Today was the day the Regent would ride through Hell's Glen. Today was the day Niall Campbell would await the attack of the Mac-Naghtens against the Regent and his party. And today, when no attack came, the Campbell would next turn his attention to Dundarave.

Dar couldn't afford to miss his arrival. Too much was at stake. And, though the going might be slower than usual, thanks to his injured leg, he intended on reaching his home no later than midafternoon. Once there, he could rest all he wanted until the Campbell's arrival.

"Ye should've told the others where ye were headed, and why," Kenneth said, intruding on his thoughts just then. "As the new chief, ye now owe them more information than before."

He had known something was festering within his cousin. Dar was just surprised it had taken him several hours into the ride to finally speak his mind.

"And do ye seriously think that if I'd told them why I was set-ting out for Dundarave they'd have let me go?" Dar asked with a derisive snort.

"It would've likely been better for ye if they hadn't," Kenneth muttered. "This is the most harebrained and potentially fatal plan ye've ever devised. Not to mention, ye now have an even greater obligation to the clan to stay alive."

"Aye, well I know that." Dar sighed. "But I gave my word, Cousin. And of what value am I as clan chief if I go back on my word?"

"Under the usual circumstances, I'd agree with ye. But the proscription sets everything askew. And I say yer first loyalty must always be to yer clan."

"Do ye imagine I haven't thought long and hard on this?" He shot Kenneth a sharp glance. "Even now, I wonder if I'm doing what's truly best. But it's more than just the giving of my word. It's—"

"Och, well I know what else is involved here!" There was now anger in the bard's voice. "It's Caitlin, isn't it? Ye imagine that if ye continue to cozy up to her brother, there's still a way to win her for yerself. Admit it, Dar. Ye're still willing to risk everything, even the clan, to have her."

"Aye, I want her," Dar ground out, "but honoring my word isn't cozying up to Niall Campbell. I do what I do solely because it's the right thing to do. Besides, with the life and death straits Clan MacNaghten's in right now, he'd never give her to me. To do so would be to condemn her to our fate. And that's a verra sad fate indeed."

"That's the first thing ye've said that makes any sense. Still, this plan of yers is daft and will likely get us both killed. Ye're no longer a broken man, ye know. And that makes ye as marked a man as me."

"I'm well aware of the danger." Dar looked to his cousin. "Mayhap it's best ye turn around now and hie yerself back to Ben Vorlich. There's no point in both of us dying."

"Nay." Kenneth shook his head. "I'm as much to blame for the fine state of affairs that rescuing Athe got us in. I'll not desert ye."

"Still, if the Campbell's willing to let me take the punishment for the both of us, I want ye to return to the clan. They'll need to know what has happened to me, and why. They're not to blame Niall Campbell in the bargain, though. This isn't his doing—whatever happens to me. It's my doing, and mine alone."

His cousin gave a strident laugh. "Och, and well I know whose doing it is! But what will it matter? Ye'll be dead, and we'll once more be without a chief."

"A bad chief is worse than no chief at all," Dar shot back, beginning to tire of this particular discussion.

"Aye, I'm sure they'll see it that way as they mill around, leaderless, with no idea what to do next."

Dar didn't have any further reply, so he lapsed into silence. Beside him, Kenneth fumed for a time then settled down for the rest of the ride to Dundarave. The familiar landmarks indicating they were nearing the tower house came none too soon for Dar. Though they had walked the horses nearly the whole way, his wounded leg had begun to throb fiercely several hours ago. He yearned to rest for a while.

As they crested the last hill, Dundarave came into view. The first thing that caught Dar's eye was the closed front gate. It was almost as if someone were already there and had taken possession of the tower house.

But who? Surely not Niall Campbell. Dar doubted the Regent had ridden through Hell's Glen at dawn, but more likely mid morn at the earliest. In any event, Niall Campbell and his men couldn't have covered the distance between Hell's Glen and here quite this quickly.

"Hold back here while I approach," Dar said, reining in his horse within a stand of trees several hundred yards away. "The gate may have somehow swung closed on its own, but it's best we have a care. If someone's in Dundarave, it most certainly can't be Niall Campbell."

"So, ye're thinking it might instead be outlaws or others who intend us harm?"

Dar shrugged. "It could be anyone intending aught. Nevertheless, there's no sense both of us riding into a trap, if a trap it really is."

"Suit yerself." Kenneth pulled his horse well back into the shade of the trees. "But if ye're set upon and need aid, ye've only to call and I'll come."

"I know ye will." Dar smiled. "If I'm not happy with whoever is there, ye can be sure I'll hightail it out of there posthaste. So be ready to join me as I ride by."

At his cousin's affirmative nod, Dar urged his horse forward. He halted only when he was close enough to be heard but far enough out of crossbow or pistol range.

"Hallo!" he shouted. "Whoever's in there, show yer face!"

For what seemed several minutes but was probably half that at best, no one came up on the parapets or replied. Then, just as Dar was about to give it one last try before riding down to check the gate, a gray-haired, bearded man poked up his head. Beside him popped up a lad.

There was something familiar about the both of them. Dar signaled his horse to slowly move toward the tower house. Then, as he recognized Goraidh, his heartbeat quickened.

With a cry, the lad disappeared suddenly, soon followed by the hermit. Dar urged his mount forward at a fast walk. Just as he pulled up several feet from the gate, it swung slowly open. He awkwardly dismounted, wincing as his wounded leg touched ground. Then, just in case Goraidh and the lad weren't alone, and perhaps were even being held prisoner, he unsheathed his claymore.

The gate was only half open when the lad slipped through and ran out, heading straight toward him. He was slender, his face smooth and flushed with a becoming shade of pink. Dar blinked, not quite believing what his eyes, his heart, told him.

Then she was there, tears in her beautiful blue green eyes, his name on her lips, her arms reaching up to encircle his neck as she flung herself into him.

"Dar. Och, Dar!" Caitlin cried, her gaze brimming with joy. "Ye won. Ye lived. Och, thank the Lord. Thank the Lord!"

He tugged the bonnet from her head. Thick, ebony hair tumbled down onto her shoulders and back. He couldn't help himself.

Cradling her face between his hands, Dar leaned down and kissed her. Kissed her tenderly but with a glad, hungry yearning. Kissed her until both were so breathless they had to stop.

"What are ye doing here, lass?" he asked at last, his voice husky. "And how did yer brother get here so quickly?"

"Niall's not here yet." Caitlin smiled up at him. "It's just Goraidh and me. Once Niall and his men rode off to Hell's Glen, Goraidh and I set out. We traveled all night to get here in time."

"Ye came all this way with only Goraidh for protection?" At the realization of the danger, Dar's anger boiled up. "Are ye daft? Ye could've been killed—or worse!"

She laughed. "Which is why we dressed so poorly, and I came as a lad. And we both had swords, in the event we may have needed them."

He expelled a long, exasperated breath. "Och, but yer brother's going to be livid when he arrives to find ye here. And for what reason did ye do this, lass? It makes no sense, even for one as impulsive and headstrong as ye."

"Aye, ye likely *would* think it made no sense." Caitlin disengaged her arms and took a step back. "But I did it because I couldn't bear to stay behind and wait. I didn't know if ye'd survive yer battle with Athe or not, but in case ye did, I wanted to be here when ye arrived. Be here to speak with ye."

Dar eyed her guardedly. "Speak with me about what?"

"And is that all ye can do?" She gave her head a toss. "Ask me questions and look at me with suspicion? For a moment there, I actually thought ye were glad to see me."

"I am glad to see ye. That has naught to do, though, with my concern and confusion over why ye're here." He took her by both arms and tugged her back to him. "It makes no sense, Caitlin. No sense at all."

"Well, it makes sense to me." Fire flashing in her eyes, she glared up at him. "I've come to convince ye to leave here before my brother arrives. Staying places the both of ye in an untenable position. A position in which ye'll not come out the winner, much less live."

"I know that," Dar quietly replied. "But I gave my word."

"I'd rather have ye alive and doing what's sensible, than dead and honoring a futile promise. I'd wager Niall isn't particularly hoping to find ye here, either. I know him. He lacks the stomach to see ye imprisoned again or dead."

"It doesn't matter. I—"

"Hish." She put a finger to his lips. "Listen to me. I love ye, Darach MacNaghten. I want to be yer wife. And Goraidh's a priest. He can wed us. Then we can leave, go where we must. But at least we'll be together. Together, as we've always been meant to be."

Staring down into her eager, hopeful eyes, Dar struggled to comprehend all she had said. Caitlin wanted to wed, to be his wife? Even the consideration of such a deed made his pulse quicken with a giddy joy.

But to break his word, to ride away, even with her at his side, wouldn't solve anything. He would only be doubly blamed by her brother. And doubly doomed, if the clan death sentence wasn't enough as it was.

"It cannot be, lass," Dar softly replied. "I won't take ye to wife. I cannot be that selfish, or think only of my own desires. Clan chief though I now may be, I've naught of any value to offer ye."

"Yer love's more than enough for me." Caitlin gazed up at him imploringly. "I don't care what the hardships will be. I don't care that I marry into a proscribed clan. I love ye, and ye love me. Niall will understand. Once we're wed, he'll have no choice *but* to understand. He'll have no choice but to release ye from yer agreement, to allow ye to go free. Ye'll be my husband, after all, and he loves me. He'll have to let ye go!"

That was indeed a strong possibility, Dar thought. And it would solve so many things. He'd have Caitlin and be free to return to his clan, to be the chief it so desperately needed. But it wouldn't be right. It still wouldn't be honorable. Even love didn't justify dishonor and deceit.

"Aye, in such circumstances, yer brother likely would feel compelled to let me go," he said. "But yer brother has treated me far more generously than I deserve. Indeed, he has even given me his trust. In return, it's not right for me now to force him—to manipulate him—into freeing me out of love for ye. Not to mention, such an act might ultimately be his undoing. Would ye have me risk that? Risk him, and mayhap even his family, to satisfy our needs?"

Dar saw the precise moment the defeat hit her. Caitlin's shoulders sagged. Tears welled and trickled down her cheeks.

"But it's not f-fair," she cried, sobbing. "It's just not f-fair! Aren't we ever to have a chance at happiness?"

"Och, lass, lass," he crooned, pulling her to him to hold her tightly in his arms. "Wasn't it ye who told me once that ye had to do what was right no matter the cost to self, or there was no self worth saving?"

Sniffling, Caitlin looked up at him. "Ye like that, don't ye? Turning my words against me whenever ye can?"

He chuckled. "Only because I'm rarely able to do so." Dar touched her cheek. "Och, lass, we've done all we could to make things right. It's in the Lord's hands—"

The sound of pounding hoofbeats rose in the air. Dar released Caitlin and turned. There, just cresting the hill, was a large group of riders.

"Cruachan!" came the Campbell battle cry.

Dar looked to Caitlin. "One way or another, it seems the decision has just been taken from us. There's naught more we can do. Yer brother's coming, lass. Coming for me. And, whether he knows it yet, also coming, once again, for ye."

22

As Dar had feared, the look on Niall Campbell's face, as he rode toward them and recognized who was standing at Dar's side, was far more foreboding than encouraging. Two men rode beside him. One Dar recognized as the Campbell's tanist, Iain Campbell. The other he had never seen before.

"If yer brother's expression is any indication," he muttered, "ye won't soon hear the end of this ill-advised escapade."

Beside him, Caitlin gave a snort of disdain. "Niall's more bark than bite. And it isn't as if I haven't been the source of his ire a time or two before."

"Only a time or two?" Dar chuckled softly. "Somehow, I find that hard to believe."

"Believe what ye want. Leastwise, he may go easy on ye. Ye, after all, honored yer word to surrender yerself to him."

Then there was nothing more that could be said. Niall halted his horse and dismounted. His long strides quickly carried him to stand before them.

He glared down at his sister. "What are *ye* doing here? Last I saw ye, ye were still at Kilchurn."

To her credit, Caitlin didn't shrink from her brother's blistering gaze. "I came in the hopes of convincing Dar to wed me and then run away with me," she replied. "Stubborn man that he is, though, he refused, claiming a prior commitment to ye."

"Then he showed more sense than the likes of ye. But we'll speak more of that later."

She smiled ever so sweetly. "I'm sure we will, Brother."

"So, MacNaghten," Niall then said, turning to Dar, "ye're clan chief at last."

"Aye," Dar replied with a nod. "For what it's worth. I still owe ye eleven more months of service, if ye're even of a mind to permit me to live."

"That power ultimately doesn't lie with me." The Campbell half turned and motioned his two companions forward.

Dar watched as Iain Campbell lithely leaped from his horse and hurried over to assist the other man. The stranger looked to be in his late thirties, tall, dark-haired, with a long, narrow nose with a bulbous tip, thin lips, and a wispy mustache and beard. He wore a black, embroidered doublet with braid-decorated sleeves, padded trunks with full-length silk stockings, and fine leather shoes. A short, black, well-made cape was on his shoulders, and a small, flat, velvet hat with a luxuriant feather trim topped his head at a jaunty angle.

This was some man of wealth and position, Dar thought. He was also not of the Highlands. Niall Campbell's respectful demeanor and half bow when the man drew up only confirmed it.

"M'lord," the Campbell said to the stranger who, even before they were introduced, Dar had already surmised was Scotland's Regent for the infant King James, "this is the man responsible for averting today's possible disaster."

Niall then turned back to Caitlin—who had likewise finally recognized the nobleman and made a hurried curtsey—and Dar. "Darach, this is the first Earl of Moray, James Stewart, Regent of Scotland."

Nothing was served in rudeness, Dar well knew, even if the man had been the one to sign the proscription and set the horrible retribution against his clan into effect. Besides, he told himself, he was paying respect to the office even more than to the man. He bowed.

"M'lord," he said as he straightened.

"It seems I'm indebted to ye, lad," the Earl replied. "Truth be told, I'd never have expected such mercy from a MacNaghten. Not these days, leastwise."

"There are still some men of honor alive and well in the clan, m'lord. And we could prove it to ye—*I* could prove it to ye—if ye were ever willing to consider lifting the proscription."

Beside him, Caitlin sucked in a soft gasp and clutched his hand. Dar knew he bordered on the brink of presumption, if not outright audacity, in so boldly confronting the Regent about the punishment he had set upon Clan MacNaghten. There was nothing left for them to lose, though.

Humor glinted in the Regent's eyes. "And are ye duly designated to speak for yer clan, lad?"

"Aye." Dar met the other man's piercing gaze, well aware of his vaunted cleverness and political acumen, and that he might be talking himself straight down the road to certain doom. "I am. As of last eve, I'm now the MacNaghten."

The Earl arched a dark brow. "Are ye, indeed? Yer clan's gone through a few chiefs of late, hasn't it? But a burning question remains. Is one any better than the next? Is one more honorable than the other?"

"I can vouch for Darach's honor and trustworthiness, m'lord," Niall Campbell spoke up just then. "Indeed, he wouldn't be here awaiting me if he lacked either. And that, not knowing what the consequences would be, or if he'd even live to see another day."

The Regent angled his head to briefly regard Niall. "Yer endorsement surprises me. I thought Clan Campbell was dead set on eliminating Clan MacNaghten. Besides a wee holiday, that *is* part of the reason for my visit to the Earl of Argyll, ye know. To discuss the distribution of MacNaghten lands. Lands Argyll apparently believes should be granted to him."

"I can't speak to the Argyll Campbells' desires, m'lord," Caitlin's brother replied tautly. "The Breadalbanes, however, have no need to seize the land of other clans."

"Yet ye spared no effort in capturing and imprisoning the last MacNaghten chief. Why is that?"

"Athe MacNaghten was intimately involved in the MacNab affair. Likely even more so than his sire, if the tales are accurate. He, leastwise in my mind, represented the true reason for the proscription. And the reason I felt it best to separate posthaste such a dangerous, unprincipled madman from his clan, as much as from all other Highlanders."

"But not this one," the Earl said, motioning to Dar. "This one ye feel differently about?"

"Aye, m'lord. Verra differently."

"Well, in that case"—the Regent shrugged as he met Dar's gaze—"it seems ye come verra highly recommended, lad. And, because I've little taste for the legally sanctioned murder of any of my people, I'm willing to give ye a chance. A chance to save yer clan."

Dar's heart gave a great lurch before resuming a regular if far more rapid beat in his chest. Had he heard right? Was it possible?

"Exactly how would I be permitted to carry out such an opportunity, m'lord?" he asked, taking the greatest care with his words, even as Caitlin gave him a strong, excited squeeze of her hand.

"How else? If ye promise to keep a tight rein on yer clan henceforth, I in turn promise to lift the proscription on Clan MacNaghten. But I want no more murderous feuds, no reiving of other clans' cattle, and no other such unpleasant incidents. Is that aught ye think ye could manage?"

"I'll manage that and more, m'lord, or die in the trying."

For a long moment, the Regent eyed Dar intently. Then, he nodded.

"Aye, I believe ye will, lad." He turned to Niall. "It's past time I set out for Inveraray. Argyll won't be happy to hear he's not gaining MacNaghten holdings, but the man's land wealthy enough as it is. Send one of yer men with me, though. Once at Inveraray, I'll need to write out a document for the lad here, officially putting an end to the proscription. Once it's signed and sealed, yer man can bring it to him."

Niall nodded. "It'll be as ye ask, m'lord." He glanced at Iain, who nodded, then turned and strode back to their men.

Dar bowed to the Regent. "Words are insufficient at a time like this, but nonetheless, I thank ye from the bottom of my heart. Ye're a most merciful and kind man. Clan MacNaghten will never forget it."

"I'm only returning the favor ye first granted me, in averting my possible assassination." The Regent smiled grimly. "It's not the first attempt, ye know, nor will it likely be the last. I need all the loyalty I can muster."

"Ye have Clan MacNaghten's, m'lord," Dar said. "I swear it."

"Good." The Regent signaled that his horse be brought to him. "Just see to it that ye keep that unruly clan of yers well contained. And ye'd do well, in the bargain, to maintain the close alliance ye've already begun building with the Breadalbane Campbells."

Dar nodded. "I'll do my verra best, m'lord."

They watched in silence as the Earl mounted his horse, offered one final wave, and then, accompanied by a large party of his own retainers, rode away. Once they were well out of sight, Caitlin gave a joyous cry and flung her arms about Dar, gave him a fierce hug, then ran to her brother and did the same.

"Och, what a wonderful day!" she cried. "Can ye believe it?"

She released Niall and hurried back to take both of Dar's hands. "More so, can *ye* believe it? The proscription's over! Ye and yer clan are free men once more!"

"Well, that's not exactly true," Niall offered with dry humor from behind them. "There's still the wee matter of Darach's servitude to me. He did sign a legal document to that effect, ye know."

Caitlin dropped Dar's hands and wheeled about. "But ye can't hold Dar to that now. He's the chief of Clan MacNaghten. He needs to be with his people, not plowing some field or mucking out some stall for ye!"

"Wheesht, Caitlin," Dar said, taking her by the arm to gently ease her back to him. "It's a wee matter, at any rate. The work, I mean. But what does matter is that I honor the promise I made, and I will do that."

Niall chuckled. "Of course, though I've no difficulty in the MacNaghten chief working for me, I am a bit adverse to my future brother-in-law doing so."

He looked from Dar to Caitlin, who were both, at that moment, standing there with their mouths agape. "That's my wedding present to ye two. Or are ye both so slow-witted ye've yet failed to have reasoned that out?"

Dar was the first to regain his addled thoughts. "Er, I haven't even asked yer leave to court Caitlin, much less proposed to her."

"Well, then know ye have my leave," the Campbell said. "Now, I suggest ye propose to her posthaste. She's not the sort to wait around forever, ye know."

"Och, aye, I am," Caitlin said, throwing her arms about Dar's neck. "I'd wait forever for the likes of him."

"Well, I'd never make ye wait quite *that* long, sweet lass."

Dar pulled her to him. His eyes burned with traitorous tears, but he didn't care. If any day were a day for tears, it was this day. But tears of joy, not sadness. Tears of victory, not defeat. Tears of gratitude . . . for God's infinite mercy and love.

"I know I've repeatedly turned aside yer offers to wed ye," he said, his voice gone hoarse and low with emotion. "But, I'm asking ye now. Will ye be my wife, lass? Will ye remain here with me at Dundarave and help me rebuild my home? And will ye be friend and sister and mother to my clan?"

"Aye," she whispered, "I'll be that and more. I've one boon to ask of ye, though."

"Ask it and it's yers, sweet lass."

She turned to where Goraidh had come up to stand a few feet behind them. "I want yer father to wed us. I'll have no other."

Dar dragged in a deep breath. Then, disengaging himself from her, he wheeled about and walked to meet the hermit.

Goraidh eyed him, his gaze calm yet at the same time resigned, accepting. "I'll tell her I refuse to do it," he said, "if that's what ye want. I wouldn't come between ye two for aught in this world."

"I know that." For one last time, Dar battled his lingering pain and resentment and, at long last, defeated them. "Today, however, begins my new life. A new life that has only been made possible by the love and faith of people who believed in me and never lost hope. And ye were—are—one of those people."

"So much has been lost to us, passed us by," Goraidh murmured. "I mourn that. Mourn that with all my heart."

"As do I." A smile twitched at one corner of Dar's mouth. "But, the Lord willing, there's still so much more time left us. Time I'd like verra much to spend with ye at my side. I'll need all the wisdom of yer years to advise me, after all, if I'm ever to be a worthy clan chief. I'll need ye beside me as my mentor. As my father."

At Dar's last words, Goraidh laughed. "That's one role I've

had little practice at. I've a lot to learn to be a good father to ye, lad."

"And I, in being yer son. But we can learn together." Dar held out his hand. "I'd like verra much to try."

His father grasped his arm, hand to elbow. "As would I."

"So, is it safe to assume ye two have finally come to some sort of peace?" Caitlin asked, joining them. "Because if ye two can't get along, what hope is there for the rest of yer clan?"

"None at all, I suppose." Dar released his father's arm and turned to face her. "Why do ye imagine I've just made up with him?"

"Och, ye made up for more than the clan's sake, Darach Mac-Naghten," she said, laughing. "I know ye too well for that."

He took her into his arms, savoring the feel of her soft, woman's curves pressed now so possessively to him. Knowing, at long last, he had every right to do so, that she was finally his. And it felt good. So very, very good.

"Aye, ye always *have* known me for the knave I was," Dar said, his voice tight with emotion. "And I knew ye. Always, from the verra first moment I laid eyes on ye."

Caitlin smiled, her gaze brimming with love. "Aye, ye did. Ye always did—deep down to the depths of my soul."

Kathleen Morgan is the author of the bestselling Brides of Culdee Creek series and *As High as the Heavens*, as well as the These Highland Hills series. She lives in Colorado.

Discover more love and betrayal

IN THE SCOTTISH HIGHLANDS

from KATHLEEN MORGAN

"Morgan's skilled pen transports readers to another time and place."
—*Library Journal*

Meet the other

BRIDES OF CULDEE CREEK

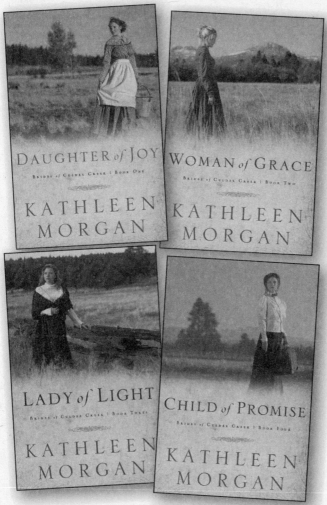

"A spectacular series." —*Library Journal*

"Kathleen Morgan writes with deep emotion and feeling." —*Reader to Reader*

Revell
a division of Baker Publishing Group
www.RevellBooks.com

Available Wherever Ebooks Are Sold